Convergence

Michael Koogler

Convergence
By Michael Koogler

ISBN: **978-0-9961537-2-0**

Book editing by Elizabeth Humphrey
Bookworm Editing, Littleton, Colorado USA

Book cover art, packaging and design by
Kreative Storm Press, Coralville, Iowa USA

Map Illustration by Clayton Chambers. ©2015 Clayton Chambers.
Chambers Studios, LLC. All Rights Reserved.
www.chambersstudios.com

Other works by Michael Koogler:

Novels

Antivirus

Hade's Gambit

The Rise of Cain

Short Stories

"Jigsaw", **Sadistic Shorts**

"The Summoning", **Sadistic Shorts**

"The Agent", **Never Fear**

And Coming Soon!

Mirror, The Earth War Saga, Book 2 (2016)

Antivirus 2, The Awakening (2016)

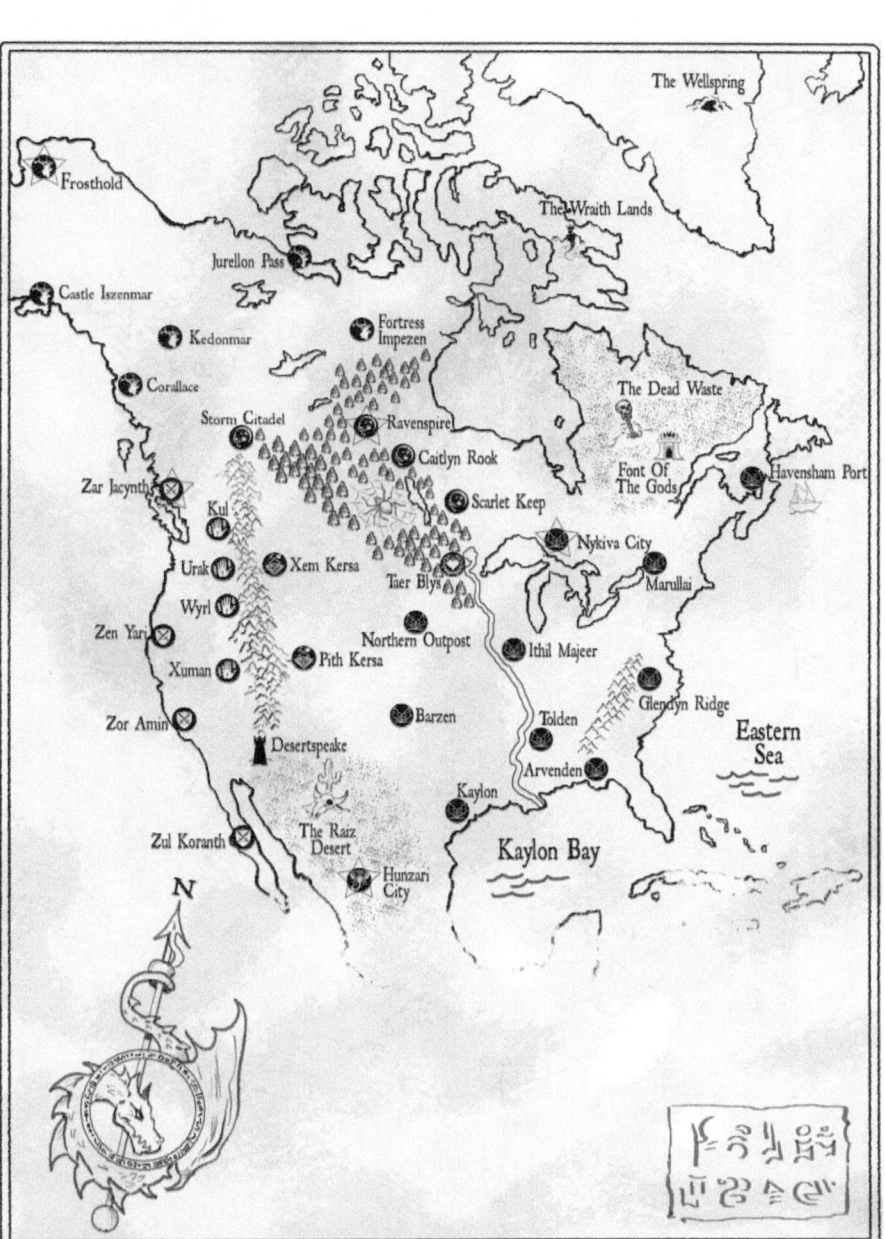

For Anthony "Toad" Hardman

July 7th, 1989 to May 30th, 2005

I really debated whether to do a Preface piece because, let's be honest, very few people read them, right? However, I would be remiss not to add a couple of short notes here for those people that do read a book's Preface and might find the words here interesting and uplifting. Besides, a few words on the dedication are in order.

Let me first offer up a few thanks right off the bat. I want to thank Karen Moeller Matibe for convincing me to condense over two decades of work into a story that doesn't ultimately need a Dramatis Personae to keep track of the cast. The song "*I Need a Hero*" now rings loudly in my head every time I sit down to work on a project. Thanks to Elizabeth Humphrey for her incredible editing skills and for helping polish the story. I mean, who needed those 10,000 extra words anyway? And special thanks go to Scott Kaalberg, Douglas Cloven, Aaron Baxter, and the supremely talented Rachel Aukes—author of ***100 Days in Deadland***—for their thoughts, remarks, and invaluable assistance as beta-readers. You're awesome!

Now, a few words on the dedication. I started formulating the idea of Convergence almost 25 years ago. It was the first full length manuscript I ever put together and when I read some of the original passages from it, I have to chuckle. All I can say about it is that my writing has come a long way since then. Over the years, Convergence has been written, revised, and rewritten several times, as I attempted to give it a unique voice in a world full of great fantasy literature. That bar is set extremely high by some of my personal favorites like RA Salvatore, Terry Brooks, and Jim Butcher—authors I respect and admire greatly for their vision and dedication to their craft.

In Convergence, I have worked very hard on building a believable world that exists on its own and yet, ties in quite nicely with our own reality. I believe characters make the story, so I try to create rich and diverse personalities that you can cheer for, fall in love with, and curse at. As I write, I find that, more times than not, my characters mirror what I see in reality. They are, in a lot of instances, based on people-watching, life interactions, and generally interesting people I am fortunate enough to run across in my life. And nowhere is that more relevant than in the character of little boy named Anthony, who shows up about midway through the story.

Anthony Hardman was born in July of 1989 and was probably all of 4 or 5 years old when I met him and became acquainted with his family. His mother, Julie, and father, Gale, were as down-to-earth and easy-going people as I've probably ever known. Anthony was their youngest child and he was special. It was not because he was born with Larson's Syndrome, a connective tissue disorder characterized by multiple joint dislocations. He was special because of his indomitable will and zest for life. Here was a little boy that, despite his handicap, quite literally hopped around everywhere on his hands, earning the nickname 'Toad,' a moniker that he loved. Anyone that didn't know the family might react in shock, but it was who he was and he made no bones about it. He was into everything and everyone. I learned a lot about life from Anthony, as I think anyone that met him did.

Anthony's life was tough. He was tougher. His medical issues were extensive and required numerous surgeries throughout his short life. If that wasn't enough, his father, Gale, died unexpectedly of a heart attack in August of 1996. It could be truly said that Anthony was one of those special spirits given a hard test in this mortal life, one that most of us probably couldn't imagine dealing with ourselves. He bore burdens that most of us pray we will never experience. And he did it without complaint; without anger or bitterness toward the lot he had been given in life. Finally, in May of 2005, before he turned 16,

Anthony passed from this life into the next, where I'm sure Gale was waiting, ready to welcome his son home.

This book—this journey of **Convergence**—is dedicated to Anthony and his memory. It's dedicated to the life he lived and his attitude of never quitting and never giving up. Anthony is portrayed in this book exactly as he appeared in real life. Anthony…Toad…is who he is. He's gone from this mortal world, but will live forever in the memories of those who knew him. Dedicating this book to him and immortalizing him as a character, is simply the least I can do for such an incredible young man. His journey on this world is over. His journey in the next life and within the pages of Convergence and beyond, will go on forever.

Prologue

He was youthful in appearance, perhaps no more than twenty years of age; strong, muscular, attractive. He was, in fact, centuries old, far older than anyone else in the world, save the Arcai. And it was specifically due to him avoiding those godly beings at all costs that he continued to outlive generations of his people. The Arcai would kill him immediately if they stumbled upon him.

It was ironic then, that the form lying on the raised pedestal before him would be so connected to those. Yet, despite the danger, he had not fled. Self-preservation should have sent him far away when the assassin came calling, bathed in the aura of demigods. But strangely, his curiosity won out and he accepted the assassin's request.

He walked slowly around the raised pedestal, his dusky eyes watching the slow rise and fall of the slumbering assassin's chest. The woman was deeply asleep now, her body draped in black silk linen, fully under the spell he had woven. It was nearly time.

He paused at the head of the platform and reached out, tracing his fingers lightly across the assassin's forehead and down her cheek. It was the intimacy of touch that facilitated his powers, and the images flashed in his mind of a time in the assassin's recent past. He saw the forest, felt the tree branch beneath her feet, sensed the thrumming magic of her weapons.

Withdrawing his hand, he again slowly circled the assassin, closely watching the woman's face. It remained peaceful and serene. The assassin had not been aware of the intrusion; her sleep continued uninterrupted. The time had come to enter the woman's dreams. The time had come to feed.

The Dream Walker sighed in anticipation and slipped under the silken sheets, pressing his body close to his prey and wrapping her in his arms. Gently, he pulled the woman's head to his chest, allowing the assassin to hear his heartbeat, drawing her further into the enchantment. There was nothing sexual about it, yet it was the most intimate form of contact. His nearness to the assassin allowed the Dream Walker to slip silently into her thoughts and dreams, to become part of her. He would see as the assassin saw; feel as she felt. And slowly, little by little, he would feed on her life force as he sifted through her thoughts. That was his way. Never enough to kill. Only enough to sustain.

At least until tonight.

Closing his eyes, he fell into his magic. In moments, he became the huntress…

…crouched motionless on a tree branch high above her unsuspecting prey. Patience – a lot of patience and a little bit of luck – had finally brought her to within striking distance. However, finding her elusive target and actually eliminating her were two entirely different tasks. She watched her prey intently while letting her mind play over the events that had brought her here to this pivotal moment.

"Can you do it?" was the simple question after she had looked at the slip of parchment that had been handed to her.

The assassin smiled, her beautiful crystalline eyes taking in the hooded stranger and noticing that there wasn't anything telling about him. He was plain and non-descript and obviously a front for someone else pulling the strings from deep within the shadows. She had been in contact with him for the better part of the last two weeks, but always through an innocent intermediary she had chosen, usually one of the many homeless urchins who prowled the streets of Nykiva, looking for something, anything, to sustain their meager lives for one more day.

Tonight was their first face-to-face meeting and it would

ultimately be their last. Ever wary of a jealous rival looking to eliminate her, she had set the time and place through the very same intermediaries and then changed it several times to throw any potential enemies off-guard. Now, sitting in the shadows of the seedy tavern's darkest corner, she could only shake her head in amusement.

Still smiling, she slid the scrap of parchment back across the dirty table. "Utter foolishness," she replied.

The assassin watched her quarry move about the small campsite with relaxed ease, obviously not worried about what might be lurking in the shadows around or above her. Then again, why should she be concerned? With her target's inherent abilities, she would be more than a match for anyone not of her own kind. And if one considered the target's companion—a companion who would typically not be too far away—anyone thinking to move against her would be foolish beyond words.

And yet here she was, prepared to do just that.

"But what of the gain?" the man pressed, undaunted by her anticipated refusal. "Surely you can see the potential for fulfilling such a contract."

"Indeed," the woman agreed. "But the gains must be attainable. These are not. This is not some random mark; this is one of the sixteen, a demigod. There is precious little you could offer me to undertake such a risk."

"Perhaps I can alter your perception," the man said softly. "Let us say for the sake of argument, you accept my offer. Tell me what it would take for you to complete the task? What would you need to kill the mark?"

"Only an Arcai blade, a dragon-forged weapon, can accomplish the feat," she answered quietly. "However, such blades are rather difficult to come by, since most dragons are unwilling to help create any weapon that could potentially be used against them or their companions."

This time, it was the man who smiled.

With silent movement born of years of experience, she freed the two long knives from their individual boot sheaths and grasped the handles in a way that the blades lay flat against her forearms.

She took a moment to gaze again at the fine weapons. An assassin of her elevated standing always had a wide variety of tools at her disposal, but these Arcai blades were among the very finest and most valuable she would ever own. They would have to be. Only weapons such as these were capable of inflicting a mortal wound upon an Arcai, and throughout the world, there were only a few such dragon-fired weapons.

She now had two.

She looked at the blade that was partially pulled from its sheath while its twin still rested on the table, the man's hand lying protectively across it. The blade was forged from a dark blue-black metal and, as she looked closer at the weapon, she noticed the faintly glowing runic lines of powerful magic woven into the metal during the weapon's creation. While she couldn't read the language, she had no problem recognizing it as dragon-speak. "Where did you obtain these?" she asked, her voice carefully controlled. "Only a dragon can forge such a blade."

"And they do so very hesitantly," the man agreed with a knowing smile.

"You still have not answered my question," she pressed.

"You will hunt one of the most formidable opponents you will ever face," he said evasively, "and you will do so with a pair of weapons that are unmatched in all the land. If you choose to accept the task, the weapons are passed on to you. What does it matter where I obtained them?"

The woman wrapped slender fingers around the two sheathed blades. "At the moment, it is not important," she agreed, feeling the weapon's magic practically hum in her grasp. "Very well, I accept the contract."

As light-footed and perfectly balanced as a panther, the assassin slipped downward from branch to branch until she was a mere ten feet above her target, who was relaxing by the fire, sipping hot root soup from a battered clay mug.

The huntress paused only a moment more before she stepped off into space and dropped to the ground beside her prey.

Nearly an hour after accepting the blades, the woman watched from a nearby rooftop as the robed man finally emerged from the little tavern. He paused for a moment, his eyes scanning left and right, before he set off hurriedly toward an even seedier side of town.

Unfortunately for him, he never looked up.

The assassin drew back her bow and sighted it on her contact. She had no more use for the man and knew he was only one contact in many that would exist between her and the unknown benefactor who had come into possession of the two incredible blades that she now owned as payment for the job she was about to do. A person capable of that would also undoubtedly know that she would not let his messenger live after they had completed their business. Such a person would also know when she completed the contract.

She let the arrow fly.

As she landed beside her mark, the assassin slashed out with her right hand, allowing the blade to extend from beneath her forearm. But her target was no ordinary mortal and was already rolling to the side, avoiding the initial strike. The blade slide harmlessly through the air, but the killer followed it up with another, her well-trained body flowing effortlessly in the deadly dance. This time, the weapon slid along the side of her target, slicing through leather and into flesh. Blood welled immediately from the wound and an amorphous red glow seemed to flow from the wound and into the knife as the blade drew off part of the woman's life force.

There was an audible gasp of pain, but no word as the target rolled to her feet and pulled a long slender sword from a scabbard at her waist. Normally, she would have preferred her bow, but it was lying harmlessly near her bedroll along with her arrow-filled quiver. She would have to make do with what she had, realizing that her attacker would give her no quarter.

The assassin moved like the wind, effortlessly circling her prey, her weapons dancing and diving through the air. The victim moved her own blade back and forth in a brilliant display of defensive swordplay, yet she began to realize that it would not be enough. In all her many centuries of life, she had never before considered possible what was about to happen and, for the first time in her life, she felt fear.

The blades of the huntress scored another hit, this one across her victim's midsection, then a third, a long bloody gash down the woman's forearm. The hunted staggered backward, weakening as the enchanted blades siphoned more of her life force away. She knew she was mere moments away from death, but fought on even as she sent her thoughts skyward, seeking her companion.

"Help me."

The assassin moved in, parrying down a weakened thrust as she rolled down the blade, bringing her face to within inches of her prey. The two women locked gazes for a moment, the fathomless brown eyes of the near immortal locking with the glacier-blue eyes of the most feared assassin in all the land.

And then the killer slid the blades home, piercing the victim through each side, angling them upwards so that they sheared through her lungs and into her heart. She held them there, buried to the hilt as her prey's eyes widened in sudden terror. The assassin felt the magic of the blades feast on the fading life of the woman and only when her expression froze and her eyes became fixed and unseeing, did she finally lower the dead woman gently to the ground.

She withdrew the weapons and spun them each into their individual boot sheaths, not a drop of blood showing on the dark metal. With a reverence not expected after such a brutal act, the assassin crossed her victim's hands over her breast and gently closed her eyes. There had been no malice in her act of murder. She held only respect for the now-dead woman. But she had been given a contract and she had filled it. It had been her duty.

A roar of anguish echoed through the forest and she looked up, unafraid. It was the woman's companion, but he was distant and the severing of the life bond between the two of them had weakened him considerably. She would be safely away long before he could drag himself to the body of his beloved.

She stood then and paused for a moment more to reflect on the monumental deed. She had slain an Arcai. She had widowed a dragon. It was something that had never before happened in the history of her world. The gains to her reputation were boundless, but the ire of her enemies would be great.

But in time, none of that would matter. She could not know that her actions were the carefully orchestrated opening moves in a chain of events that would usher in the destruction of all that she held dear and ultimately change the very fabric of her world's reality.

She could not know…

…but the Dream Walker did.

With a groan of distress, the ancient vampire bolted from the bed and scrambled away from the assassin. The magic broken, Vendetta was quick to awaken and she rolled to her feet, drawing the sheets around her body as she faced the strange enchanter.

"I tasked you only…to read my dreams," Vendetta gasped, feeling the weakness weigh heavily on her. It had been a calculated gamble, allowing the vampire the opportunity to feed on her life force, while trusting he would hold to his word. "I would not have begrudged you a taste, demon."

But the Dream Walker was pressed up against the far wall, his glowing eyes wide with alarm of his own. "Would that I had slain you when you slept," he said softly. "It might prevent what is to come."

"Why?" Vendetta asked, fear raising the hairs on the back of her neck. Beneath the sheet, her fingers slipped around the hilt of the dagger she had kept strapped to the inside of her thigh, before disrobing. "What is coming that would frighten someone like you?"

"I sensed it in you when you first came to me," the vampire answered, gathering his own courage in the face of what he had seen. He had witnessed the end of everything in the assassin's future—the clash of races, the crush of worlds, the fall of the gods, the end of time. Everyone's time. The woman's future was bleak indeed, awash in approaching encounters with other Arcai and their companions. But that would mean nothing when the gods went to war with each other. When that happened, the fate of the assassin would matter not at all. Nor would the fate of anyone else. Including him. Unless he acted.

He took a deep breath and straightened, his eyes never leaving those of the killer. "You are touched by the gods, Vendetta, in ways that far outstrip your abilities to fathom."

"I killed the daughter of a god," the assassin countered. "Nothing more."

"That is where you are wrong."

"They hunt me then?" she questioned, raising an eyebrow in doubt.

"Nothing so simple, dear girl."

"Then what?"

The Dream Walker only shook his head.

"Then what!" she fairly shouted, stepping toward him, forgetting for a moment who she was dealing with.

The ancient creature moved with incredible speed and was suddenly upon her. A blade appeared in his hand as he spun her around and pressed it against her throat. "Did you believe I would let you live?" he hissed, tightening his arm around her chest, the metal edge of the dagger drawing a line of blood on her neck.

"Why would you kill me like this?" Vendetta asked, her voice catching slightly in fear. "The blade is not your way."

"It began with you, child, when you accepted the contract," he answered, "when you took the weapons. Only your death might prevent what has been set in motion."

"It was an assassination."

"No!" he shouted in sudden anger. "It was more than that! More than a mere contract! It was the beginning, my dear, the beginning of the end and you are but a lowly pawn, a worthless tool given a task you could not hope to comprehend. It began with you." His voice dropped and his eyes narrowed. A quick slice and it would be all over. "It began with you," he repeated, "and it can end with you, as well."

"What are you speaking of?"

"The convergence," he replied, lowering his lips to her bare neck. He should kill her outright by cutting her throat, he knew it. But her blood called to him, tempted him to feed in the old way. "The merging begins with you; with the brats you will usher into this world," he breathed, his voice husky with hunger.

"A child?" she gasped.

"Indeed," the vampire answered, opening his mouth and baring his fangs.

"I have no children and I never will," she feigned alarm. "I do not understand."

"You wouldn't," he sniffed arrogantly, drawn into complacence by the timber of her voice. "You are but a mortal and mortals die."

"But you are not immortal, either," she whispered back, the fear suddenly gone as she turned her head to catch his eyes. Before he could react, she slid the Arcai blade deeply into his side.

With a howl of pain and rage, the Dream Walker twisted away, throwing his would-be victim to the floor. But it was too late. The magical blade—a tremendously powerful artifact itself—was embedded to the hilt between his ribs, the ornate handle seeming to absorb the growing red mist that was being pulled from his body. The blade drank his life, peeling away the centuries of youth from his countenance in a matter of seconds. The Dream Walker could not speak, his mouth working in a soundless scream as his skin wrinkled and his flesh shriveled and then sloughed away from his bones. Moments later, his skeletal remains collapsed to the floor, smoking and blackened as the blade feasted on what remained of his essence.

Vendetta pulled the sheet tighter about her chest, though there was no one now to see her. For the longest time, she stood silently and stared at the pile of smoldering bones on the floor. Her weapon lay amongst the remains, now cool and dormant. It had begun with the blade, the vampire had told her. A dragon-forged gift to kill an Arcai.

For the first time since the assassination, she began to consider the question she had long since ignored.

Why?

10 years later…

Part 1

Strangers in a Strange Land

Convergence

A lone warrior stood atop the highest hill overlooking the large bastion of humanity on the central plains – the Dom'Ithi stronghold known simply as Northern Outpost. It was a plain name for the large trading town, one of three stone and timber walled outposts that extended the Dom's influence perilously westward past the great Lira River and into the immense flatlands and rolling hills of grasses and timber, much still covered by the melting snow of early spring. Most would agree that it had always been a bold move for the land-hungry Dom'Ithi people to extend their influence westward as far as they had dared with their three border cities and countless settlements and farmsteads. They were, truly, the greatest race in all the lands, at least as far as land area was concerned. However, others would contend that the dangers inherent in such an expansion were too great to overlook and the boldness of the Doms should have been tempered with care. On this particular day, the latter group would be proven right.

The day was warm, with spring nearly ready to take complete hold of the land, leaving those people who were in immediate peril, hoping they would somehow escape the death and destruction that would descend upon them before night would fall again. They knew that behind the single solitary warrior, and hidden by hills and trees that were common in this part of the plains, were the armies that the warrior commanded, gathered together and awaiting the first taste of blood in a campaign that would allow them to sweep through the midlands and into the heart of the Dom empire.

The people of Northern Outpost knew it and they were powerless to stop it.

Savage dark-skinned U'Raati from the foot of the Dragon's Teeth Mountains, nearly three thousand strong, brought up the fore of the impressive fighting force. They were clad in the skins of various animals and even humans, with bones and skulls decorating the more prominent warriors of the clans as if to emphasis their higher standing and greater blood-letting abilities in battle. Their weapons varied widely—usually bone hammers of varying size and shape or blades and other weapons taken from past unfortunate victims. They had all the appearances of a ragtag band of wild men, but despite their unorganized and savage look, they were vicious fighters and greatly feared, barbaric in nature and with little need for order and even less for spoils of war. They lived only to kill, and it was something they did exceedingly well.

Greater yet were the formidable and heavily-armored warriors of the coastal dwelling Gol'Athi—disciplined and militaristic, yet cold-blooded in their own deadly fighting prowess and generally bitter enemies of the U'Raati, not to mention the Dom'Ithi. Most of the Gol forces were common soldiers and clad similarly in heavy plate or chain mail with crests depicting their home cities or villages emblazoned on their chests. Each soldier was similarly armed with a variety of blade, as well as a crushing hammer or mace. The Gol heroes and generals, however, were more unique in their trappings, sporting ornate armors and powerful weapons as they stood at the head of a group of standard soldiers. All together, the Gols numbered more than twice that of the Rats, their battle lines straight and their battalions well-ordered as they awaited the signal that would spur them to encircle the condemned stronghold.

All was in readiness. More than ten thousand strong, the entire army outnumbered the fighting men of Northern Outpost more than three to one and they were led by the greatest warrior to walk the land. It would be a slaughter.

Draven smiled as he looked down upon the town, anticipating

the coming battle and tasting the fear of the men who would fall to the might of his army before the day was out. He, himself, wore no armor save for a leather skirt and a pair of silver bracers, his powerfully-muscled body mostly bare and majestic in its perfection. With the bracers, he had little need of any other clothing or armor, for the metal bands were crafted of impossibly strong alloys and bore magical properties that lent him a large degree of protection should an enemy's blow ever be lucky enough to get past Dread, the mighty dragon-forged claymore that was strapped to his back. His features were sharp and defined, his golden hair blowing in the slight breeze, and his blue eyes were deep and penetrating as they gazed down at what would be the first target in his intended military sweep across the great lands.

Below him, the inhabitants of Northern Outpost awaited his assault, knowing fully two days past that his army was approaching their town and that he meant to destroy them completely. Draven, himself, had been responsible for alerting them, having sent a captured Dom trader back to the town, carrying the severed heads of two other Doms that his scouts had come upon and taken. With the grisly gift went a message detailing his intention of killing everyone that lived in Northern Outpost, should they attempt to oppose him. Few had fled, despite the dire threat, as the townsfolk simply could not allow themselves to believe what was coming.

"The carrion birds will feast well tonight," spoke a quiet voice as a figure slipped out from behind a copse of pin oak trees at the far side of the hill and walked easily toward the great warrior, her long strides covering the ground quickly.

Draven turned to look at the newcomer, a tall and statuesque woman clad in a full suit of gleaming blue chain mail, leaving only her forearms, hands, and head unprotected. She was nearly as tall as Draven's own seven-foot frame and heavily armed with a great sword strapped to her waist and a pair of smaller long swords sheathed across her back. Her hair, long and colored the silver of liquid metal, was pulled back into a tight warrior's braid that fell to the middle of her back. Her facial features were hard, but beautiful, with ice-blue eyes glittering dangerously as they took in the scene before her.

"I think the U'Raati will likely feed better," he said with a twisted smile, turning back to look at the small forms of the town's people scurrying about in preparation for an attack that they could not hope to survive. "The Rats can almost smell the blood in the air and it becomes taxing to keep them in line."

"Then perhaps you should make the challenge," offered the female warrior, turning to regard him. There was an unspoken bond between the two and her eyes flashed warmly as she addressed him before turning and looking back down upon the town. "All is in readiness," she continued. "There is no further need to delay, my lord."

"Perhaps you are right, Zarandrae," he agreed with a smile before turning and striding to a boulder on the far side of the hilltop. Jumping atop it and looking down at his assembled forces on the other side of the hills that separated them from their target, he held up a hand and then tightly clenched his fist and brought it to his heart, signaling his generals to begin readying the army for the assault. A roar rose up from the gathered soldiers and, without waiting to see the expected result, he turned and walked back to the woman. He knew that at his signal, his Gol commanders were already forming up their respective ranks of soldiers and preparing to march forward, while the Rats were being worked up into a killing frenzy by their tribal leaders and shamans. His war machine was primed and ready, awaiting the inevitable outcome of the warrior's challenge.

"Do you think the Doms will acquiesce to the old laws?" asked Zarandrae, referring to the ages-old and revered custom of two chosen warriors facing each other in open battle before their respective armies clashed.

Draven shrugged. "Why not?" he replied confidently. "We are marching openly and have even warned them of our coming. We have obeyed every edict of the warrior's code. They have no reason not to comply and, if they don't, then may the gods cast their wretched souls into the Nether." He spat the last comment in disgust, having no room for cowards who lacked honor.

The armored woman turned to regard him, a knowing look in her eyes. "The laws of war apply to mortal men, Draven," she softly reminded him. "I have my doubts that if they knew who championed the armies of Shayene, they would not send their own champion to do battle as the law dictates."

"Perhaps," he replied thoughtfully, reaching up and stroking his smooth chin. The mortal fools might very well consider his coming an easy way to avoid the challenge, and the disappointment of possibly missing the chance for physical combat almost pained him. But he knew that he would eventually get more than his share of opportunities to best mighty warriors in combat as the campaign progressed. Northern Outpost was but a hovel compared to the majesty of the greater Dom cities, so there would be opportunities in abundance later on. With a widening smile, he turned to face the woman, a gleam in his eyes. Without hesitating, he placed a hand on her shoulder and said almost playfully, "Now that I consider it, you are absolutely right, my dear. They cannot possibly realize who they are facing. So, I choose to have a second fight in my stead. You will represent me."

For a moment, her beautiful face was as stone, but it passed quickly and a smile played at her lips. "You would not jest with me?" she challenged, excited at the thought of crossing swords in battle with a champion, even one from a smaller town like Northern Outpost.

Besides, it was certainly more exciting than simply eating one, as she would normally do.

"Of course not," he replied honestly. "Besides, why should I have all the fun? Once Northern Outpost is ours and the supply lines are established, we will move on to Ithil Majeer and there I will slay their champion, Kelemaur."

"Your skills are unmatched, my lord, but Kelemaur is a mighty warrior," she said, her eyes narrowing again as she reminded him of something he certainly already knew. "He is one of the finest fighters in all the land." She placed a long-fingered hand gently over his and moved closer to him, her voice soft as she pressed her body to his. "Do not let your confidence be your undoing, Draven. Your kind is not above being slain by a mortal. Remember well the daughter of Desha."

Draven looked at his companion and lover, and smiled warmly. His confidence was unshaken and he leaned forward and kissed her roughly. "Jayra was a fool," he said contemptuously, referring to the untimely death that the goddess Desha's Arcai daughter had suffered at the hands of a Vi'Raaji witch some years before.

"All the same," Zarandrae said firmly, not backing down, "do not underestimate Kelemaur. He is a worthy opponent and he possesses a dragon-forged weapon. He can hurt you."

"Which is precisely why it will be I who will slay him," Draven finished quickly, his eyes flashing dangerously. "As mighty as he supposedly is, he has yet to face me."

"And Northern Outpost?" she asked, quietly dismissing her companion's stubbornness and changing the topic. On a deeper emotional level, she feared for her lover's safety in battle, despite who he was. But if he was confident in the outcome of a fight with Kelemaur, she knew she should be the same. Right now, though, the more pressing issue was the champion of Northern Outpost and the idea that she would be the one to challenge him or her.

Draven shrugged again. "I do not even know if this city has a champion. A victory over one with no renown would be without meaning for me anyway, even if they accepted the challenge. For you, however, it will allow you to hone more of your already impressive fighting skills." He paused as his eyes roamed over her armor-clad body with a knowing grin. "At least in your present form."

Her smile returned as she contemplated his words and, for a few moments, she was silent. She was as old as any of her kind, but had never had any real opportunities to face a human in combat in their own form. That had changed only recently when Shayene had broken with Arcai law and had begun marshaling her forces against mortal man and Draven had accepted her request to lead them. Now Zarandrae looked forward to crossing swords in battle with seasoned warriors, having sworn to keep her true form hidden for the time being. Finally, she looked at him, her decision made. "Very well, my lord. I will accept your charge," she said confidently as she held up three fingers, sharp blue nails flashing in the sunlight, "and I will challenge three."

"That's my girl," Draven said easily, then turned mock serious. "No cheating, either."

Zarandrae returned a shocked look to him and then playfully brushed her lips to his. "I need no tricks to claim victory in this manner," she said silkily.

"I know," he replied with a smile. "But seriously, make your challenge and be finished with them. Do not take the chance of having to revert to your true form. It would not do well to have Ithil Majeer preparing for a dragon when we march up to their gates. Your true nature is to be kept a secret for now, for it will make your appearance to them all the greater and lessen the risk to you if they are not fully prepared."

Zarandrae nodded solemnly and stepped back. "Your reasoning is sound, my lord," she said quietly, "but I do not fear humans," she paused before finishing, "in any form." She turned and began walking down the hill toward the settlement. "I will bring victory to your sister's cause," she said loudly as she broke into a run and charged down the hill in anticipation of the battle she would soon face.

"Of that, I have no doubt," replied Draven quietly to himself as he watched her go.

Zarandrae stood about fifty yards from the gate, her massive great sword held out easily before her as she slowly turned, keeping her eyes on the three armored Dom warriors who circled her at equal distances, their wary eyes locked on her flowing movements. She had descended the hill quickly and come before the gates, where she made the standard challenge. When the first warrior immediately answered her call, she had called for two more, angering the first and sending murmurs of apprehension through the soldiers who were manning the walls of the town. In a few short minutes, though, her request had been heeded and the three warriors now faced her, the terms of the challenge set according to the laws of old. If she successfully defeated the three fighters, it meant an immediate and brutal attack by the waiting army that would not halt until Northern Outpost had fallen. However, if she failed and her enemies defeated her—which was not likely—the people of Northern Outpost would be given a full seven days to prepare in whatever fashion they wished and those who did not desire to remain and fight could leave safely and not have to worry about being pursued. Such were the laws of war and the way of the challenge, ancient standards that the Arcai, Draven, adhered to religiously.

The four fighters slowly circled, each side measuring the other and looking for that opportunity in which to launch a crippling first strike. The three Dom warriors had quickly moved into a triangle around the woman, forcing her to turn continuously to keep them all within her range of vision as much as possible and therefore increase the risks of her making a mistake.

"You must think highly of yourself, wench," growled the first warrior, still bitterly angry at her request for two additional champions; a request that he viewed as a terrible insult to his honor. "You may look like a warrior," he finished mockingly, "but you are still a woman and your place is tending the cooking fires. Perhaps I will spare your life and let you live out the remainder of your pitiful life in servitude to me and my house."

"You speak as a fool and a coward," Zarandrae replied icily, ignoring the nervous laughter of the man's two comrades. "As far as I am concerned, there is no honor to be gained from killing an idiot such as yourself in the warrior's circle." She spun her huge sword effortlessly in her hand as if to punctuate her cutting statement.

The man harrumphed, slapping his hand loudly against his bronzed breastplate. "Bah! I am Delgor and I am champion of Northern Outpost!" he challenged boldly, his mouth curling into a sneer. "And when this battle is through, I will see to it that you admit that fact with your dying breath."

But Zarandrae did not answer, instead moving like a cat even as the man boasted. She spun toward him, her great sword slashing through the air toward his midsection. His swaggering nearly got him killed, but his own considerable fighting expertise allowed him to drop his own sword to take the brunt of her initial strike. As it was, the force of her swing jarred Delgor's blade from his hand, driving through to dent his armored torso. An expert swordsman himself, he quickly fell backward with the strike as she followed through and his defensive movement lessened the great sword's impact on his ribs. He hit the ground and immediately rolled back to his feet, snatching up his dropped blade as he did.

But the woman was already moving past him, her great sword swinging around to deflect the second warrior's heavy mace that was whistling toward her unprotected head. The weapons came together with a ringing clash of steel, and the superior quality of her dragon-forged blade sheered through the metal haft of the man's mace in a shower of sparks. The surprise and shock of the shattered weapon cost the man his life as Zarandrae allowed her momentum to carry her full circle. As she came back around swinging her two-handed weapon at full strength, her massive blade cleaved completely through his leather-armored body. The man was dead even before the two halves of his corpse hit the ground. She continued her pivot expertly, coming back into a defensive posture before the remaining two warriors could act to take advantage of her position. She then backed away so that she could hold them both within her peripheral vision and therefore be ready for their counterattack.

It was well-executed and came almost immediately, nearly proving disastrous for her. Oblivious to the gruesome death that had befallen his ally, Delgor darted in with a hard thrust, causing Zarandrae to bring her huge sword around quickly to pick off the blow. Too late she realized that it was merely a feint to draw her away from the other warrior and it was only pure instinct that allowed her to escape serious injury as he came on in a rush, his long sword cutting through the air in a vicious arc toward her head. She dove wildly to the side, the man's deadly blade missing the intended mark, but still drawing a line of blood down her forearm. Her great sword was knocked from her grip as she rolled through the blow and came back to her feet, her hands already going to the pommels of the twin long swords that were sheathed across her back. In a flash, she had them out, instantly deflecting and parrying strike after strike from the two fighters now bearing down on her from either side in a savage fury.

For several long minutes, the battle raged with nothing more to show for it but the ringing clash of weapons and the grunts and curses of the combatants. Delgor and the other warrior pressed in on the woman relentlessly, slowly driving her backward toward the settlement's outer wall, hoping that she would tire and they would be given the killing opportunity they both sought.

But Zarandrae was not the human they thought her to be and therefore not subject to the endurance limits of their own bodies. She was a tireless fighter, her stamina greater than that of any living thing, even that of her own kind, and as such, she was just getting started.

Her twin blades whirring in a blur of motion, she drew next blood as she parried down a vicious thrust by Delgor with one of her swords and, at the same time, slashed her other sword tip across the cheek of the other warrior who fought beside him. The man spun reflexively away to avoid any serious damage from the cut, but her backhand swing with her other sword exploited the opening, quickly taking his weapon arm off at the elbow in a spray of blood. With an agonized groan, the man dropped to his knees, the shock of the horrible wound only too evident on his stricken face. Frantically, he grasped at the stump of his arm in a vain attempt to stem the flow of blood and perhaps save his life. He failed.

Zarandrae offered no quarter, spinning easily to deflect another savage cut by Delgor with one of her weapons and then continuing around in a beautiful pirouette to bring her other blade down swiftly, the finely honed edge of the sword cleaving easily through the wounded man's skull, killing him. Then, with a twist of her wrist as she continued her spin back toward her last remaining enemy, her gore-spattered sword came free and she was facing Delgor with both her weapons at the ready, even as her second victim slowly pitched forward in death behind her.

With an enraged shout, Delgor dove in quickly, thrusting his sword forward and immediately twisting the strike upward, hoping to impale the woman on the end of his blade. But by now, Zarandrae was moving so quickly that her form was almost a blur and she twisted effortlessly away from his stroke, expertly bringing her swords together in a pincer-like movement as she spun by him, a move that took Delgor's weapon right out of his hand and sent it flying. Then, she was behind him, both her blades poised for a final strike before his sword even hit the ground.

For a moment, Delgor simply stood there, unable to believe what had just occurred. Finally, stunned and beaten, the weaponless man fell to his knees and placed his hands on his thighs, while lowering his head in supplication. The challenge was over. She had beaten him and he knew what must come next. It was the one inevitability of just such a battle and honor demanded it.

Zarandrae quickly sheathed her twin blades in one fluid movement and then leaned down to sweep her great sword back into her hand. She then swung the huge blade down to rest against the back of her defeated opponent's exposed neck, the razor-sharp edge leaving a thin line of blood. "Are you at peace?" she asked.

"Be done with it," he growled savagely, all pretense of honor given up at the knowledge of his impending death.

The victorious woman gave him a steely gaze and then after a moment, she removed her sword from his neck and placed her foot between his shoulder blades, before shoving him forward. Delgor sprawled on the earth and quickly rolled to his back, propping himself up on his elbows while looking at her with an incredulous stare.

"How dare you?" he seethed, the implication of her actions all too evident on his face. It was bad enough that he had lost the battle, but she had disgraced him by sparing his life and denying him a warrior's death.

Zarandrae simply smiled at him, her features cold and without pity. "You are beaten, Delgor, and I am within my rights to spare your life if I so choose," she said quietly. "Yet the fact that I am a woman blinds you to the honor you have been given even in defeat."

The beaten man climbed to his feet, his face twisted in rage. "You took away that honor when you called for the others," he said venomously as he swept his hand around at the two corpses that lay lifeless in the blood-spattered grass. "Do not forget that it was you who first tarnished the sanctity of the challenge!"

Zarandrae shrugged, looking past him to the men who were upon the walled battlements, concern lining their faces and fear in their eyes. She noted with satisfaction that more than a few bows were already drawn and trained on her. With a shiver of excitement, she turned her gaze back to Delgor and brushed aside his charge. "Return to your people," she said coolly, slowly sliding her great sword back into its sheath at her waist, her eyes never leaving his. "You will be given another chance to fight and I promise you will have ample opportunity to reclaim the honor that you seem to think you have lost."

Delgor inclined his head, indicating the high hill behind her. He could see a lone figure standing off in the distance and it brought to bear the weight of what he and his people would soon be facing. He had been present two days ago when news had come of the large army marching toward Northern Outpost; an army that he knew now lay just beyond the hills in the distance. "We will fight you," he said quietly, mustering up his courage in the face of overwhelming odds.

"So be it," she said easily, still smiling. "But we are ten thousand strong, Delgor, and more than a match for you and your defenders."

He returned his look back to her, his own eyes blazing. "Northern Outpost may be yours in the end," he agreed calmly, already knowing the inevitable outcome of what would likely be a short and bloody battle. "But you will take it at your own peril, I promise you." He crossed his arms defiantly as he finished. "And if you intend to march on Ithil Majeer, know that Kelemaur will turn your minions back and stake your head outside the city gates as a warning to others."

Zarandrae smiled and took a step toward the man, her form seeming to ripple and grow, causing him to shrink back from her in sudden unexplained terror. "When we reach Ithil Majeer," she began icily, "there will be another in my stead to face Kelemaur. And for him, so much the better." She offered him a dangerous look, one that promised something very different from what he had faced in her. Then abruptly, she turned away from him and put her back to the city, her very actions a contemptuous barb aimed at the archers on the town walls. "Be gone, Delgor," she said as she walked back toward the hill. "Your time grows short. Nightfall will find you either dead or running for safety and if I catch you running, you will find me far less charitable."

The man needed no more prodding. He turned quickly and hurried back to the gates of the town, even as the war horns of the Gol'Athi began to blow.

The attack came quickly, some three thousand screaming U'Raati killers racing around and over the huge hill and across the small expanse of flat grasslands toward the walled town. From the hilltop, Draven and Zarandrae casually watched as the Rats reached the settlement and began swarming over the walls, oblivious to their own losses as they tore down the men and women defenders of Northern Outpost with savage and relentless precision.

Behind them, the Gol warriors had begun their own orderly march around the hill, splitting into two columns that would converge on the doomed border town. The Gol soldiers knew they would fight little this day, their real purpose in this battle being to drive away whatever semblance of hope the beleaguered defenders might have against the Rats. As it was, even their imposing presence was not needed. The savage U'Raati tribesmen were already well on their way to victory by the time the Gol generals finally ordered their soldiers into battle.

In eight hours of fighting, Northern Outpost had fallen.

The next day, the first rays of the morning light fell upon an occupied town that was bustling with activity as the western army continued to bolster and fortify their position within the captured Dom stronghold. Smoke from Rat cooking fires still hung heavily in the air, carrying with it the strong odor of burnt human flesh. The scent of death was carried far on the spring breeze and was the first thing the wounded man noticed when he opened his eyes and tried to rise.

Delgor's strength quickly failed him and he pitched forward. He rolled over, his face looking upward through blood-encrusted eyes as the events of the past day came flooding back to him. The defeat to the female warrior and the slaughter that quickly followed when the Rats attacked his town overwhelmed him and brought tears to his eyes for the loss. For his own worth, he had fought well, slaying more than a dozen of the wild savages in the battle and then leading some of the remaining survivors to safety beyond the battle lines, intending to catch up with those few men, women, and children who had already fled. However, he had taken many wounds in the fierce fighting and had eventually fallen behind, but urged the others on. Once the ragged group had crested a far ridge and disappeared from sight, he had collapsed from exhaustion and loss of blood. That had been before the sun had set the previous night.

Now it was morning and the smell of death from the fallen town sickened him. He struggled back up into a sitting position and forced himself to consider what was next. Taking stock of his injuries, he knew they were serious, but he thought he could survive them if he was careful. He had several deep gashes on his body, including one that had opened up his side and exposed the white bone of his ribs. There was also a jagged wound across his forehead where he had narrowly escaped losing the top part of his skull to a Rat short sword. In addition, his left arm hung limply where a Gol war hammer had crushed the bone above his elbow, but in his right hand, he still held his sword, the same Gol's blood still slicking the blade from where Delgor had run him through.

Using the sword now to steady himself, he climbed slowly and painfully to his feet and then stood staring at the ridge to the north, knowing that he had a long journey before him to reach Ithil Majeer. Summoning his resolve, he silently vowed that he would indeed reach the city and he would again stand with his Dom'Ithi brothers and sisters, this time in victory. The vile Rats would once again taste the blade of Delgor and he would revel in the spilling of their blood, as well as that of the Gol invaders. Strengthened by his desire to fight again, he took a deep breath and began slowly walking.

Distracted by thoughts of battle and vengeance, the wounded

man never saw the massive blue-scaled head hidden within the morning shadows of the nearby trees. Reptilian eyes watched him intently, having been locked on their prey now for the past hour.

The dragon took her time eating him.

Chapter 2

With a last desperate hope, the bone-weary man delved deeply into his arcane power and drew on his magic for what would be the last time. The wall before him began to shimmer as if distorted by waves of rippling water, and a slow hiss could again be heard. The man, a small and stooped figure kneeling before the stone wall, seemed to shrink even further into the depths of his fraying and tattered gray robes. Yet, his concentration was utterly complete as he drove his thoughts deeper into the magical forces that swirled within his mind and body. Raising a wrinkled hand, he pressed it to the surface of the rough wall before him, sending even more pronounced undulations of power through its solid mass. A shiver ran through his age-wasted body and it seemed that he continued to grow smaller, as if the task was draining him of his very essence.

Directly behind him, another figure stood, silently watching the spectacle. Cold gray eyes glittered within the depths of a hooded cowl and black silken robes billowed out from a slim body as if carried by an unseen breeze. The woman's beautiful, but shadowed features, were expressionless, no hint of emotion on her face. She simply watched and waited for the old man to do what only he could. Only then, when he had succeeded, would she act to complete the ritual.

The shifting waves of energy within the wall began to twist and turn more violently and the stone blocks seemed to warp, before quickly curving into rounded objects that seemed to fit together almost seamlessly. As the change became more pronounced, the old man felt himself begin to falter. He knew that he had little more to give. But of himself, he would give everything that remained to succeed. He had to. Failure meant an eternity of damnation for his beloved wife and children. Whatever the cost of this ritual, he could not allow them to suffer any longer. They must be freed, and only he could bring that to pass.

He allowed himself to open his eyes and caught his breath at the scene that was playing itself out before him. The euphoria of imminent success threatened to invade his consciousness and immediately the vision before him began to waver, once again twisting the stone into insane patterns as it tried to revert back to its original solid form. Instinctively, he knew that his concentration had slipped—in part due to his weakened state, but also because of his heartfelt desire to save his family.

Clenching his fist in grim determination, he strengthened his resolve and prayed silently to the gods that he could hold out for the sake of his loved ones. He summoned forth all the emotion and torment, all his anger and rage, and began to channel it back into his task. As raw emotion fed his desire, the tattooed whorls and glyphs on his hands and arms began to glow pale blue in the shadows and he felt hidden reserves of power open up within him. The effect was instantaneous. As more of his magical energy surged through him and into the wall, the dream-like effect in the stone began to change from watery translucence into solid reality.

Before him, a small hole had opened up in the wall, ringed with stone that seemed to melt as it rippled in and out of reality. A deep and impenetrable blackness filled the opening and the putrid stench of death and decay emanated from within, filling the huge ritual chamber with its stink. Sounds could be heard coming faintly from the deep blackness, wails and screams of tortured souls and the guttural cries of blood-starved creatures that defied description.

The portal had finally been opened. The gateway to the Nether was before him. While the old man stared in a mixture of horror and relief at the pinnacle of his skills as a gatekeeper, creatures imprisoned for millennia were fast making for the spot of light that had suddenly appeared in their eternal prison, a promise of freedom not tasted for ages gone by; a promise of vengeance on the living for taking what had been rightfully theirs after the gods had sent the Earth Storm to destroy them millennia ago.

As the portal opened before the withered old man, the black-robed woman behind him finally moved. The faint trace of a smile passed over the smooth features of her face before disappearing just as quickly as she began her own work to complete the ritual. She raised her arm from her side and her left hand snaked out of the confines of her dark robes, her skin pale but perfect and without flaw or blemish, with the exception of her own set of magical glyphs that gracefully encircled her fingers and worked their way onto her hands and up her arms; magical runes that marked much of her body, an indication of the immense power she controlled. From a distance, the runes resembled only an elegant patterned design with varied shades of blue, purple, and black. However, if one were to look closely, one could see the intricate images of skeletal warriors, zombies, specters, wraiths, and worse worked into the body markings. They were the symbols of a magical power of the vilest nature and few in all the land were marked in such a way, while none were marked anywhere near as impressively as she was.

Reaching forward, the woman placed her delicate hand on the old man's stooped shoulder, her long fingernails pressing into the thin folds of his gray robes, cutting through the frayed cloth and into his withered flesh.

If the old man felt the pain of her claws biting into his shoulder, he did not show it. Nor would it have mattered anyway, for his duty was nearly complete and he knew his life was now forfeit. But his loved ones would be freed. He had won.

He turned his head ever so slightly, looking once more upon what remained of his beloved wife and three of his five children, their lifeless forms shackled to the wall next to him so that he could easily see the horrible torture they had endured and what had finally become of them. Although their lives were already gone and their bodies little more than dried husks, he could still hear their frantic screams of terror and agony echoing inside his head. The few leech-like creatures that still hung to their desiccated skin appeared fat and bloated from their long meals.

His family had suffered immensely, for the creatures that had slowly devoured them were well-known for the indescribable agony they caused their unfortunate victims. But it was not the shriveled corpses of his wife and children that he was looking at. It was the single solitary ruby gem that floated in the air before each one of them – four soul stones housing the spirits of his dead family; spirits that had been ripped from their dying bodies and imprisoned within the gems by the woman who even now stood behind him, forcing him to do her will.

Before he had undertaken this final task, the gem prisons that contained the souls of his family had been hers to do with as she pleased. A sorceress as skilled as she could easily cause unimaginable torture to a soul thus imprisoned and she had demonstrated her power over their souls a number of times already, all for his benefit. Now though, he had done what she had asked of him. She would have to honor her word and set them free by destroying their gemstone prisons and allowing them to move on to their eternal rest. The woman was, after all, the daughter of a god and would be loath to break a promise. Of that, the old man was certain. He had to be.

The woman must have sensed his thoughts and his yearning to have his family freed, for she gripped his shoulder even more tightly, her own strength driving her fingernails deeper into his flesh. Two words came from the shadows of her cowl, her voice a soft, almost imperceptible whisper. "Not yet."

With a sigh of resignation, the old man turned back to view the height of his power one more time before he died. The gateway that he had opened had finally coalesced into a solid reality. His hand, once pressed against a solid stone block, was now immersed halfway into the inky blackness before him and he watched almost dispassionately as a wraith-like appendage slipped from the pit and translucent fingers entwined about his wrist. His wrinkled skin immediately began to wither as the creature on the other side began to voraciously draw his life force out of him, its insatiable hunger spanning countless centuries and greedy for even the slightest taste of the living.

He felt himself beginning to die, the bitter cold of death's embrace creeping up his arm and into his body as it sought to rob him of his last breath. But his time was not yet come, for the woman had yet to complete the ritual. For the sake of the souls of his family, he knew he must hold on until that moment. Strengthening his resolve, he felt his magic flare to life one final time. He was a gatekeeper, a member of the highest circle of sorcerers in all the land, and his considerable magic, augmented by that of the sorceress, would sustain him until he had completed her task. A glint of defiance shone in his eyes as a hollow cry of frustration emanated from the blackness before him and the wraith relinquished its deadly hold on him, slipping back into the gloom. The old man allowed himself an empty smile of victory as he echoed the woman's words. "Not yet."

But as powerful as the old man was, the woman standing behind him was beyond even his ability to comprehend. In all the lands, she had no equal and even the power of a gatekeeper ultimately paled in comparison to the dark powers that she commanded. Yet despite her talents, she could not do what the gray-robed old man kneeling before her could do. She could not actually open the portal. Only the gatekeepers—mages of the Gray Circle—had that ability. The man before her was just such a man. In fact, he was the most powerful of his kind, a man who had lived quietly with his family, never using the great power he controlled, remaining unknown to any and all. Even the Consortium had been unaware of him. But they were fools, one and all, and where they had erred, she had long known about his existence. And she had watched him for years. When she knew he had strength enough to accomplish the task she would set before him, she had taken his entire family and dangled them before him as bait.

It had taken much persuasion from her to force him to do her will. Threats had meant nothing to him. Pain had not moved him. In the end, his wife and three of his children had died horribly before his eyes, their deaths lasting many long and agonizing days as their lifeblood was slowly drained away and their organs eaten from within by the creatures that fed on them. And still he refused her, knowing what the consequences of her request would be. It was only when she had finally torn their souls from their dying bodies and caged them within their gemstone prisons that he had finally broken and agreed to trade his powerful abilities for their release.

The agreement made, he had done what she commanded. He had done what no one had ever done before in the history of his order. He had opened the gate. But this was not just an earth gate to another world. It was a portal to the most horrifying world of all. The Nether was an eternal prison of darkness for the first race of man that had been destroyed by the gods centuries ago in the Earth Storm. It was a portal to the realm of the First Born. It was a gateway to hell.

The woman behind the old man gazed at the creation before them. She felt the dark power behind the gate and the hatred of billions of souls that were neither living nor dead. The air beyond the stone portal seethed with the energy of death magic. She fed on it, drank it in, bathed in its vile essence, and she smiled.

It was time to complete the ritual.

The woman, Shayene, slipped her other hand free from the confines of her robes, lifting the glittering weapon she had held hidden, high over her head. It was an incredible piece of craftsmanship, a deadly looking mace of unparalleled power. Its handle was long and beautifully engraved with strange magical runes and markings and its pommel resembled that of a dragon's claw fastened around a glittering orb. But it was the mace's head that bore the most interest. In the shape of a grinning skull, it had numerous wickedly sharp spikes protruding from it, looking oddly like some perverted crown atop the foul head of a terrifying demon. Crafted of the blackest obsidian and tempered with some of the most intricate and powerful of death spells, Varankyl, the Mace of the Damned, was the only artifact in the world that could give permanence to the gate that was even now pulsing before them. It knew this. And it saw the potential in the woman that wielded it.

Summoning her own magical power, Shayene held the weapon above her and concentrated on the old gatekeeper kneeling before her. Varankyl, thinking the woman's mastery of it had slipped, once again tried to exert control over her. But her strength was beyond mortals and more than a match for it. At least for now.

You serve me, she imparted her thoughts directly to the sentient artifact, bending it back to her will. *And you will do so until I have no more need of you.*

As you wish, Varankyl replied deep within Shayene's thoughts and yet, still it attempted to sway her, to subtly twist her will to more serve its own. It was well aware of the Arcai's strength and what she intended to do and it gloried in it. It desired the chaos that would descend on the world when it was used for its purpose. But it was an ancient being—nearly as old as the Arcai—and it craved control. It could no more deny that desire than it could deny the pleasure it would take in the blood it was about to shed.

The woman's hand that grasped the gatekeeper's shoulder began to glow with a sickly purple light as she channeled more of her own considerable power into the old man. Up to this point, she had only amplified his magic, funneling her energy through him, where it combined with his, strengthening him for the final task. Now that the gate was opened, she intended to burn through him with every bit of arcane power she possessed, fusing her essence into the gateway itself.

His body responded immediately by beginning to twitch and jerk spasmodically as her powerful magic began to flow into him, filling him up. But her magic was much too great for his weakened state and his body could not contain it. Smoke began to seep from his robes and the skin of his hands and face started to blacken and burn. Mercifully, the old gatekeeper never knew what happened, his mind destroyed as the power of the woman's magic consumed him.

His spirit gone, his body nothing more than a conduit now, she forced more of her arcane energy through him and into the gate, strengthening the doorway between the worlds. The old gatekeeper's task was nearly finished. What remained of the ritual would be completed through his withering corpse.

The gateway itself began to shimmer, again becoming a watery image, before it quickly grew larger, suddenly encompassing much of the stone wall before them. When the portal had reached a circumference of roughly twenty feet, the widening effect began to slow and the woman used that exact moment to strike. She swung the mace downward, smashing into the top of the gatekeeper's head.

Varankyl hummed with glee as bone was crushed and gore was splattered across the pulsating gateway, where it sizzled as it disappeared into the blackness. The artifact fed on the old man's life force and absorbed his blood into its crystal, then turned its attention to the one who held it. It felt the woman's life force and thrilled at the amount of power that was there. She would make a fine meal.

The frenzied screaming from beyond the ethereal hole grew louder and more fevered as the creatures within tasted of the bits of flesh that were flung to them. Battling to keep her identity against the growing strength of the artifact, Shayene wrenched the spiked head of Varankyl from the old man's ruined skull and again swept the weapon downward. This time, it descended down in an arc and drove into and through his spine. The old man's chest exploded outward, flesh and blood once again spraying into the void. Varankyl struck as well, drawing in part of the woman's life force and then channeling it into the gate, enjoying every moment that her essence passed through it.

Finally, a low rumbling noise came from the pit and the gateway again began to shimmer, before quickly coalescing back into solid form, this time for good. After a few moments, it was over. The ritual was complete, the gateway opened – a permanent link to the underworld, a doorway created by the sacrifice of the old gatekeeper and infused with the life force of the master of Varankyl. Sated, the artifact rested.

For now.

Her eyes closed, Shayene took a deep breath and steadied herself. She had been prepared for Varankyl's assault on her body and her mind, but the sheer power of the artifact had been almost too much for her. The moment had passed and she had maintained her mastery over it and Varankyl had fallen silent. Finally, she opened her eyes to view her accomplishment.

The portal was there in all its permanent reality. It existed and would not be closed until she desired it. Several of the unspeakable creatures from beyond it wasted no time in crossing that threshold.

The sorceress took several shaky steps backward, still weakened from her encounter with Varankyl, as the first of the undead world's denizens slipped through the gate to stand once again in the world of the living. Slightly taller than a man, yet hunched over as if a great weight were upon their shoulders, the creatures were little more than tattered skeletons, bits of rotted flesh hanging from protruding bones. Despite their decrepit appearance, green eyes burned with a fierce hatred of the living and long crooked fangs protruded at all angles from their oversized jaws. Mortals knew them as scarecrows and they were creatures of nightmare. They were powerful killers and even one was a formidable opponent for a skilled warrior.

Few people had the power and the ability to summon such a creature. She was one of those capable of the feat. But summoning individual demons and monsters to do her bidding was a long and arduous task, even for one such as her. With the portal now opened before her and the actual task of summoning no longer a requirement, she could quickly form an army of them as they freely passed from their world into hers.

There were three of them at first and they paused to gaze hungrily up at the woman standing before them, almost as if in expectation. For a long moment, she did not move, merely appraising the first of the many creatures that would come through the newly created portal. Finally, she smiled, her control over them complete. They would not attempt to harm her. They were not mindless creatures. Even in their maddened desires to feast on the living, they knew they were here at her behest and they realized if she could bring them forth, her magic could just as easily destroy them. With a dismissive wave of her hand, she turned away from them and walked across the chamber, her strides long and full of purpose, her strength returned. Behind her, the three monsters instantly fell upon the shattered body of the old gatekeeper and tore it to pieces.

"So it begins." The quiet words came from a dark-robed robed man standing far back in the shadows of the chamber as the woman came to stand before him. He was tall and slender and, upon first glance, one would think him almost skinny. But there was a powerful aura about him, an emanation of complete and utter supremacy over any who stood in his presence. His hair was long and jet-black, framing an angular face, and glittering eyes of the blackest night stared out from under eyebrows that arched over them like scimitars. Even more compelling were the man's hands. His fingers were long and thin with black razor-sharp nails that extended fully two inches from the ends of his fingers, and the arcane markings of his order were the colors and shades of violet and purple, though darkened as if in shadow.

Right now, his right hand was fastened tightly around the upper arm of a young man who cowered and whimpered in terror before him. The young man was clothed in the robes of the Gray Circle and the runes on his hands and wrists were of the same order as his now-dead father, murdered before his eyes by the sorceress that stood before him.

"Indeed, my love," the woman replied softly with a nod and a knowing smile. "The lands beyond my tower are prepared for their coming," she continued, sweeping an arm before her in a grand gesture. "The armies will assemble quickly."

"You still believe the outworlders you intend to bring here will be safe from these creatures you summon forth?" the man asked, a hint of doubt in his voice. "They will be, after all, not of this world."

She waved him off. "I have seen them, my dear Kraegor," she

explained easily. "They are soldiers and they will be well-armed. Once I have purged their number of the weaker ones, they will be all the safer. The damned will not bother them, so long as they are under my command."

Kraegor dipped his head in agreement. "And of the Gols?"

"They march already," she stated confidently, looking down at the kneeling prisoner as she spoke. "The savages precede them and Draven is at their lead. The Northern Outpost will be the first to fall."

"What of this one?" Kraegor asked menacingly as he looked down at the terrified young man he was holding prisoner. He would have preferred to eat him, but he knew his companion would not permit it, at least not yet.

The woman reached out and gently placed her hand on the young man's head, causing him to tremble even more. "His task will provide us with the conduit we will need to bridge the worlds," she answered sweetly. With her other hand, she held up the blood-spattered mace and continued. "But his are gates that I shall only need open for short durations. Varankyl has served his purpose."

With that, she uttered a quick incantation in an ancient language and the deadly artifact broke apart in her hands with an audible hiss. In an instant, she held the haft, while Kraegor reached out and snatched the head out of the air before it could fall to the stone floor, taking care to avoid its deadly spikes. In doing so, he released his hold on his terrified prisoner, who quickly collapsed before them.

"It would not be wise to leave the pieces where they can be found and reassembled," Kraegor said quietly. He knew of the artifact's immense power and intelligence, but separated as it was now, it was much more docile. That didn't make it any less dangerous. "With your life force now tied to the gate through the ritual, you are vulnerable."

"It is a price I am willing to pay for the gain it presents," the woman replied, looking hard at him. She turned to the suspended bodies of the dead gatekeeper's wife and children. With a slight motion of her hand, the iron shackles that had held them prisoner were magically unlocked and the hollowed husks of their bodies dropped unceremoniously to the floor, where the ravenous scarecrows immediately set upon them, devouring what little remained. The four pulsating rubies that imprisoned their souls floated slowly over to her, where she plucked them out of the air one by one. She handed the gemstones to Kraegor. "Some new playthings for you to practice your magic on."

Kraegor's own smile widened as he quickly slipped the gemstones into a hidden pouch within his black robes. "And of your promise to the old man to free them?" he deliberately mocked the young prisoner.

"What do I care of promises," she laughed. "The old man is dead and, as far as I am concerned, so are any promises that I might have made to him."

At that, the quaking young man on his knees finally found his voice. "But, my father…," he began, his voice quivering with terror. "Please, my lady," he pleaded, his voice breaking and tears welling up in his eyes. "I beg of you to honor your word. My father has done as you have asked and I swear to you that I will do the same. My allegiance is yours for as long as you require it. But please free the souls of my family and spare my sister." His last words came out in a pitiable wail and he grasped at her robes, bowing his head.

For a moment, the woman looked down at the young man as if she would address him, but then returned her gaze to her dark companion. "Do what you will with the soul stones," she said coldly, as much to the young man as to him. "But first, take the head of Varankyl to Nykiva and give it to our colleague there – a bauble to remind her of what she may yet attain while in my service."

"What will you do with the haft?" he asked.

"I am certain that once I have reduced the outworlders to those that will serve me best, I will be able to find a suitable hiding place for it on their world," she said slyly. "A determined enemy might succeed in finding one piece on this world. A true threat will be one that finds a way to bridge the worlds to retrieve the other piece. Only in that way will Varankyl will ever be reformed."

Kraegor bowed low, his gleaming smile never leaving his face. "Truly inspirational, my lady," he replied. "I will do as you wish, of course," he finished with a flourish.

"Very good," she said, reaching down and taking the arm of the terrified gatekeeper's son. She pulled him to his feet. "The young gatekeeper and I have some tasks to perform before you return and I send you after the outworlders." Turning her cold gray eyes on the young man and speaking directly to him, she continued. "Then, I may decide to release you from your servitude and you may at last join your father and be free of this wretched world. As for your sister, she remains safely locked away and her fate depends greatly upon your cooperation."

Kraegor watched the woman gently support her sobbing charge and then lead him slowly out of the chamber while whispering soothing words of encouragement to him.

In moments, the dark man was alone in the chamber, acutely aware of the presence of the shuffling scarecrows as they busied themselves scavenging the stone floor for the last few remaining scraps of the old man's body and the corpses of his dead wife and children. Kraegor turned and looked past them to the newly-opened portal again, truly a masterpiece of arcane power. The magic that had been used in its creation would forever be awe-inspiring to him, despite his own unique powers, and not for the first time he felt a momentary pang of jealousy that those particular powers would forever elude him.

But the moment passed quickly and he smiled as he noticed that several more scarecrows had joined the initial trio, as well as the ghostly form of a lesser wraith. He himself had nothing to fear, though, for two very good reasons. In the first place, he knew that as the creatures emerged from the gate and into the world of the living, they fell instantly under the sway of Shayene, his life-long companion. They would then find their way from the tower into the barren lands beyond, there to begin assembling into the horde that she had long envisioned.

More importantly, though, was the simple fact of who and what he was.

He turned quickly, his own black robes flowing out behind him as he strode through the chamber doors and into the passage beyond. He passed quickly through the deserted stone halls until he came to a particularly wide spiral staircase leading upwards into darkness. A long but effortless climb brought him at last to the top of a wide stone tower, a flat parapet that stood taller than the numerous other towers and spires that were part of the vast stronghold of the woman who ruled the land all about.

It was midway through the night, the ever-present fog of the Wraithlands adding to the impenetrable gloom that seemed to always cloak these dark lands. He paused, raising his head and sniffing. Taking in the night air felt good and he knew that it would feel even better to stretch his wings. Truth be told, he had been in his lesser form for the better part of two weeks and he was more than anxious for the freedom of the skies again. Now, with his companion's requests to see to, he could once again revert to his true form for a while.

Hunching over, the bones in his back immediately began to stretch and lengthen and he felt his own unique arcane powers flare to life as they leant energy to the transformation he was undertaking, a physical change he had undertaken countless times before. Turning his face upward, he allowed himself a roar borne of primal pleasure and searing pain as his features contorted, changing from that of a man into that of something far larger and insidious. Glittering black scales began to take the place of pale human skin, while arms and legs continued to lengthen. Black nails grew longer, hooking and curving into deadly talons, while his face began to elongate and vicious-looking teeth sprouted from growing jaws. From his back, great black leathery wings began to grow.

It was a truly remarkable transformation and in a few moments it was over. Kraegor arched his long neck, feeling with satisfaction as the vertebrae aligned themselves with an audible crack and he felt the strength flow through his powerfully muscled limbs. Opening his mouth, he cracked his huge jaws, stretching the tendons and marveling at how good it felt to be himself again. Several drops of green saliva dripped from his black-scaled chin, where they hissed and bubbled as they struck the stone flooring of the tower parapet.

Finally, with a ground-shaking roar of satisfaction, Kraegor the Black spread his great wings and, with a few easy beats, rose effortlessly into the air. For a moment, he surveyed the darkened landscape about the stronghold, seeing easily into the darkness with eyes sharper than that of any other living thing in the world. Then, clutching half of the magical weapon in one of his clawed hands, the great dragon flew southward, heading for the city of Nykiva.

Chapter 3

Major Rick "Brickhouse" Branson peered through his binoculars for a second time, confirming that he was seeing what intel had said he would be seeing. The sub had indeed breached the surface of the Nachvak Fjord and lay motionless in the ice. There were no markings on the sleek black metal of the coning tower, so he couldn't tell if it was Russian or not. And there was no movement at all on the deck. As far as he could see, the vessel was a dead stick. That didn't mean that it was, though, and he was well aware of the precariousness of the situation.

He tapped his radio man on the shoulder. "Tuner, inform command that we've got a visual."

"Yes, sir," Lieutenant Eric Johansson replied and then quickly set to work.

Branson turned to another man nearby, one of his best soldiers and his closest friend. The two had been together for years, starting in boot camp and then progressing through three combat tours. They had saved each other's lives several times over and both figured they were getting toward the end of their active duty. "Get'em up, Swan," he went on, addressing his friend by his nickname. "We need to get hoofin'."

"Tell me again why we didn't just come up the strait?" Lieutenant Gabriel Swanson grumbled as he checked his clip on his M16 assault rifle. He snapped it back into place, ready to move, the countenance on his ebony face one of complete dedication to duty, despite the complaining.

The major shook his head. "No one is supposed to know we're comin'," he replied. "We go in weapons hot and eliminate anyone that gets in our way. Simple as that."

"They call that an act of war back home, bro," Swan reminded him sarcastically.

"Only if they know about it," Branson replied and slung his own weapon over his shoulder.

"You think it's the Russians?"

Branson shrugged. "No idea. But whoever it is, they aren't supposed to be here," he answered. "Let's just get in, get the sail team aboard, and get back home."

"Roger that," Swan sighed, then turned and loped back into tree line, giving orders as he went.

Branson watched him go and then raised the binoculars for another look. If he had to hazard a guess, he'd say Swan was right and it probably was the Russians. It would be just like them to bring a sub into the strait in North American territory, even if it was in Canada. But he was still hard pressed to figure out why. Granted, relations between America and Russia were strained almost to the point of war breaking out, but this was really pushing the boundaries.

"We've got a green light to proceed, sir," Tuner reported from nearby.

"Secondary orders?"

"No survivors."

"Figured as much," he growled and then clicked on his radio. "Alright gentlemen, it's time to go. Weapons hot and no questions asked."

The sub was only about two miles upstream from them now. Three days ago, they had put into the brush some twenty miles downstream, deep in Newfoundland's Torngat Mountains National Park, and then moved strictly at night to avoid detection. Their insertion point also gave them access to the water, so they could monitor if anyone made an attempt on the sub through the fjord. No one had, so he and his men had made decent time, staying mostly to the timber when possible, though the heavy equipment had to stay closer to shore where it was a little easier going. It had taken nearly three full nights of covert movement to get within position and, now that they had made visual contact, the time for secrecy was over.

"Swan," he went on over the radio, "you got your snipers in position?"

"Yes, sir," his second-in-command reported immediately. "We'll start moving ground troops in ten."

"Roger that," Branson replied. "We got any movement reports?"

"Negative," came the reply. "It's really quiet."

"Which means it's probably ready to blow up in our faces," Branson sighed. "All right, let's get paid."

"We're out."

"Davis?" Branson went on.

"Yes, sir," came his other team leader's voice, a man leading about fifty soldiers on the other side of the fjord.

"Report."

"Locked and loaded, sir," Davis replied. "Snipers are placed. We'll start moving the rest shortly."

"You heard the orders. Eliminate any resistance. No survivors."

"Affirmative."

Branson held up a hand and circled it in the air. As one, he and his men began moving out of the trees and onto the beach, along with several armored assault vehicles. The AV's took point and begin working down the shoreline, flanked and followed by heavily-armed soldiers. Altogether, Branson had over a hundred soldiers under his command. There were nearly fifty more on the operations team who would take possession of the sub and sail it back home, once he and his soldiers took the boat.

Other than the sub itself, they still didn't know what they were up against. Under constant drone surveillance, no one had seen anything in the way of movement or life around it since it had first been discovered. His team had been dispatched to take possession of it with strict orders to do so with extreme prejudice.

Resistance came at less than half a mile out, when one of his AV's went up in an explosion of flame and debris as a shoulder-fired missile blew it apart. The radio immediately lit up with status reports and automatic gunfire rang out from both sides of the river.

Branson heard the screams of the first men to die, but he was a soldier first, and in war, men died. He had seen it plenty of times. He quickly moved into the trees, barking orders as he went. His team was one of the best and had reset themselves, returning fire in just a few seconds. Sniper team reports began coming across the radio, giving him all the intel he needed as the snipers worked to take out the enemy as quickly as they could see them.

The resistance was centralized around the sub on both sides of the river. Branson did not think they had been there long because there had been no intel on movement and, had the enemy been in the area longer, his team would have met resistance further out. As it was, his team had the greater firepower and numbers on their side and it didn't take long for the gunfire to begin to taper off, finally stopping altogether. More reports came in over the radio, along with shouts of "Cease fire!", something that greatly surprised him.

Branson picked up the pace and, a hundred yards out from the sub, he encountered a situation that hadn't been on his list of possibilities. Swan and a dozen more of his men were fanned out around a pair of AV's, everyone with weapons ready. Not far from them, scattered along the beach and into the nearby woods, were a number of "enemy" soldiers, all with weapons up. It was a standoff that Branson knew could go south in a hurry. What surprised him, though, was that the enemy sides hadn't reduced each other to hamburger already and he wondered how long the impromptu cease-fire would last. They were, after all, under orders to exterminate any resistance.

One of the enemy soldiers was standing face-to-face with Swan. Both men were obviously pissed and yelling at each other.

"Good men are dead because of you!" the enemy soldier was practically screaming at his second in command.

"You still haven't told me what you're doing here!" Swan yelled back and it appeared that both were ready to come to blows.

That's when Branson realized what the problem was and why the cease fire. The enemy was not Russian. They were French. "All weapons to ready position and ready position only!" he spoke quickly into his radio as he hurried toward Swan and the newcomer.

"Are you in charge?" the man turned burning eyes toward him as he approached, his accent heavily French.

"I am," Branson replied, keeping his demeanor cool as he sized up the man. The guy was definitely French military, likely part of a Troupe de Marine division. But what the French were doing here was beyond his understanding. "I'm under direct orders to take possession of this vessel and eliminate any hostiles."

"*Merde*," the man snapped angrily, looking around. "Do we look like hostiles to you? You have fired on an ally!"

"With all due respect, sir," Branson said coolly, silently considering the men who had died when the AV went up in flames, "you fired on us first and I have men dead because of it."

"You are interfering with a top secret military project, Major, and we've got ourselves a serious problem here," the man went on, stepping up to face him directly. Rick Branson was over six and a half feet of solid muscle, which gave him his nickname, and this soldier was every bit his size and then some.

"I agree with that assessment, sir," Branson replied, trying to take stock of the situation. Unfortunately, it made no sense. An American and a French fire team in the same area as an unknown sub stranded in the ice of the Nachvak Fjord simply did not compute. There was no way the French could have known about the sub, unless it was actually theirs. And if it was a French vessel, what was it doing in North American waters? "Maybe you should tell me what you and your men are doing here." He paused to turn to Johansson, who was right behind him. "Tuner, inform command of our situation. Tell them..."

"You will do no such thing, Major," the man snapped. "We will maintain radio silence at all costs."

At this, Branson actually smiled. "I don't take orders from you, sir," he said, laying the disdain on thick. "This is an American military op and my commanding officer is an American, not a Frenchman."

The French commander started to protest, but what happened next froze the words in his throat. It began with a low buzzing sound that began to grow in pitch, drawing all eyes toward its source. The phenomenon suddenly appeared in the air not more than twenty yards from Branson and his French counterpart, starting small and then growing in size until it was a circular field of energy some fifteen feet in diameter. To Branson, it appeared first as a watery reflection of the surface of the fjord until he realized he was looking into it and could not see the stranded sub across the strait. It was as if he was looking through a doorway into a darkened room.

Even more compelling was the stranger who unexpectedly stepped through the gate, seemingly materializing out of the air. He was extremely tall and dressed in flowing black robes, complete with hooded cowl. His face was hidden in shadow and his hands were folded and concealed within the long sleeves of his robes. Under normal circumstances, the man would have been on the ground and immobilized in seconds, but so shocking was his appearance that no one had found the ability to act. To Branson, the man could have walked right out of a horror novel.

If the stranger was concerned about the firepower that surrounded him, he did not show it. Instead, he walked directly toward Branson, who felt himself go cold inside as the man drew nearer. Branson wondered for a moment if the French commander was feeling the same thing he was.

"Which of you commands these forces?" the man said, his voice heavily accented but understandable.

"Um...I am," Branson found himself stammering in shock.

"*Je suis*," the Frenchman said at the same time and both military leaders turned to stare at each other angrily.

The stranger just smiled, a cold thin look of contempt. "My mistress has need of your services. You and your men will accompany me," he finished, leaving no doubt that his words were not a request.

"Uh...say again?" Branson asked uncertainly.

The figure stared at him before replying. "I believe my words were quite understandable."

"Who are you?" Branson snapped, growing angry.

The stranger looked first at him and then the Frenchmen, then turned back toward the gate. "I understand you have questions," he replied. "The answers, of course, are on the other side."

With that, he stepped back into the vortex and then turned and waited. So shocking was the whole experience that every soldier just stared, unable to move. For a moment, Branson wondered if the gate—for that's what it appeared to be—would disappear. It remained open. Finally, he looked at his French counterpart.

"I know you're wondering the same thing I am," he said softly. "But I can assure you this isn't ours any more than it's yours."

"*Irez-vous avec lui?*" he asked, nodding toward the gate.

Branson stared at the vortex. Then, coming to a decision, he was moving toward the gate, speaking into his headset. "Tuner, get word to command and inform them of our situation. Tell them I made a field decision to investigate this anomaly. Davis, you keep your men on that side of the river and be prepared to come running if we need help. In the meantime, roll tape. Get as much of this on video as you can."

"You are going in, no?" the Frenchman asked in English this time, matching him stride for stride.

"No sense in letting an opportunity like this get away. Care to join me?"

The Frenchman did not answer him directly, but quickly peeled away, issuing orders to his own men as Branson continued speaking into his own headset. "Swan," he said. "Get our men moving and into the portal or whatever this thing is. Everyone on this side goes in."

"All of us?"

"Affirmative," he replied. "I don't have any idea what we're getting ourselves into, but we're bloody well going in armed."

"Roger that," Swan sighed. "We're moving."

Twenty minutes later, more than eighty fully-armed marines had vanished through the gate. With them went an entire contingent of French soldiers, forty-seven strong. When the last man had stepped through the portal, the gateway vanished as if it had never even existed.

It had begun.

Chapter 4

Twelve days later, Rick Branson blew an exhausted sigh and leaned back against the rough trunk of a long-dead tree, closing his eyes and wondering once again how they had gotten into this nightmare. They had been fighting for nearly two weeks now, although who could count days in this God-forsaken land of darkness. It would have been nice to still have his watch, but he and his men had been stripped of everything shortly after they had walked through the mysterious portal, a decision he now considered his worst in an otherwise stellar military career. Trapped in a strange world, all they had been allowed were their uniforms.

"Twenty-five," Shayene had said, after informing them just what would be expected of them. The man that had unbelievably walked into their world from another—Kraegor he had called himself—had introduced them all to the woman when the gate had winked out of existence behind them. She had wasted no time in telling them what would happen. She needed warriors, only the best. It would be a small group of twenty-five, no more.

Branson had foolishly thought that it would be a simple matter of picking the best soldiers from both his own forces and those of the French commander and the rest could then go home, but she had dispelled that notion with a laugh that had chilled him to his very core.

"No," Shayene had said. "You will all be expelled to the lands about the castle, where you will remain until twenty-five of you are left. Those," she had continued, "will be my chosen warriors and return to my side. Serve me well in my campaign and I will return you to your world. Refuse me and you will still serve me, but in ways you will find most disagreeable."

Soldiers, both American and French, had immediately objected to her statements by drawing their weapons. The next thing he knew, every last weapon and piece of equipment they possessed had vanished. Shayene had then demonstrated her meaning by randomly choosing half a dozen men and horribly murdering them before their eyes. Branson, for the first time in his life, had witnessed true and terrible magic and the devastating effects it had on the unfortunate soldiers. As he watched her magically strip the flesh from their bones while they screamed, he realized fully that they had all descended into a nightmare that defied explanation. The demonstration was over in minutes and the dead soldiers, only skeletons now with bits of bloody flesh still hanging from their bones, remained upright, empty eye sockets glowing red as they took up positions behind the woman.

"As I said, most disagreeable," she explained. "The choice is yours. You may serve me as these six now do or you may sort out the twenty-five that I require, yourselves."

The question was asked as to how exactly those twenty-five would be chosen, to which she had answered simply, "The strong will kill the weak."

With that, she had vanished. Or rather, they had. The next thing Branson knew, he was opening his eyes in the complete darkness of night. Even when his sight had become accustomed to the blackness, he could still barely see anything. He spent his first few hours on that strange world ascertaining his predicament. He was on damp ground, spongy and pungent-smelling. He would realize later that the whole of the land they were in was nothing more than one big foul-smelling swamp, covered with diseased cypress trees and more bog than dry land. Crouched silently in the darkness, he heard a few shouts, some American, some French. He heard curses and even some sobbing, too. But he remained quiet, taking stock. He had nothing with him, save his uniform. His weapons and equipment had not been returned to him and he was fairly certain no one else had regained their gear. If this did not turn out to be some kind of sick game, he knew the inevitable combat would all be done by hand.

The morning of the first day came, only marginally improving his ability to see, and that's when he realized that what they were experiencing was all too real. The slaughter began with a scream of pain and the sounds of a struggle somewhere in the trees behind him. As silently as he could, he made his way toward the fight. As luck would have it, it turned out to be Swan. A French soldier already lay dead, his neck clearly broken and Branson's second-in-command was engaged in a brutal struggle with another French marine, who had him on the ground and was trying to lock in a guillotine-choke hold. Branson made his first kill there, breaking the Frenchman's arm and then pushing the man's head into a foul-smelling pool and holding him there until he finally ceased struggling.

From there, it only got worse.

The first two days were brutal, one fight after another separated only by a desperate search for food and water. The water in the swamp turned out to be drinkable, if stomach-churning, but the only food they found were small black frog-like amphibians. These at least, turned out to be everywhere and, as disgusting as it was to chew and swallow the slimy, bitter-tasting creatures, they at least had sustenance.

Knowing they wouldn't starve, Branson and Swan and those who joined them over the next two days fashioned weapons out of broken branches, first creating spears and then adopting them as staves. By the third day, sides had been formed. He could not know it then, but at that time, there were five distinct groups ranging from four to eleven in number. Besides his own with seven soldiers, the French commander led another group and three of his own men were leading the others. Those who remained unattached were hunted down and killed, if they were deemed not worthy or refused to join a side.

On the fourth day, Branson and his small group found a somewhat defensible position on a small hill deeper in the swamp. They quickly constructed deadfall traps out of the seemingly unending supply of dead trees and scattered branches and then began creating crude javelins, easier to wield in the tight spaces of the swamp than spears or staves.

The first group came at them on the dawn of the fifth day, thirteen strong at that point. They were led by an American who Branson knew to be an overbearing and bullying sergeant from his outfit. Briggs was his name and he had no leadership abilities save brute strength. Branson, on the other hand, was adept at shaping a battlefield and when the fighting was over, only three of the attackers were still alive, while Branson's seven soldiers had suffered only minor injuries. Branson killed Briggs himself and took the other two into his group. One was Tuner, who Branson was extremely relieved to find alive. Tuner was barely nineteen, a frightened kid who somehow made it through basic back on their own world, and because of his uncanny knowledge of mechanics and communications equipment, had been assigned to Branson's platoon as a radio man. The other was one of the few female soldiers that had been under his command back in their own world, a tough-as-nails Jewish gal name Debra Winestein. The men just called her Boozer. Whether that was because of her last name or the proven fact that she could drink most of them under the table, no one really knew or cared. What mattered was that she was one of them.

Now, nine strong, Branson and his soldiers began scouting the land. They found numerous bodies and several living soldiers, both French and American, most of them wounded, starving, and near death. These they mercifully killed, save one. He was a French marine, silent and brooding, who stood them off for an hour with a sharpened spear, his back to a tree. When it was obvious what the outcome would be, he finally threw it to the ground and surrendered, allowing Branson to take him prisoner.

Today, the man they had come to call Paris, because the name Arceneaux was incredibly irritating, was at the top of the hill, his hands safely tied to a tree as the fighting around them continued. The battle—if it could be called such—had been going on for most of the day, and night was falling. Branson knew this would be the last of it. Several brutal fights had already taken place, some of them with soldiers switching sides in the middle of the fight when it appeared they were going to lose. He had lost a couple men to that desperation and gained a number more. He had no idea how many remained on either side, only that they had to be getting close to the magic number.

Twenty-five.

A figure moved out of the shadows, slinking toward him. Branson tensed for a moment before he realized it was Boozer. She was holding a pair of smooth sticks, both of them spattered with blood. A large cut ran down one of her cheeks and she was limping noticeably.

"Sitrep," he whispered, feeling his own wounds acutely, including a broken left forearm, earned when the last man he killed had managed to slam a heavy tree branch against it.

"We found him," she replied, her voice husky. "Tuner did, anyway."

"That French prick?"

"Yep, the one you should have capped before the gate opened."

"How many are following him?"

"Hard to tell," she shook her head. "I think he's hurt, though, and he's got several guys protecting him, including a couple of our guys."

"Any ID's?" Branson asked, hoping he might know who it was and if it would be possible to convince them to follow him instead.

"No, just grunts."

"How far?"

"Less than half a click in that direction," she replied, pointing back down the hill and off to the right. "Tuner is still there, trapped behind enemy lines. They extended their perimeter as we bugged out, but he didn't make it, so he scooted up a tree. I don't think they know he's there, though. At least they didn't when I started hoofing it back here."

"Okay, we don't have a lot of light left, so let's go get him," Branson said, pushing himself to his feet with a grimace. "Maybe we can cut the head off this snake and end this."

"Roger that," Boozer said and she disappeared into the trees back in the direction she came.

Branson was right behind her.

They picked up two of their scouts as they pushed onward, slogging through knee-deep water a couple of times, leaving them soaked and shivering. One of the scouts reported that Swan had a squad of five moving in on the enemy's flank, hoping to pick off the French Commander before the darkness got too thick. Emboldened by that, Branson pushed his makeshift team quicker toward their target until Boozer held them up. She was up against the trunk of a withered tree, looking up into the darkness.

"Tuner," she hissed.

When she received no answer, Branson moved up beside her, sending his scouts out to either side.

"He's gone," she said, a trace of concern in her voice. "He was up this tree, but they must have found him."

"You sure it was this one?" Branson asked, peering up into the darkened branches, hoping she was wrong. He could see nothing through the black and diseased leaves.

"Yes, sir," she replied, her expression worried.

Before he could reply, a shout arose from the right, disturbingly close. It was followed by more yelling and an occasional scream of pain. The battle had been joined. They moved quickly now, not needing orders. All of them instinctively understood that the end was upon them.

They came out of a tight group of trees, behind the enemy line. Branson could see the French leader, standing over the still form of a soldier. Whether it was Tuner or not, he couldn't tell, but he could not let it matter. They were committed. Swan and his men had engaged soldiers in hand-to-hand, leaving the leader unprotected. While Boozer and the other two soldiers moved to bolster Swan's outnumbered forces and flank the enemy, Branson crossed the distance to the commander quickly, holding his broken arm close to his body. At a dozen feet out, the Frenchman suddenly turned, locking eyes with the American.

Branson could see clearly enough to note that the man was indeed wounded. A crude javelin had been shoved through his upper thigh, the bloody point protruding from just behind his knee. But he turned nevertheless, grinning maniacally. In his hand, he held a sword. It was battered and streaked with rust, but it also dripped with blood, attesting to the fact that it had been used recently. That likely explained why both American and French soldiers were fighting for him. For them, he was their best chance of getting through this alive.

The major pushed aside the thoughts and waded into battle, leading with a three-foot section of tree branch. He had picked up the make-shift club when his broken arm had made using a spear or staff impossible. Now, he swung the club one-handed, hoping to overwhelm his opponent. The French marine brought his sword up, blocking the blow and then turning the sword and slashing it downward. Branson dove awkwardly to the side to avoid the blow, his broken arm slamming into the soft ground.

An involuntary shout of pain escaped him as he rolled to his feet, turning and bracing himself as his enemy thrust the sword forward. The blade went wide and Branson used the moment to swing the club again, this time scoring a glancing hit against the man's shoulder, sending him stumbling to the side.

Gritting his teeth against the agony radiating from his shattered forearm, Branson reversed direction and swung again, aiming for the man's head. This time the sword came up again, catching the club, the blade cutting deep into the rotten wood. With a yell of defiance, the Frenchman jerked the sword backward, taking the tree branch right out of Branson's hand.

Weaponless, the American backed away, seeking something to defend himself with. But there was nothing but dead reeds and a scraggly bush. With a growl of victory, the Frenchman limped forward, holding the sword before him. "I'm going to gut you, American," he seethed, his face a mask of rage. "I'm going to bleed you and end this. Then I'm going to kill the witch and get me and my men out of here."

Branson continued moving backward slowly, keeping a safe distance from the threatening blade. Shouts and grunts and cries of pain surrounded him as the fighting continued around them. Men were dying. Soldiers that were once squad mates or allies were killing each other. "This isn't right," he replied, his eyes on the eyes of his enemy. But he saw no understanding there, only madness.

Then, he was falling, his feet tripping over something as he retreated. There was no way to save himself. His wounded arm went out, bracing the fall and this time snapping fully as his weight came down on it. The bone popped through the skin near his elbow and the wave of pain and nausea robbed him of all strength. He rolled to his back in agony, seeing the Frenchman burst forward, sword raised high, a primal scream of victory on his lips.

It would never fall.

A bloody branch was driven up into the man's groin. Tuner, his face spattered with blood and tears, held the other end as he rose to his knees, eyes on his captor. It was the boy that Branson had tripped over, but he wasn't dead! No, the Frenchman had captured him and brutally beaten him, planning on using him as a trump card if the need arose. His mistake had been in not killing him.

Face white with pain, the sword dropped from nerveless fingers as the Frenchmen looked incredulously at the young American. Tuner twisted the embedded branch as he climbed to his feet, eliciting a strange mewling sound from the man.

Branson was on his feet as well, fighting back his own pain and sweeping up the sword in his good hand. "It's all right," he said softly to the young soldier, stepping in front of him. He raised the sword, looking into the eyes of the doomed man. He saw only defiance and madness. Any humanity left in him was gone.

Branson started to bring the sword down to cleave the man's skull, but it was suddenly gone, his hand empty. Moments later, their surroundings vanished as well and he found himself standing in a large stone-walled room, flaming torches set into sconces at even intervals all around the room. Looking around in disbelief, he realized he was not alone. Tuner was with him, as were others, all of them speechless and looking around in wonder.

Shayene stood upon a dais at the far end of the room, her

hands clasped in front of her. Her cowl was lowered, revealing her face, her gray eyes glittering in the torchlight. "Well done," she said silkily, offering them a smile as she scanned the group. "Twenty-five remain."

"Wait a second," Branson was the first to speak up, drawing her eyes to him. "What about the French commander? He was still alive."

"He will die soon enough, as will the others who are too wounded to be of any value to me," she replied evenly.

"You'll just let them die?"

"There are things in the swamp that will make a meal of them," she said with a shrug. "Either that, or I can return you to the swamp to finish them off." She raised a hand as if she intended to do just that.

"Why?" Branson asked, shaking his head at the madness of everything. "What did you accomplish with any of this?"

"You come from a very different world," she answered, stepping toward him, still smiling. "Here, only the strong survive."

"I don't believe that," Branson replied, realizing that his humanity depended on it. The French commander had given that up and had fallen into madness. Branson had seen that in the man's eyes and wanted no part of it.

Shayene stopped before him, looking up. She was actually quite small compared to Branson's six and half foot frame. He had a fleeting thought that he would kill her right now and end the nightmare, until she reached up and placed a hand on his shattered arm. Pain unlike anything he had ever felt before exploded through his whole body and he sank to his knees, tears streaming down his face. Rick "Brickhouse" Branson had not cried in years, not since he was a kid. He had lived a rough life, enlisted in the military, and been in truly deadly situations. He had seen comrades die and had experienced truly agonizing battle wounds over the years. But nothing compared to the cold pain that threatened to obliterate his entire being as she maintained her grip on his arm.

"This is my world," she went on. "Here, magic rules. Strength rules. Weakness is purged." She leaned forward, bringing her eyes level with his. "I like you, Rick Branson," she purred, smiling demurely. "Therefore, I appoint you leader of your people." Leaning forward, she placed a kiss on his forehead, freezing his blood. "You are healed."

She released his arm and stood up, her eyes sweeping over the other survivors. Branson, still kneeling before her, looked at his arm in amazement. It was no longer broken, now straight and strong. The torn skin where the bone had popped through had been healed as well, a waxy and scarred impression of her hand in his flesh all that remained. "You are all here because you survived," she said, her voice commanding now. "I required twenty-five and twenty-five you are. You will serve me as Rick Branson serves me. He is your commander. I am his master." She returned to the platform, taking her place at the head of the room. "I will broker no dissent, either. If you displease me, I will kill you in ways you cannot even imagine."

She paused, looking around, her eyes meeting the startled or fearful gaze of the soldiers. None of them spoke. Branson climbed to his feet, daring to step forward. "If we do what you ask, will you send us home?" he questioned, swallowing his fear despite the powers that she had just shown. He had little doubt she could obliterate him with just a thought.

"When my campaign is complete, I will return the survivors to your own world," she answered. "But that will be some time, I am afraid. Much still has to happen."

"And if we refuse?"

"Then I suppose I must demonstrate my resolve," she sighed. "A good object lesson will serve all of you well."

She raised her tattooed hands, energy crackling at her fingertips.

Rick Branson would scream for days.

Chapter 5

It had been years ago when it happened, back when Branson was still a sergeant, and it had happened while on patrol with four other marines. It was a route they had patrolled nearly a dozen times in the weeks prior and without fail, it had been little more than a boring walk through a burned out village. The insurgents had long been rooted out and his platoon hadn't seen action in quite some time. That's why it had been a surprise when the attack came. It was quick and lethal, automatic weapons fire coming at them from three different directions. Two of the soldiers had been cut down immediately. He and the other man had been wounded badly enough that fighting back was not an option. So, they had been taken prisoner.

During the three days he had been a captive of their enemies, he had been tortured in ways that were clearly spelled out as atrocities in the articles of the Geneva Convention. His friend had succumbed by day two, the man's body little more than mutilated meat by that time. Branson would have quickly joined the man in death, had it not been for the rescue party. Swan had been part of that group of marines that had swooped in and saved his ragged ass in the nick of time. The last thing Branson remembered about that horrible time was watching an enraged Swan carve up one of his captors with his combat knife. Then blackness took him.

It would be more than a week before he would awaken in a hospital bed, wrapped in bandages from his head to his toes. When he awoke, Swan was there, telling him he looked like a tic tac toe game. His friend was laughing about it, but it was laughter born of relief, not amusement, and Branson felt himself grinning tiredly in spite of the horrifying truthfulness of that statement. His body was indeed crisscrossed with now-healing scars. His captors had enjoyed using a knife. And yes, they had actually been playing tic tac toe on his flesh.

As he felt consciousness begin to return, the nightmares of the past began to recede. It was different this time—a different place and a different enemy. But as he opened his eyes, it was once again the familiar visage of Swan that was leaning over him.

"Good to have you back, sir," Swan said softly. The only difference this time was that his best friend wasn't grinning. There was a haunted look in the man's eyes, one that left Branson feeling cold inside.

"What…happened," he croaked, his voice dry and cracked.

Swan disappeared from his view for a moment and then was quickly back, holding a battered metal cup. "Here," he said. "Drink slowly, man. You've been out of it for a couple days now."

Branson nodded and the slight movement shot brilliant flashes of agony through his body. Closing his eyes, he reached up and weakly took the cup, trying his best to ignore the pain. Swan held his hands steady as he drank, forcing him to take only small sips of the stale water. It was heaven on his parched tongue and throat. "What happened?" he repeated after he had drank most of the water, his voice a little stronger.

"It was bad," was all that Swan would say before turning away from him, a truly uncomfortable look on his face.

"So spill it," Branson said, feeling his strength returning, but in sharp little jolts.

"You don't wanna know," Swan said, shaking his head. "Leave it at that."

Branson started to protest before another set of hands were on him, gently taking him by the arm and helping him into a sitting position. "She took you apart," Boozer explained softly, helping him place his feet over the edge of the ragged bed he was laying on. "It's best that you know," she finished, shooting Swan a disapproving look.

"What's that supposed to mean?" Branson asked.

Instead of answering, Boozer took his hand and raised it to his face so that he could see his flesh. He saw immediately what she was talking about. His hand was covered with scars, as were his arms. These were not the scars caused by psychotic animals carving X's and O's into his flesh; these were scars that ran long and deep, caused by horrendous wounds that should have killed him. They were fresh and burned with pain at every movement and, judging by the way he was feeling, he was pretty sure they covered his whole body.

"She made us watch," Boozer went on, her voice tight. "She would take you apart and then put you back together. No knives or weapons, sir. Just her magic or whatever kind of power she has."

"How...long," he asked, his voice hollow as his eyes traced the shiny lines on his hands and arms.

"A few days, maybe a week," she shrugged. "She kept telling us to learn well from your mistake."

"My mistake?"

"Disobedience is not tolerated, bro." It was Swan again, his arms folded as he leaned up against the nearby stone wall. "You should be dead, man. What she did to you..." He trailed off, unable to finish.

"Well, I'm not dead," Branson replied, trying to sound strong, but truly frightened at the prospect of what she had done to him. He was beyond grateful that he couldn't remember any of it.

"Maybe not, but with all due respect, you look like Frankenstein, sir," Boozer added with a nod.

"I reckon so," he agreed, trying to stand, but failing. It was much too soon and he allowed Boozer to help him lay back down. He was incredibly weak and his body was on fire, a result of the healing scars, he hoped. "Where's she at now?"

Boozer shook her head.

"She comes and goes," Swan offered. "When she felt we'd seen enough, she brought you here and left you with us."

"What about the others?"

"Locked up in cells all up and down the hallway, sir," Swan replied, nodding toward the metal bars that comprised the door of the room. "Twenty-five little birds, all in their cages."

"Tuner?"

"Couple doors down, near as I can tell."

"She say anything about what she wants?" he asked, quietly relieved that the young soldier was alive.

"Nothing beyond our unwavering obedience," he answered and then suddenly, he was on his knees before the bed, his eyes almost frantic. "This is a bad one, Rick. As bad as any psycho we've ever come up against," Swan hissed, his voice desperate. "I ain't never seen anything like what she did to you and I'm not up to seeing it again. We are in way over our heads here."

"Tell me about it," Branson agreed, closing his eyes.

Footsteps in the hallway silenced any remaining conversation and Branson looked up as Shayene's tall companion appeared before their barred cell door. "Ah, so our guest has finally awakened. I trust you have had a restful sleep?" he grinned, flashing brilliant white teeth.

"It's Kraegor, right?" Branson said, refusing to be baited.

The man inclined his head, a sharp look in his eyes. "I'm surprised you remember," he said.

"What do you want?"

"It's not what he wants, but what I want," Shayene answered instead as she suddenly appeared out of thin air before them. She wasn't on the outside with Kraegor, but on the inside of the cell with the three of them. If there was any doubt about the power she held over them, it was dispelled the moment Swan and Boozer moved quickly to the other side of the cell, nearly cowering in her presence.

"And what do you want?" Branson asked, trying to keep his composure.

"I believe your companion phrased it best when he mentioned unwavering obedience," Shayene replied with a knowing smile. "So tell me, Rick Branson, are you ready to offer that to me?"

"Do I have much of a choice?"

She shrugged and turned away. "You have always had a choice, outworlder. What you have failed to understand is that there are consequences to making the wrong choice." She turned back to face him, her smile gone. "I caution you against making the wrong choice again."

"Meaning what? That you'll not put me back together this time?" he snapped, slowly pulling himself to his feet, ignoring the pain as best he could. "I don't know who you think you are, but I don't scare that easily."

"No, you don't," she agreed. "But I made your friends watch as I made an example of you. Do you think you could stomach the same thing when I make an example of one of them?"

The blood in Branson's veins froze and he stared at her with open hatred. There was no threat there. He knew she meant every word. For a brief moment, Branson wondered what it would be like to watch her dismember Swan or Boozer or Tuner. That was all it took for him to lower his head. "Enough," he said quietly. "I will do as you say."

"I thought as much," she replied, reaching out and placing her fingers lightly on his forehead.

Agony once again flared through him, but was gone before he could stagger backward. When it vanished, so did his pain. He slowly raised his hand and looked. His scars were still there, though somewhat whiter and shinier. The pain behind them, though, was completely gone. He found that he hated her for it; for the control she had over him.

"You have us here for a reason," he said, placing his hands behind his back, hoping to hide the trembling rage that was growing within him. "Obviously, we're not going anywhere. Maybe you should tell us what exactly you need us to do."

"A task," she answered plainly, "likely the first of many."

"Are we here to fight a war for you?"

"Nothing so straightforward," Shayene replied. "I have an army quite capable of carrying out my orders and if I needed more soldiers, I would not have forced you to cull three quarters of those you brought through the gate."

"Then what?"

"Reconnaissance," she replied.

"Don't you have your own spies for that?"

"This is a little more than simply skulking from shadow to shadow, eavesdropping on conversations. There is much going on here, Branson, and much more still to come."

"And we're a part of it?"

"You are actually the reason for it," she said slyly. "Let me ask you a question. Do you understand what it was that brought you here?"

"No more than what we learned from your pet," he replied, casting a baleful glance at Kraegor, who continued to stand outside the cell door. The man stared back at him, his face emotionless.

"You should have a care not to insult my *pet*, as you call him," Shayene warned, a hint of danger in her voice. "Kraegor is unlike anything you could imagine. He is definitely not an enemy to trifle with."

"I stand corrected then," Branson said, not meaning a word of it.

"To continue," Shayene went on, "you were brought here from your world to mine through a gateway created by a special kind of sorcerer. That, in itself, is a truly monumental feat, something I doubt you can appreciate at the moment."

"And that means what to us?"

"It is something that has never been accomplished, at least on a scale such as that. The fact that it was possible at all means that the time is right."

"Right for what?"

"All in good time," she answered, smiling. "If one day you warrant a clearer explanation, I will be happy to provide it to you. In the meantime, your assignment will be a simple one. There is a rather large city far to the south, Nykiva by name. I would have you go there."

"To do what?"

"Why, to be seen, of course," she replied as if it was the most obvious thing in the world. "I wish you to visit the city, specifically the inns and taverns and ask for information."

"And what information am I looking for?"

"Does it matter?"

"Ma'am, I really don't have the first clue what you're talking about," Branson responded helplessly. "Care to elaborate a little bit?"

Shayene stepped closer to Branson, her silken robes brushing his tunic. She looked up at him, her pale eyes glittering. "You cannot possibly comprehend what is happening in this world," she said softly. "Or in yours."

"I'm not following," he said weakly.

"You only need to follow directions," she explained. "Go to

Nykiva. Ask questions. What you ask makes no difference, because no matter what, you will appear out of place in our world. You will draw attention to yourself. I would know who takes an interest in you beyond the norm."

"And what will that accomplish?" Branson snapped. "If you're planning on a war, sending us down there is not only going to get people riled up, but it's likely going to get them wondering what's coming."

"Which is precisely what I wish to happen," she agreed. "You may say anything you wish about my plans for their city. My forces will be there before winter sets in as it is. Whether they know about it or not matters nothing to me. The city will be destroyed in the end, either way."

"For what gain? A pile of useless rubble?"

"I care nothing for the city," she smiled. "I care only that the people are broken."

"Why?"

"The worship of a beholden populace is a powerful thing, Rick Branson," she said with a wink, before turning away from him and walking to the cell door. Once there, she glanced back at him. "You will choose nine of your soldiers to accompany you. I will outfit you as mercenaries and have a gate opened that will bring you to within a few leagues of Nykiva. Do as I command, Rick Branson, and the rest of your people will be spared."

"Go south and ask questions," he said. "I got it. How hard can that be?"

"That's the spirit," she smiled and waved a hand toward the barred door. It vanished, leaving the doorway open to the hall. "You and your soldiers are free to reunite and begin planning, although I advise you to stay within the halls you are currently in. Should you venture to another floor, you will find creatures that will think nothing of eating you alive or worse. At the moment, my magic wards them from this level."

"Understood."

"Oh and before I forget, I would caution you to remember who you are serving. If you betray me, the fifteen soldiers that remain here will suffer unimaginable horrors."

"Lady, you're practically sending me there to betray you," Branson argued. "You told me to go there and start talking and to feel free to speak about your plans for attacking them! How can I possibly betray you any more than that?"

"There are other, far deeper betrayals, Rick Branson. See to it that you do not fall into one of those traps." With that, she stepped into the hall and vanished. Kraegor remained a moment longer, his silent eyes boring holes into the marine, before he, too, disappeared.

"I think it's safe to say that we are officially screwed," Swan finally spoke up after they had gone, his voice barely above a whisper.

"I'm not betting against that, Swan," Branson replied, staring at the empty hall. "Come on you two, let's start figuring things out."

A short time later in a lower part of the keep, Shayene watched as several more undead creatures stepped through the portal and into the land of the living, this time three shambling ghouls and a rotting zombie. They paid her no heed and shuffled directly through the chamber and into the passage that would lead them to the outside.

"You play a dangerous game, my love," Kraegor said softly. He stood behind her, one hand laid gently on her shoulder.

"It's not a game," she replied. "We have a betrayer in the midst of Nykiva. I wish to be certain it is who I believe it is."

"Do you suspect her?"

"I am almost certain that she is the one."

"Then why would you consent to give her a piece of Varankyl?" the dragon asked incredulously. "She will surely exploit this opportunity."

"That she will."

"But why?" Kraegor asked again.

"Because she will attempt to unite the pieces and reform the artifact, believing that will give her the power she needs to close the gate and defeat me."

"She would be correct," Kraegor scoffed.

"I care nothing for the gate," Shayene replied. "By the time she is successful in reforming Varankyl, the gate will have already long since served its purpose."

"Now you are speaking in riddles, my dear."

"You should look beyond the obvious," she said, turning into his arms.

Kraegor pulled her close, looking deep into her eyes. "You believe she will retrieve the other piece of Varankyl?" he asked.

"I'm counting on it."

"That will require a gatekeeper."

"It will."

"Might I remind you that you have the only other one in the land?"

"And he opened the portal to Branson's world with a fair amount of ease," she pointed out. "If the time is indeed right, logic dictates that there will be others that are capable of such a feat or they will be very soon."

"You believe she will be able to accomplish it?"

"That or she will find someone who can," she replied. "She is quite resourceful and in doing so, she will hasten the convergence."

Kraegor stared at her, dumbfounded.

"My dear companion," she said, reaching up and gently stroking his face, "this has never been about our world. We could crush this world and rule over it at any time we chose."

"But all of this?"

"Merely a ruse," she replied. "Surely you must have suspected."

"You have purposefully set yourself up to fail?"

"Yes, at least in their eyes," she nodded. "This will end as I have predicted; with the reformation of Varankyl and the destruction of the gate, as well as my exile to Branson's world."

"If Branson's world is your destination, why not just go there now? Why this elaborate deception?"

"Because events must remain in motion in our world to ensure that the convergence is not delayed," she answered. "Branson's world is a world of science; magic does not exist. That, my dear one, is the key to everything."

"You seem certain of your course."

"As certain as I care to be," she replied. "But as with all things, I will keep my options open."

"Fair enough," he said and then changed the subject. "What of the other?"

"What of him?" her voice took on a sharper tone and she stepped away from him.

"You have dreamt of him for some time, have you not?" his voice was just short of accusatory.

"You act as if you believe he can replace you, my love."

"Hardly," he snorted disdainfully. "He is mortal, an aging sack of meat."

"Yet he threatens you," she said, smiling playfully now.

"You hold him in higher regard than you should," Kraegor snapped. "I only question your need to subjugate him, nothing more. You are the daughter of a God. What purpose could a mere mortal hold for you in all of this?"

"It is a complicated issue, my dear Kraegor," she replied quietly, "and one I am not yet willing to share beyond my own thoughts."

"You know I would never challenge you on that," he said, nodding. "I am only concerned, nothing more."

"I know and I will tell you in time," she answered. "Trust me, my reasons for finding him are valid."

"Will you use the outworlders for this?"

"No, not for this. Branson will serve my purpose well enough just by being a stranger to our world," she replied. "As for Terion, I will allow our colleague in Nykiva to arrange his capture."

"You place a lot of trust in her, when you know she intends to betray you. First Varankyl, now the mortal."

"I trust her to do exactly as I wish, although she will never know that," Shayene replied.

"And by the time she finds out?"

"Then I give you leave to eat her," the Arcai replied with a dark smile. "But only when she has completed the tasks she is unknowingly working on for me."

"That can be arranged," Kraegor said, grinning. "Until then, I will watch your work with great interest, my love."

"As will the gods," she replied, her voice suddenly bitter, "for as long as I let them."

Chapter 6

Branson took another sip of the bitter drink and decided he'd had enough. He pushed it aside and stared across the table. There were four of them tonight, three others besides himself. Swan had been along on just about every bar hop they had been on and, at the moment, was looking just as angry as he was. Boozer seemed right at home, slowly working her way through her drink, while Tuner kept looking around, wide-eyed and nervous. It was hard to blame him. Branson had to admit he was feeling much the same way.

They had been in this strange city now for several weeks, their mission not at all a difficult one. See the sights, ask questions, be seen. It was an easy assignment, if not a boring one. For the life of him, he still could not understand Shayene's game, though. What he could understand was that fifteen of his people had remained back in that dreadful castle of hers. Shayene had been very upfront with him about what would happen to those soldiers should he fail her. After the torture he had already endured at her hands, he had no problem believing the worst.

So they had come to Nykiva, ten in all, sent through a portal not unlike the one that had brought them to this world. Outfitted now in clothing suitable for the new world they were in, they had been doing their best to blend in with the populace and yet stand out at the same time. Branson had considered asking her for their old uniforms back, but he figured that would probably be too obvious. She wanted them seen subtly, given time to cultivate the attention she knew they would draw. Once in Nykiva, Branson had split them up into random groups that he shifted around every day, so as not to draw attention too quickly, and for the last several weeks, they had been wandering the city. They went from inn to bar to inn, sampling the food and drink and listening to just about every conversation they could, although Tuner did the lion's share of that work. The young radioman seemed to be able to hear multiple conversations at once and was always scribbling notes on pieces of paper he had torn from a book they had found in one of their rooms.

Branson had to admit that as strange as this world was, it was not at all unlike being back home. The taverns were full of working folk, as well as the occasional off-duty soldier. Most of them were grumbling about their day, others were BS'ing with friends. It was no different than a gathering at a local bar in the states, pulling at beers while talking smack and watching football. Only here, there were no TVs. That did not mean they didn't have entertainment. Bar fights and other feats of strength seemed commonplace in this world, as did betting on the winners. Most of the fights were fisticuffs, although he saw a couple of fighters that he knew were trained in some kind of martial arts. Those guys—and one gal—almost always won. The fight would happen, the winner would generally help up the loser, and they would all go back to laughing and drinking, though not necessarily in that order. There was something about the whole thing that struck Branson as almost honorable. For the most part, they weren't fighting out of anger; they were fighting because it was what they did.

Unfortunately, not all of the contests turned out that way. He had seen a couple bouts that ended up with some people badly hurt and, in one instance, a man dead with knife in his heart. Those fights that were born out of ugliness were the ones to watch out for.

"I know what you're thinking," Swan said, leaning low over the table and resting his chin on his folded hands. "What are we doing here, man? Be honest."

"What we have to in order to keep our people alive," Branson replied, already knowing what Swan was going to say next.

"How do you know she hasn't killed them already?"

"Keep the faith, brother," Branson sighed, but he had to admit he was having a hard enough time doing that himself.

"There are ten of us," Swan went on. "I hate to say it, but we might not have a better opportunity to get away from her with as many troops as we have right now."

"I can't leave them to die, Swan. You know that."

"And if we go back and she's already killed them? What then?"

"Can't think that way."

"Even if she hasn't, if we try breaking our people out, she'll kill all of us. You know what she can do."

"Only too well," Branson said quietly. "We just need to walk the line right now, Swan. We'll break free of her, but we're going to do it with as many of us as we can. At the moment, I'm not up to leaving fifteen soldiers back there for her to tear apart."

"Well, I hope you know what you're doing."

"You and me both," Branson said pensively, before turning to Tuner. "What are you hearing tonight?"

"Pretty much the same," Eric Johansson replied with a shrug. "Couple guys talking about trouble in some place called Ithil Majeer, but no one seems worried."

"Don't you find that a little strange?" Swan spoke up.

"Not really," Tuner shook his head. "They don't have any kind of rapid communication in this world, sir. They don't know it because they haven't seen it. Can you imagine what TV would do to these people?"

"No different than what seeing real magic has done to us," Branson replied, just a little bit angry at the wave of helplessness he suddenly felt again. He had been in plenty of tight spots back on their own world, a couple times wondering if he would even survive. But here, even roaming free on a recon mission for a sadistic witch he had every intention of killing when he got the chance, he felt as helpless as he had ever felt.

"Head's up," Tuner added. "Fight brewing."

Boozer perked up and looked around. "Who is it this time?"

"At your two o'clock," the young man replied, nodding toward two men who were nose-to-nose, while others around them prodded them on. "This one is going to be ugly."

"That'll be our cue to move out," Branson nodded, pushing his chair back. "We don't need to be around if it goes south."

"And why's that?" a surly voice spoke up as a heavily armored guard suddenly appeared out of the crowd of people. He smacked a hand down on the table and leaned forward, his face coming closer to Branson's. The marine could smell the liquor on the soldier's breath, but his eyes were hard and calculating. He wasn't drunk and this wasn't a random encounter.

"I'm sorry, but I don't know you," Branson replied icily, quickly on his guard. His eyes picked up several more soldiers lurking on the periphery and he mentally kicked himself for not seeing them sooner.

"No, but I'm for knowin' who you are," the soldier replied.

"Maybe some other time," Branson said, stepping away from the table, putting himself in a position that would allow him to maneuver should things get out of hand. "Now, if you don't mind, we'll be on our way. We're not looking for trouble."

The others stood up at those words and immediately four more soldiers stepped out of the crowd, surrounding them.

"Maybe trouble is looking for you," the soldier said dangerously, leaning closer. "I'll ask you one more time, who are you?"

"Who wants to know?" Swan spoke up, but Branson quickly

held up a hand to quiet his friend.

"We're just travelers," Branson said, keeping his voice calm and trying to diffuse the situation. If it went crazy, he knew there was no chance of it turning out in their favor. "We've been spending some time in the city, just taking in the sights, nothing more."

"Travelers, eh? Where do you hail from?" the guard pressed.

"West of here," Branson scrambled, realizing that the line of questioning was going to put him at an extreme disadvantage. He didn't know a blasted thing about the geography of this world.

"Meaning?"

"Meaning west," he answered with a scowl. "Look, I don't like where this is going, soldier. If you have a problem with me, then spit it out. Otherwise, my friends and I are leaving."

It was at that moment that one of the other guards reached out and grabbed Boozer by the arm, a leering grin on his face. The female marine responded by peeling the man's fingers off her, breaking two of them in the process. His howl of pain was abruptly ended when Boozer drove an elbow into his face.

The result was a foregone conclusion and Branson immediately found himself staring at a dagger that had suddenly appeared in his antagonist's hand. He dodged one lunge and then a second, before he was able to get a grip on the man's wrist, bringing them both in close. Branson was a big man, but clad only in leathers. His opponent, while measurably shorter, was protected by fine chain mail and metal plating over the more vital areas. Using his armor to his advantage, the soldier drove himself into Branson, sending them both over a chair and to the floor. As Branson wrestled with the guard, he was only vaguely aware of the crowd of people pressing in closer, all of them shouting and yelling encouragement to the fighters.

Swan found himself in a similar situation, only his opponent was not the equal of Branson's enemy. The marine quickly disarmed his attacker and sent him flying back into the crowd. Armed now with the soldier's dagger, he faced no less than three similarly clad guards as well as an overzealous citizen. As one, they swarmed him under, bearing him to the ground, Swan shouting curses at everyone as he slashed and fought.

Boozer had a little more luck, at least in the early going of the fight. Her initial assailant had been pulled back into the crowd, his nose smashed and bleeding by the elbow shot she had given him. Only another single guard had moved toward her and she easily parried a clumsy thrust of his blade, grabbing his wrist and quickly turning it back toward him. The man howled with pain as she stretched his wrist to the breaking point and held him there, watching to see who would come to his aid. She never saw a dark cloaked man on the other side of the table raise a small hand crossbow and fire. The bolt took her in the spine, directly between her shoulder blades. Her entire body went numb and, with her eyes wide with shock and fright, she slumped to the ground.

Tuner saw the whole thing happen. He had seen the man step out of the crowd and raise the weapon, but his shouted warning had come a moment too late. Now, with his friend injured and maybe dead, the young man simply snapped. With a primal yell of fury, he leapt at the attacker, his hands going toward his enemy's face. But the assailant was more than just a town regular and he side-stepped the radioman's frontal assault, bringing the crossbow up and across the young man's face with a crack of wood on bone.

Stars detonated behind Tuner's eyes and he stumbled sideways, the world suddenly off kilter. He was roughly grabbed by several bystanders and quickly propelled back toward the crossbowman, who used his off-balance momentum to quickly and painfully hip toss him to the floor. Before Tuner could move, the man dropped low, slamming his knee into Tuner's chest, driving the wind out of him. Tuner vaguely saw the blade appear in the man's hand and descend toward his throat. At that moment, complete and utter helplessness began to drown him.

That's when the whole world exploded.

The town guard would interview dozens of witnesses, all of them saying the same thing. The young stranger was on the ground and looked like he was going to end up dead at the hands of his enemy. Where the blast of magic came from, no one had any idea. But they all described the same thing…a swirling sphere of blue and purple energy that was there one moment and gone the next and when it vanished, the young man was nowhere to be seen. His assailant—or what was left of him—had tumbled to the floor. He had been cut in half at the waist, his legs gone along with the boy. There was little blood as the man's devastating wound had been burned closed. Nevertheless, he died quickly, repeating the word "what" over and over again as death took him.

Rick Branson had no idea where he was. He, too, had seen the flash and in the momentary blindness, had been knocked unconscious with a vicious head butt from the helmeted guard. When he finally regained his senses, he was seated in a chair in a small circle of light, his hands tied together behind him. He could see nothing outside the glow, save the slight figure of a woman before him, her form carefully cast in shadow. She had been attempting to interrogate him for the better part of a half hour now and Branson was pretty certain he had found the person that Shayene was looking for.

"Despite what you may think, I am not your enemy," the woman said quietly, her face hidden as much by a deep cowl as by the shadows she was cloaked in. Her voice was soft but strong, and her tattooed hands were folded at her waist. That much Branson understood about this world—the markings indicated she was a sorceress.

"Then show yourself," Branson growled, once more struggling against his restraints. It was no use; his wrists were fastened securely to the back of the chair he was sitting in. He had no idea where his people were and the woman had not given up anything substantial.

"As I have told you, that is not yet relevant to our conversation," she replied.

"The way I see it, we're not having any conversation until you tell me what I want to know."

"Your friend, the one you call Swan, is alive and being tended to by my healers," she replied. "Your woman is dead. The boy is missing."

"Then let me see the bodies," he demanded.

"All in good time."

"I really hate that excuse," he growled. "When will that be?"

"When you see fit to answer my questions," she replied with a shrug that sent a ripple through her robes.

"What more do you want to know?" he asked helplessly. "We're here visiting Nykiva and a bunch of town soldiers decided to pick a fight. Next thing I know, I'm here and my people are missing."

"I'm not disputing that at all," she said, "and I will deal with the guards appropriately for causing this tragedy. What I want to know is where you came from."

"And I told you, we came from the west."

"Indeed," she said patiently. "Perhaps we should try a different track."

Branson stiffened involuntarily, thinking of what that meant with Shayene. The torture he had endured at her hands had been unreal and he would be lying to himself if he said the thought of reliving it did not shake him. But the woman's next question completely blindsided him and the thoughts of torture were suddenly far away.

"Tell me of your world."

For the longest time, Branson couldn't answer. He simply stared at her, blinking in the candlelight. He was right. This was definitely the person Shayene was looking for.

"Come now," she went on, her voice lighter. "You don't honestly expect me to believe you are part of this world, do you?"

"How...why would you ask that?" he stammered.

"We live in strange times," she replied. "This world is ruled by prophecy as much as anything else. Though few know of it and even fewer understand it, there is one such prophecy that talks about travelers from a different world, their arrival heralding the end of all things."

"What makes you think that has anything to do with me?" he asked, finding a measure of strength in his past military training.

"Because I have read your thoughts and sensed your loss, Rick Branson. When you were brought to me, beaten and unconscious, you cried out for home, a place we have no knowledge of. Your thoughts betray you. You do not belong here, am I right?"

Rick Branson had no words to answer her.

For the first time, the woman stepped forward into the light and slowly took a seat in the empty chair opposite him. Her robes were deep scarlet and appeared to be made of silk and they clung to her body. She reached up and slowly lowered her cowl, showing him her face. She was young and pretty, her skin pale and her hair dark, cascading in waves over her shoulders. With a smile, she waved a hand in the air and Branson immediately felt his bonds disappear. He slowly brought his hands back in front of him, rubbing his aching wrists. "I am not your enemy," she said again, her voice soft and inviting. "Tell me of your home, Rick Branson."

Branson could not help himself. He told her everything.

Hours later, the woman stood in another room, this one dark and silent. There were two others in the room with her, both lying unconscious upon soft beds. Their tending healers would return shortly, but she had a moment to contemplate and consider what everything meant. Contrary to what she had told Branson, his people were all alive and accounted for. The one he called Swan was in a cell in the city lockup, alone and silent in the dark. He had killed a man during the fight, likely two if a second succumbed to his injuries. That would be enough to get him executed, if she saw fit to allow it. The female fighter—the one who had taken the crossbow bolt in the back from one of her agents—was lying on one of the beds before her. The healers were unsure if she would live or die, but if she did live, she would be paralyzed. The bolt had severed her spine and her injuries were beyond their ability to heal.

However, it was the young man that most intrigued her. Branson had called him Tuner and she had pressed him hardest about information regarding the young soldier. Tuner was a loner, Branson had said, an outcast among many but a great friend to those who were close to him. Branson could shed no more light on the magical phenomenon that had quite literally teleported him out of the battle. People from his world did not possess powers like that. Branson was desperate to find him, that much was certain.

But she was not yet willing to reveal his location to the marine, particularly if her intuition was correct. It had been pure luck on her part that her own people had come across the young man, lying in an alley not far from the tavern where the fight had occurred, the lower half of his assailant lying next to him. Now that she had him, she intended to make very certain she was right about him.

"Can you truly be?" she asked softly as she moved toward him. She looked down at his sleeping face and then seated herself on the edge of his bed. Muttering softly to herself, she reached out and traced her finger across his forehead and down his jaw line. Then closing her eyes, she began to fall into her magic. Within moments, she began to sift through his thoughts.

Eric "Tuner" Johansson whimpered in his troubled sleep.

Convergence

Part 2

The Beginning of the End

Convergence

"They are coming, my lord," the weary man said with a slight bow of his head, partly out of respect for his leader and partly because of his nearly exhausted condition. He was a scout, his armor consisting of a lightweight leather jerkin and leggings, and his arms were bare, save for a thin metal bracer fastened tightly to each wrist. He was bruised and cut and streaked with mud and wet grass from his rapid flight back to the city of Ithil Majeer. Blood still oozed from the broken stump of an arrow that was imbedded high in his shoulder, giving credibility to his ominous words.

"How many?"

The wounded man shook his head helplessly, wincing at the pain in his shoulder. "I do not know, my lord," he answered quietly. "But I do know that the survivors from Northern Outpost were far short in their assessment of the army that moves against us."

"Then they have been joined by reinforcements," a third man said matter-of-factly as he stepped out of the shadows where he had been listening intently. He was a powerfully built warrior and was fully armored in gleaming chain mail, having been summoned to this emergency meeting during his duty watch. His face was marked by several scars and he had a perpetual frown to match, giving him the appearance of having been carved from stone. The shadows cast upon his face from the flicking lamplight of the room enhanced the power of his presence, and even the lord of the city seemed smaller in comparison to him. "What was needed to take Northern Outpost was all that was committed in the original attack," he continued. "What will be needed for an assault on Ithil Majeer will be a far greater force. Whoever commands this army would know that and has prepared accordingly."

He turned away from the battered scout and gazed hard at the richly dressed leader of the city. "I told you this would be so when word first arrived from the survivors of the Northern Outpost massacre, my lord," he finished, his voice just short of being accusatory. "We should have gone forth many days ago and taken the battle to them. We could have ended this by retaking Northern Outpost and sparing our city. Now we are forced to defend our own homes from our doorsteps."

Garamon Whiteblade, Lord of Ithil Majeer, turned away from the other two men and ran his hands through his graying hair as the weight of their desperate situation began to settle about his aged shoulders. While not as imposing as the huge warrior who dwarfed both he and the wounded scout, he still carried a presence all his own. He had been a champion of Ithil Majeer many years before, a powerful warrior in his own right, and had earned his current position through his dedication to duty and a great amount of compassion for the people of his city. Today, he was much loved and respected by the populace of Ithil Majeer and, as their leader, he wanted nothing more than to see them prosper and grow in safety. Now, all that he knew was threatened by the approaching shadow of war.

Nearly two months had passed since he had heard the tales and rumors of approaching war from the survivors of the massacre. He had filed them away, thinking the attack on the Dom outpost nothing more than that of a rogue force, one that could not possibly hold together to fight a sustained campaign against a nation as powerful as their own. Still, he had quietly petitioned the ruling Dom council in the capital city of Nykiva concerning the possibility that there might yet be a greater threat to their people than they realized. But the council's thoughts mirrored his own and he found peace in that.

Nevertheless, the council had sent a small cavalry force to

march on Northern Outpost and more than two thousand riders had ridden through Ithil Majeer a week past to do just that, cheered on by thousands of peasants and noble men and women who stood in the streets and urged them on to victory. At that time, Garamon had been counseled by his young successor and urged to match the force of Nykiva riders by sending several regiments of Ithil Majeer's own army to aid in the reclaiming of the outpost. Instead, he had chosen not do so, thinking it better to leave his forces in place, just in case. Besides, the cavalry's general had not requested additional reinforcements from him, having been supremely confident that he and his soldiers would quickly retake and hold the Dom stronghold.

Now, it appeared likely that the riders had been destroyed. That truth burned deeply within him and he had been forced to accept the reality of the situation. Somehow, an impossible alliance of Gols and Rats had been forged and was, even now, moving toward Ithil Majeer. If such an army was marching together, then the two races were held together by someone of incredible renown – a person who had somehow circumvented the seething hatred between the two bitter rivals in order to bring together the terrible war machine. Considering that Garamon could only think of one individual capable of such a feat, he had little doubt that he and his people would be soundly defeated, whether his soldiers had joined the Nykiva riders or not.

Still, it was a bitter reality to accept and he cursed his own shortsightedness and that of the council. "How long before they reach our outer defenses?" he finally said, breaking the silence in the room and ignoring for the moment the imposing warrior's veiled allegation that he was responsible for what would soon happen to his people.

Again the scout shook his head, either unable or unwilling to see the tension between the two men. "Four or five days, no more," he replied solemnly. "I have no idea how hard they march, but I had to slip through several scout lines on my return."

"Then they are already here," Garamon said quietly.

"There is still the matter of the challenge," the huge warrior countered, interrupting him. "Four days to reach us, a week more to wait after I kill their champion. That is plenty of time to get organized and set our defenses and make them think twice about attacking us. We can end this here."

"My friend," Garamon went on as he stepped back into the lamplight to finally address him, "I appreciate your confidence in the abilities of our people, but there is more to this than you know."

"I warned you two months ago of the numbers that might be arrayed against us if they should march on our city," the warrior went on. "I remind you again that we should have marched with Nykiva's riders and stopped this before it came to our gates. Together, our numbers would have been great enough to retake Northern Outpost and crush this incursion."

"I do not speak of numbers!" Garamon snapped back, slamming a hand on the table in emphasis. "I was well aware of the possibilities at the same time you were, perhaps even sooner," he went on. "You forget that before your time as champion of this city, it was I who answered the call of the challenge."

Kelemaur straightened at the rebuke and a shadow passed across his face. But if he was angered at the older man's words, he did not show it outright. "My lord," he remarked calmly, "I apologize if I have overstepped my bounds. But with all due respect, I am champion now. We have not taken the fight to them and our opinions will always differ on that. But their weakness now lies in the warrior's challenge," he explained as he leaned forward and placed his own hands on the table. "This is an army of Gols and Rats that threatens us, and you and I both know that the Gols would not willingly serve with Rats unless they held their leader in the highest regard, a man who viewed honor as the only thing that mattered. Therefore, the challenge will come. When it does and I have killed my opponent, we will be given the time we need to either convince them of the folly of their ways or to continue readying ourselves to repel them. Either way, our victory is assured. Ithil Majeer will never fall."

Instead of answering immediately, the older man turned to face the wounded soldier. "Tend to your injuries," he said softly, his voice both kind and sad at the same time. "Your service to me and to the people of our city will be duly noted. However, I fear that in the end, there will be no one left to sing the praises of your heroics."

The man bowed his head. "I understand, my lord," he replied solemnly, bowing his head. "Will there be anything else?"

Garamon nodded. "Indeed," he answered thoughtfully. "Wake my servants and have them send word to the heads of the city council that we will convene an emergency session in one hour. We must begin immediate preparations to evacuate the city and the lands about."

"Yes, my lord," the man said once more and then turned and pulled the huge door open with his good arm before vanishing into the darkness of the hall beyond.

When the door had closed again, Kelemaur let his anger finally show and turned on the older man, his eyes blazing. "You give too much credit to this rabble that marches against us!"

"And you give too little credit to the one who leads them," was the older man's quick reply.

It was enough to set the warrior back on his heels a bit, but he did not rest his stance. "I remind you that we have beaten invasion forces before," he said. "We have the soldiers and we have the defensive plans to safeguard our home, even against a great many enemy soldiers. So why should this time be any different?"

"We have been at peace for nearly ten years," Garamon began.

"All the more reason for this army to come against us, I would think," Kelemaur said quickly, pounding a fist on the oaken table to illustrate his point. "Peace and prosperity breed greed and discontent in our enemies. You, as well as anyone, know this to be true. So why should we be surprised that our enemies have decided to strike?"

"It is not the invasion force that I fear," the older man replied. "It is the person who leads them."

Kelemaur shook his head, his dark eyes flashing. "I do not understand your concern here. Do you fear the challenge will not be made?"

"No," he replied. "Of the challenge, I am most certain. You are indeed correct in your assessment that the man who leads this alliance holds honor in the highest regard."

For a moment, there was no reply. But as the meaning of the old man's words became clear, Kelemaur straightened and scowled, drawing a deep breath and folding his arms across his broad chest. "Then you fear I cannot defeat him," he stated almost bitterly.

Garamon did not even hesitate. "You cannot," was his quiet reply.

"You cannot be serious," the warrior scoffed, clearly offended. "I know of no one who is my equal on the battlefield, and I do not say that in boasting. I speak only the truth."

"No *mortal* is your equal, anyway," said Garamon quietly.

Kelemaur narrowed his eyes in suspicion. "What are you talking about, old man?" he asked, reverting to his common name for his mentor and leader, a name he only used when no one else was around. "Are you saying that whoever leads this army isn't mortal?"

"That is precisely what I am saying," Garamon replied, nodding slowly.

For the longest while, the big warrior was silent, his forehead creased in disbelief as he pondered the implications of what had been said. When he finally spoke, his voice was quiet and, for the first time, there was the smallest hint of doubt in it. "There were no reports of any such man leading the attack on Northern Outpost," he said slowly as if trying to piece things together as he went along.

"But there were reports of a warrior woman putting forth the challenge instead and fighting not only their champion, but two others besides," the old man replied.

"But we know of no immortal daughters that..." he began, but faltered.

"No," Garamon conceded, holding up a hand, "but we do know of a son. And everyone knows that the son is always accompanied by his companion."

Kelemaur took a step back as if struck and he looked at his mentor with pure incredulity. "You cannot be serious," he said in a voice barely containing his disbelief. "The Arcai are forbidden to interfere in the destiny of mortals. Such is the decree from the gods themselves. Yet here you are saying that not only is one interfering, but so is his companion!"

Garamon offered the younger man a tired smile. "This is an army of Gols and Rats, joined together to come against us," Garamon replied. "They have been at war with each other for a hundred years and I know of no mortal alive who has the ability to force these two races to put aside their genocidal feud for any length of time, much less to get them to join together and march as a single army. Even you, Kelemaur, could not bring about such an alliance."

"And because you believe that I could not lead an army such as this, you think that only an Arcai can?"

"They are the sons and daughters of the gods," Garamon

replied softly, stating a simple fact that everyone knew. "If anyone is capable of uniting the Gols and the Rats, it can be no other. No, my friend, there is no doubt...it is him."

"But what of their forbiddance to interfere?" Kelemaur countered. "Surely there would be reprisals from the gods themselves. They would not allow it."

"Perhaps not," agreed the old leader. "Perhaps the gods would even intervene on our behalf on the battlefield, but unfortunately it is not for us to know what aid we might expect or what those reprisals against a wayward immortal son might be. How simple our decisions would be if that were so."

"I would think that the fear of such a punishment would keep even him from violating that oath."

Garamon shrugged. "It has never stopped this one from interfering before."

"But to lead an army?" the younger man objected. "It is one thing to declare yourself the greatest warrior in the world and make it a point to go around challenging and defeating warriors and champions in mortal combat. It is quite another to put together an impossible alliance and go around exterminating other races."

"Agreed," was the reply. "But can you think of any other explanation for such a coalition as this?"

Kelemaur could only shake his head. "No," he admitted slowly, "I cannot."

"Then we will make the necessary preparations to leave," stated the older man finally. "We must evacuate Ithil Majeer."

"You cannot evacuate everybody in four days, old man," Kelemaur protested. "Ithil Majeer has existed for hundreds of years and has never been abandoned in the face of an attack."

"It has never faced an enemy quite like this, Kelemaur."

"So we will turn and run?"

"We will save as many as we can."

"He can be stopped," Kelemaur said quietly, trying to sound confident. "I can defeat him."

"I admire your bravery and devotion, my friend," Garamon said sadly, "but believe me when I tell you it is not possible. No mortal can defeat an Arcai in open combat."

"What about Jayra? She was killed by a mortal."

"She was assassinated by a mortal," corrected the older man, "and a Vi'Raaji assassin at that. It is one thing to kill by stealth. It is quite another to face an Arcai on equal terms. If you try to do so against the man who leads this army, he will kill you."

Again, silence filled the room as the two men regarded each other. Finally, Kelemaur spoke, his voice once again quiet, but resigned. "I cannot run away, old man," he said. "Honor demands that I defend my home and my people."

"Honor demands that the two warriors meet on equal ground. This is hardly equal ground."

"I will not run," Kelemaur stated again.

"Then Draven will kill you," the older man stated bluntly, pointing a finger at his friend. "He will kill you and his army will march on Ithil Majeer and destroy it anyway. You will gain nothing by dying under his sword," he finished, his voice almost bitter.

"If that is my destiny, then so be it," was the warrior's calm reply. He turned and walked toward the door, his point made. Grasping the handle, he pulled it open, then turned to look once more at his mentor and friend. "The Arcai are forbidden to interfere in our lives," he stated one more time. "I have to believe that the gods will find favor in me and I will emerge victorious." With that, he turned and quietly left the room, pulling the huge door closed behind him.

Garamon remained silent, staring for the longest time at back of the closed wooden door and wishing for simpler times. But he knew he would not get it, just as he knew the great soldier whom he had groomed from a young lad into the man he was today would certainly perish. Kelemaur would die in an unfair battle and never assume the mantle of Lord of Ithil Majeer. Sadly, Garamon also knew that he would never be able to sway the honor-bound man from his sense of duty, either. And as Kelemaur's determined footsteps faded down the hallway beyond, Garamon could only sigh wearily, before finally leaning over the table and beginning to map out the evacuation of his beloved people. Kelemaur would die and so, too, would he, when it was all over. But he would make sure that his people survived.

He must.

Chapter 8

Unfortunately, Garamon's wounded scout had been wrong in his earlier report and estimation of how much time they would have to prepare, just as the survivors from the Northern Outpost massacre had been wrong about their appraisal of the size of the invasion force that would be coming for them, and just as the Dom Ruling Council had been wrong in their assessment of the limited potential of being drawn into a terrible war. As it was, little more than three days had passed from that fateful meeting in his private chambers with Kelemaur before war descended with sudden savagery upon the city of Ithil Majeer. Already, thousands of Doms had fled the city for the safety of Nykiva, far to the north and beyond the great inland seas. However, many still remained in the city, over-confident and perhaps even arrogant in their belief in their ability to defend their homes and families against any enemy arrayed against them. As the invasion commenced, they quickly found out just how hopeless it truly was and by then, it was already too late.

The initial attack came just after dawn had broken above the horizon, and now almost five hours later, Garamon could still hear the fierce fighting as his soldiers battled the blood-thirsty Rats on the flat grasslands surrounding the huge city's formidable walls.

When it had begun, the painted savages had come screaming out of the trees on the south side of the city, still half-hidden by the morning mist. They had been met almost immediately by four regiments of mounted cavalry that Kelemaur had ordered readied three days prior. At first, Garamon had resisted the idea, thinking that it would be best to get as many of his people safely on the road toward Nykiva as possible. But in the end, many of them simply did not want to leave their homes, had in fact refused to abandon what they had built over the years. With the reluctance of so many people to evacuate, Kelemaur had convinced him to be prepared in case the attack came early.

When morning had come and the man had been proven right, Garamon had wondered for a brief moment if his friend might also be right about his chances against the nearly invincible Arcai that he knew had to be leading the attack. However, as the armies clashed on the battlefield, it was a fool's hope that he did not entertain long. While the Rats engaged Kelemaur's riders on the southern plains, Garamon's scouts were reporting the movement of massive numbers of soldiers through the forests and hills that surrounded Ithil Majeer. The Gols were surrounding them. The time for flight was past.

Draven had not issued the formal warrior's challenge, either, but then again, Garamon did not expect him to at this point in the battle. It was far too early for that and this initial skirmish would be fought only in the fields before the city walls. The challenge would come before the city itself was attacked and the old man knew that before the challenge, the Arcai would first send his expendable soldiers to battle in the fields before the city in order to gauge not only the preparedness of the city defenders, but to wear down and thin out their ranks while the Gols took up their positions around the city. Garamon doubted not the least that Draven looked upon the savages with as much disdain as every other race in the land, and any commander in his stead would have done the same.

The Lord of Ithil Majeer also knew more about Draven than most other mortals did. Although he had never met the legendary son of Karasika, Goddess of War, he had heard a great deal about him, more so than he had heard about any of his immortal brothers and sisters.

The Arcai, in a sense, were a secretive group; sons and

daughters of a union between a god and a mortal. There were only sixteen originally—thirteen now—a son and a daughter for each of the eight gods of their world.

They had existed for centuries, ageless men and women coming into this world in the early years of the third age, which would make them somewhere near four millennia old, at least in spirit. For it was said that although Arcai were blessed with nearly immortal life spans, the godly parent of one could effectively rebirth them, allowing them to grow once more from a babe in a mother's womb and experience life all over again. Whether there was truth to those words or not, Garamon did not know, and if one of them could even return to life from death, his own lore told him nothing.

What he did know was that for almost four thousand years, the Arcai had adhered to the dictates of their godly parents and had stayed away, refusing to meddle in the affairs of man. However, time changes all things and the son of Karasika eventually took a different path, brazenly disregarding the laws of the gods.

It began nearly fifty years ago during the Festival of the High Arena, the annual Gol'Athi gladiator tournament featuring the greatest living Gol warriors battling each other in tribute to their goddess, Karasika. It was a Gol warrior's greatest honor to be named to the tournament, and this yearly celebration marked their most anticipated holiday. The winners became champions, while the dead were interred with honor in sacred burial chambers across the land.

At this particular festival, the son of Karasika unmasked himself and announced his desire to be the greatest champion the Gols had ever known. He promised honor and glory to them and the highest of honor in his mother's eyes to any warrior who stood against him in combat. Many that faced him were killed and few challengers survived; but the Gol people quickly revered their new champion, believing he had been sent to them by the goddess herself.

Since then, Draven was said to roam the lands, seeking out the greatest warriors of any race to engage him in mortal combat. Many men and women rose to the challenge, the lure of possibly earning the title of "God Killer" enough to dull their senses to the reality of what they were facing in battle. Each one died as he or she came. In time, there was talk that none could stand against an Arcai in combat and be victorious.

But ten years ago, a Vi'Raaji witch proved otherwise, tracking down and killing Jayra, the daughter of the Goddess of the Mountains. There was never any formal declaration of the kill and most people in the world would never know the real reason for the killing. But the whispered rumor told of an ominous warning to Draven to never think he was beyond death. This, more than anything, incensed the powerful Arcai. A short time later, he would seek out and kill another immortal, taking the title of "God Killer" for himself. The fervor to stand against Draven rose to a fevered pitch and many great warriors came against him once again. As before, each challenger died and Draven's fame grew legendary.

However, back then, it was for honor and the glory of defeating another in battle. Now, things had changed. Draven appeared to be no longer content with one-on-one battle for glory – he was now leading an army that was killing thousands. That was the most troubling thing of all.

From the battlefield beyond the city walls, a great shout of victory arose, shaking Garamon from his contemplation, and he immediately recognized it for what it was. Kelemaur and his riders had finally broken the U'Raati attack. Almost on cue, there was a rapid knock at his study door and before he could answer, one of his aides pushed open the door, his face beaming.

"That Rats are beaten," he fairly shouted, his joy evident. "They are fleeing even as I speak, my lord!"

"Do not let hope cloud reality," he addressed the aide firmly as he pushed back his chair and stood up, his richly embroidered robes falling open and revealing the gleaming metal armor that was now strapped to his body. "This is only the beginning."

Ten minutes later, Garamon was standing atop the south gate of the city, silently surveying the carnage on the battlefield. Hundreds upon hundreds already lay dead or wounded, many more of them Rats than his own people. The riders of Ithil Majeer had indeed been successful in beating back the attack and Kelemaur stood proudly in the stirrups of his horse far out onto the killing grounds, facing away from the city and watching as the last remnants of the Rat marauders slunk back into the trees. Many Dom soldiers, some mounted and some on foot, were already busy combing the battlefield for wounded. Wounded Rats were put to death immediately, while fellow Dom soldiers were thrown across horsebacks or shoulders and brought back into the city to be treated, if they could, or buried when they could not.

As Garamon watched the grim scene unfold before him on the battlefield, there was a slight rustle of heavy robes as another man joined him upon the battlement. The newcomer was breathing hard, but whether from exertion or fatigue, he did not know.

"So it comes to this," the man said quietly, his thick voice heavy.

"Yes, my old friend," the Lord of Ithil Majeer answered sadly. "I believe the end comes for us all."

"You do not believe we can defeat them?" asked the man.

Garamon turned his deep-set eyes on the other. He was a

portly man, clad in heavy robes of the deepest red with embroidered bands of gold all up and down the rich material of his sleeves. His jewelry-adorned hands and wrists were encircled with magical runes and glyphs of red, orange, and yellow – markings that extended far up his arms, showing his mastery over the elemental sphere of fire. He was a good man, fair in his dealings with others and well-respected within the city of Ithil Majeer, particularly since he was the only wizard of real power that resided there. More importantly to Garamon, though, the man would give his life for his city. When he answered the wizard, his voice was sad. "It would be foolish to think we could win. The Rats are nothing more than bait and the Gols have already surrounded the city. There will be no escape from what awaits us."

"And yet, we will fight," the wizard continued matter-of-factly.

"We can do little else," Garamon replied with a shrug. "But it will not change the outcome. After hundreds of years, Ithil Majeer will finally fall."

The mage stroked a graying beard, his blue eyes lost in thought. "Is there any hope in the challenge?" he finally asked, looking up, but already knowing what the reply would be.

"You already know that an Arcai leads them," Garamon replied, shaking his head. "Kelemaur swears to fight him, but he will die just as surely as we will."

"Then we will show these invaders what it means to bring war to our people," the wizard retorted. "We will show them this is only the beginning."

"Yes," Garamon stated sadly as he looked back out over the battlefield where so many had already fallen. "This is indeed only the beginning."

As if to answer his desperate thoughts, the air was suddenly split by the sound of many Gol'Athi war horns, each one being sounded by a seasoned warrior who would soon take the field with the intention of slaughtering anyone who stood in the way of their conquest.

Draven was coming.

The blare of the horns faded away and for a few moments, there was nothing but silence, punctuated only by the cries and moans of the wounded and dying on the battlefield. Garamon could see the Dom soldiers frozen on the blood-soaked southern plain, every one of them looking away from the city, watching the lines of trees for the first appearances of the Gol army and the man that led them. When they finally appeared, reality came with them.

The first lines of Gol warriors marched out of the trees surrounding the city, still almost a mile from the walls of Ithil Majeer. Led by standard bearers, the Gols were powerfully built and heavily armored in gleaming chain and plate mail, and every one sported a myriad of blades and crushing weapons. Wherever Garamon looked from his vantage point, Gols were marching toward them and he knew that the same act was being played out on every side of the city. With a sinking feeling, he knew it would be a slaughter. Had he sent his forces along with the riders from Nykiva two weeks ago, they would have been overwhelmed and destroyed, and this would still be happening. Here, at least, they might die defending their homes and families.

The appearance of the army also brought life to the victorious soldiers on the south field. Most were quickly gathering up nearby wounded comrades and heading back toward the relative safety of the city gates, while fifty or so riders wheeled their mounts about and were heading toward Kelemaur to join him.

But the champion of Ithil Majeer was not waiting for them. Seating himself in his saddle, he slowly and purposefully turned his horse, presenting his back to the approaching invaders, and began a slow high-stepping parade canter toward the city, his riders falling in smartly beside him and reigning in their own horses to match their leader's pace. It was a sign of contempt and a trump card well played, at least in the mind of Kelemaur. He was signifying his disdain for the approaching army. It would produce the desired effect.

Kelemaur had reached the city gates when it came. The Gol armies, still filing out of the trees, were now some ten to twelve deep in places when a large corridor opened up between two columns of warriors on the southern battle line. More horns blew, this time at a different pitch, signifying the coming of their leader. It was enough to make the champion of Ithil Majeer stop and wheel his mount around to watch as the unarmored Arcai strode through the opening created by his soldiers. The Gol fighters stood at attention, saluting him with fists clutched at chests as he swept by them and onto the battlefield. An equally tall and well-armored female warrior accompanied him, and the two walked purposefully toward Kelemaur and Ithil Majeer. Halfway there, the woman stopped and folded her arms, her visage stern and unreadable from the distance.

Without even looking back, Draven continued his solo march. Except for the whinny of an occasional warhorse and the cry of one of the wounded still on the battlefield, there was little other sound. All eyes were on the spectacle that was about to take place. Fifty yards from the southern gates of Ithil Majeer, the man stopped and reached around behind him to grasp the pommel of his huge sword. Effortlessly, he pulled the mighty blade free and swung it through the air in front of him before turning it downward and plunging it into the ground.

"I seek Kelemaur!" his voice boomed as he stepped forward. "By the laws and decrees of the warrior's code, I formally issue the call to challenge!" He took another step forward and folded his arms across his massive chest.

After a few tense moments, the champion of Ithil Majeer kicked his mount forward and rode back out onto the battlefield, his eyes locked with those of his foe. When he was but a dozen yards from the Arcai, he wheeled his horse to a stop and dismounted, all in one motion. With a slap on the rump, he sent his warhorse back toward the city gates and then faced the man he would now fight to the death.

"I am…" began the Arcai.

"I know who you are," Kelemaur spat angrily, cutting the huge man off. "And if I'm not mistaken, you are interfering in the affairs of man."

Draven looked long and hard at the man he intended to kill and then simply laughed. "Is this a sign of cowardice from the great Kelemaur?" he asked in a voice laced with contempt. "Do you now intend to go running back to hide behind the safety of your city gates and pray the gods will deliver you?"

"Hardly," replied the champion of Ithil Majeer, his voice firm and betraying nothing. "I fear no one, including the likes of you, Draven."

"Well, you should," replied the Arcai, his tone icy.

"I do not fear my death," Kelemaur replied, his voice full of conviction. "Nor do I fear the one who brings it to me. If that one turns out to be you, then so be it. If you slay me, then I go to my death with honor. I can stand before the gods and hold my head high when they judge my life and my accomplishments. My reward, then, shall be justified." He paused before continuing, his voice strong and unwavering. "However, Draven, your time on this world is not without end. You believe yourself to be immortal, but we all know that you bleed and die just like any man. And when you die and stand before the council of gods, I doubt your reward will be anything like mine."

"You fear for your life, Kelemaur," Draven said easily, ignoring the man's pointed words, "and rightfully so. So, if it pleases you, instruct your archers on the city walls to let loose their arrows. Slay me where I stand and be done with me."

"That is not the way of the challenge," the champion answered calmly. "You have come here to fight me and I shall not dishonor myself. I will fight you, Draven, and I will leave it to the gods to decide the outcome."

At that, the powerful Arcai turned and spat on the ground, the contempt now fully evident on his face and in his voice. "The gods decide nothing when it concerns Draven," he shot back. "My destiny is my own to create and to fulfill."

"Think what you will," answered Kelemaur as he pulled his sword from the scabbard strapped to his back. "But be done with the idle talk."

Draven smiled and took several steps forward until he stood only paces from the warrior, where he once again folded his massive arms across his bare chest. He made no immediate move to retrieve his weapon, still stuck into the ground behind him, and he only watched in amusement as Kelemaur inched toward him carefully, his own blade poised to strike.

"Take up your sword," Kelemaur commanded, his voice growing tight as he tried to decipher what the Arcai was up to. "Retrieve your weapon or I will strike you down!"

Still, Draven did not move.

"I give you one last chance to take up your weapon, Draven," he said again. "If you do not, I will assume that you have thrown yourself upon my mercy and I will act in accordance."

"Act then," was the Arcai's only response.

It happened in an instant. Kelemaur surged forward, the point of his sword driving for the heart of his opponent. At the last possible moment, the Arcai moved, bringing his right arm up in a lightning fast motion, his metal bracer connecting with the thrusting blade and shoving it aside in a shower of sparks. The clash of metal brought both sides of the conflict to life and the roar of the two opposing armies rose up, urging their champions on as the warrior's challenge began.

Kelemaur had not been caught unawares, though, and reacted with polished skill. Knowing his thrust would certainly be blocked, he allowed his momentum to add to his next strike and he spun quickly on his heel, bringing his weapon toward his opponent's neck. But as good as Kelemaur was, Draven was better. In battle, he sensed the moves of his opponents better than anyone and when the decapitating swing came around, he was already under and behind it, spinning to launch his own blow. His bare fist slammed into the warrior's armored side, propelling Kelemaur off balance several yards away.

The champion of Ithil Majeer realized the counterstrike was coming a split second before he felt the hit. He relaxed his body to absorb the force of the blow but even still, he felt and heard several of his ribs crack from the powerful blow. Pain coursed through his body but he fought it back and turned again, bringing his sword to bear as Draven stalked toward him, still weaponless. As the Arcai stepped into range of his weapon, Kelemaur feinted with a thrust and then pulled back at the last moment, bringing his sword down in an overhead strike while ignoring the pain from his broken ribs.

Draven didn't have time to dodge the blow this time, instead bringing both his hands together against the flat of the blade in a clapping motion and catching the strike before it could split his skull. For a moment, neither man moved and the spectators on both sides held their breath. Then everything happened at once. Draven thrust his hands sideways in hopes of dislodging his opponent's weapon, but

Kelemaur realized what was going to happen and twisted the blade between his opponent's hands even as he yanked it backward.

Draven howled in pain as the razor sharp sword—a weapon that had been forged by a dragon—opened up the flesh of both his palms, forcing him back several steps. Kelemaur pressed his advantage immediately, again thrusting toward his opponent's heart. This time Draven was back on his heels and could only twist away, unable to launch any kind of counter. The defender of Ithil Majeer drove the Arcai back, three successive swings drawing closer and closer to the mark.

By the fourth swing, however, Draven had regained his composure and brought his bracer-covered wrist up to deflect the blow in another shower of sparks and ring of metal on metal. He sidestepped and allowed Kelemaur's momentum to carry him forward and then he lashed out with his foot.

Without broken ribs, Kelemaur might have been able to avoid the martial kick, but he was already hurt and moving slower than normal. As a consequence, he took the full force of the kick directly to his already injured side. The force of the blow was devastating to the warrior, his fractured ribs shattering on impact, despite his chain mail armor. He felt the splinters of bone being driven into his lungs and blood burst from his lips as he spun away and crashed to the ground in agony. He tried to roll to the side to regain his feet, but Draven was there, his next kick catching him in the stomach and lifting him a full three feet off the ground, where he crashed back down in a blaze of pain. One final time, he tried to rise and bring his weapon up, but the Arcai was there once more, this time slamming his foot down on the wrist of his mortal opponent's weapon hand and crushing the bones.

As quickly as it had begun, it was over. Kelemaur was beaten. He lay in a haze of blazing agony, staring up as Draven towered over him. Blood dripped from the victor's cut hands, but on his face was a smile of victory. Without a word, Draven reached down, grabbed the edge of the beaten man's metal shoulder guard and pulled him roughly to his feet. Kelemaur had no strength remaining and his legs buckled. He would have fallen back to the ground if not for the huge warrior spinning him around and locking a huge arm tightly around his neck.

"Bear witness, Garamon!" the huge Arcai shouted as he looked up at the ruler of the city standing upon the battlements above the city gates. "Here is your champion!" At that, he shook Kelemaur like a rag doll to emphasize the sarcasm that dripped from his words.

Atop the gate, Garamon could only watch helplessly, knowing what was about to happen. "Leave him," he managed to say, his voice nearly breaking. "You have proven that you are the better warrior."

"Leave him?" Draven shot back contemptuously. "Why? His fate will be no different than yours."

"Allow me to tend to him then," Garamon called down to him. "Your armies have moved much quicker than I had foreseen. At least allow me some more time to evacuate those who remain. I will gladly give over my life to you if you grant me that and spare his life."

Draven threw back his head and roared with laughter, but in an instant, the laughter disappeared, replaced by cold, emotionless fury. Slowly, he lowered his head and for a moment was motionless, time seeming to have frozen. Then he reached up with his free hand and cupped it over Kelemaur's chin before savagely yanking the man's head sideways, breaking his neck with a sickening crack. Kelemaur's final breath was a quick gasp and his body twitched once before Draven tossed it aside with a contemptuous shove.

On the wall above the gate, Garamon felt his heart sink. His friend and protégé was dead and it was only a matter of time before he and most of the others who remained in Ithil Majeer would be dead, too. Nevertheless, he pleaded for the lives of his people. "Grant me the time, at least," he asked, trying to keep his voice strong. "You have won the challenge. Your soldiers will win the day and the city will be yours. At least spare those who remain."

For the longest time, Draven stood motionless above his enemy's broken form, his own body rigid and his gaze intense. Finally, without a word, he raised a hand and brought his thumb across his throat, giving Garamon his answer. And as if on cue, the horns of the Gol'Athi army once again rent the air.

The battle for Ithil Majeer had begun.

Dawn was breaking over the horizon the next morning when the fighting finally ended. The doomed defenders of Ithil Majeer had put up a valiant defense, throwing back the huge army of Draven during the day-long assault. That initial victory had lent a small semblance of hope to the fighting men and women of the city, but it turned out to be nothing more than a cruel hoax.

As dusk finally started to enshroud the battlefield, the Gol soldiers began an organized withdrawal from the fighting, retiring to the fields around the city. By all appearances, it seemed as if they were preparing to set up camp and wait for the following morning to begin their assault anew. Ithil Majeer was a large city and, despite the previous evacuation of many of its people, the city defenders could hold for several days or more before the might of Draven's armies could finally crush it. But as the sun disappeared beyond the horizon, the first unearthly screams erupted from deep within the Temple of the Gods that lay at the heart of the city.

Outside the great temple, confusion reigned and none could know the horrors of the massacre that was transpiring within. They would get their answer soon enough. A short time later, terrifying legions of First Born began to boil up from the building's lowest depths and passages, pouring out into the streets. The maddened and ravenous creatures fell upon the people of the city, devouring them alive even as their hearts continued to beat. Men, women, and children perished under the killing claws and demonic fangs of the undead intruders, torn to shreds to feed their unholy appetite.

As the vicious undead tore down the shocked and terrified defenders from behind the city walls, the Rat savages came on once again, screaming out of the trees and rushing toward the city gates. Gol battering rams, free from any defensive counter attacks, quickly blasted down the gates of city. The Rats swarmed into the city, desperate for their own taste of blood.

Now, as the first rays of the morning sun peeked over the distant trees of the forest, Garamon found himself kneeling before the shattered southern gate of his own city, the victorious Draven standing over him, the flat of the Arcai's great sword, Dread, lying casually against the old man's slumping shoulders. They had been like that for more than two hours, Draven forcing the old leader to watch as his remaining people were run down in the streets and slaughtered one by one by the savage Rats and the marauding First Born. Scarecrows, skeletons, ghouls, and worse could be seen darting from shadow to shadow, hunting what remained of the living, while others were busy consuming what scraps remained from victims who had already been slain. Hundreds of hollow-eyed men, women, and children had already been led from the city in chains where they would become slaves, or worse, to the victorious Gols and Rats.

The entire time, the Arcai had not spoken a word. He had not needed to. The scene playing out before them was enough. Now, as the sun rose higher, the creatures from the Nether sought solace from the light, forsaking the dead and the dying and disappearing into buildings and shadows where they would remain until the sun set once more.

At long last, Draven spoke, his voice quiet and firm. "You see now the futility you face?"

Garamon had no words, his mind almost numb with grief.

"The Doms are a formidable people," continued the victorious Arcai, "and against a strong enemy, an even greater army needs to be arrayed. Before your eyes, you see only the beginning, Garamon." He paused and leaned forward. "We march on Taer Blys before midsummer," he finished quietly.

At that, the old man stirred, tearing his eyes from the few torn and bloody corpses that still lay strewn in the street before him. He looked up at the murderous leader and felt a flame burst forth within his soul. "The Taes are a race of healers," he said quietly, but with as much force as he could muster. "While we Doms will fight you, they will not."

"I am well aware of the Tae's lack of military desire," the warrior answered. "Yet, Taer Blys is the staging area I need for what lies ahead."

Garamon's eyes narrowed and he understood clearly what the man meant. "You mean to march on Nykiva," he challenged with certainty.

"Indeed," replied Draven evenly. "That much should be obvious. And I intend to do it before winter sets in, which is why I must have Taer Blys. If all goes well, the might of your people will be crushed before the snows come and the resistance of the other races will be weakened. At the very worst, Nykiva may hold out until winter arrives, but the winter will be long and hard and I am certain that, before spring blooms again, Nykiva will have fallen and your people will bow to me."

Garamon shook his head. "But why?" he pleaded. "You are the son of a god, Draven. What could you possibly gain from this madness?"

"What I will gain from this is beyond your comprehension, mortal," Draven replied, "and I do not intend to waste my time explaining it to you."

"The gods will not tolerate your interference," the old man countered. "It is your punishment that will be beyond comprehension."

"You may believe what you will, Garamon," Draven answered. "But to think that I have not fully explored all possibilities is to give me too little credit. You can hate me for what I've brought upon you and your people, but understand that I have my own best interests at heart."

"Your vision is clouded, Draven. You forget that the gods have our best interests at heart. It is we who offer them praise and worship, not you."

For a moment, the Arcai tensed, his corded muscles rippling as anger coursed through his body. But in another moment, his tension was gone and his voice was calm. "Enough," he said flatly and then hefted his massive sword in the air. He held it high over the old leader's head, then in one deft motion, spun it overhead and slid it into the huge sheath strapped to his back. "You are free to go, Garamon," he said, backing away a couple of steps. "Take word to the people of Taer Blys. Tell them that the armies of Draven will march before midsummer."

Stunned that he was being spared, Garamon slowly climbed to his feet, wincing at the ache both in his old bones and in his heavy heart. He had fought hard in the battle, staining his own sword and armor with the blood of his enemies. But he had eventually been overwhelmed and had spent the past several hours on his knees, witnessing the bloody slaughter of the innocent. He glared up at the big warrior, searching his mind and heart for what he could say.

Before he could speak, the Arcai picked up a burlap sack from the ground. With a flick of his wrist, Draven tossed the sack toward him and it landed at his feet with a wet thump. The Lord of Ithil Majeer let his eyes drop slowly to the bag and he could see the crimson stain that had soaked through the material. He was certain he knew what the sack's grisly contents were.

"The head of Kelemaur," Draven answered the unspoken question. "Take it to the champion of Taer Blys and give him my regards."

"The Taes have no champion," Garamon answered softly.

"Then tell them to find one," the Arcai answered contemptuously. With that, he stalked back onto the battlefield, leaving Garamon alone with his grief.

Chapter 9

The Battered Keg did a brisk business nearly every night, and this evening was no exception. Located in a rougher section of the Dom capital city of Nykiva, it was the right kind of atmosphere for tonight's meeting. Most of the patrons were already drunk and rowdy, and those that weren't were too busy with their own back alley deals to worry about what anyone else was doing. All of this suited Balgar Mud just fine, although he could do with something a little more refined than the swill the joint was serving as its house ale.

He took another sip from his chipped mug and winced as he swallowed the bitter brew. The beer was warm and stale, though less for the fact that he had been sitting there over an hour and more due to the lack of care the pub took with its wares. Waiting for so long had dulled his sense of excitement for the meeting, as well as his tolerance for the stale drink. He would have already left if his employer hadn't made him swear to wait as long as possible for his contact to arrive. And because of who the contact was, he thought it best to obey.

He was waiting for a Vi'Raaji assassin and not just any killer, either. No, this one had earned her name, no small feat in their world. The Vi'Raaji women were some of the best martial fighters in all the land and most possessed inborn arcane powers. They were not evil, but they honored no strict codes of conduct, either, working toward whatever gained them the most at any given time. Many were well-known throughout the land as exceptional mercenaries and assassins, selling their skills to the highest bidders. Occasionally, if a witch gained enough honor in the eyes of her people, she would go through a secretive Vi'Raaji ceremony known as the Harrowing. During the ritual, the witch would be stripped of her birth name and given a new one— one that the rest of the world would quickly come to recognize and fear. It was the mark of true power and the one thing that each and every Vi'Raaji woman aspired to. A witch who gained her name was afforded the highest standing within her people and her original name was stricken from all records. All others were then prohibited, under penalty of death, from ever uttering the woman's birth name again.

Balgar didn't know how Vendetta had earned her name beyond whispered rumors and truthfully, he wasn't interested. All that mattered to him was that she accomplish the jobs she was given. He looked around in irritation, wondering for the hundredth time when she was going to show or even if she would. His employer had told him to expect the assassin in person this time, but he hadn't believed it at first, thinking she would likely send another street rat to set yet another meeting. He knew of the woman's legacy and employing her would be time-consuming and expensive. He wasn't yet sure if it was worth it.

He snapped his fingers as one of the waitresses hurried past him. "Oy, woman!" he shouted, getting her attention. "I'm hungry," he said, tossing a couple of copper coins on the table in front of him. "Bring me something to eat."

"What do ya want?" she snapped through a mouth full of yellow teeth. She was thin and her dress hung on bony shoulders. There wasn't much meat to her and she was far from pretty, but Balgar wasn't interested in anything more than her taking his order. There would be time enough later for other interests to be indulged in with a more palatable woman.

"Just give me the house stew," he answered gruffly. "And bring me a loaf of bread so I can stomach it."

The woman snatched up the coins, muttered something incomprehensible, and disappeared into the press of people. Balgar leaned back, glanced around again, and then closed his eyes for a moment. He hated waiting, but he had to look at the bigger picture.

With the removal of this particular thorn in his side, he would take control of the council. Regardless of what his employer took from that arrangement, he had no problem imagining the wealth and power that it would bring him personally. That was enough to bring a smile to his face and, with an appreciative chuckle, he opened his eyes.

He immediately stifled a yelp of surprise as he looked across the table at a stranger who had silently joined him. It was hard to see what the assassin looked like, for she wore a dark cloak and hood pulled up far over her face. He could see her eyes, though, and they seemed to glow a soft blue from the shadows of the cowl. "Blast it, woman," he seethed, getting himself quickly under control. "You could have given me a heart attack."

"There are far better ways of inducing heart arrhythmia," she said, her voice almost a purr. "You are not who I expected to meet tonight, Balgar. I had assumed it would be your employer, if this contract is as important as I have been led to believe. Does your employer fear me?"

"Most do," Balgar answered plainly, trying to catch a glimpse of her features in the shadows. She was a master assassin, but Balgar had heard of her rumored beauty and feminine attributes as well. With the power he stood to gain at the completion of this contract, he had no problem considering a future where she was at his beck and call, both for business and for pleasure.

"Do you?" she pressed.

"Should I be?"

"That depends on whether you care if you live out the evening," she replied evenly.

"It took two months and three intermediaries to get to this point," he said, leaning across the table with a sneer, temporarily forgetting the carnal thoughts he had been entertaining. "You give a couple coins to some homeless child that wanders free after delivering your message, yet one of my men ends up dead in an alley somewhere. I'm here because my employer desires an end to the negotiations and an end to the senseless killings of our messengers."

"It is only senseless to one that doesn't understand the world like I do," she replied. "There are others out there I must be cautious of and you still haven't answered whether or not you care about dying tonight."

"You won't kill me," he boasted, but careful to keep his voice at a minimum. "I'm far too valuable to my employer and I'm fairly certain you know that, so I think we'll reach an agreement on our mark tonight."

"You forget that other arrangements can be made."

"Not this time," he snapped, supremely confident. "Do we deal or not?"

The woman leaned back in her seat, crossing her arms over her chest as her pale blue eyes stared across the table at the politician. For some moments, she remained silent, appraising the man. He was obese and rather ugly, but he wielded a fair amount of power in Nykiva City. She also knew that, with the removal of the target he had in mind, he stood to garner a lot more of that political clout, which could be advantageous to her in the future, as it would allow her to extend her network deep into the Dom capital city.

"Very well," she finally said, noting that Balgar's stare never left her face to travel elsewhere during the long silence. She knew what was going through his mind earlier and it spoke well of his devotion to the cause, that he refused to let his baser instincts take over, at least for the moment. "What are the contract stipulations?"

"She needs to be removed," he answered, leaning closer and lowering his voice. "It has to be an obvious murder. So, only a blade will do."

Vendetta nodded, reaching into a pocket deep within her cloak and producing a small glass vial stoppered with wax, which she offered to Balgar.

"Didn't you hear me?" he immediately shook his head angrily. "No poisons. It has to be by a weapon. Others need to suspect an assassin, not someone from within putting poison in the food."

"Someone like you?" she asked with a smile in her voice, reaching out and pressing the vial into his hand despite his objections. "Fear not, Balgar, for this will not kill her. It will only rob her of her magic, at least temporarily."

"Do you fear you cannot handle her power?" he suddenly smirked, taking the flask nevertheless and slipping it into his own pocket.

"I would prefer to not cause the complete destruction of her tower when we meet," the assassin replied. "She is a formidable woman, one of the strongest of her order. If you want this to appear as you wish, then you will do as I say. Place the potion in her drink. It will dampen her abilities and ensure a clean kill."

"I know of no brew that can do that," Balgar said doubtfully. "How do you know it will work?"

"Because it's my own creation," she replied. "That is all you need to know. Now, can you manage it?"

"I can," he replied. "The council will meet by the next moon. It must be done by then."

"If the circumstances are right, then it will be done at that time," she answered.

"That's not good enough. We must have assurances it will be done when the council next meets."

"I will assure you of the completion of the contract," she said, "and nothing more. If you are successful in getting her to take the potion, then it should be done then. But I will not do so blindly."

"And I'm telling you it needs to be done then, regardless of what happens in the council chambers."

"Then perhaps you should find yourself someone else," she said, pushing her chair back from the table.

"Now, let's not be hasty," he said quickly, realizing he had overstepped his bounds.

"I warn you, Balgar, that I am not to be trifled with," she went on icily. "I will complete the job on my own terms and will not have it dictated by someone with no understanding of what is involved. Do you understand me?"

"Yes, yes," he said hastily. "Let me just say that it would be advantageous to us all if the job is done during the next council. Is that fair?"

"That is," she agreed, "providing it's understood that you complete your own task and the final decision on timing is mine."

"Agreed," he sighed, knowing he could go no further.

"And what about the other? I understand there is a second mark?"

"He, at least, must be taken alive," Balgar answered sourly.

"Employers rarely make use of someone of my particular skill set to arrange a simple kidnapping," she said with a smile.

"Consider this a bonus," Balgar stated. "He has been away from some time, but I am told he is returning to Nykiva very soon."

"Summer is not even here," she countered. "He has several months of good adventuring weather before him. Why would he return now?"

"He has likely heard of war breaking out," Balgar shrugged angrily. "By all accounts, Northern Outpost has fallen and Ithil Majeer is threatened. I am told that he and his band of miscreants are due back in the city before the next council. If so, he will be there."

"I have no intention of taking him at the council," she said plainly. "His capture will require some additional planning and is secondary to the main goal."

"Well, we are in agreement on that point."

"What if he cannot be taken alive?"

"I am told that is non-negotiable," Balgar answered. "There are other parties interested in him being captured alive and I'm certain they would not take too kindly to having his head delivered to them instead."

"If it can be arranged, then I will see to it," she said. "Beyond that, we will simply have to wait and see what happens."

"You don't have some sort of potion that would render him helpless?" Balgar sneered.

"For what purpose? He is well-known with the blade and would present an excellent opportunity to test my own skill."

"He's dangerous."

"All my marks typically are," she replied sweetly. "Isn't that why you are hiring me?"

"As long as you complete the main task, we can worry about the other piece later," he replied. "Now, let's discuss payment." He reached inside his shirt and pulled out a leather pouch. It wasn't overly large, but it was heavy, filled with a literal king's fortune. He carefully laid it in the table and slid it toward her. "Fifty flawlessly cut diamonds out of the mines at Pith Kersa—half of the agreed upon amount. The other half will be paid upon completion of the main contract. Another twenty-five more if you can hand that wandering fool over when he returns."

"What about the sorceress's personal belongings?"

"I don't care about her knick-knacks and baubles," Balgar waved her off. "But there are several items that must not be taken."

"Such as?"

"I am not at liberty to say at the moment," he replied. "Not that I know what they are, anyway," he quickly added.

"You are a bad liar," she said, taking the pouch of gems and tucking them away inside her cloak. "But nevertheless, we are in agreement for now. You will be able to handle your task?"

"I can get it done," he said importantly.

"See that you do," she replied. "If I make the attempt and her powers are at full strength, I will hold you accountable for additional costs for me to complete the contract."

"I'll get it done," he repeated. "You just make sure you don't fail."

"I never fail, Balgar Mud," she said, pushing herself away from the table as the waitress arrived and set down a bowl of watery looking stew and a crust of bread in front of him. She was gone a moment later, not even bothering to glance at the assassin.

"Care to join me for dinner?" he asked her, happy that the deal was complete and he could get back to considering other possibilities.

"Have a care, Balgar," she replied icily, leaning forward so that her face drew close to his. "I tolerate you because you present a means to an end for me, nothing more."

"Don't forget that I'm the one doing the hiring," he growled, meeting her gaze. "You work for me."

"If it pleases you to think so," she countered and then straightened. "In the meantime, enjoy your meal." With that, she was gone, slipping through the crowd of people like a shadow.

Balgar scanned the mass of patrons, his eyes seeking her form, his brain both angry and lustful. Then with a muttered curse, he snatched up his spoon and dipped it into his stew. Balgar screamed as the bowl full of spiders scattered in all directions.

Convergence

Chapter 10

The dream came again and he was surrounded by darkness – an impenetrable gloom that snuffed out all light. In the blinding blackness, he felt time and space race by him as he spun through the vortex and into the dreamscape where he knew he was destined to die. He became aware of the creature's presence as he neared the end of the tunnel and he felt a moment of despair and a surge of fear. He knew he would have precious little time to defend himself.

He suddenly broke out of the blackness and had only a moment to glimpse his surroundings before the thing was upon him. It rushed forward with frightening speed, its ponderous bulk pounding across the stone floor as it bellowed its hateful rage.

The man flung himself out of the way of the initial deadly charge and then rolled quickly to his feet as he desperately tried to shake the disorientation that dogged his steps. It would be several moments before he could hope to challenge the beast, so he settled for ducking behind a stone pillar and wincing as the monster let out an ear-splitting roar. Enraged, it struck the column with one massive clawed fist, sending cracks running through the stone from floor to ceiling as the man sprinted for the other side of the chamber.

He was in a large stone-walled cavern with no adornments save for a few thick pillars and a gateway of swirling darkness at the far end of the room. He knew the gate to be the origin of the creature he now faced and the portal's very existence was enough to chill him to his very soul, for beyond the gate, countless more nightmarish creatures awaited their opportunity to enter the land of the living. The thing that was trying to kill him was only the first.

As he fled, the monster's misshapen head swiveled immediately, its murderous eyes quickly locking on its prey. It was in pursuit in a moment. With only a few seconds' head start, he pulled his sword from the scabbard at his back. It thrummed with arcane energy, but the magic offered him little consolation. This particular fiend was a reaver, a powerful undead creature from the Nether, its primary purpose being to crush the life from magic wielders. While the man did not count himself among the small number of spell casters in the world, he knew that would not save him. It killed men and women alike; it killed the powerful and the weak; it killed anything it could find, particularly if it sensed magic, such as that which it sensed emanating from his blade. It was a relentless hunter and a devastating killer.

What perplexed him most, though, was not his certain death. It was the gateway that had spawned the demon, a portal that spoke of happenings far beyond his understanding. He knew instinctively that it was an earth gate and, as incredible as that was, he also knew that the gate was permanent, bridging his world with that of the Nether.

No, the situation could not be much worse.

He didn't have to be a scholar of history to understand the significance of the gate. The creatures beyond the portal were what remained of the first born of the gods, a race of man so perfect that they had evolved beyond any need for their creators. Angered at the affront, the gods had destroyed the bodies of their children in the Earth Storm and banished their souls into the endless void for eternity. Behind that unbreakable wall, their black spirits had festered and changed into representations of their inner hearts, turning them into monsters and demons of savage hatred and insatiable hunger.

Despite the occasional summoning from that world by a powerful dark sorcerer, most of the First Born remained safely imprisoned and locked away from the Second Born. But all that had suddenly changed with the existence of the portal. This earth gate was a doorway left wide open between the two worlds, and the First Born's ravenous hunger would draw them to it and then into the world of the living. In the end, he knew that meant only one thing. It would mean the end of the Second Born.

All of them.

He slipped into the deeper shadows near the far wall, but the creature would not be fooled. It thundered toward him, a monster dredged from the much of a child's worst nightmare. The reaver was fully twelve feet tall, a tangled mass of rotting flesh and shattered bones, held together in the shape of a humanoid figure. A flat, noseless face featured a pair of large red-rimmed eyes that burned with hatred and a huge gaping maw filled with jagged teeth that were capable of biting a man in half.

With another bubbling roar, the monstrosity launched itself across the room, a single leap bringing it nearly on top of him. But he was ready this time, dropping low under the reaching claws and slashing his weapon across the reaver's lower legs. The blade bit deep into the putrid flesh, the sword's enchantments sending ribbons of sparking energy into the wounds. But as quickly as the magic surged to life, the energy dissipated, sucked directly into the slashes left by his weapon, the torn flesh mending almost instantaneously.

A massive fist smashed into the floor, sending shards of stone flying in all directions. But the swordsman dove aside in the nick of time, avoiding the blow. He swept his blade in a backhand strike, slashing the creature across the face, leaving one of its eyes an oozing, steaming hole. Once more, the wound began to close, but not completely this time. The eye remained dark, the damage more severe.

Enraged, the monster swung its long arms forward, razor-sharp claws slashing harmlessly through the air, barely missing the fleeing man. Ducking behind the last remaining pillar, the warrior quickly pivoted and reversed course, slashing upward with his blade as the reaver reached for him. He scored his most serious strike, his weapon slicing through the creature's arm above the elbow, the sword's magic blasting into the flesh. Bits of ash, charred meat, and shattered bone flew in all directions as the creature's massive arm was severed. However, the attack barely slowed it and it struck quickly, the curved claws from its remaining hand slashing through the flesh of the warrior's side.

Blood sprayed from his lips as the talons drove deep into his entrails and up into his lungs. He felt himself lifted off the ground, pain suddenly blazing through his torso, before he was savagely flung across the room like a rag doll to slam into the unyielding wall. Stars exploded behind his eyes as he struck, blood from his head and body smearing the stone. As his hands went instinctively to his mortal wound, he felt his strength drain away and he knew that his injuries were fatal. Death would likely come quickly. He rolled over to his back, helpless and already fighting just to stay conscious.

His eyes filled with tears of helplessness as he heard the creature's approach. A moment later, its hulking form loomed over him, its remaining eye casting a malevolent look down at his broken form. Blood bubbled from his nose and mouth as his breathing became more and more labored.

But the creature did not resume the attack. With almost relaxed casualness, it lumbered over to the other side of the chamber and picked up its severed arm. Without a sound, it jammed the charred stump back into place.

The dying swordsman watched with detached curiosity as rotted flesh seemed to swell and grow around the wound, sealing it and reattaching the appendage. In a few moments, the monster was whole again, the only apparent damage being that of the eye that still remained dark.

Its body healed, the First Born monster returned to him and wrapped its clawed fingers around his throat. He wanted to scream, but no sound would come as the creature carried him to the edge of the portal. There it stopped, holding him inches from the numbing coldness of the earth gate.

"Well fought," came a soft female voice from further back in the cavernous room. "But then again, the outcome was fore-ordained. All that remains is to toss you through the gate, where you will suffer beyond your worst nightmares as your body is torn apart and devoured by the First Born and your soul is tortured for eternity in hell."

With a mighty struggle, the man turned his head slightly. His eyes settled upon the slight figure of a woman draped in robes of shimmering black silk, her face hidden deep within a shadowed cowl drawn up purposefully around her features. There was something about her – something about the way she carried herself that stirred to life forgotten memories deep within that had been long lost to the passage of time.

This is what he had fought for; what he needed to discover, and it was tantalizing close, a promise that the dreams could finally end. However, as quickly as the images came, they fluttered away once more as leaves on the wind. Another wave of pain washed over him, pulling him inexorably down into the waiting blackness of death.

The figure came forward slowly, gazing upon the dying man. Eyes glittered within the shadows of her cowl as she spoke. "My dear Terion," she said in a voice barely above a whisper. "You stand upon the threshold, but even now, while there is still a breath of life left within you, all is not yet lost." She drew closer. "You may still choose the right path and be saved," she finished, reaching up and placing her hand on his bloody forehead, connecting her mind to his. "You may still bring an end to this fate that awaits you."

The dying Terion screamed, a thousand terrible visions and twisted images slamming into his mind and assailing his consciousness. They were shimmering ghosts of a time not yet come and she held him fast in her power, showing him what could be. They flashed in through his mind's eye in a mere instant, weaving a terrible story and showing him power beyond compare, rampaging armies beyond count, and death beyond calculation…all of it under his own guiding hand. It lasted but a moment, but when she had finished with him, he felt as if he had lived a lifetime.

A single solitary tear rolled down his cheek. He knew what she wanted, but the price for saving himself was more than he could bear. His life would be forfeit, but he would remain steadfast in who he was. He would not give in to her wishes. He would not be a part of the destruction of his world.

Turning his head away from her, he stared directly into the face of the creature. "Be… done with… it," he gasped, every word a struggle as dark blood ran from his mouth.

For a long moment, nothing happened. Then the black robed woman simply shrugged. "As you wish," she said quietly.

The creature raised the dying man's body high in the air and flung him effortlessly into the void. Terion's unending scream floated back through the portal, bringing to pass the woman's dire warning of what horrible fate awaited him within.

Its task completed, the huge monster slowly trudged across the floor, a low rumble in its throat. In a few moments, it had vanished through a large doorway in the opposite wall, leaving the woman alone. She stared at the writhing blackness within the gateway, wondering what might have been. Finally, she too, turned away. "Good-bye, Terion," she whispered softly as she departed the room.

Chapter 11

Terion awoke from the dream as the last vestiges of terror and pain faded away, his body bathed in sweat, a silent scream at his lips. He climbed to his feet, grateful for the darkness of the night, and silently padded away from the glowing embers of last night's campfire, quickly losing himself in the trees. He paused, allowing his heartbeat to slow, as the safety of reality set back in. He was awake in the real world now, camped out in the woods, his four companions all quietly sleeping around him.

The dream was nothing new. He'd had it many times before, each time ending the same way, even if the path he took within the dream was different. Sometimes he fought better; other times he died quicker. Sometimes the mysterious woman spoke to him; other times the reaver killed him before she appeared. He wasn't so concerned with dying, whether in a dream or in reality. The threat of death was always part of his vocation. No, what concerned him was how real the dream had been and it left him with a hollow pit in his stomach.

He felt a pang of despair as he thought of the woman again. There was something about her that struck a familiar chord, but he couldn't place what that was. He didn't know her; he couldn't know her. He only knew of a handful of wizards and spell weavers in the land and only a few of those on a personal basis, rare as they were. But the woman in the dream? In all his travels and adventures, he had never come across anyone similar to her. The level of power she displayed frightened him beyond anything and yet, somehow, she knew him.

He gazed up into the star-filled sky and let the realization slowly settle upon him. He had enjoyed his time away from Nykiva, traveling the lands with his companions, letting the wind take them where they may. Their travels had taken him back to a happier time, a time when his love walked, fought, laughed, and slept beside him. But those times were long past and she was but a memory. The dream had reminded him of that, and he knew it was time to go home. It was time to face the present, one he wasn't certain he wanted to face.

"You had the dream again," a voice spoke up from the darkness behind him, soft and gentle. Arianna was the youngest of Terion's little band of adventurers and was also the newest. They had rescued her, a beautiful young Tae, from a group of slavers far to the south, before the winter snows the previous year. She was a wanderer, a rarity for her people, and Terion's plan had been to eventually return her to her home of Taer Blys. That was before he discovered her penchant for alchemy, using the abundant plant-life of the swamps and forests and plains they traversed to brew all manner of potions and droughts. As a healer, she had quickly become a valuable member of his group and had also made it clear that she had no intention of returning home. So the band of four had become five and Terion had quickly found he was grateful to have her along. "Every night for the past two moons, it has come to you," she added, stepping into the moonlight, her forehead creased with worry.

"Not every night," he replied quietly.

"But enough," she said, reaching out and placing a delicate hand on his shoulder, not as a lover would, but as a daughter would. And to her, Terion was just that—the father she never had. She loved the man as dearly as she loved anyone, and while he had filled that particular void in her life, his companions had filled the other and become her family. As a Tae, she was expected to remain grounded to their city and their reality, offering her healing to those that required it. But her family had been killed when she was but a toddler and she had been bounced from home to home until she knew nothing of family. As she grew into her teenage years, she soon realized that her home would not be with the others of her kind. So she had left, journeying wherever a caravan or traveling company that might accept her, would go. Her travels took her to many different places and eventually as far south as the Raiz Desert. It was there, that fate intervened again.

Her caravan was attacked and decimated by brutal slavers and she alone had been captured, certainly destined for the pleasure den of some abusive desert lord. Terion and his huge mute companion, Notyet, had stumbled upon the slaver camp three nights later quite by accident. They had liberated her, as well as some of the criminal's ill-gotten gains, and escaped into the desert. She had been with them ever since. Now, despite the dangers she faced as part of his little band, she had never known happiness like she knew today. She had never had a family like what she had now.

"Perhaps you should seek out someone that can explain it to you," she finally offered.

"I think not," Terion managed to chuckle, patting her hand affectionately. "That would require a trip to Ravenspire and a meeting with a witch that I'd much rather avoid. No, I do not think that would be the best idea at this time."

"Then what about the gods?" she pressed. "Surely this is important enough to consider taking your question to them. You have said that these dreams foreshadow a threat, even to them."

"The gods would demand too much in return," Terion replied abruptly, turning away from her. "Besides, it's a journey that few could survive and not worth asking about a silly dream."

"It's not silly if it plagues you like this."

"It is to me."

"Others go."

"Most of them either perish or turn back," he answered bitterly. "The Font of the Gods is not a place to be approached lightly.

It shouldn't even be approached at all."

"But you've been there," she stated softly after a few moments of silence, recognizing his anger for what fueled it. "It must have brought you great loss, for it to anger you so."

"It might have," interrupted another voice, gruff, but kind. "And it's not something he's meanin' to talk about with a youngster."

"Am I to be given no peace at all tonight?" Terion sighed, letting the demons of his past quickly fall back into the recesses of his mind.

"Bah," the other man replied, crunching through the brush toward him. "You prefer the company of Notyet because he has no voice to bother you with. At least with me, I offer the voice of reason and you don't have to read me fingers to figure out what I'm sayin'."

"Aylan speaks just fine and yet he doesn't pester me like you do, Cavanah."

"That's because he's got his nose in them spell books all the time," Cavanah answered. He was a big man, more portly than muscled. But his girth hid a panther-like grace completely unbecoming of one of his stature. When he wanted to, he could walk through a pile of dry leaves and dead twigs with little more than a whisper and he was an accomplished fighter, whether with a blade or the small hand crossbow that he favored. He trudged up to Terion and leaned against a nearby tree, huffing with exertion. "Always with you, we have to be outside, traipsing through woods and up hills and mountains, when an inn and a bottle or three of wine would be much more accommodating and restful. I'm just sayin'."

"There are no inns within a hundred leagues of us."

"Then maybe you should let me set our destination."

"If you will leave me be, maybe I'll consider it," Terion couldn't help but smile.

"Dawn will break in a few minutes," Cavanah said, his voice becoming serious. "Might be that's long enough to come clean with what's going on in that head of yours."

"It's not that easy," Terion began, but it was Arianna who cut him off.

"Not that easy to do what? Share something that troubles you with your friends?" she asked as she grabbed his arm and turned him back to face her. "I owe you a debt for rescuing me and taking me in, Terion. Give me something, anything, to begin working on repaying it."

"It's just a dream, Arianna," he said softly, offering her a small smile.

"It's more than that," she replied, refusing to back down.

She was right and he knew it. He had been plagued by the dreams for weeks now and slowly withdrawn from his friends, becoming moody and introspective as each night brought the same vision. "Very well," he sighed, looking up at the stars. A hint of violet to the east told him that the darkness would soon be replaced by the morning sun. "You're right. It's more than just a dream."

"Do you fear the beast?" Arianna asked.

"No," he shook his head. "Death comes eventually to all of us and cannot be avoided. If this dream foretells my end by this creature, who am I to change it?"

"If you do ever end up facing this thing," Cavanah cut in, "I would hope you would do your level best to beat it and not just lie down and accept something that a stupid dream told you would happen."

"I'm not going to roll over and die, if it does come to pass," Terion answered with a sad smile. "Besides, that whole fight is secondary to the woman."

"You haven't spoken much of her in what little you have shared," Cavanah said acidly, purposefully baiting his long-time friend.

"I haven't told you what she showed me while she was asking me to join her," Terion said quietly. "That's what concerns me." He paused for a moment, gathering his thoughts before continuing. "As I was dying, she showed me a vision of what she is planning on doing. She is gathering an army and intends to subjugate all the lands."

"We live in a world at war, which is why we have jobs," Cavanah said. "Someone's always fighting with someone else. She will be no different than any other power-hungry would-be despot that we've seen, some of which we've helped topple."

"She will be different," he replied. "She already is."

"What makes you say so?"

"Because she will win," Terion replied matter-of-factly.

"You're daft, man," Cavanah snorted. "Ain't no one ever succeeded in the foolish idea of world domination. How many of these high and mighty rulers have bawled like babies after we've gone in and tossed them out on their arses?"

"You're talking about petty tyrants and dictators who are only concerned with a single town or settlement. This is different."

"Ain't no different," Cavanah persisted.

"She has an open gate to the Nether and she has control over the creatures coming through it. The First Born are beyond anyone's count and they give her the means to overcome the world. It is completely different," he finished.

"Meaning no disrespect, but even if somehow you are really receiving visions from the gods in these dreams, you're off your bean if you believe a gate to the Nether truly exists."

"This one does."

"Bah!" Cavanah exclaimed, throwing up his hands in

exasperation.

"Don't be so quick to dismiss the gate," a new voice replied and a young man stepped out of the trees beside Arianna. He snapped his finger and a ball of light appeared in the palm of his hands, casting a muted blue glow over the group. He was a young lad, barely a man, his jet-black hair and dark skin giving an indication that he called the desert his home. He was clad in a loose short-sleeved tunic and breeches that were favored by the desert-dwelling people that he was descended from. However, unlike most of his people, he bore the tattooed hand markings of a young mage. The glyphs covered his hands that entwined his fingers and circled his wrists. From a distance, they resembled nothing more than swirling patterns and whorls of various shades of brown and green. Upon closer examination of the arcane runes, one could see the tiny images of mountains and stone, trees and rolling hills, indicating his continuing studies into the elemental sphere of the earth. At the moment, he seemed quite pleased with himself.

"Where's Notyet?" Cavanah asked, looking past him.

"Likely still asleep," the young mage, Aylan, replied evenly.

"And why aren't you?"

"I prefer the early morning hours for study."

"You and your books," Cavanah sighed and shook his head. "Bottom line, there ain't no gate to hell that exists in the world. Period."

"How do you explain the First Born then?" Aylan asked. "They exist, Cavanah. We have fought them on several occasions."

"Only because some blasted dark sorcerer sees fit to summon them."

"The woman in my dream is a dark sorceress," Terion took control of the conversation again, "and she has figured out how to create a gateway to let them in, rather than worry about summoning them one by one."

"That would take a gatekeeper," Cavanah answered. "And you and I both know those gray robes have been gone for a long time."

"That is where you are mistaken," Aylan explained. "My master…"

"Loken is a crackpot," Cavanah interrupted in a huff. "He ain't been out of his tower in years. Ain't that why you left?"

"My reasons for leaving are my own, Cavanah," Aylan said icily. "But I left with his blessing, contrary to what you think."

"That still don't…"

"Enough," Terion cut him off, raising a hand to hush his friend. "I know your feelings, Cavanah. We all do. But let Aylan explain."

"Whatever you think of Loken, he's a brilliant wizard and I owe him my life for taking me in and sponsoring me in the Consortium's test," Aylan said, referring to the ruling council of wizard's disturbingly dangerous Iron Circle test for apprentice mages. "During my years as his apprentice, he spoke often of the four circles, including the grays. The whites existing for good, the blacks for evil, the reds for balance, you know, all of the normal stuff.

"Then there are the grays and…well, the grays exist for a whole other reason. No one knows the true purpose in their creation, but Loken hypothesized that they were once the chosen mouthpieces of the gods; priests if you will. Their magical abilities would seem to allow them to open up a conduit to at least converse with the gods, so that's a distinct possibility for their origin. I asked him once if the grays—the gatekeepers—still existed. He said that a few do, but they remain in hiding."

"Why would they be in hiding?" Arianna asked.

"To prevent someone from doing just what happened in Terion's dream," Aylan was quick to answer. "If what Terion has told us is actually happening and the woman does indeed have a gate, she got it by employing a gatekeeper. There is no other explanation."

"But would a gray join forces with the woman in his dreams?" the young woman questioned. "Granted, I have just heard tales of them, but they never struck me as being anything but decent and kind. If what you say about them being true priests and priestesses of the gods, I can't believe one would willingly join her."

"The woman in my dreams was incredibly powerful. If the gate is the work of a gray, I doubt it would have been by choice," Terion put in.

"It wasn't," Aylan answered confidently.

"How can you know that?" Arianna asked.

"Because the gate in Terion's dream is permanent, at least by what he has shared with us. For that to happen, it would require the sacrifice of the gray performing the opening of the portal."

"You mean he would have to be killed?"

"Precisely," Aylan nodded. "When the gods divided the magical elements, the grays were given the most power and also made the most vulnerable. They could learn no other magic, only that which could open up temporary portals and gateways. It made for ease of traveling, and history states they became great ambassadors between the races, but they could accomplish little else in the way of magic. And the fact that they would have to give up their lives to make a gate permanent made it a foregone conclusion that none likely ever would."

"So what about the gate in my dream?" Terion asked, looking directly at the young mage. "This was a gateway to the Nether, a portal to hell. Since when can a gatekeeper open up a gate into another plane of existence?"

"That's just it," Aylan replied. "They can't. Or at least, they aren't supposed to be able to."

"Then explain this one."

"I can't," Aylan shook his head. "Not with any certainty, anyway."

"Then hypothesize," Cavanah said with a wink.

"I suppose it's possible for a gray to grow powerful enough to open a gateway into another world," Aylan said slowly. "That's really how magic works; the more you study and practice, the greater power you come to wield."

"But you don't believe that's what happened here, do you?" Terion asked, picking up on the young man's reluctance.

"No," Aylan replied somberly. "I think it is something much more serious. I think it has to be because of a weakening of the barrier."

"A weakening of the barrier?" Cavanah scoffed. "You mean a convergence?"

Aylan nodded, his face grim.

"That's not even remotely possible!" Cavanah bellowed. "That would mean the end of the world!"

"Why would it not be possible?" Aylan countered, his voice low. "Just because it has never happened before, doesn't mean it never will."

"I don't understand any of this," Arianna sighed. "What's a convergence?"

Aylan started to answer, but Terion held up a hand, knowing his young friend would launch into a long philosophical discussion about the gods and the worlds they created. "Simply put, we can see our world around us, Arianna, and we know it's a gift from the gods," he said, motioning to the land about them. "But we do not see the gods as our caretakers. We all know they exist, but some people believe in their existence more or less than others. Lore states that when the world was organized and created by The One, there were countless gods in His presence who were set to become gods of the world He created. Consequently, there were many discussions about which gods should be in power over which elements, crafts, seasons, even emotions. Despite all the possibilities, there were still far too many gods for the world. The One solved the problem by creating multiple copies of earth and allowing the gods to choose where they would rule and how they would populate their new world," he went on. "Countless worlds came into existence and the gods organized themselves into groups, becoming caretakers of their chosen earth."

"I understand all that, but what is the convergence Aylan mentioned?"

"It is the weakening of the barrier between worlds," Terion answered. "The One created a barrier between each world so as not to allow interference between the gods of different worlds and the mortals that existed on each world. This barrier not only keeps the gods away from each other's earth, but it prevents people from traversing between the worlds."

"And if the barrier weakens?"

"The worlds come together."

"So our world is going to merge with hell?"

"If this gate is actually opened to the Nether, then it won't matter whether it merges or not," Terion explained. "The First Born will come through the portal and ultimately overrun every corner of our world. It may take some time, but in the end, we will all die."

"Unless we can close it," Cavanah spoke up.

"That still doesn't address the possibility of a convergence," Aylan said. "Closing a permanent earth gate into the Nether is going to be next to impossible. But even if we are successful and the barriers are actually weakening, there is nothing we can do about that. A convergence will eventually happen and when it does, it will be the end of everything we know."

"Must you be so blasted optimistic?" Cavanah snorted. "Always the same with you wizarding types."

"Nevertheless, he's right," Terion said. "I have no idea what it's going to take to close a permanent earth gate and that might be a task we cannot even hope to successfully complete. The bigger question, though, is if it even matters. If a convergence is coming, it cannot be stopped."

"What will happen?" Arianna asked, looking pointedly at the young mage.

"Two worlds become one in a convergence," Aylan shrugged. "Imagine two different earths, both with cities, buildings, people, laws, etc., and suddenly they are one. Theoretically speaking, the lands would stay pretty much the same. But the rest would be in ruins. If a city in our existence was occupying the same spot as a city on another world and a convergence occurred, imagine the destruction that would occur, not to mention what would happen when the people of two different worlds come together."

"I'm guessing that would be a war to end all wars," Cavanah mused.

"Or worse," Aylan said thoughtfully.

"That said, I think it's time to go home," Terion said. "We need to figure out what's going on."

"Because of your dreams?" Cavanah asked, but there was no disbelief now, only concern.

"Exactly," Terion answered.

"So, why you, my friend?" he asked.

"Why the dreams?"

"No, why is this dream sorceress of yours asking you to join her? Why you?" Cavanah went on. "Granted, you're pretty good with the blade and a capable leader, but if she's a dark sorceress with an open gate to hell, what does she need you for? She already has an unlimited army."

"Maybe the better question is what does she *want* him for?" Arianna spoke up thoughtfully and all eyes turned to her. "She knows you Terion. You mean something to her."

"But what?" Terion questioned, once more looking into the night sky. Dawn was beginning to break over the eastern horizon and the stars were fading into the lightening sky. Somewhere, up there, he knew the gods were watching. What did they know about what was happening? What would they take from him if he sought them out once more? Whatever it was, it couldn't be worse than what they took the last time. "Maybe it's time to find out," he whispered, a single tear rolling unnoticed down his cheek.

Chapter 12

"They are coming," the weary man said at last, completing his tale to the council seated around the table before him. Garamon Whiteblade felt old and tired and saw in the eyes of the council member that most did not believe him. That war seemed to be threatening was not a surprise to the men and women he had just addressed. But the tale of an Arcai leading an army of thousands against Ithil Majeer, a crown jewel of the Dom empire, was almost too fantastic to entertain. Those seated around the table were looking at him with various looks of thoughtfulness and skepticism.

Finally, a tall man with piercing eyes and sharp features broke the silence. His name was Myngar and he was responsible for much of the Dom'Ithi people's wealth and success in his position as Minister of Finance. He was a master strategist when it came to trading with the other races and, under his guidance, the Doms had grown and prospered beyond any other race for more than two decades. "We appreciate your report and your candor, Lord Garamon," he said quietly. "Unless you have anything more to add, you may leave."

The old man nodded his head and rose from his chair, grief and weariness lining his face. "I've nothing more to add," he said quietly, "beyond a warning."

"And what is that?"

"Send aid to the Taes," he said, "whatever you can spare."

"To go to the aid of the Taes, when so many of our own people have already been killed or driven from their homes, is foolhardy," Myngar replied.

"Since when has it been called foolhardy to aid another race and save the lives of innocent men, women, and children?" Garamon countered, his voice bitter. He had known that the council would resist his words, particularly his claim that an Arcai marched at the head of the enemy. "The Arcai, Draven, will march on the Taes from Ithil Majeer and from there, he will launch his attack on Nykiva. If you send aid to the Taes, you can delay or even stop his march before he can turn his sights toward this city."

The minister ignored the outburst and continued undaunted. "We have our own people to protect," he said softly. "Our efforts should be directed at reclaiming Ithil Majeer."

"Have you not listened to my words?"Garamon asked. "Ithil Majeer is overrun and occupied by forces beyond anything we have ever faced and they are led by the God Killer. We should not be considering how to retake Ithil Majeer, but how to best protect Nykiva and the Taes."

"Come now," Myngar said, offering Garamon a weak smile. "You speak of an alliance between the Gols and the Rats and that may be true, though everyone knows the two races hate each other. You have told us of scores of First Born creatures that attacked from inside the city at night and even that may be possible. But to think they are all led by an Arcai is almost absurd."

Garamon nodded as he saw how well his own words had been turned against him. Myngar had read and played him perfectly, giving the others reason to doubt as well. "The words of a crazy old man, then," he said with a tired sigh. "I understand," he finished and turned and left the chambers, his shoulders slumped.

"Your words, not mine," Myngar said softly to himself in genuine sorrow, for he truly did not like putting the man in such a difficult position. He did only what he felt he must for the safety and continued well-being of people of Nykiva. Having them stirred up in fear due to fantastic tales of marauding armies and terrifying undead, all lead by an unstoppable foe, would do more harm than good. So he had been forced to play the other side, something he actually felt deep regret for. But at least now, they could keep their own soldiers home and quietly prepare in case Draven was indeed on the march.

As the doors shut behind Garamon, another voice spoke up, this one from a man further down the long oaken council table. He had sat in silence during the proceedings, hunched over with his chin resting in his meaty hand as he listened intently. "I would have to concur with our fine minister of finance," Balgar Mud said importantly. "We must first look to our own, if what we have been told is the truth." He sat back, crossing his arms across a broad chest that had gotten that way from an over-indulgence of good food rather than from physical activity. He let his gaze travel around at the others in attendance. "What proof do we have of this anyway?"

"I did not say that I disbelieve him," Myngar spoke up, somewhat angered that Balgar would build upon his own arguments to make accusations that did not need to be made.

Balgar waved him off. "Perhaps you are swayed more than you let on, Myngar," he challenged. "But I am not."

"Then what do you suggest?" another council member asked, leaning forward as he stroked a long white beard.

"I recommend that we put together a small group of scouts to travel to Ithil Majeer and ascertain the real threat," Balgar replied. "Perhaps we can even impose upon our own wise council leader to do a little conjuring of her own. She might speed things on their way and we can quickly be done with this silly business," he finished almost contemptuously, looking down at the end of the table to the woman seated there.

"You would have me teleport someone to Ithil Majeer?" the woman asked quietly, locking her deep blue eyes upon those of Balgar. "You would consign someone to an almost certain death by sending them into the middle of an occupied city."

"You do not know that to be true," Balgar scoffed. "For all we know, Ithil Majeer may have been besieged by a bunch of half-witted rogues and illusionists."

"Would you go then?" the woman asked, looking hard at him. "If you wish me to send someone to the high tower of Ithil Majeer, then perhaps you should be the one to volunteer for such a task, Balgar. If you are so certain that the words you heard today are without merit, you should have little to worry about." She offered him an almost pitying smile, but her blue eyes were cold as ice.

At this, Balgar paled, shrinking down into his chair. "I only meant..."

"I know exactly what you meant," she interrupted him, her voice steely, "and we will speak more of it later, when it better suits me. For now, the matter before the council is plain." She looked up, her countenance firm, and regarded each of the dozen members in the room. Keiran, arch mage of Nykiva, was a born leader, wise and knowledgeable and used to the almost constant bickering of the council. She herself detested politics, being much more favored toward quietly studying in her tower. But her considerable power made her the logical choice to head the ruling council of the Dom'Ithi people. As a sorceress, she was among a select few in all the races who were complete masters of their craft; as a politician, though, her wisdom gained from long studying those powers gave her a keen insight into the minds and souls of men, allowing her to govern a ruling council both justly and intelligently. As such, she had ascended to the head of the Dom council nearly eleven years before and had ruled wisely ever since. "The task is before all of us," she continued, then turned her eyes on Balgar again. "Even you must be a part of the decision we make, Balgar, for you are also part of this council, for better or worse."

She then swept her gaze across the others. "For myself, I believe the words we have heard. We are in danger."

"My lady," said another man, who leaned forward in his chair as he spoke. Terion had been back in the city for a short time and had cleaned up rather well from the road. He was a striking individual and middle age had been kind to him. He was tall, with deep set dark eyes and long black hair pulled back tightly into a ponytail. His skin was darker than most, whether due to his parentage or the time he spent in the sun, no one really knew. As a whole, his presence was imposing. "May I speak?"

"The floor is yours, Terion," she replied with a nod. "It is good to have you back among us and your counsel is always welcome here."

"Thank you," he said, rising from his seat as was his manner when addressing the council. In battle, he was nearly unmatched with a blade. In the political arena, he was a dynamic individual and a master of speech, eloquent and intelligent. Hands behind his back, he began to walk slowly around the table. He was sharply dressed now, having changed out of his traveling leathers into a billowing white shirt and black leggings, while around his waist, a crimson scarf was tied. Supple boots of black leather were on his feet, rising nearly to his knees, and he looked like he had just stepped from the deck of a great masted sailing ship flying the skull and crossbones.

"For a number of years, I called Ithil Majeer my home and I know Garamon personally. I have no reason to doubt what we have heard today," he said. "On our return from the southwest, we spent two nights behind the walls of Ithil Majeer, before the attack occurred. Even then, there was much talk about trouble in the west. It is not a stretch to believe our enemies seek to destroy us, and taking out Ithil Majeer would be a sound tactic."

"Ithil Majeer is well defended. It should take weeks to breach its walls," Myngar spoke up. "Garamon said the city fell in two days."

"An easy task for an Arcai," Terion pointed out, "particularly if his companion was with him."

"Surely you jest," began Balgar, trying to get an upper hand in the conversation, but Terion quickly silenced him with a glare.

"I do not question that this has happened, nor should any of you," Terion went on, his voice even. "It would certainly take an Arcai to unite the Gols and the Rats, but I wonder, why would Draven lead this army? To what end would an Arcai wish the subjugation of another race? The Arcai are immortal – or as close to immortality as they can be. Because of that, they already have a certain dominion over mortal men. So why lead an army against us?"

Myngar cleared his throat and straightened in his chair, already knowing that the silent opinions of the council had shifted in those first few moments of Terion's speech. He was glad that they had. "You truly believe that Draven is at their head," he said, his eyes narrowing.

"I do. Lord Garamon is not a doddering old fool and besides, everyone knows the tales of Draven anyway. If I had to pick an Arcai that would dare to do this, I would choose Draven above all others. For many years now, he has forsaken his vow of non-interference and has been obsessed with matching his strength against others. Is it such a stretch to believe he could have taken it to this level?"

"But why a war?" Keiran asked, her voice quiet and concerned.

"That is something known only to Draven and those closest to him," he replied with a shrug.

"Then perhaps we should seek to question one of those closest to him," Myngar pressed. "Surely, there must be someone else who knows what his goals are."

Terion chuckled and shook his head. "Do you forget who walks at his side? If anyone knows the mind of an Arcai, it is his or her companion. And given the choice, I would face neither."

"I find myself agreeing with you, Terion," Myngar sighed.

"Well, I still do not believe it," Balgar cut in as he pushed his chair back abruptly and rose to his feet, his face red with anger. "The words spoken here today are madness and you are fools to believe them! I do not believe that an Arcai marches against us anymore than I believe Keiran should head this council!"

There was a collective gasp of amazement from the council members at his direct words. Balgar had always been considered a coward and everyone knew of his hatred and jealousy toward Keiran. He coveted her seat at the head of the council, and for him to speak up as he just had, hinted of things happening within the man's mind that no one else would have thought possible.

"Despite what you might believe, Balgar, at the present time, I *do* head the council," Keiran said, her voice soft but firm. "Of course, if you see fit to test my authority…" She trailed off, letting the unspoken threat hang in the air as she locked her glittering eyes on him.

But Balgar had found some measure of courage where it was nearly always lacking in him and, for the first time that anyone could remember, he stood his ground. "I have spoken against you from the first, Keiran, and I will do so again. You lead this council only by the grace of the grand baron and it is by his word that I serve his interests on this council."

At that, the sorceress stood up herself, her slender form seeming to grow. When she spoke, her voice was deep and power flowed through her, making everyone present cringe at the thought of her fury unleashed. "The grand baron rules the city of Nykiva, Balgar, and no one, least of all me, dares to challenge that fact. But when it comes to ruling the Dom'Ithi people as a whole, that charge falls to myself and this council. Your allegiance to the grand baron is admirable but your petty charges against me and your continued attempts to thwart the actions of this council are repulsive. Therefore, as of this moment, I relieve you of your duties as a council member. I will petition the grand baron to replace you with another member of his own advisors as quickly as opportunity allows." With that, she slowly sat back down into her high-backed chair, her gaze never leaving the disgraced man.

"You cannot dismiss me," Balgar sputtered, his voice coming out in a whine. "I was appointed to this council by the grand baron himself!"

"And you are being dismissed by the ruling head of the Dom'Ithi people," spoke a different voice, this from another woman who sat nearer to Balgar and had, to this point, been silent. She was clothed in the robes of a sorceress, dark scarlet in color, and she pointed at Balgar with a glyph-encircled finger. "I suggest that for your own sake, you heed her words and remove yourself from the council's presence," continued Ranora, apprentice to Keiran herself.

"You cannot threaten me!" Balgar fairly shouted, turning his gaze upon the younger sorceress.

But Ranora silenced him as she rose to her own feet. "Be gone!" she shouted back, thrusting her arms free of her long sleeves, her rune-covered hands and arms beginning to glow with arcane energy. Blue sparks arced from fingertips and the very air in the room crackled and smelled of ozone. "My mistress may stay her hand out of goodness, but I will not! Leave this room before I reduce your bloated corpse to ash," she shouted angrily.

Her final threat was little needed, for Balgar was already making for the door. Huffing in terror and exertion, he shoved through it and slammed it shut behind him, stopping to catch his breath. For a few moments, fear ruled his features, but he quickly brought it under control and calmed himself before an evil smile suddenly appeared on his face.

He wiped a hand across his sweaty brow, believing the whole scene had gone as well as he could have hoped. He could live with the disgrace of being banned from the council, just as he could deal with the embarrassment of having fled from Ranora. He knew he would not be gone from the council long and, when he returned, it would be at its head. He had planned it all so perfectly and he silently congratulated himself on pulling it off as well he had. Taking a deep breath, he slipped his right hand into the sleeve of his left and pulled from it, the small crystalline vial the assassin had given him. The time had finally come to finish things with Keiran. Palming the vial, he turned and hurried down the corridor.

While Balgar plotted his final revenge, Keiran was restoring order inside the council chambers, directing a mild rebuke at her apprentice. "While your enthusiasm and devotion is appreciated, I caution you to hold fast your emotions, Ranora," she said gently. "Balgar is not worth fretting about."

The younger woman nodded as she sat down, her composure restored. "I understand, my lady," she said quietly, "and I offer my apologies to you and to the rest of the council for my outburst."

"Believe me," said Terion, an amused smile on his face. "I myself rather enjoyed that little show. Balgar should have been put in his place quite some time ago."

There was a murmur of agreement from several other council members until Keiran held up her hand. "Enough," she said. "We will speak no more of it. What we must decide now is how to proceed."

"If you'll permit me," agreed Terion, walking back to his seat,

"I have a suggestion."

"Go on," Keiran urged as she sat back in her chair and folded her arms, prepared to listen.

"If we are to believe what has happened, then the actions of Draven are indeed disturbing," Terion explained. "But as terrible as they might seem to us, they must be a complete affront to the gods themselves. Why would the gods allow this to happen? Why would they turn a blind eye to the actions of one of their own immortal children?"

"You intend to ask them directly?" Keiran asked quietly.

"You must admit, much could be learned," Terion replied.

"None have traveled to the Font of the Gods in many years," she countered, referring to that sacred temple that stood alone deep within the desolation of the Dead Waste, many leagues northeast of Nykiva. "At least none have done so and returned to tell the tale."

"The Dead Waste is treacherous, my lady, particularly to the unlearned," he answered knowingly, tightening his control over his own emotions, still raw after so many years. "But I have traveled there before and I know what dangers await."

"I will not attempt to dissuade you, Terion, because it is a sound suggestion. But I caution you to take few others with you," she said. "Seeking an audience with the gods with a large armed contingent can only end in disaster."

"I will bring only Notyet and a few others," he answered. Despite what he had told his companions in the past, he had been planning on going already. This task would help him justify the dangerous journey. "A dozen, no more," he finished.

"That's a reasonable plan," she agreed, "but so, too, is Balgar's." Ignoring the looks of disbelief on several of the council member's faces, she went on. "Therefore, we will send two groups at dawn tomorrow. Terion will go north to seek counsel with the gods. The other group I will send south to Ithil Majeer. They will travel by horseback and then by foot, to scout the situation. Only this way can they ensure their safety."

"Cavanah could best lead the south road," Terion added, a sly smile on his face.

"Were it not for his fondness for the grape and the pint, I might agree with you," Keiran answered doubtfully.

"Yet few can match his abilities in the timber, regardless of his state of mind."

"It is unconventional wisdom, Terion," Keiran sighed and shook her head. "But I will again agree with you. You will inform him that he has been called to duty?"

"It will be my pleasure," Terion answered with a mischievous gleam in his eye.

"Thank you," the sorceress added. "Will there be anything else?"

"As a matter of fact, yes. We seem to have quickly adopted the mindset that we are standing against an Arcai with no hope of defeating him. But I remind you that Draven is only one Arcai. There are others, and one in particular who might have reason to stand against him."

"That is a possibility," she said slowly, her eyes distant and thoughtful. "It would prove most beneficial to have an equal to Draven standing opposed to him. Very well, I will consider it. In the meantime, you will begin preparations immediately. The two groups must leave no later than dawn's first light. I will supply each member with a gem of return. I have few of those remaining, but enough to spare for those who will be riding into peril."

"What of the Taes?" Terion asked. "Should they be warned?"

"You know they would not listen," she answered sadly. "The Taes are a peaceful people and they will not leave their city or their lands, no matter the threat. However, I will consider what aid we can send."

"And the presence of the First Born, my lady?" Terion continued.

"To that, I have no answer myself," Keiran replied helplessly. "The undead have always walked freely about the land, but never in such numbers. How they came to be behind the walls of Ithil Majeer is a mystery at the moment. For now, though, let us tend to the present and proceed with our designs."

There was a chorus of agreement and the woman stood up with a rustle of her white robes. "If there is nothing more, we stand adjourned," she said to the council, looking around and silently gauging the looks of the individual council members. Myngar, despite his earlier refusal to fully believe the story the old man had related, now appeared almost fierce in his agreement. Ranora looked grim and nodded her head. The other men and women, individual voices in the council, but always united, looked at her expectantly.

There was a soft knock at the door before it opened slowly. After a moment, in came two young child stewards bearing trays with wine and water. "Are we too late?" asked one of the children, a boy of about thirteen.

"We hurried as quickly as we could," said the other, a pretty young girl of about the same age. "We were told to bring water."

"The council is completed," Keiran said with a soft smile. "However, we shall be grateful to accept what you have brought us."

Smiling happily, the two children quickly set out simple cups of finely blown glass and then began pouring the drinks.

Chapter 13

"Awake!" shouted Terion as he slammed open the door and made straight for the man in a bed on the far side of the sparsely furnished and darkened room.

"You had better be bringing me tidings of riches or beautiful women," growled Cavanah's surly voice from beneath the covers. "If not, I will…"

"You will what?" Terion interrupted him as he grabbed hold of the linen and pulled it aside with a flourish. "You dare threaten me when you lack the strength to stand or even grab your weapon?"

"It wouldn't be a fair fight," the other man moaned, rolling over to huddle against the wall. "Now leave me be or fetch me several pints from the inn down the street."

"There is no time for drinking today, my friend," Terion continued as he walked to the window and threw open the shutters, letting the warm light of the late spring sun stream into the room.

"By the gods, we just got here! Shut the window and leave me in peace!" Cavanah shouted, throwing an arm across his face. "My eyes are not ready for the full light of day."

"Then get them ready. It's time to rise, my friend. You have been appointed to a task of great importance."

"Appointed? More like volunteered by you, I'll wager," Cavanah said grumpily as he rolled back over the bed and finally swung his feet to the floor. With a moan, he rubbed his temples and opened one squinting eye, which he fastened on Terion. Taking in the man's pirate garb, as he liked to refer to it, Cavanah nodded. "I see you were at council," he remarked.

Terion nodded.

"Did Keiran finally turn Balgar into a toad?"

"No, but Ranora nearly set him on fire," he chuckled. "I think she would have if Keiran had not been there."

Cavanah harrumphed. "I always liked that girl. She's got spunk. So why are you bothering me anyway?" he went on. "We just got back to civilization. Would it kill you to let me enjoy it for a few days?"

"Ithil Majeer has fallen," Terion said abruptly, his voice suddenly grave.

"Bah! You can't be serious," Cavanah started to laugh, but the mirth quickly died on his face as he saw that his friend was not joking. "You are serious?"

Terion nodded solemnly.

Cavanah shook his head in disbelief. He had journeyed to Ithil Majeer many times over the years and had many fond memories of the city, its taverns, and a few female acquaintances that he had shared a number of magical moments with. "How did it happen?" he finally asked.

Terion told him, relating Lord Garamon's story about the army of Gols and Rats, as well as the Arcai that was leading them and the appearance of hordes of First Born.

"First Born, huh?" Cavanah asked, raising an eyebrow. "Do you think there's any connection to your dreams?"

"Too much of a coincidence for there not to be."

"And what about this Arcai?"

"That's what we must discover."

"So how do I figure into this?" Cavanah asked suspiciously. "Am I being ordered to go see for myself?"

"I merely volunteered your services," Terion replied with a small smile. "You may decline if you wish."

"Not likely," Cavanah snorted as he tried to stand. For a moment, he looked as if he would collapse, but he steadied himself by grabbing the bedpost. "I'll go, since you and I both know I really have little choice. But what are you going to do in the meantime? Will you sit idly by here in Nykiva or will you travel with me?"

"I will do neither," was the answer. "My road lies in a different direction."

"If I'm going south," he asked, squinting at his friend, "where are you going?"

"The Dead Waste," Terion plainly stated.

"Are you out of your mind?"

"Can you think of any better destination?"

"A few," Cavanah snorted. "Why the blazes would you want to travel to the Font of the Gods? You of all people should know the gods will give you nothing but grief, and that's if you even complete the journey."

"I have to try."

Cavanah shook his shaggy head. "For what purpose? To discover why we are suddenly at war with one of their brats?"

"I've been there before. I know what to expect."

"Yes, and what did that get you?" Cavanah challenged.

Terion was silent, a look of deep pain passing across his face. He had indeed braved the Waste long ago, a brash young man with visions of grand adventures, seeking the wisdom and the guidance and perhaps the very treasure of the gods themselves. Four of them, friends since toddling about their parents' homes, had made the journey. Two of those friends had died in the wastelands and his beloved had been torn apart by the guardian, a savage monster that prowled the catacombs of the temple. He had returned from his journey alone, a man wounded of body and broken of spirit, and he had carried the scars ever since.

Cavanah lowered his head, realizing too late he had stepped

into an area he should not have. "I'm sorry, Terion. You know I didn't mean it that way."

"I know what you meant," Terion said softly. "At least I know you care."

"Do you really think going there will provide you with answers?" Cavanah asked.

"I hope that it provides me with something," Terion answered. "They certainly cannot be pleased with Draven's meddling in the affairs of man, which is why I have to believe they will let me succeed in reaching them."

"You're putting a lot of stock in the hope that the gods will decide it's okay to meddle in the affairs of man."

"There are no guarantees, to be sure," Terion agreed. "I go because I must. If the gods will give me any information, we need to know what it is. And I have to believe that my dreams have something to do with this, as well."

"Well," said Cavanah as he stretched his arms behind him to relieve the tension in his large frame. "I think I would much rather travel south myself, into the very teeth of Draven's army, than to tempt the Dead Waste."

"That's why you're going south instead of north," Terion smiled knowingly.

"Are you taking Notyet?"

"Yes," he nodded. "I'll need his fighting skill in the Waste. Your task relies on stealth, not fighting. He would be a poor companion for you."

"You're probably right," Cavanah grunted. "I'm sure if Notyet came with me, Draven would know of our whereabouts before we were within one hundred leagues of him. What about the young'uns?"

"Arianna and Aylan will remain here. They are much too

inexperienced for these tasks."

"They'll fight ya on that."

"They already have," Terion replied ruefully, recalling the long argument he'd had with them earlier in the morning.

"I'll bet," Cavanah chuckled. "So when do we start?"

"Tomorrow morning, first light."

"Good," the big man growled as he started toward the door. "Then I have time for several meals and some good drink to boot."

Terion looked at him gravely and grabbed him by the arm. "Do not forget yourself. You and your men will ride for Ithil Majeer at first light. They do not need a drunken fool falling from his horse as their leader."

"They will not have it," Cavanah said briskly as he shook himself from Terion's grasp and opened the door. "Now go prepare for your own journey and allow me to prepare for mine as I will. I will meet you before the sun rises in the morning."

With that, he clomped down the hall. Terion watched him go.

The sun was almost an hour from breaking fully over the horizon when the two groups began gathering outside the city gates, torches in hand. Ironically, Cavanah was the first to arrive and he was busily tending his horse, ensuring that his provisions for the journey were well-stocked, when Terion arrived. With Terion was a monster of a man, huge and well-armored, standing a good head taller than most others. Both of them were leading horses of their own.

Cavanah looked up from his task and smiled. He was dressed in drab green and brown clothing, with leather bracers fastened to each arm. A short sword hung in its scabbard at one hip and a small hand crossbow and a leather quiver of quarrels hung at the other. He was dressed to move easily and quickly and, despite his size, he was one of the best trackers in the land. He watched the other two approach, then raised a hand and began moving his fingers rapidly, signing his greeting. *Good morning.*

The huge warrior raised his own hand and silently rattled off several signs himself. *And to you, my friend. You're early. Did the inn run out of drink?*

"Oh you're a funny one, you are," Cavanah said sourly, not bothering to sign his reply. Then with a chuckle, he went back to his work. He liked the big warrior and the two of them were well-known for their good-natured ribbing of each other.

Leave him be, Notyet, Terion signed rapidly to his mute friend. *He knows what his task is and he will not fail.*

The huge man only smiled as both men began checking their own gear and provisions. Terion was no longer clad in the flashy clothing he had worn to the council the day before, having traded in his outfit for his traveling leathers. He wore chiefly black, his well-maintained leather armor dyed to pitch. Tall black leather boots accompanied it and he had a dull-looking metal bracer strapped to each wrist. At his hip, he wore a long sword hidden by a battered old scabbard, a contrast to his other raiment, and he had several knives sheathed and strapped to his body at his waist, on his forearms, and slipped down into his boots.

Notyet, on the other hand, was dressed as if he was going to war. We wore a heavy coat of polished chain mail and his leather leggings were studded with metal rings. While his massive upper arms were protected by the chain coat that he wore, to his lower arms there were strapped long strips of metal plating that continued down across the top of his hands and halfway down his fingers, so that if he clenched his fist, he could present several sharpened metal ends that jutted out, making a mere punch from the man a deadly thing indeed. While Terion wore no helm, Notyet had a chain hood that was fastened around his head by a circlet of metal, while the chain itself flowed down his back, protecting the back of his neck. Strapped to his back was a plain leather and steel scabbard, which housed an enormous great sword and at his hip, held only by a chain loop on his belt, there hung an impressive long sword. A great bow was also slung across one shoulder and behind him, an oversized quiver full of arrows was already strapped to the flank of his horse.

The others began arriving soon after, ten riders who would travel north with Terion and Notyet, and eleven more scouts clad in similar fashion to Cavanah, to travel south with the big tracker to Ithil Majeer. Last to arrive was the Lady Keiran.

"Good morning," she began somewhat tiredly, looking at the assembled riders as she greeted them. "I trust you are already aware of your tasks. You leave on missions of utmost urgency. On one hand, we must know what is transpiring in the south and how quickly Draven intends to move his soldiers toward Taer Blys. On the other hand, we must know if the gods will offer us any hope or guidance against one of their own children gone astray. Both quests are equally important and both are dangerous."

At her finely woven belt, there hung two leather pouches and these she now detached. She handed one to Terion and the other to Cavanah. "Inside each, you will find a dozen magical gems of return," she continued. "They will bring you and your men instantly and safely back to the gates of Nykiva after you have completed your tasks." She stopped and closed her eyes, then passed her hand across her forehead as if in distress.

Terion stepped forward immediately, looking concerned. "Are you well, my lady?" he asked, looking at her intently.

"I'm fine," she answered softly after a moment, opening her eyes and waving him off. "I am just feeling a touch out of sorts – weak, if you may. But it will pass. Besides, my health is far less important than what you are setting out to do."

Terion looked doubtful, but nodded anyway. "If you insist."

"Go," she said finally, turning to face the others. "Ride swiftly, but ride carefully. May the gods look upon you in favor."

With that, the riders mounted swiftly and in a few moments, were thundering away from the city, two groups in opposite directions. Had any of them chanced to look back, they might have seen Keiran once more put her hand to her forehead, then take several steps before stumbling and falling to the ground.

Part 3

Of Gods and Men

Convergence

Keiran fell to the floor, the weakness overpowering her. She had returned to her tower, thinking she simply needed to rest. But the feebleness had not left her and had only grown worse. She lay on the floor now, fixing her eyes on the pinnacle of the ceiling in her private chambers, hoping to understand the strange fatigue that seemed to hold her in a vise-like grip. She felt as if she had just poured every last bit of her arcane power into a duel with another arch mage. However, she had cast no spells lately, which added to her uncertainty.

"I am as helpless as a newborn babe," she whispered to herself as she heaved a great sigh and slowly pulled herself to unsteady feet.

She had taken only two faltering steps when she grabbed the edge of a nearby table for balance. However, it was not the fatigue and weakness that stopped her this time, but rather the presence of someone else in the room. Perhaps, had she been all right, she might have known earlier that an intruder was in her tower. Unfortunately, her senses were dulled and the figure had remained carefully hidden.

Until now.

Slowly, Keiran turned to face the presence and she fought to keep calm at what she saw. With a feeling of despair, the fatigue that had mysteriously and suddenly shackled her now made perfect sense. She could in no way defend herself and she understood that it had all been by design.

The intruder was a woman, dark-skinned and beautiful. She was tall and lithe and her movements were fluid and cat-like, honed to perfection over years of martial training. She was dressed lightly in the alluring fashion of her race, a long black silk skirt that was slit to the hips up both sides, revealing strong thighs and knee-high boots of black leather. Above her waist, she wore a long-sleeved blouse of black silk, knotted just below her breasts and leaving her flat stomach bare. Around her waist was a fine golden chain, and a small sapphire glittered from her navel. Her features were flawless and captivating— dark skin and high cheekbones almost befitting royalty, framing eyes that resembled pools of the clearest mountain spring. Her long hair was fair, almost white, the lightness of it contrasting sharply with her skin and her clothing, and it was pulled back from her face and tied with a dark silken scarf of midnight blue.

To the unlearned, the woman facing Keiran might have been mistaken for one who sold herself for a night of gratification to the highest bidder. However, to the sorceress, her adversary was well-known. With a feeling of hopelessness, she knew her time in this world was finally at an end.

The assassin took several more steps toward the weakened mage, her ice-blue eyes locked with those of her victim. Three steps away, she stopped and smiled. "I read your eyes, sorceress," she said in a sultry voice that matched her looks perfectly. "Your fear is evident."

"I do not fear you," Keiran objected plainly, working hard to keep her voice strong. She thought of yelling out, hoping someone would come running quickly enough to save her, but it was a fool's hope. The woman facing her was well-armed, a fine chain whip coiled at her waist, and a long black-bladed dagger in her hand. The hilt of another dagger was evident at the top of one of her boots and the sorceress could only imagine what other weapons the assassin was hiding. "But I do know your intentions," she continued quietly, resigning herself to her fate. "I know you intend to kill me, though I do not pretend to know why."

"My reasons are my own, Keiran," the woman replied softly, holding the dagger up for Keiran to plainly see. She then slowly folded the weapon back in her hand so that the black blade rested flat against her forearm.

"The purse must be rich," Keiran continued. "I know a Vi'Raaji witch cannot be bought with but a little gold."

"It depends on the witch. But then again, I am not just any witch," she replied, her voice like ice.

"And I am not just any victim," Keiran countered and as she spoke, she acted in one last desperate bid for survival. Her arms came up, a weak orange fire gathering at her fingertips, but even as she did so, she knew that she was already too late.

Moving so quickly that she was almost a blur, the assassin stepped forward and spun herself around, the dagger flashing out from her arm. She was behind the dying sorceress before the blood even started pouring from the slit in her throat. Flipping the blade around in her hand even as she moved, the killer slid it expertly between Keiran's ribs and into her heart, feeling the Arcai-forged blade siphon off what remained of the woman's fading life force.

Keiran was dead before her mind even registered what had occurred, and the assassin allowed her body to sink slowly to the floor. For a moment, the killer looked down at her prey and then quickly slipped her dagger into a sheath that was concealed under her blouse. Not a drop of the dead woman's blood was on the blade.

"You can come out now," Vendetta said easily, glancing toward an ornate divider that concealed a small changing area on the far side of the room. "There is no more need to hide like a beaten cur."

There was a huffing sound as if someone had released a lungful of pent up air and slowly the form of Balgar peeked out from his hiding place. "She is dead?" he asked suspiciously.

The woman laughed, a sound both light and almost cheerful, and yet full of venom. "Do you think I would be bandying words with you if she was not?"

Balgar stepped forward to where the assassin still stood over the body of the former leader of the council – the woman he had hated most in the world. He carefully skirted the growing pool of blood as he looked down with distaste. "The potion worked," he muttered.

"Of course it worked. It is my own brew. But, I give you good marks for getting it into the drink that was served at the council meeting yesterday. A sorceress without powers is like a helpless newborn babe," she mimicked the dead woman's words, before her voice once more turned cold. "Unfortunately, such an easy deed is without satisfaction."

"Yes, yes," Balgar said, suddenly irritated and looking around quickly as if he expected the town guard to suddenly break down the door and catch him with the dead woman and her killer. "But you will get more than your share of a challenge when you go after Terion. Remember, he must be brought back here to be dealt with properly."

"He has already departed for the Dead Waste," the woman said dismissively. "I will consider it, should he survive and return."

"Perhaps you should consider going after him now."

"Does your puppet master have a plan in which to get me there quickly?"

Balgar nodded and reached into the folds of his council robes that were drawn tightly across his portly belly. He pulled out a small leather pouch. "Indeed, although I am loathe to give this up to you."

The woman's knife was out of its sheath and pressed against the man's throat before he could even finish his breath. Leaning forward, she put her beautiful face close to his. "Do not trifle with me, Balgar," she said in a deadly whisper, "or I shall leave your corpse here with that of Keiran. Do not forget that I have powers of my own." A flash of purple energy flared down her arm and across the drawn blade, causing the defrocked council member to jump back with a painful yelp as the magical energy snapped at his neck. "Such a thing would go a long way to explaining what happened here," she finished the threat with a dangerous look.

Balgar's hand went to his throat and his eyes were wide with terror. Only then did he realize that she had taken the pouch from him, snaring it when she invoked her own magical power."You burned me," he whispered harshly, rubbing the loose folds of skin at his neck.

"I will do far more than that the next time you see fit to consider withholding something from me," she said, giving him a venomous stare. She sheathed the deadly dagger before undoing the rawhide cord about the top of the pouch. Turning it upside down, she dumped the contents of the pouch out into her hand and let out a low whistle of admiration.

In her hand, she held a single palm-sized emerald gem, priceless as a simple treasure and cut and fashioned in a most unconventional way. It seemed to possess a faint inner light. "I know this is far more than what it resembles," she said almost excitedly. "Tell me, Balgar, is this what I think it is and if so, how did you come by it?"

"It is exactly what you perceive it to be and from Keiran's own little treasure chest," he replied, still rubbing his throat. "I spent many weeks discovering where she hid it and many more planning on how to claim it."

The assassin nodded appreciatively, her eyes still on the priceless gem that she held. "Only three of these artifacts exist and their locations are not even known, save this one now, the weakest of the three. If the other two stones are even in the possession of a living creature, they would be well-guarded and their secret kept hidden. How did Keiran come by this one?"

Balgar shook his head. "I don't know. Obviously I never spoke to her about it. To do so would have been pure stupidity."

"You're right," she answered matter-of-factly, holding the gem up to the light and peering closely at it. "If she knew that you had discovered her little secret, she would have killed you immediately or imprisoned you forever, despite her ties to her precious code of honor. By the gods, had I known that she possessed this, I would have come for it a long time ago."

"Well, it was I who discovered it," he said importantly, forgetting the precariousness of his situation and allowing his eyes to quickly dart over her body. "That should be worth something, at least."

"The Star Stone," the woman said almost dreamily, ignoring his lecherous gaze. "Who would have thought that it would be found in the collection of a sorceress like Keiran. This gem is worth a king's fortune a hundred times over." She regarded the man slyly. "You could have walked away with it, Balgar, and sold it for a most tidy profit, not to mention a fair share of power. In fact, I'm sure that thought has already crossed that cunning little mind of yours. Am I right?" She leaned seductively toward him, her beautiful face again only inches from his.

Balgar smiled crookedly, mistaking her intentions. "There is much that I can get you, should you desire it," he said hungrily as he licked his lips and his eyes openly strayed downward.

But she was away from him in a moment and the back of her hand caught him sharply across the face, dropping him to his knees. "You disgust me, Balgar. And if I did not know that your master had more use for you, I would carve out your eyes for your transgression."

The fat man cowered on the floor at her feet, holding his hands over his head. "Please don't hurt me," he whined. "I only thought..."

"I know what your thoughts were and if I were you, I would think no more unless it be how to save your own worthless skin." She held up the gleaming gem before her and then closed her fist around it, smiling as she did so. "Inform your master that I require no more compensation. I will complete her tasks and keep the Star Stone as payment."

"Impossible," Balgar hissed angrily, daring to look up. "That was not part of the deal! My master desires the gem, but would have allowed you to use it to complete your tasks. Beyond that, you can have all that Keiran has. That was the deal."

"I am altering the deal," she countered. "I have completed the first part of our contract and I claim the stone as compensation, as is within my right. Once I complete the second part, our business will then be completed and I hereby absolve your master from any future compensation for my services."

"You risk a wrath greater than you could know," the man warned dangerously.

"It is my risk to take," she answered quickly.

"You will go after Terion then?" Balgar said hopefully, understanding there was nothing more he could say to dissuade her. He could only hope his master would understand that when he reported back to her.

"The power of the Star Stone can take me to any place I have been before," she smiled. "Regretfully, I have never been to the Font, so I will simply wait for his return."

"But...but you can't take it, then!" Balgar sputtered. "You mustn't!"

"I already have," she replied and with that, the Star Stone began to glow. A greenish light emanated from it and quickly enveloped Vendetta's body, giving her already intoxicating beauty an ethereal look.

In another moment, the deadly assassin was gone, leaving Balgar alone and despairing in Keiran's private chambers, the sorceress's dead body lying in a pool of blood on the floor next to him. His master would be most upset with this change of events and he feared that anger would be directed at him. Visibly quaking, it took him only a moment to rouse himself from the floor and hurry from the room.

Chapter 15

While Cavanah and his small band of scouts rode along the miles and miles of forest roads and paths, making their way southward with as much haste as possible toward Ithil Majeer, Terion and his group of warriors rode hard toward the north, unconcerned with whatever eyes might be watching their journey. Their steeds were swift, covering the leagues quickly and effortlessly, given magical strength and endurance through the powers of Keiran's apprentice, Ranora. They rested little, pausing only long enough to partake of meager meals and catch what little sleep they could. There was little talk and no merry-making, for their destination was among the most dangerous in all the land and even the bravest of them held an uncertainty about whether or not they would return safely.

It was after many days of riding that they came to the fringes of the Dead Waste. Where northland trees and grasses, some still sparkling with ice or under the few remaining patches of melting snow, had marked their way north all the way from Nykiva, now the new springtime growth gave way to ever-widening patches of death. Gray scrub marked these areas and the skeletal limbs of ancient long-dead trees still stood here and there, warning the riders that they were drawing nearer the place where no living thing could grow.

The twelve riders continued on, their horses finally beginning to slow—whether from fatigue or fear, they could not know—until at last the greenery gave way and disappeared altogether. Rich earth turned to gray dust and rough sand, and even the scrub grasses were no more. Before them, nothing lived.

The Dead Waste spanned the horizon. It was a sickly land of limitless sand dunes and mounds of poisoned earth. Only one place in the world was darker – the Wraithlands, even further north. Little was known of how the Waste came to be, many scholars claiming that it had come into being through a great evil that cursed the land countless ages before. Still others claimed that the gods themselves created the land, a sea of death to test the mettle of those who would dare to approach their holy shrine. For it was in the Dead Waste that the Font of the Gods lay, an ageless temple of unknown construction, and it was that place that Terion and his men hoped to reach.

The Font of the Gods was an almost inaccessible dwelling where supposedly resided the spirits of the eight gods themselves. It was said that within the shrine, one could actually converse with them. Those who traveled to the shrine rarely returned. And those few who did return spoke nothing of what they encountered there or what secrets they might have learned.

Terion reigned in his horse and the others behind him did likewise as he stared out into the desolate plains. After a few moments, he dismounted and looked back at them. "From here, we proceed on foot. Our horses will not venture any further and it would be cruel to force them to carry us against their will."

"It will be a long journey without them," one of the men spoke up, a tall and rangy looking warrior clad in armor pieces of red and gold, mementos from past adventures and battles. Falduron was a seasoned soldier and had been one of the first men chosen to travel north.

"Agreed," replied Terion with a nod. "But on foot we will go."

Good thing the temple lies near the southern edge, Notyet signed as he dismounted from his own horse.

"Indeed," Terion responded in voice and then turned back toward the men as they began unpacking their horses. "Notyet points out that the shrine lies not too far from the southern edge of these lands. That alone improves the chances that some of us will return alive."

"That's cheerful," said another man as he tightened his belt and checked his sword.

"I'm not trying to cheer you, Menon," Terion said, clapping the man on the shoulder. "I don't want to cheer any of you. Many deadly things prowl this land."

Notyet tapped his companion on the shoulder and began to sign vigorously. *You have said nothing of what happens once we reach the font. The journey will be dangerous enough, but what of the guardian?*

Relax, my friend, Terion replied with his hands. *Keiran gave me something that should delay the beast for a while. We should have time enough to spare within the shrine to accomplish what we need to do.*

I hope you're right.

"Have I ever been wrong before?" Terion asked aloud with a forced smile.

Notyet only gave him a withering glance before going back to unpacking his horse.

"What will we find once we reach the temple?" asked one of the warriors, a short and compact soldier named Goron, as he fingered the blade of his war axe. "I know you have traversed the Dead Waste before and even visited the shrine, so I ask you – what awaits us?"

"It was many years ago and my time within the font was short," he answered solemnly. "There are a few creatures within that we may have to defend ourselves against, but none that should present much of a problem for a well-armed party," he went on. "However, there are likely to be more that will leave us alone so as not to draw undue attention to themselves."

"Why?" Goron asked.

"Because they fear a beast known only as the guardian," Terion answered quietly, unable to prevent himself from thinking back to the one time he had met the creature and the horrible death that his beloved had endured because of it.

"The guardian?"

"It is a worm-like creature of unholy savagery. It stalks the catacombs beneath the temple, devouring anything it comes upon. What few other things that we may find in the temple are creatures that have long ago learned to avoid it. Their fear of discovery should be our greatest ally against them."

"But what of this worm you speak of?" Goron pressed. "What will keep it from us?"

"I have procured a bit of magic for it," he answered softly. "We should be safe enough."

"I suppose we will soon see," the warrior said as he slid the axe into a loop of chain at his belt. "Let us move quickly."

There was a murmur of agreement from the other men as they, too, made ready to enter the deadly land.

"You will all follow my lead," Terion said, removing a pack from his horse and slinging it over his back. "We shall journey in a straight line and you should follow in the footsteps of the man before you. Step lightly and quickly and do not tarry."

"Why is that?" questioned another.

Terion gave him a knowing look. "Because there are dangers beneath the sands, as well as above," he answered and then slapped his horse on the rump, sending the steed trotting back the way they had come. The other horses quickly fell in behind the stallion, only too happy to leave the Dead Waste behind. "They will find their way home eventually," Terion said of their horses. "Now, let us find our way forward." He turned and walked into the desert.

Night was closing in as Terion led the way quickly and quietly through the shifting sands of the Dead Waste, cringing at every footfall of the nine men hurrying behind him. They had traveled swiftly on foot for six days and, by his reckoning, they would reach the font by midday tomorrow, if the creatures that had been pursuing them for the past four days did not decide to make another attack.

The first two days in the Waste had been uneventful, and at the time, Terion had begun to harbor some small hope that they might reach their destination without serious mishap. Even the men had seemed a little more at ease as the second day drew to a close. However, they had only traveled an hour the following day before tragedy struck and a pack of voracious sand sharks found them. The creatures were terrible predators that lived beneath the sands of the waste. While their ancestors were marauders of the sea, these were killing machines in their own habitat. They resembled their sea-going cousins of the deep, though they possessed short and powerful limbs instead of fins, which enabled them to move quickly through the shifting sand of the Dead Wastes. They were efficient and brutal killers, serrated teeth capable of rending through almost anything except for steel or stone.

Early that third morning, the predators had taken Menon and torn the screaming man in half before pulling what remained beneath the bloody sand. Terion had ordered torches lit as they ran desperately for rockier ground. A second man had fallen during the flight, a young warrior of considerable experience, and his fate had been the same as Menon's.

Once on less sandy ground, the ten men had turned their torches and swords on the attackers, striking more at shifting sand than at the creatures themselves. After a short while, they had driven the creatures back, mostly because of the shark's intense dislike of light and flame. The group had then gone quickly from rocky area to rocky area, keeping their torches low to the ground as they went. They saw no more of the menace, but they knew the creatures still pursued them. Every now and again, the soft sound of moving sand could be heard as the killers patiently followed their prey and there was little doubt in Terion's mind that the pack was growing with each passing mile.

Night began to fall upon the waste and Terion led the way toward a rocky outcropping, so that they could camp for the night without fear of the deadly creatures pulling them under. Once there, the men set fires at both ends of the tiny rock shelf and set themselves up for a restless night of fitful sleep and uncertainty.

Terion sat thoughtfully alone near the edge of the firelight, looking out into the deepening night, when Notyet walked up and sat down beside him. The big man nudged his companion and then began to sign. *There are howls on the wind. Do you hear them?*

I do, Terion replied back, his hands moving quickly. *I have heard them for two nights now. They are the cries of men. Many have already been taken by the sharks, but there are many more and they draw closer with the passing of each day. They do not rest when darkness comes and are either heedless of the danger or they simply do not care.*

They pursue us with great purpose then.

Terion nodded.

That means we are betrayed.

Again, the man nodded solemnly, having already come to the same conclusion.

They intend to stop us from reaching the temple, Notyet continued.

I believe you are right, Terion signed back. *But they will fail. We should arrive at the shrine before midday tomorrow if we rise early and leave at first light.*

What then? the big warrior asked. *We are greatly outnumbered.*

With a little bit of luck, we can accomplish our task and return home before our pursuers reach us.

Do you intend to tell the others? Notyet signed after a few moments of silence.

Terion nodded. *I have intended to all along, if they do not yet already know. I have simply waited until we were ready to begin the last sprint. Our pursuers will not come upon us this night.* He turned and pointed back toward the fire. "Now go and rest, my friend," he said quietly aloud. "Your sword will be needed before this is all over."

The next morning, the little group roused themselves before the cold light of the dawn shone through the gloom. Terion sat on the edge of the rock, as he had the entire night, staring out across the sands back the way they had come. One by one, each of the other nine remaining men joined him, looking at what held his gaze. There was silence among them, for no more than three leagues distant, a line of flickering torches was moving steadily toward them. Shouts and screams could also be heard, echoing in the early morning air.

"I would say better than one hundred," Falduron finally said, breaking the silence. "They are running hard, whether to catch us or to escape the sharks, I don't know. But they have been following us for several days."

"And more than twice that have already fallen," agreed Terion quietly. "Whoever they are, they mean to catch us."

"Then what do we do?" asked another warrior, a grim-looking man named Hayron, his sword laying against his shoulder.

Terion did not answer immediately, his eyes thoughtful as he watched the torches approach. Finally, he looked up. "They draw the sharks to them," he said as he quickly climbed to his feet. "Leave everything but your weapons. We will need no more provisions, for we will reach the temple by midday. If we are to make a stand, we must make it at the font."

"We race for our lives then," Goron growled darkly.

The men strapped on their weapons and gathered up their remaining torches, which they lit in the flames of the watch fires. Leaving everything else, they quickly gathered around their leader, their features grim and determined.

"Now we run," Terion said evenly as he turned and leapt off the rock shelf, running hard. Without a word, the others followed and the race was on.

Chapter 16

Cavanah stopped and held up a hand, motioning to his trackers to freeze. It was nearly dusk and they were still some leagues from the city of Ithil Majeer, but they had been seeing signs of the occupation for quite some time already. On several occasions now, they had come across small patrols from the marauding army, ranging far in their own scouting expeditions. Cavanah was not sure whether the enemy was expecting trouble or if Draven was simply being cautious, but it was unnerving to find them scouting this far from the city.

The first patrol they had encountered had been a pair of Rat scouts and the two parties had met quite by surprise. Cavanah's men, however, were well-trained and they reacted quickly, cutting down the two savages before they could call out or flee. After hiding their bodies high up in the branches of a nearby tree, the group became more cautious, slipping in and out of the trees like shadows in the darkening evening. In that way, they had avoided a pair of heavily-armed Gol soldiers, talking idly about what they would do should they come across any Rat patrols. It was somewhat of a comfort to Cavanah, who figured that if the bodies of the two Rats they had slain were found, their deaths could easily be blamed on the genocidal feelings that existed between the two races. Those thoughts were confirmed when they came upon yet another group of the enemy and Cavanah quickly and silently ordered the halt.

Ahead between the trees, he could hear men arguing and, in the light of torches in the hands of a pair of Gols, he could faintly see what was happening. Half a dozen Rat savages were standing their ground against three Gol warriors, two of which were holding the torches in one hand and fingering the hilts of their swords with their other. The third Gol, obviously the leader by his more elaborate armor and by the way he was talking, was ordering the Rats back to the city.

"I remind you that we are far from camp," he was saying, his voice cold and clipped. "While we are in camp, we will tolerate your stink for the greater purpose of Lord Draven. Out here, you will find that things are much different."

"You over-estimate yourself, Gol," one of the U'Raati snarled, waving a spiked cudgel in front of him. "You are little more than pawns in his game. He uses you to crush his enemies and when this war is over, he will send you back to the sea and you will obey him like the dogs you are. We fight with him because he allows us to taste the blood of our enemies."

"You will taste the edge of my blade if you tarry here any longer," the Gol leader replied dangerously. "I order you once more to return to camp."

"I would rather taste *your* blood!" screamed the Rat suddenly as he brought his cudgel up hard toward the face of the Gol leader.

The experienced warrior reacted quickly as he brought one armor-plated arm around to deflect the strike harmlessly to the side, even while he was drawing his sword with his other hand. At the same moment, the other Gols sprang forward, one of them swinging his torch and crushing the cheekbone of the nearest Rat. The wounded savage stumbled back, screaming and clutching his burned and broken face, but the soldier gave him no quarter, drawing his sword and bringing it down to split the Rat's skull. He turned immediately, but the other Rats had started their own attack. Before the soldier could react, a Rat short sword was buried to the hilt in his throat and he fell forward with a strangled gurgle, clutching frantically at the blade's hilt even as he died.

The Gol leader, after having deflected the initial cudgel blow, had lashed out with his metal-gauntleted fist, knocking the offending

Rat warrior backward with a powerful blow to the savage's jaw. Two others leapt at him, but he had already swept out his sword and swung it in a wide arc. The lead Rat pitched forward, his head rolling off his shoulders and into a nearby thicket. The other savage tried leaping aside, but the Gol pivoted around, bringing his sword low. The blade slashed across the man's midsection, slicing through flesh and disemboweling him.

While the third Gol soldier fell back, the Gol leader finished off the stunned cudgel bearer by quickly beheading him. He then buried his blade into the back of one of the remaining savages, the point blasting through the man's chest. It was enough to put the final Rat to flight, but the Gol leader was quicker, whipping a dagger from his belt and throwing it. The weapon struck the fleeing savage directly between the shoulder blades, driving him forward to his knees, nearly paralyzed and gasping for breath. The Gol general casually walked up to the wounded man, yanked the dagger from the man's back and slit his throat with it. When the Rat was dead, the Gol shoved him to the ground with a snort of contempt.

The fight was over almost before it had even begun. Two of the three Gols remained alive while the Rats had been wholly slaughtered. The Gol leader was unscathed, but his surviving subordinate had suffered several nasty gashes. The third Gol was dead, the Rat sword still buried in his throat. Without a word, the two survivors picked up their dead companion and bore his body back toward the city.

Cavanah remained motionless the entire time, though he briefly thought about killing the two Gols before they could return to the city. However, the leader's fighting prowess could not be denied and the big man opted for the safety of his men. Knowing it was the right decision, he slipped back the way he had come and gathered his men.

"With some luck, they'll all kill each other before they ever march on Taer Blys," he whispered when they were all together, gathered in the deep shadows of the forest.

"One could only hope," agreed another with a half-smile.

"We'll move away from this area and rest for the night," Cavanah continued, looking about at the darkening shadows. Evening would descend very shortly and he did not like the idea of stumbling forward in the blackness, only to run into more of the enemy. "We'll take to the trees, three together. Split the night into three watches and get some rest. Tomorrow morning at first light, we go on."

With that, the twelve men split up into four groups and found suitable trees some distance apart. They quickly scaled them and settled in, where they took meager meals and passed the night in vigilance. Morning dawned and once more, Cavanah gathered his small group and set out for Ithil Majeer.

It was after midday when they drew near the ruined city. Their trek had been dangerous and they had been hard pressed to avoid scouting patrols. However, their luck had held out and they had escaped detection. Through breaks in the trees, they could see columns of smoke rising in the distance, and the smell of death was growing stronger with every step. Cavanah called another halt.

"We go no further as a group," he said quietly when they were gathered together, somewhat sheltered by a copse of overhanging bushes. "From here, four will go at a time. I will make my way around the city and approach from the south. Trae will scout the east, Faran the west, and Delanor will approach straightaway from the north. The rest of you will remain hidden here. Draw no attention to yourselves and do not engage the enemy. Give us until this time tomorrow to return. If none of us do, then send four more to scout in the same fashion and again the following day, if needs be."

"And if none of us survives?" asked Delanor quietly.

"Remember the gems Keiran gave you," Cavanah answered. "If you are attacked or look to be taken, use the gem and return home with whatever information you have. But use it only if your situation looks hopeless. We need to know as much as we can about what's going on here."

There was a murmur of agreement and Cavanah turned away to look toward the ruined city. "Let's move," he said finally.

Cavanah drew his cloak tighter about him and crept silently through the black shadows toward the city proper. In the dead of night, he would have been difficult enough to see by the eyes of alert soldiers on watch, had there been any. However, with the city of Ithil Majeer firmly in the control of Draven and with no immediate threat of retaliation, there was little reason for alert guards, at least in the U'Raati part of camp that he was creeping through. Cavanah had specifically chosen this area to penetrate, knowing that it would be easier to slip past the uncaring Rats than the military-minded Gols. And so far, he had not encountered any trouble.

Earlier, he had scouted the outer area of the camp from the safety of the trees and had despaired at what he had seen. The city was ringed with the armies of Draven, the Gol and Rat armies carefully divided, and the land about the city walls was barren and trampled. A number of huge pits had been dug near the edge of the forest and were full of charred bones and ash, the remains of those who had been killed in the battle. The air was heavy with the stench of death and decay, and several times he had to pause to breathe deeply into his cloak to mask out the putrid smell.

When night had finally fallen, the sky was filled with low-hanging clouds. The moon was well hidden and the shadows deep, all serving to make his final foray a little easier. With his magical gemstone held tightly in his hand, he had slipped out of the trees and into the open, dodging from shadow to shadow and praying he would remain invisible to the savages as he moved through their midst.

It was a circuitous route that he took through the camp toward the city walls and he had to backtrack several times before he gained the outer walls of Ithil Majeer. For several long minutes, Cavanah crouched deep in the shadows of the base of the high stone wall, evaluating his next move. He had little doubt that the main gate would be much more heavily guarded, most likely by Gol soldiers. So his only other options would be to scale the wall, which would expose him to any roving eyes, or look for a breach in the stone that he might sneak through. He opted for the latter and began moving cautiously away from the main gates, hugging the deep shadows as he went.

He had not gone far when he found what he was looking for. Most of the battle hadn't damaged Ithil Majeer's protective walls. However, in several places there were fissures and rifts in the masonry where Gol war machines had breached the defenses. Cavanah had found just such a crack and with an inward smile, he grabbed the edge of the stone and pulled himself quickly into the city.

Normally, the streets of Ithil Majeer would be alight with lamps and torches. But tonight, the city was dead and the streets darkened and deserted. What survivors there might have been from the battle would have already been sent to slave pens somewhere within the city. While his heart sank at the loss, he was grateful nevertheless that his movements would not be hampered. So, with skill borne of years of practice, he silently moved toward the center of the city and hopefully, some answers.

Chapter 17

Terion never even paused as he leaped from the sands of the waste onto the first steps of the temple and raced up the stairs at a dead run. Behind him, his men were already nearly spent, but they knew they could not pause—their pursuers were almost within bowshot.

Terion and his companions had been harassed by the sharks and worse yet, slowed, on the last leg of their journey to the font and it had allowed their pursuers to catch up to them. Many of the enemy had fallen to the sharks, yet their force was still better than fifty strong—more than a match for Terion and his tiny band.

"Into the sanctum," the charismatic leader shouted as he paused at the top of the stone steps to allow his warriors to move past him and into the temple. After the last man had entered, he stood for several moments more, watching their enemies approach with reckless abandon. Then, with a deep sigh of regret, he turned and stepped into the darkness within.

Inside, Terion quickly rallied his men. "Listen closely," he said as he took off a small pack he had slung over his shoulder. Opening it, he pulled out the remaining torches and a small object wrapped in a heavy cloth. "I had hoped we could move through the temple with great care. But with our pursuers nearly here, we must hurry. The denizens of this temple are dangerous, but they should avoid us. The guardian, however, will not. Since we do not possess the means to kill it, we have another way to keep us safe. But I dare not use this bit of magic until we have reached the inner sanctum."

"Then let us go quickly," said a severe looking man named Luron. He pulled a slender long sword from his scabbard and held it before him. Its sheen was dull and the blade already heavily notched from their flight through the sand shark infested waste. "I fear I will need another weapon before this day is through."

"Let's hope that before the day is through, we are all back in Nykiva with this safely behind us," said Terion, before looking at each of them in turn. "Each of you must keep your gem at the ready. You may have little time to use it."

Gathering up the remaining torches, he took a flint to one and then quickly had them all alight, passing them around as they flared to life. Finally, with the last one held high before him, he headed off down the main passage, his companions following closely behind. The temple layout was unknown to all of them, save Terion, but each man knew they were in mortal peril.

That fact was driven home less than ten minutes later.

They had passed down several large, musty passageways, moving deeper and deeper into the huge shrine when the attack came as they moved into a wide and pillared hall. The creature lunged out of the darkness with a guttural roar, long muscular arms reaching for a victim. It stood almost eight feet tall and was humanoid shaped, but with green and brown scales instead of skin. Its face was hideous, most of it taken up by a gaping mouth lined with jagged teeth. Two small reptilian eyes were situated over the terrible jaws, slitted and yellow in the torchlight.

"Troll spawn!" shouted Goron as he immediately swept his axe around and charged toward the creature.

But the monster was quicker and its grasping claws caught one of the young warriors by the upper arm and lifted him high in the air. As the man screamed, the monster savagely slammed his body into a nearby stone pillar with a sickening crack of bone. The warrior was dead before his broken body fell to the ground.

Goron and several others were already leaping toward the

creature with weapons drawn, when a second troll-like creature struck from the opposite side. The alternating attack of the two creatures had been disturbingly coordinated and Luron died immediately, his head savagely torn from his body by powerful claws.

"Stand fast!" shouted Terion as he darted in toward the second monster, his blade slashing across the creature's midsection.

Though the tough scales deflected most of the strike, the huge creature turned its full attention on its attacker. With a roar, it lashed out with one of its claws, only to have the nimble man quickly dodge to the side. The monster pivoted, hoping to corner the man and crush him, but Terion's feint had done exactly what it had been intended to do. An arrow fired from a great bow blasted through the back of the monster's neck and tore out its throat on the way out. With a gurgling moan, the creature turned back around, clumsily trying to zero in on its new attacker. Notyet's second arrow disappeared into the creature's eye. It was dead even as it pitched forward.

With shouts of victory, the remaining men turned their full attention to the second creature. But with its companion dead, the fight had quickly left it. It turned to flee, pausing only to snatch up the dead body of the man it had crushed against the stone pillar.

The mute warrior shot his bow for third time, this arrow imbedding itself into the monster's upper left shoulder. With a roar of pain, it dropped its intended meal and turned to defend itself. However, Goron was there and his axe bit deeply into the creature's muscular leg just above the knee. Even as Goron wrenched the weapon free and spun to the side to set himself up for another swing, Falduron drove his sword through the monster's chest. With another roar, the falling monster struck out wildly, its claws slashing down across Falduron's chest and opening up several bloody furrows in the man's torso. But Goron finished the fight, his axe cleaving down through the creature's skull and dropping it dead to the stone floor.

Before the monster had rattled its last breath, Terion was kneeling beside the wounded man. "How bad?" he asked grimly, looking at the dark blood seeping around Falduron's hands, which were pressed tightly to his torn chest.

"I've...had worse," the injured man answered through teeth clenched in pain.

"Your journey is done here, my friend," Terion said, reaching into a small belt pouch and pulling forth a pinch of white powder. "Now move your hands and remain still."

The injured man slowly removed his hands. There were three long slashes that had opened up his leather armor at his right shoulder and all the way down his chest and across his left side, exposing his ribs. The blood flowed freely when he moved his hands away, but Terion acted quickly, blowing the dust into the wound. There was a flash of acrid smoke and Falduron howled in pain. But immediately, the bleeding slowed and the edges of the torn flesh darkened, almost as if they had been burned.

"There," remarked Terion grimly. "Now at least, you will not die so quickly."

"Pity that," Falduron said, his face white with agony. "I think I would almost prefer it."

"We must hurry," Goron spoke up, moving back into a battle stance with his axe. "More are coming."

Another of the trolls lumbered into the edge of their torch light. However, it quickly disappeared after grabbing Luron's dead body. In the darkness beyond, they could hear the horrible snapping of bones and tearing of flesh as the creature began to feed.

Swallowing the bile in his throat, Terion pulled a small leather pouch from Falduron's belt. Quickly, he dumped the small gemstone out and then pressed it into the man's bloody hand. "You have served well," he said solemnly. "Now return home."

The wounded warrior started to object, but Terion raised a hand. "We must be quick and you will only slow us down. Now return home. I will send someone back with you to help you to a healer."

"All right," the wounded man grimaced. "I'll go back. But I expect a full report from you when you return. I want to know if this whole thing was worth it."

"You shall have it," answered Terion as he motioned one of the remaining warriors over. "Go with him," he said plainly.

The man nodded as he pulled his own magical gemstone from a belt pouch.

"May the gods go with you," Falduron said quietly, looking up at Terion. A moment later, he vanished in a swirl of glowing energy as he activated his magical gem. The man who Terion had commanded to accompany him, quickly followed.

"Let's go," Terion said at last as looked around at the men who still remained.

"I don't think they will be willing to attack us so quickly again," Hayron pointed out as more sounds came from the darkness. "But what of the guardian? How are we to defeat it when we are already so few?"

Terion shook his head. "We don't. There are other ways to deal with it."

"Will the trolls pursue us?" asked a man by the name of Jagra. He was a wily and smart fighter, but his face was full of doubt.

"No," answered the dark-haired leader flatly. "I doubt they will venture any closer to the sanctum. But I do expect our friends from the waste to arrive at any time." He picked up one of the scattered torches and then hurried down the hall. The others quickly followed with

Notyet bringing up the rear, his great sword held out before him at the ready.

They had only a short way to go to reach the doors of the inner sanctum – two great stone slabs engraved with strange runes and set upon two massive metal hinges. Terion did not bother to read the etchings as he placed his hands on the cold stone. With little effort, he gave a slight push and the two doors swung silently inward on well-oiled hinges. A massive room opened up, its stone walls hung with rich tapestries. Torch sconces were set into the walls every ten or fifteen feet, the pitch already burning. It was a beautiful room, but barren of any furnishing except for a single pool of dark water in the center of the chamber. It was to this that Terion hurried. As he reached it, he turned quickly and pointed to his remaining companions. "Bar the doors," he instructed. "Let nothing…"

Suddenly there was a surging spray of water from the center of the pool and something monstrous emerged, shooting toward the ceiling. With cat-like agility, the creature spun in midair, a dozen taloned feet easily gripping the stone above. For a moment, it hung from the ceiling and the survivors got their first look at the guardian. It was long and lithe, with twelve scaly legs sprouting at uneven intervals along a sinuous body mottled black and red in color. At its tail was a long whip-like appendage, barbed at the end with a wickedly-hooked stinger, while its head looked like a cross between an insect and a lion. Huge feline jaws snapped open, revealing glistening rows of razor sharp teeth, while multi-faceted insectoid eyes missed nothing. It was a nightmare combination of animal and insect and its mere presence froze them all in fear.

Then, with an ear-splitting scream, the guardian sprang from the ceiling toward the men. Before anyone could react, it had struck Hayron full in the chest, slamming him to the stone floor and pinning him under its legs. The monster's tail whipped over its head, its stinger plunging deep into Hayron's stomach, even as it whipped its head around, jaws snapping for Notyet's face. But before they could close over the head of the powerful warrior, the creature froze, as if time had suddenly stood still.

Goron jumped at the opportunity, bringing his axe high overhead to strike.

"Do not attack!" Terion yelled, one hand held up in warning and the other hand holding a small item. "If you do, the magic will fail and we will all die!"

Goron hesitated, his eyes narrowed in suspicion as Notyet carefully withdrew his head from the massive jaws and what would have been certain death.

"What magic is this?" Goron asked, his axe still at the ready.

"It was given to me by Keiran," Terion explained, carefully holding up his hand. In it, he held a small hourglass housed in an intricately carved wooden frame. The sands could be seen trickling slowly through the narrow stem, beginning to make a small mound in the bottom. "We have precious little time. The sands will only last so long and when it runs out, the creature will be freed."

"Then why not kill it?" Goron asked again, raising his axe higher and desperately wanting to deliver the blow.

"Because the guardian cannot be slain by mortal weapons," Terion answered. "To strike at it would cause it no harm and would release the magic that currently binds it."

"But what of Hayron?" Goron continued desperately, finally dropping the axe to his side and kneeling beside the wounded man.

Hayron was holding up as best he could. A powerful poison had been injected into his body from the guardian's stinger, which was still buried in his belly. His face was white with pain and sweat ran freely from skin that was growing hotter by the moment. "The wound is mortal," the injured man whispered in agony. "The venom…"

Terion shook his head. "I know of no cure for the poison," he answered solemnly, kneeling himself. "But we do not know how much has been injected. Hayron, do you still have your gem of return?"

The dying man nodded almost imperceptibly.

"Good," continued Terion. "Then activate it and return home. Jagra, you return with him and get help immediately."

Without a word, Jagra knelt and pulled Hayron's magical gem from his belt pouch, pressing it into the fevered man's palm. A moment later, they vanished, leaving the guardian frozen in its attack. The only movement was from several drops of Hayron's blood dripping from the end of the monster's deadly stinger.

"Let's finish this," said Goron bitterly.

"Agreed," said Terion as he straightened. "Bar the door and stand ready. I will make the attempt." He walked back toward the pool while his three remaining companions pulled torches from the wall to wedge under the door and between the hinges.

Terion gently set the hourglass down on the floor near the edge of the water. Then with a deep breath, he stepped into the water and vanished.

Chapter 18

It took Cavanah the better part of an hour to carefully make his way to the central square of the occupied city. Isolated patrols of Rat savages were leisurely roaming the city, plundering already-ruined houses and shops, but he saw no survivors. He only saw scattered and brutalized remains that could no longer be recognized as ever being human.

Several times he had been tempted to release his own anger by attacking some of the Rats, but he reminded himself that his mission was not one of vengeance. There would be time enough for that later. For now, he needed information and the likeliest place he might find it would be in the center of the city.

His suspicions were confirmed a short time later when he settled down behind an alley rain barrel and looked out over the city's central plaza. It was a typical Dom'Ithi city design, a large spacious inner square intersecting a number of main streets and centralizing the commerce and trade of the city, while acting as a gathering point for the populace. The plaza was wide open, carefully cobbled with red stone, and would usually be teeming with the carts and mobile markets of vendors selling their wares. Tonight, however, it was full of enemy soldiers.

At the far end of the plaza, there stood a beautiful temple dedicated to the god Benovan. It was flanked on either side by equally-beautiful stone structures. From past visits to Ithil Majeer, Cavanah knew that one of those secondary structures was the manor house of the ruling lord of the city, while the other, a small tower of sorts, was home to the arch mage of Ithil Majeer. However, whatever they were in the past, they were home to others now and he was reasonably certain that the Arcai, Draven, would be found in one of them.

A scream of agony tore Cavanah's eyes from the buildings and he looked out across the plaza. He caught his breath, almost crying out at what he saw.

In the center of the square was a row of thick rough-hewn wooden poles driven into the ground. There were twenty of them and each pole had an iron ring imbedded into the top. From each iron ring there hung a pair of heavy chains, each of those ending in a manacle. Most of the manacles were encircling flesh, holding a tortured man or a woman a good three or four feet off the ground. Even from his distant vantage point, he could tell that most of those who had been manacled to the cruel poles were either dead or very close to it. However, there were two in particular that caught his eye.

Two of his companions had been captured and now Faran and Trae were both hanging in chains from individual poles, their clothing stripped from their tortured bodies. Faran might already have been dead, his body bleeding from a dozen different horrific wounds. Trae on the other hand, was very much alive and it was his agonized scream that reverberated through the plaza as a Rat shaman slowly peeled the flesh from one of his legs using a razor-sharp dagger.

Cavanah bit his lip and fought back the tears as he watched the torture continue. As the Rat completed his knife work, a large Gol stepped forward, torch in hand, and immediately pressed the burning end into the bleeding leg, cauterizing the wound and stopping the flow of blood. Trae screamed in unimaginable anguish again. Cavanah felt as if he would burst forth from his hiding place to demand that the inhumane torture cease. However, he held himself in check, knowing there was nothing he could do to help his doomed companions.

He caught a glimpse of movement far to the right, away from the glow of the plaza. A minute passed before he saw it again and his heart lightened somewhat as he watched Delanor slip effortlessly over the peak of a nearby building roof and creep down the slope, taking care to keep himself cloaked in shadow. He watched the tracker reach the edge of the roof and set himself before slipping his bow from his back.

Another tortured scream from Trae tore through the air and Cavanah winced, turning his attention back to the square. He knew that Delanor was preparing to spare the man any more torture. Cavanah tensed, praying the shot would be true. Then, as Trae screamed again, he heard the twang of Delanor's bow and the shriek was suddenly cut short. Cavanah watched as Trae's head lolled forward, the arrow imbedded deeply into his chest.

A shout rose up as several of the Gols quickly realized what had happened and began moving toward Delanor. Cavanah watched as the scout fit another arrow to his bow and then calmly shot the leading Gol through the throat. More of the enemy, both Gol and Rat, began moving now and he realized that he could use the distraction that Delanor was providing.

Shouts arose as several of the enemy spotted the scout and the chase was on. Gols and Rats streamed across the square toward their prey and Cavanah watched as Delanor reached the peak of the roof and swung a leg over. He hung there for just a moment and looked straight toward him. Cavanah nodded grimly. A moment later, Delanor was gone. The man had mercifully ended Trae's torture and, in doing so, had given Cavanah the chance he needed to get closer to their quarry. He began moving quickly along the walls of the building.

Cavanah made the other side of the square in just a few minutes and ducked into an alley, planning one working himself around to the back of the manor house. The frustrated shouts of the pursuers were growing distant and he smiled, imagining Delanor using the rooftops to keep the chase going for as long as he could. The big tracker crept around another corner, crouching low and he surveyed the grounds before him.

The rear entrance to the manor house was a pair of large heavy wooden double doors set at the top of short but wide stone stairs. At the top, a pair of Gol warriors stood, their large swords cradled in their arms at the ready. At the bottom, there were two more identically-clad warriors. He knew he wasn't getting in that way. He glanced around, thinking he could find another way in, when he heard the slightest rustle of cloth on stone behind him. Suddenly, a thin piece of rope slipped over his neck from behind and was jerked tight.

Cavanah threw his head backward more out of desperation than an actual counterattack, but he was rewarded with the sound and feel of his head smacking hard against the face of his attacker. There was a muffled grunt and the rope around his throat fell slack, allowing him to quickly regain his balance. However, the four manor guards were quickly moving toward him and he knew he was in trouble.

He pulled a dagger from the sheath at his belt and gauged the situation. His attacker, a man clad in the black clothing of an assassin, had stumbled backward, one hand over his face, trying to stop the flow of blood from his shattered nose. Cavanah knew he was out of the fight, at least for the moment, so he spun again to face the four charging Gol warriors.

He sidestepped the first overhand sword swing and turned neatly down the Gol's outstretched sword arm, allowing his momentum to give more force to the solid elbow he threw to the soldier's jaw. The Gol dropped to his knees, but Cavanah was already moving past him to engage the next one.

The tracker grabbed the second man's wrist and yanked him close, driving his knee up between the soldier's armored legs. The Gol dropped like a stone, moaning in agony, as Cavanah moved to take down the other two.

Seeing what had befallen their companions, the two Gol's split up, moving around so that the big man was between them. The first soldier darted in, a feint, pulling up short. The other Gol, thinking he would have an easy kill, suddenly jabbed forward with his weapon. But Cavanah twisted around, parrying the blow. Once again, he allowed his momentum to carry him through the spin and the Gol pitched forward with a strangled cry, blood pouring from his opened throat. Cavanah flipped the bloody dagger around in his hand, ready to finish off the last one.

Suddenly the black-clad killer who had started the whole thing moved into the open area. He pulled a curved knife from his belt and began to stalk in, mumbling curses, as the other Gol circled around in an attempt to get behind the Dom scout.

Cavanah knew that his momentum had played itself out. The Gol was the closest, so he lunged toward him, forcing the man to retreat, giving him the opening he needed. He dashed past the Gol and toward the steps of the manor house's rear entrance. But even as he gained the lower stair, the door burst open and several more Gols came charging out.

Without breaking stride, Cavanah jumped from the stair back to the ground. He raced around the corner of the huge house, the pursuit heavy behind him. He knew he could not outrun them and a sudden thought came to him. He shifted his direction again, this time turning toward the nearby temple.

The temple had a standard pyramid-like shape, with stairs running up all four sides, each leading to an entrance near the top. He leapt up the steps two at a time until he gained the landing. Stopping, he looked back and saw a huge man striding toward the temple. The newcomer was clad only in leather breeches, his chest and feet bare.

Bronzed skin shone in the light of the torches and a huge sword was held easily in one hand. Cavanah knew immediately that he was facing an Arcai.

"I see we have a little mouse loose in the house," Draven said loudly, looking directly up at Cavanah and smiling. There was nervous laughter from the Gols, and Draven came to a stop at the bottom of the stairs. "Come down, little mouse. Come down and I will make certain your death is quick."

"I decline," Cavanah replied, fighting hard to keep the fear out of his voice as he faced the son of a God. "I prefer the temple halls over the crucifixion poles you have staked in the city square."

"I will spare you the pole if you come down," Draven offered again.

"Like you spared my companions?"

Draven shrugged. "I made no such offer to them. But I make it to you. Surrender yourself to me and I will kill you right here."

"I would tell you nothing," Cavanah countered. "You would gain nothing from torture."

"I have no need of anything from you. I already know all that I need," the Arcai replied. "Two of your men hang dead in the city square and the other soon will be. The eight that wait for you in the forests will be killed before the sun rises. You are alone, Cavanah. Accept my offer and die quickly."

Cavanah glared at him. He was terrified that the Arcai knew his name, but he was not going to give the immortal the satisfaction of knowing that. "Sorry, but I think I'll take my chances," he replied.

Draven's smile disappeared and, without taking his eyes off Cavanah, he directed his next comments at the men around him. "Make certain our little mouse does not leave the temple. I would hate for him to miss out on the opportunities that await him within." Then he turned and stalked back toward the manor house, not sparing Cavanah another look.

One of the Gol's raised his bow and released an arrow just as Cavanah ducked into the temple entrance. Cavanah heard the arrow clatter harmlessly off the stone as he turned and hurried down the dark tunnel.

His encounter with the Arcai had terrified him and he briefly thought of returning home that very moment. But something he had heard earlier about dark things coming from the temple during the battle of Ithil Majeer prompted him to explore further. Perhaps the temple would provide him answers to questions that had not yet been asked.

He only went a few dozen yards before he had to stop, unable to see in the all-encompassing darkness. Dom temples were usually alight both within and without. But all the torches and lanterns inside had been either extinguished or broken. He reached into one of the pouches at his belt and pulled out a small stone bowl, in which he set a small candle. In moments, he had it lit and was looking around.

He was in a long tunnel that sloped downward with intermittent doors set into the walls on both sides. There was no dust, and cobwebs were rare, but the air had a terrible mustiness to it and there was an unmistakable chill that penetrated to his very bones. He quickly found a usable torch and lit it with the small candle flame.

He sheathed his dagger and loaded his small hand crossbow, then started forward cautiously, trying first one door and then the next. Each one was locked and he felt he was too pressed for time to worry about picking any of them. Besides, if they were locked, it was probably because the Gols had not yet plundered the temple. Had he paused to give thought to why they had not done so, he might have decided not to go further.

He continued downward into the bowels of the temple. The hall opened into a small square antechamber, with passages leading from it in four directions. He paused to consider his options, when he heard a hard scrabbling sound, as if something was moving quickly through one of the tunnels toward him. He had no time to hide, so he raised his crossbow and quickly put his back to one of the corners. He saw the eyes before he saw the rest of the creature—green slits that seemed to glow in the gloom of the passageway. When the scarecrow shuffled out of the darkness, Cavanah promptly put the crossbow bolt into the creature's eye.

With a terrible scream of rage, the First Born leapt forward, but Cavanah was already running down the left passage, his torch held out before him, the flame wavering wildly.

Only one thought coursed through his brain as he fumbled with the pouch that held his gemstone. Survival. Gripping the leather bag tightly, he ran on, the creature close behind. His path took him steadily downward into the depths of the temple. As he went, more creatures took up the chase and, on two occasions, he barely escaped the grasping claws of several monsters that he simply bowled over as he ran. Finally, the tunnel opened up into a larger chamber and Cavanah skidded to a stop, the torch dropping numbly from his hand as his brain quickly grasped the enormity of what he saw.

Before him was an enormous portal, some twenty feet in height and spanning almost the entire wall of the chamber. Through the portal, he saw an evil-looking landscape of dead trees and barren earth, with what looked like a fetid swamp or a bog off to one side. Beyond that, he could barely discern the outline of a tower. Over everything, an eerie mist shrouded the ground. The light of a nearly full moon cast an ethereal glow on everything and his heart froze, for he knew he was looking directly at a portal to the Wraithlands.

The first pursuing scarecrow burst through the tunnel and slammed into him, sending both man and monster through the gateway in a tangle of limbs, the pouch with his magical gemstone spinning out of his hand. The breath was blasted from his lungs and he felt the creature's claws tearing at him as he rolled with the blow and tried to come to his feet. But the undead monster was on him in a moment, its deadly maw snapping forward to tear his face off. Cavanah desperately thrust a hand upwards, slamming the monster underneath the chin and driving several of the oversized teeth through the dead flesh of its nose. Using the shift in momentum, he threw the creature clear, rolled to his feet, and ripped the dagger from his belt as the creature came at him again.

Cavanah spun outside of the outstretched claws and tried to get behind it. But the scarecrow was incredibly fast and, as it lunged past the man, one hand clasped down in a vise-like grip on his arm, claws digging into flesh. With a howl, Cavanah brought his dagger down hard, just below the creature's elbow. The blade sliced through the rotting flesh and bone, severing it, and Cavanah leapt away, his eyes on the leather pouch lying perilously close to the edge of the bog. He dove forward, his hand closing on the small bag as another figure exploded from the stagnant water immediately in front of him, clawed arms whipping through the air.

Cavanah tore at the drawstrings with frantic fingers, even as he rolled to the side to avoid the grasp of the zombie-like creature. As his fingers closed around the gemstone, a sharp crack of thunder filled the air and time seemed to freeze. For a brief moment, his eyes settled on a man. He was tall and dressed in strange clothing, and he was not alone. There were others behind him and in the gloom, Cavanah could make out their clothing's odd shifting patterns of varying colors of green. The man before him held a metal rod and it was pointed right at his chest. As Cavanah willed the magical stone to life, he thought he saw a flash of fire leap toward him.

He never heard the shot.

Chapter 19

Terion was suddenly thrust into a twilight world of featureless gray. There was no land or sky, only an emptiness that was oddly illuminated enough for him to see. For a moment, he was alone, but he soon became aware of figures standing before him. He knew immediately who they were and bowed his head in reverence.

"My creators," he said simply, with as much respect as possible before looking up. There were eight of them, as expected, all dressed similarly in robes that appeared both colorless and yet shining with every color known to man. Each stood with his or her arms folded, hands hidden deep within sleeves, and each bore a somber look.

After several moments of silence, the figure in the center stepped forward. To describe a deity would be foolhardy and in later years, Terion would have no words with which to match the power of the god's presence.

"Terion," the god Benovan said softly, his voice seemingly ancient and young all at once. "You have braved much to speak with us and your companions have suffered greatly to speed you here."

"I would never have come if our need was not of great importance," he answered, his head still bowed. He dared not look at them.

"But you came once before," the god went on, "when you had no such need."

"I did," the mortal admitted, "but I was much younger then. I am a lot wiser today."

"Are we to believe you have achieved wisdom in such a short amount of time?" asked another of the gods, her eyebrows arching condescendingly.

Terion knew immediately that the speaker was Karasika and it was primarily her words that the warrior was seeking. "No. But if there was any other way to receive guidance, I swear I would have sought it."

"And you believe that we will give you this guidance that you so desperately seek," challenged Karasika. "You know that gods will not meddle in the affairs of mortal men."

Benovan turned his head slightly and raised his hand. "Allow him first to speak, my sister," he said. "Then you may judge whether or not an answer should be given."

Karasika nodded and fixed her eyes on the man and waited.

Terion felt utterly insignificant, realizing that his considerable oratory skills would not avail him here. Here, in the presence of the gods, he knew that his heart was already known to them, so eloquent speaking was both unnecessary and unwanted. "As you know, a great evil threatens us," he finally said after clearing his throat.

"Evil is such a subjective term," said Karasika lightly.

"Nevertheless, we are threatened on a scale we have not had to face before. It comes to us from a source we cannot defeat."

"So you would come to us begging help with every little problem?" she scolded. "If we are to solve all your troubles as we did with the First Born, then what would be the purpose of having created you?"

"Under normal circumstances, I would agree with you," Terion dared to reply. "But this problem goes beyond mortality, for it is your son who causes our grief. The Arcai, Draven, has declared war on our people, despite his sacred covenant not to do so."

Karasika chuckled while the other gods remained stoic and silent. "On one hand, you are correct, Terion, but on the other hand, you are mistaken."

Terion shook his head. "I apologize for my ignorance, but I am a mere mortal and I do not understand."

"The actions of Draven are known to us," the goddess continued. "But it is not his aspirations that should concern you."

"He has banded together the races of the Gol'Athi and the U'Raati," Terion argued. "He has mastered a force that will sweep over the lands and destroy all in their path. As mortals, we can settle our own affairs, but against your son and his companion, we have no hope. We cannot defeat the son of a god."

"But was not the daughter of Desha slain by a mortal?" Karasika asked slyly.

At this, the goddess Desha herself spoke up, her voice quiet and reserved. "The death of my daughter has no relevance here. It is your children that are the issue."

"And I will deal with my children as I see fit," Karasika said flatly, her gaze never leaving Terion.

"But why does Draven do this?" asked Terion.

"For him, his actions serve a two-fold purpose, Terion," Benovan said as he raised a hand to silence Karasika before she could speak further. "Nothing more can we tell you."

"Will you not aid us at all?" he pleaded, desperation edging his voice.

"The answers you seek are within the words that we have spoken, both for questions asked and for dreams unspoken," Benovan said, his voice deep and soothing.

"My dreams?" Terion asked abruptly.

"Your dreams are a looking glass into the future, Terion. You will find that your questions about Draven and the dreams that plague you, have origins in the same place."

"Can you not tell me anything else?"

"Karasika has been most helpful, even if you do not immediately see it," Benovan explained. "You may have to speak with others to discern the meaning of her words, but that is all part of your mortality and your voyage of discovery, both as a man and as a race of men. This was the downfall of the First Born. It will not be the ruin of you."

"So, is there no fault to be found in an Arcai that breaks his oath then? Or in an Arcai that murders his brothers and sisters in some profoundly disturbing quest for glory?" he dared to say, giving voice to the knowledge that Draven had killed other Arcai in the past.

"There is," Benovan answered solemnly. "But that is for the gods to deal with."

"And you will tell me nothing more?" Terion pressed.

"As I said, much has already been explained, though you cannot yet see it," he answered almost sadly. "And we can tell you nothing further. This is as it must be."

Terion bowed his head, knowing that he had heard everything that he would hear.

"Now, return to your companions," Benovan continued, raising his hand and pointing behind him. "Your time here is at an end and your friends are in peril."

The gray void vanished and Terion found himself standing ankle-deep in the dark water while a battle raged before him. Their pursuers—soldiers and mercenaries from Nykiva, some of whom he knew by name—had finally caught up with them and had forced open the doors of the inner sanctum. Almost a dozen already lay dead or wounded while more continued to force their way into the room. Goron and Notyet fought side-by-side, their weapons keeping the others at bay, but both were bleeding where enemy strikes had found their way past their weapons and the two men were slowly falling back. Of the third man, Terion could see nothing and he knew he must have already fallen.

Terion stepped out of the water and picked up the hourglass. With a glance, he knew that the time was nearly up and he raised it high into the air as he shouted at the top of his lungs. "Enough!"

The battle slowed slightly and both Notyet and Goron moved quickly backward, putting some distance between themselves and their attackers, knowing their time in the temple was finally over. More of their enemies rushed into the room and fanned out to surround their prey. But where the attackers were filled with elation and expectation of the kill one moment, the next saw them looking around in stunned amazement as both of the fighters suddenly vanished before their eyes. Only Terion remained, standing defiantly on the edge of the pool.

"Some of you I recognize," Terion said sadly, drawing the full attention of the men. "Some of you have even served Nykiva honorably as soldiers. But your hearts have been twisted and you have betrayed the trust of your city and the people you have sworn to protect. And now, you must pay the ultimate price for your betrayal."

With a miserable look, Terion lowered his arm. The hourglass fell to the floor, where the glass shattered and the sand was scattered. With the magic released, the guardian of the temple was suddenly a blur of deadly motion, this time amid a large group of doomed men. As Terion activated his magical gem, the screams of the dying echoed in his ears. He knew that none would survive.

A moment later, Terion found himself standing in the long grass just outside the walls of Nykiva, Keiran having chosen a relatively safe place for their magical gems to return them. His mind was jumbled and he was already wondering if the journey to the font had been worth the price they paid. Notyet was already there, his bloody sword plunged into the ground, and he was angrily pulling off his metal gauntlets. Goron was silently kneeling beside the body of Hayron. The seasoned warrior was dead from the guardian's venom, though Jagra was even now racing back through the city toward them with a healer. Of the twelve men that had set out, six had died.

Notyet placed a hand on Terion's shoulder and signed to him. *Were they helpful?*

Terion shook his head slowly and placed a hand over his friend's. "Not like I had hoped," he answered quietly. "Still, they would have me believe that they told me more than I heard."

Riddles?

"To an extent."

Do they not care?

"They care, my friend. But there is much that we must do ourselves."

How many more must die?

"I am afraid to answer that," he replied somberly, remembering Benovan's final words.

At that moment, Jagra came running down the path, half dragging a white-robed man behind him. As he approached, he slowed, his eyes going to the still form of Hayron. A look of grief passed over his face and he let go of the healer.

"You're too late," Goron said quietly, his eyes never leaving the face of his dead friend. "Hayron is dead."

Jagra shook his head sadly and turned toward Terion. "There's more news, I'm afraid," he said slowly.

"What?" Terion asked.

"It's Keiran," Jagra said. "She is dead, as well."

Notyet and Goron looked up sharply, but Terion only nodded slowly, somehow not surprised at all.

"She was assassinated in her private chambers two weeks ago, shortly after you departed," the healer added, bowing his head in sorrow. "Balgar now leads the council."

Terion was silent, taking in the news. Then he looked up at the sky. "A little bit of help is all I ask," he muttered quietly and turned toward the city gates. He had not walked a dozen paces when another figure appeared suddenly before him, arriving in a wash of magical energy. Cavanah stood frozen and then slowly fell to his knees, blood soaking through the front of his leather armor.

"Cavanah!" he exclaimed, quickly rushing to his friend.

The big man looked directly at Terion, his eyes glassy, his face white. "That really hurts," he finally whispered and then pitched forward on his face.

"Healer!" Terion yelled, kneeling down and rolling his big friend over to his back.

The man was kneeling before him in a moment, pulling at the wounded man's leather jerkin. Blood was everywhere and, as he stripped it off, Terion saw the dark hole in his friend's chest, as if an arrow or a spear had run him through. The healer worked quickly, pressing his hands to the wound and muttering incantations.

"What happened?" Terion asked softly, placing a hand on the man's forehead.

Cavanah's eyes fluttered and he looked at Terion. "I know...how they did...it," he gasped.

"What?"

"The city," he said, taking a rattling breath. "Ithil Majeer is... no more," he coughed, gritting his teeth in pain. "The city... is occupied, the... people enslaved. In the temple...a gate."

"A gate? To where?"

Cavanah coughed again. "The Wraithlands," he finally answered.

"But how?" Terion was incredulous.

The big tracker shook his head. "Strange men.

Strange…weapons."

And then his eyes rolled back and Cavanah was gone.

Chapter 20

"Your ignorance is astounding!" Terion shouted, slamming his fist onto the table in an uncharacteristic display of temper. He was normally a man very much in control, but the last hour had proven even more than he could handle. Three days after their return from the font, he and Notyet had arrived to report to the council—or more specifically to the new head of the council, Balgar Mud. Yet Balgar had spent the entire hour trivializing his words and Terion had finally had enough. "We are in the midst of the gravest danger we have ever faced and all you can do is play king of the court!"

The rotund leader leaned forward, his beefy face flushing. "You should learn to hold your tongue," he snapped angrily. "I will not tolerate such an outburst, especially from you."

"Keiran tolerated your outbursts and so you will learn to tolerate mine," Terion snapped, his eyes narrowing as he folded his arms across his chest in defiance. He was not about to let the weasel force him into submission.

"Keiran is no more," Balgar said with just a touch of smugness, something that Terion did not miss at all. "She does not lead this council anymore. I do."

"And you lead poorly," Terion countered. Notyet laid a huge hand on his shoulder, indicating that he was treading dangerous waters, so he quickly changed his tactics. "You know nothing of battle plans, Balgar. If you wish to survive as leader of this council, you would do well to listen to those who do."

"I will not petition the grand baron to send our forces to Taer Blys," the man snapped as he leaned back in his chair. "That is the end of it."

"Listen to me very closely, Balgar," he said slowly, repeating words he had already wasted on the man, in a vain hope that he might finally understand. "Draven has taken Ithil Majeer. We know that Draven is increasing his army and will march on Taer Blys and afterwards, on Nykiva itself! Surely you can see this!

"However, if we meet him there with our own forces," he continued, sweeping his eyes across the other council members, "we can perhaps wound him and slow him down. We would then have time to better prepare our defenses and to rally others to our cause. We would have time to ensure that we had a chance of defeating him when he brings war to our gates."

Balgar shook his head, obviously enjoying provoking the normally calm fighter. "You are wasting our time, Terion. The decision has been made. We will not march."

"Then the Taes will die," Terion said quietly. "And in time, so will we. We cannot stand against the full might of Draven and his armies. Our only chance is to weaken him before he turns his full strength on us."

"By your own estimation," Balgar said. "And quite frankly, I am less than impressed with your abilities as of late."

"It is not my abilities that are in question, Balgar," he replied coolly.

"Oh yes, they are," the fat man said eagerly, leaning forward to rest a heavy chin in his hand. "You conveniently leave at the same time an assassin murders the leader of this council. You take some of our best veteran fighters on a foolish expedition to the Font of the Gods, getting more than half of them killed—and for what? Now you wish to take our forces westward to aid the Taes? You would leave us with nothing to defend ourselves with and likely get them all killed, as well. Perhaps we should begin an inquiry into you, Terion. Perhaps it was even by your own design that Keiran was murdered."

Terion moved so quickly that Balgar had been pulled onto the table and had a dagger at his throat before anyone else could even move. He leaned close to the terrified man, his eyes glinting dangerously. "You may say what you will about me," Terion said through clenched teeth as he pressed the dagger against the soft flesh of the man's neck. "But Keiran was a friend of mine. I warn you – you play a dangerous game with me, Balgar."

"Enough," came a quiet voice from the side as Ranora stood up. "While I disagree with the current leadership of this council, the decision has been made and its mandate will be followed. And you, Terion, are out of line."

Terion held her gaze for several moments and then moved his head closer to the council leader. "I am not so unintelligent as you might think," he whispered harshly. "If I find out that you had anything to do with the death of Keiran…" He let his words trail off, but there was no mistaking the threat in his tone. After another moment, he released the man and his dagger disappeared back into the sheath at his belt. He turned to face Ranora again. "I beg your pardon, Ranora. I acted out of turn as I am truly disturbed at the leadership of this council."

"But it is the leadership, nevertheless," she said, "and it has spoken. The council has voted and ruled, Terion. Our soldiers will not march."

"Very well," the fighter answered, snapping off a curt bow. "Then I shall no longer be a part of it."

"You cannot resign," sputtered Balgar, his hand rubbing his throat where the dagger had been. "Not before I banish you from the council!"

Terion smiled serenely. "Call it what you wish, but of my own volition, I am no longer a member of this council."

Balgar managed to stand, holding on to the table to steady his quaking. "You are nothing!" he shouted. "You have attacked a member of this council! I will see you executed for this!"

"You will do nothing of the sort, Balgar," Ranora interrupted, her voice cold. "What is done, is done and no more will be said of it. If you wish to consider him banished from the council, so be it. Let it end with that."

Balgar turned on her, wanting to say something, anything to help him salvage some sort of dignity, but he quickly thought better of it and collapsed into his chair with a resigned sigh. "Be gone," he finally said, waving his hand in the air. "You are banished from the council, Terion, and have no place here. Return again under penalty of death."

Without replying, Terion offered Ranora another nod of acceptance and left the room, the hulking figure of Notyet walking silently behind him.

After the doors shut behind them, no one in the council chambers spoke for several long seconds. "You do not agree, Balgar?" Ranora finally asked.

"His actions demand justice," the man answered bitterly. "He attacked a member of this council."

"He warned a member of the council, nothing more," Myngar interrupted, his own voice cold and calculating. He was one of only two others, besides Terion himself, to vote against Balgar on keeping the troops within Nykiva and he was more than willing to let the new council leader know just how little he thought of him. "The vote is done and you have won the day. But you would be hard pressed to find anyone in here willing to back up your charges against Terion."

Balgar glared at the man, but Ranora caught his attention again. "It is done, Balgar—let it be. Terion is a valuable ally to us and we may need his services again."

Balgar huffed but said nothing.

"In the meantime, we must begin preparations," Ranora continued. "Dispatch a courier to inform the grand baron of our decision. We must prepare ourselves for the siege."

Terion leaned back against the wall of their room, his eyes studying the flames that flickered in the fireplace across from him. Nearby, Notyet calmly ran a grinding stone down the length of his blade, restoring its razor-sharp edge. Neither had spoken much at all since leaving the council chamber. Terion still wrestled with the reluctance and stupidity, at least in his mind, of the ruling council and Notyet continued to wonder if his closest friend's outburst would have further ramifications for them, despite Ranora's assurance that it was done.

Terion finally looked at his friend, a tired smile playing at his lips. "Do you believe I was out of line?"

The big man gently laid his sword before him before answering. *Hard to say*, he signed.

"You are little help," Terion replied. "I cannot begin to tell you the depth of my frustration. To do nothing in the face of certain doom is preposterous."

That's politics.

"I hate politics," Terion answered.

Yet you are, or were, a member of the council, Notyet replied. *And you did so of your own free will and appeared to enjoy it.*

"I did so at the behest of Keiran," Terion reminded his friend. "I never would have accepted such a calling otherwise. And now she is gone."

Conveniently allowing you to step down.

Terion's eyes narrowed at the statement. "I would never have stepped down otherwise," he snapped.

Precisely my point.

Terion allowed himself to smile again at his friend's pointed wisdom. "So you believe I was out of line."

Notyet shook his head. *I believe that you could have yet been of greater service to our city and our people, had you remained on the council.*

"There would have been little I could do, now that Balgar leads it," he replied. "I don't think he even believes the threat exists."

Ranora believes as you do. As does Myngar.

"They are only two of a dozen."

Yet Ranora has a measure of control over Balgar. Together, you might have accomplished more.

Terion had no answer for that line of reasoning, so he resumed looking at the fire, thinking of his murdered friend. "Do you think he had anything to do with her death?" he asked, remembering Balgar's smug look as he spoke of the Keiran's murder.

If he did, I shall take great pleasure in exacting vengeance upon him.

At that moment, there was a soft knock at the door of their room. Terion rose and walked across the floor, casting a somewhat concerned glance at Notyet. They were not expecting anyone and only the innkeeper knew they were even on the premises. He was reaching for the latch when the heavy oak door exploded inward in a ball of fire, throwing him across the room and slamming him hard into the far wall.

Notyet was up in an instant, his huge sword already coming up to parry the lunge of a spear as several men clad in black robes and hoods stormed through the broken doorway, various weapons drawn. The powerful warrior brought his sword around in a wide arc, burying it halfway through the leading spear-wielder's torso. The man's dying scream was short, but Notyet was already moving again as he caught the wrist of another attacker, halting the man's own sword thrust. His fist crashed into the attacker's face, crumpling him in a heap, as others rushed in behind.

The force of his body hitting the wall had driven the breath from Terion and he had slumped to the ground. He quickly tried to stand but his legs buckled and he dropped again to the floor. The inadvertent action saved his life as a sword cut over his head and thunked into the wall. The sound of metal on wood cleared some of the fog in his brain and he instinctively rolled to the side, crashing into the legs of the man who had just tried to take his head off. His ribs shrieked in protest as he brought the man down on top of him and he knew that he might have cracked one or two. But the pain brought clarity and he clamped a hand around the man's throat as he pulled his dagger from his belt. Several moments later, his assailant was dead and he was standing again, the bloody knife in his hand as he prepared to face the others.

Notyet had dropped two more men with several well-placed punches, before tearing his sword free from the body of the first man who had died. Now with his feet set, his sword swung through the air, sending men diving for cover. But that would be the last of his offense as a bolt of lightning burst forth from the outstretched hands of a cloaked man still in the doorway. The sizzling tendrils of energy slammed into the big warrior, enveloping him in crackling electricity and throwing him to the floor.

Terion leapt at that moment, his dagger slashing one of the attackers across the arm as the man lunged forward with his sword. He spun away from another slash and buried his dagger in the chest of another attacker closing in on his fallen friend. But he know it would not be enough. There were still half a dozen attackers in the room and the wizard was still in the doorway, his hands leveling at him as he prepared another spell.

It never went off, though, as the point of a sword suddenly burst from the wizard's chest, driven through him from behind. Cavanah let the dead wizard slump to the floor as he stepped into the room, one arm bound up in a sling, but wielding a bloody sword with his other. Two of the attackers shifted their attention to him and advanced, only to find that even with one arm, the angry man was more than a match for them.

Terion had moved over to protect the fallen Notyet, but by then, the fight had left the remaining attackers. As one, the survivors charged back toward the door and Cavanah found himself hard pressed as they swung their weapons wildly, intent on killing him or at least clearing him out of their way. As it was, he took a glancing sword hit off his hip as he twisted out of the way. Three made it out the door, but the fourth came up short, jerking wildly and trying in vain to grasp the throwing dagger that was suddenly buried to the hilt in his back. Blood began to seep from his lips as he sank to his knees and fixed a baleful glare on the advancing Terion.

"Why?" was the only word Terion uttered as he stood over the dying assassin. But the would-be killer only stared at him, before falling forward, dead. Terion knelt down and pulled his dagger free, before rolling the dead man over. He then reached to the man's neck and tore a thin silver chain from him. Holding it up, he stared at the tiny silver emblem. It was of a snake, a viper, coiled to strike with overly long fangs protruding from its mouth.

"Looks like someone took a contract out on you," Cavanah said grumpily as he limped over to him, wincing and holding his wounded hip. He had immediately recognized the symbol that his friend now held — that of a dangerous guild of assassins known as

Fangs, and run by a master known only as the Serpent. No one knew anything else about the guild leader, but the Fangs had a presence in every major city across the continent and were universally known. They had been operating for years and over that time, a number of would-be glory seekers had claimed mastery over the guild of killers. None of those making that claim were alive today.

"Looks that way," agreed Terion grimly as he regarded his injured friend. His demeanor softened immediately. "Three days in the infirmary seems to have agreed with you. It is good to see you up and about again."

The burly scout grunted and looked at the fallen Notyet ."I expected a better homecoming. How is he?" he asked as he moved toward the big warrior. Terion quickly joined him. Notyet's eyes were open and alert and both men breathed a sigh of relief.

I hate wizards, Notyet signed with one shaky hand waving in the air.

Terion only chuckled. "Can you move?"

Notyet shook his head and signed again. *Right side only. Left side feels like it is encased in ice.*

"It will pass," Terion assured him and then turned to Cavanah. "And thanks again. Your timing could not have been better."

"Well, seeing as you owe me, I think a night at the pub on you might be in order."

Terion shook his head. "Not tonight. We have more pressing concerns. Who do you know that has the power or wealth to employ such a large number of Fangs in a straight on attack?"

"No idea," Cavanah replied. "Who have you crossed lately?"

"Besides everybody?" Terion replied ruefully. The answer to that question was all too apparent and his features hardened.

Cavanah knew it, too, the story of Terion being banished from the council already making the rounds. But he shook his head. "I don't think Balgar has the gold or the sack to hire a bunch of Fangs."

"Yet someone did," Terion answered angrily." And Balgar is the only one that comes to mind."

"You have other enemies," Cavanah reminded him. "And many who have carried a grudge for a long time."

"It's possible," Terion conceded, rubbing his chin thoughtfully, "but I find it unlikely. First Keiran is murdered and now this. It's too much of a coincidence."

A hand reached up and grasped Terion's shoulder as Notyet tried to pull himself slowly up into a sitting position. With a little help from both men, he was successful and quickly began signing with his right hand, his left arm still hanging limply. *If Balgar sent the Fangs, he may try something more straight-forward when he learns they failed.*

"Agreed," Terion nodded.

There is nothing more we can do in Nykiva, Notyet continued. *Our list of allies here grows small.*

"What do you suggest?"

Taer Blys.

Terion was thoughtful before agreeing with his companion. "Sound advice. Perhaps we can be of use to the Taes at least."

There may also be someone nearby we might enlist. I doubt Keiran had time to contact him before she was murdered.

"Even better," Terion nodded. "Perhaps providence will smile on us and we can find him."

"I am not in the best condition to travel," Cavanah groaned. "Might we find a place here in Nykiva to lay low, at least for a little while?"

Terion shook his head. "Notyet and I will leave by first light. If you feel you need to remain, find someplace you won't be found. If there is a contract out, I can't help but think your name will be on that list, too. If the purse is large enough, their next attack will likely be more successful. They are not known to fail twice."

"That's comforting," the big man grumbled.

"You will be safer with us," Terion said, standing and helping the still somewhat numb Notyet shakily to his feet. "Gather supplies, but remember that we travel light and fast. Then meet us by the west gate before dawn."

"What will you do in the meantime?"

"If Draven has his sights set on Taer Blys, we're going to need some soldiers," Terion answered.

"You think you can muster up an army overnight?" Cavanah scoffed.

"No," Terion shook his head. "But I can spread the word and then hope for the best."

"So you're going to call in some favors."

"A few and with one very big one to ask."

"That's just bloody great—another blasted Arcai. Why am I not surprised," Cavanah grumbled as he limped to the door, stepping over the bodies of the dead. "I'll go fetch the young'uns. They'd be right pissed off if we ran off and left them again." With a sigh, he was gone.

Terion turned back to the big warrior. "Taer Blys, eh?"

It is our best move, Notyet answered, his face set.

"I agree," Terion said quietly and then started gathering up his weapons. "We can also see about paying a visit to someone on our way."

Do you think that wise? Keiran said only that she would consider it.

"Do we even have a choice anymore?"

Perhaps not, Notyet signed thoughtfully. *But are you certain you can even find him?*

"I concede, I have not seen Donaran in nearly a year and then it was only by accident," Terion answered. "He is, after all, an Arcai. But if they have not left the area, I know where they may be found."

How do you know he will even speak to you? Just because Draven has forsaken his oath, doesn't mean that he will.

"Three Arcai have been slain in the past decade," Terion explained. "A Vi'Raaji witch killed one of them, but Draven killed the other two, including Donaran's sister. He has more reason to hate Draven than most."

And you believe that will make him want to help us?

"No," Terion admitted. "But I have had dealings with his companion in the past and I trust her enough to at least listen to us."

She is a dragon.

"Yes, and I remind you that our enemy has a dragon, too."

Right. The biggest, nastiest flying lizard in the world.

"You admit that we need help, then," Terion offered his friend a half smile. "Siranschae can at least give us a fighting chance."

If she will even help us, by my estimate, she is half the size of Draven's lizard. Not a good matchup at all.

"We have to try," Terion replied. "We need every bit of help we can find."

I only hope you know what you're doing. Notyet shook his head.

"So do I, my friend," Terion said quietly. "So do I."

Chapter 21

"I told you he was to be taken alive!" Balgar wheezed as he slammed his hand down on the kitchen table where he was seated, knocking over a half-empty bottle of wine. It was an expensive year, but he was too angry to care. He had been in a tirade ever since an aid had informed him about the attack on Terion, and more so when the Vi'Raaji assassin arrived in the middle of the night, questioning him about it. Him! As if he had anything to do with the attack!

Vendetta was seated on a countertop, one leg drawn up to her chin, her skirt riding to her hip and making it difficult for the man to maintain his composure. "And I told you, I do not employ thugs," she said calmly, regarding him with cool eyes, unmoved by his outburst. "The Fangs are not under my control."

"Yet they showed up and made an attempt on his life after...after...," he trailed off, his face purple with rage.

"After you threatened Terion with execution in front of the entire council," she finished smugly. "I pity your sense of timing, Balgar."

"They will think it was me!" he pleaded.

"Perhaps," she shrugged.

"You have to do something about it!"

"And what would you have me do? The Fangs are controlled by the Serpent, not by me or anyone else. You know this, for this is common knowledge."

"What do you know of this Serpent? Can he be killed?"

"I imagine the same as any man," she laughed. "But I know nothing about him, Balgar. His true identity is unknown to everyone."

"He is in your line of work. You must know something."

"He is someone I take great care to avoid," she answered easily.

"There are plenty of greedy politicians and would-be tyrants in the world. I have no need to expand my influence into areas where the Serpent holds sway."

"Then what am I to do?" Balgar whined.

"Perhaps the question you should be asking is why the Serpent would send his Fangs after Terion, if not because of you."

"I don't...what are you saying?" Balgar asked, narrowing his eyes.

"Only that this is quite the coincidence if you think about it," she answered slyly. "It's not so much of a stretch to believe you paid the gold for the hit on your enemy. You did, after all, threaten to have him killed. What will the rest of the council say, I wonder, when they find out about what happened? Your reign as leader of the Dom council will be a very short one, I imagine."

Balgar rushed across the room, falling to his knees before the assassin. "You have to find him!" he demanded hysterically. "You have to finish the contract! He has to be taken alive!"

"As we agreed upon originally," she said, looking at him disdainfully. "But I will complete it in my own good time."

"I will pay you!"

"I have already been paid," she grinned, thoroughly enjoying the spectacle of the groveling weasel. "I need nothing more than the stone I took from Keiran's treasury."

"I will double the original payment! I will pay whatever you require!"

"Perhaps," the assassin said, languidly swinging her bare leg slowly up over Balgar's head and then sliding to the floor. It was a calculated move and brought about the reaction she wished, judging by the widening of the man's pig-like eyes.

Balgar was not so far gone that he didn't appreciate the

movement, but he wasn't able to reign in his lust in time and he knew that the assassin had caught his hungry look. He felt himself cringing involuntarily, expecting her to lash out, but surprisingly, she didn't. Instead, she moved to the kitchen table and turned back to face him as she reseated herself on its edge.

"I will track Terion down as part of my original contract with your master," she finally offered. "However, because I will escalate the time frame as you are requesting, I will expect certain concessions."

"Anything," he begged, nodding his head eagerly. "Anything you need, I will get."

"You agree too quickly, Balgar. A sensible man would bargain."

"I understand perfectly!" he seethed, crawling to his feet. "I don't care what you do or what it costs! You have to take him!"

"Because you believe it will exonerate you."

"If the council knows he's been taken alive, I cannot be held accountable."

"How do you know they won't blame you for his capture? He is, after all, held in high esteem by them."

"That doesn't matter," Balgar said, finding his political center again. "I can work with a kidnapping, particularly if it's a matter of public knowledge."

"Whereas his death?" she prompted.

"Could be blamed on me too easily," he finished. "I expect you to make sure that doesn't happen."

"You expect?" she taunted.

"You mentioned concessions," he said, ignoring the bait this time.

"And you agreed to them."

"I did, as long as you find him. Now that we have established that, you may tell me what your demands are."

"They are political, nothing more," the assassin replied. "I require no additional monetary compensation. But in time, I may require something else from the head of the Dom Council. When that time comes, I will expect your acquiescence."

"As long as it doesn't cost me politically."

"You will agree to whatever I require or I will exact payment in a different way," she countered, her voice suddenly steely. She stood up from the table and took a dangerous step forward, causing Balgar to stumble backward and his bluster vanish.

"Yes, yes," he stammered. "I only meant that for me to be able to maintain the ability to help you in that arena, you must consider the political ramifications of what you may ask."

"I assure you, I consider everything," she replied coolly.

"So what is it you want?"

"Nothing for now," Vendetta answered. "But when the time comes, you will be the first to know. Can you agree to that?"

"Agreed. Now please go and find him."

"I will leave within the hour," she said. "After his altercation with you and the attempt on his life, he will be heading west to Taer Blys, I'm certain. There are plenty of inns and hamlets along the road where I can make the attempt. I assume you will want him brought back here?"

"Preferably in chains," Balgar sneered. "But yes, to me. I will deal with him publically at that point."

"Very well," she said, walking toward the door. She opened it and breathed in the night air, before turning back for one last parting shot at Balgar. "I wonder something."

"What?"

"If you truly did not send the Fangs to kill Terion, who do you think did?"

"He has enemies," Balgar snorted.

"But none with the amount of gold it would have taken to hire an entire hit squad," she countered.

"What are you insinuating?" he asked, his eyes narrowing.

"I am insinuating nothing where it comes to you and whether or not you hired them," she answered. "To be honest, I don't believe it was you. But you certainly cannot rely on my testimony in front of your precious council to bail you out."

"Then what?"

"Simply consider the facts. You have hired me to capture Terion at the behest of your master, which I have agreed to do. There is no gain for me to kill him. So the question is, who or what else is moving behind the scenes?"

"There's another player in the game," Balgar suddenly reasoned, quietly considering what that new information meant.

"One with a lot of capital," she agreed. "You would do well to employ your resources to find out who it is."

With that, she was gone, vanishing into the night.

Balgar stood staring at the open doorway, considering her words. She was right, he could not deny it. The game of power he was playing just got a whole lot more interesting, as well as dangerous. Someone with the money to hire a group of Fangs would not be a player to take lightly. He would have to carefully consider his political maneuverings in order to get the most gain out of the situation. What he knew for certain, though, was that Terion had to be taken alive. What he would do then was only now beginning to take shape within his mind.

A half hour later, as he headed up to his bedroom with a wicked smile on his face, he had it all figured out. Not only would he gain a valuable bargaining chip with a living Terion as his prisoner, but he might also be able to turn the tables on the assassin. If he played his cards right, he could bring both the Council and her completely under his sway. At that point, her concessions would be meaningless.

Balgar Mud fell asleep quickly that night, supremely confident that when everything had played out, no one would be able to oppose him. He would rule the Doms with an iron hand and for those who dared to oppose him...well, with a Vi'Raaji witch as his personal assassin, he didn't think many would.

Chapter 22

Three days out of Nykiva City, Terion and his four companions found themselves leading their horses down the main road—the only road—of the tiny lake town known as Haven. It was a small hamlet settled on the northern shore of the largest of the Five Seas, massive inland lakes that dominated the northern Midwest. Haven maintained a handful of well-kept buildings and businesses and a few nice homes, as well, being one of several small settlements on the road between Nykiva and Taer Blys that relied on the lucrative business done by travelers passing through.

At the moment, as dusk was approaching, there were a number of people walking the streets, a few travelers looking for room and board and a number of sailors looking to spend some quality time in one of the few inns and taverns in town.

"Quiet little town," Arianna remarked as she walked next to Terion, her eyes scanning the people on the road, some of which seemed to be casting furtive glances toward them.

"For now," Terion replied. "When war comes to Taer Blys, Haven won't be a quiet place when the refugees start pouring through."

"And with Nykiva as his destination, Draven will destroy this place when he comes through after that," Aylan added as he walked on the other side of Arianna. "The people here should be warned."

"They aren't likely to hear," Terion said. "We have no proof of those claims and telling them they should leave their little paradise will likely be met with contempt."

"Well, we have to do something," Arianna pressed.

"We will. We'll see if we can find someone that will agree to help us in Taer Blys," he replied. "We need someone to even things up a bit."

"Do you really think you'll find him here and that he'll agree to help us?" the young Tae asked thoughtfully, thinking of the home she hadn't seen in a year. She was not anxious to return, but she didn't want to see her people hurt, either.

"If he's here, he'll find us," Terion said, carefully watching a pair of unfriendly looking sailors who seemed to be paying them more attention than most.

"Or his dragon will," Cavanah spoke up, pulling his mount up close.

"True," Terion agreed. "And whether they choose to help us will be another story."

"You have spoken of Siranschae several times in the past, Terion," Arianna said, excitement suddenly in her voice. "I have never met a dragon."

"Few people do. The Arcai and their companions avoid mortals for the most part."

"Someone might want to tell Draven that. If he listens, we can all go home," Cavanah said sarcastically.

"If only it were that easy," Terion said, handing the reigns of his horse to the big man. "You and Notyet get the horses boarded. I'll take Aylan and Arianna and we'll get us a couple of rooms. Meet us in The Mermaid's Pearl when you're done." Lowering his voice, he leaned close. "Several sets of eyes on us. Be watchful."

"Aye," Cavanah agreed and took up the reigns of the other two horses. "Oy, Notyet! Make yourself useful and grab a couple of these. The faster we're through, the faster we can get to drinkin'."

Smiling, the mute warrior quickly dismounted from where he had been bringing up the rear, and took the offered reigns. Together, the two friends led the horses toward a stable on the edge of town, one of them complaining, the other laughing silently. Both, however, were alert and watchful.

As the group split up, a shadow detached itself from the space between two buildings and slipped behind a group of sailors heading in the same direction as Terion and his young companions. Vendetta had been in Haven for most of the day and had thoroughly scouted the tiny town. She knew where Terion would be going and she had already set the battlefield. She would wait until they'd had dinner and attack when they left the tavern. If all went as planned, she would have the warrior trussed up and stowed aboard the boat she had hired earlier, bound for Nykiva in the morning before anyone was the wiser.

The plan was to do it with as little bloodshed as possible, but if worse came to worse, she saw no issues with any of the man's companions. She could eliminate them easily enough if she had to. Loosening the Arcai blade inside her blouse, she stepped back into another alley and then quickly made her way up the side of the building, making for the rooftop.

It was almost time.

A short while later found Terion, Aylan, and Arianna sitting around a darkened table in the corner of the tavern known as The Mermaid's Pearl, while Cavanah and Notyet sat at the bar, nursing large mugs of ale. It catered to a variety of people, but mostly to the sailors that made port in Haven on a daily basis. Right now, though, it was quite busy with an equal combination of sea farers and landlubbers.

"So, tell me of Siranschae," Arianna said quietly, pushing the conversation back to the topic she was most interested in.

"There's not much to tell," Terion answered after taking a drink from his mug. "I have only ever met her as a human. To see her, you would never suspect what her true form is."

"Oh," the young Tae replied, sounding somewhat disappointed. "How did you meet her?"

"Quite by accident," he replied thoughtfully. "Siranschae prefers the desert and from what she has told me in the past, that is where she and her companion, Donaran, normally reside. But several years ago, Draven killed Donaran's sister. Donaran, of course, sought vengeance and Draven nearly killed him, too."

"I have heard that tale from my master," Aylan added. "I heard that Donaran went crazy with grief and then worse when Draven beat him during the challenge."

"Which would be correct," Terion replied softly. "Ultimately, he fled the desert and came here."

"Why here?"

"Plenty of vineyards," Terion answered with a sad shrug, but offered nothing more.

"If they are in Haven, how do you know Siranschae will come here tonight?" Arianna asked.

"Because she is already here," he answered softly as he inclined his head forward.

Arianna and Aylan both looked up and noticed the woman coming toward them. Far different in appearance than the few other women in the bar, she was small of frame, not even as tall as the young Tae, and she was clad in desert brown leather, with a well-maintained scimitar held in a fine chain loop at her waist. She had extremely dark brown eyes that glittered in the flickering light of the room and her tan skin had an almost bronze sheen to it. Long raven hair cascaded freely down her back and, underneath her warrior appearance and despite the hard look on her face, she was quite beautiful. She gracefully slipped into the fourth chair at the table and immediately stretched her hand across the rough surface to clasp Terion's offered hand.

"Terion," she greeted. "It has been too long, my friend."

"It has indeed, Siranschae. How did you know I would be here?"

"I felt your presence," she said warmly, her dark eyes flashing. "You have a touch of destiny about you. It's hard to miss it. I see you have new companions," she added, looking at the young wizard and then the Tae.

"Aylan has been with me for a couple of years now," Terion replied. "He came out of the Raiz after Loken asked me to give him some real world experience."

"I see. And how is Loken these days?"

"Cranky, the last time I saw him," Terion smiled. "But you know how wizards are. The other here is Arianna," he finished, indicating the young Tae with a mischievous smile. "She's a healer out of Taer Blys."

"I am not a healer," Arianna bristled, turning a sharp eye on Terion. She always hated that just because she was a Tae, people considered her a healer. She brewed potions and knew a fair amount about the art, but she didn't like the assumption. Terion enjoyed pushing her buttons that way.

The woman laughed, a wonderful sound. "If not a healer, then what are you, my dear?"

"I'm just...or rather..."

"She was taken by slavers early last fall," Terion rescued her, still smiling. "Notyet and I intervened."

"To the better for you, I'm sure," the human-form dragon replied, eyeing both of the young ones before turning back to face

Terion. "So tell me, what is it that brings you to Haven? You haven't been through here in almost a year."

"Business," he answered flatly, allowing his eyes to wander to the many faces in the tavern, noting that several had moved closer upon Siranschae's arrival. Too many people were seemingly interested in them. "But nothing of real importance."

"Well, it would have to be far more interesting than anything else around here lately," she grumbled.

"So how is he?"

"The same," she answered easily enough, but still somewhat sadly. "He certainly keeps the wine vendors profitable."

"So, he really is a drunk?" interrupted Arianna, looking surprised.

"It's not that difficult to believe, after what he's been through," Terion replied, laying a warning hand on the young girl's arm. "But we will speak nothing of it here. Can you take us to him?" he asked, looking at Siranschae.

"Certainly," she answered, pushing her chair back, "but I cannot vouch for his soberness. I doubt if there is anything you could say that will get him away from that cursed bottle."

"Perhaps," Terion answered somberly, standing up as well. "But I must try. Come. Time grows short."

They filed quickly through the tavern toward the front door. Terion led, with Arianna close behind him, followed by Aylan and the warrior woman. Cavanah and Notyet remained at the bar, but would follow up a few moments later, by design, in the event of trouble. They were halfway to the door when a leering sailor stepped in front of the young Tae, his rough hands reaching lewdly for her. He never got close as Aylan's hand shot out over Arianna's left shoulder and closed about one wrist and a gleaming scimitar came around the other side, angling up toward the drunkard's throat. Terion laid a hand on the man's shoulder, the warning clear. As the drunk backed hastily away, Terion leaned close to the other three. "We must hurry," he said quickly, a sense of urgency in his voice. "Others track us even now."

The four of them hurried through the tavern and out into the night.

The attack came almost immediately.

Two figures rose up out of the shadows before them, swords slashing simultaneously. Aylan threw himself sideways, shouldering the young Tae girl hard to the ground and then falling on top of her as the first blade whistled through the air where the girl's head had been. The second would have found its mark against Siranschae, but she had her own weapon out and parried the blow in a blur of motion and a ring of steel. The bronze-skinned woman stepped forward even as their weapons clashed together, then spun her body and brought her blade around, driving it through the chest of her antagonist. He fell with a strangled grunt, blood pouring from the mortal wound.

The second attacker would have killed the young mage had Terion not intervened, picking off a blow with his own weapon. As he shoved the sword strike aside, Terion threw a front kick to the attacker's chest, slamming the man into the wall of the tavern. Dazed, the assailant slid slowly to his knees, his weapon dropping harmlessly to the ground. The tavern door suddenly burst open and two more killers rushed out, blades slashing through the air as they entered the fray.

Their timing, however, put them right in front of the scimitar-wielding woman and she dropped and spun low, her weapon slashing through the belly of the first man before he even knew she was there. His eyes went wide and he grabbed at his stomach, trying desperately to hold himself together.

The second man brought his blade down toward her, but Siranschae jumped up from her crouch, bringing her own weapon straight up underneath the killer's arm. He screamed once as the blade sliced through the limb above the elbow, dropping it and his weapon to the ground. Siranschae's blade slashed through the air a final time and his head rolled from his shoulders as his body pitched forward. The whole battle was over in a matter of seconds.

"Enough," said Terion quietly as he held up a hand to keep the deadly woman from finishing off the surviving assassin.

"It has only been five minutes with you and already I have seen more action than I have in the past five years," Siranschae said grimly.

"Why would they attack us?" Arianna asked, looking down at the groggy would-be killer.

"That is what I intend to find out," he answered, reaching down to help pull the man to his feet.

At that moment, something shot out of the darkness, coiling itself tightly around his outstretched arm. Terion felt himself yanked roughly to the side, where he lost his balance and crashed to the ground. He caught a glimpse of his attacker as she hurtled out of the gloom, one hand behind her and holding tightly to the end of her metallic whip, the other hand leading, slender fingers outstretched. Missiles of green lightning erupted from her fingertips as she came on, fanning out before her and putting Siranschae immediately on the defensive.

The lithe warrior spun her body away from the bolts and very nearly escaped unscathed, but one caught her in the shoulder and sent her tumbling backward in a haze of pain. Another missile caught the surviving assassin in the head, enveloping it in a swirl of burning green fire. With a scream of agony, he grabbed his face and then fell forward as the magical energy reduced his brain to ash.

The attacker leapt over Terion with amazing agility, giving her whip a flick so that it freed his arm as she passed him. She then snapped the whip out before her, the end wrapping tightly around Siranschae's throat. Terion jumped to his feet, but the woman leapt and spun again, this time in the air. The heel of her boot slashed him across the face and sent him spinning to the ground. She landed facing Aylan and her hands flashed out, hitting him twice in the chest and driving the air from his lungs. She spun again in a blur of motion, her backhand catching him in the temple, dropping him unconscious to the ground.

She dropped to a crouch beside Terion, fastening the long fingers of one hand around his throat as she slipped her other hand into her black silken blouse. She withdrew a large glittering emerald and leaned closer, holding the gem between them.

At that moment, having been forgotten, Arianna struck, her own short sword swinging through the air toward the woman. But the assassin flattened herself on top of Terion even as she lashed out with her foot. The blow caught the Tae just above the knee, buckling her leg and driving her backward. But the Tae's ill-advised attack proved to be the turning point in the fight, for Siranschae had freed herself from the metal links of the whip from her neck and was moving forward, her scimitar held out before her.

The assassin rolled quickly to her feet and the two women faced each other.

"I know who you are," Siranschae said evenly, her dark eyes flashing dangerously.

The other woman shrugged and smiled. "It matters little," she replied softly. "I see no reason to hide my identity."

"What do you want?" Siranschae continued, her eyes carefully watching the assassin for any sign of movement. Behind her, Terion had regained his feet just as Cavanah and Notyet stepped out of the tavern, their eyes widening in surprise at what they saw.

"That is my own business," she replied quietly, gripping the emerald gem before her, "and we will finish it at a later time." A moment later, she faded from view in a swirl of magical green light.

For several moments, Siranschae held her sword before her, all her senses alert. But she felt no sign of the assassin's presence. "She is gone," she said, looking at Terion's bloody face as she slipped her sword back into her belt loop. "You're hurt."

"It's nothing," he grumbled, reaching up and pressing his fingers to the cut.

"How is it that you're outside for all of thirty seconds and someone takes a shot at you?" Cavanah said, looking at the dead and dying fighters lying on the ground. "I swear, first it's the Fangs and now it's a Vi'Raaji witch."

"That wasn't just any witch," Siranschae replied quietly. "Of all the Vi'Raaji that have earned their names through the Harrowing, Vendetta is by far the deadliest."

"Vendetta," Terion repeated the name in a shocked whisper, the recognition immediate. "Are you positive?"

"Trust me, I know." She offered him a scrap of cloth, which he quickly pressed to his bloody face, and then she turned to help the others. Aylan was regaining consciousness and Arianna was just lucky. Three inches lower and her knee would have been shattered by the assassin's martial kick. As it was, though, her lower thigh was deeply bruised and it would be some time before she could walk without a limp.

"What if she comes back?" Arianna lamented, leaning painfully against the wall.

"She won't be back. At least not here."

"What makes you so sure?"

"Because I know her kind and you do not," Siranschae replied evenly. "The Vi'Raaji are talented fighters and deadly assassins, and none more lethal than her. They use fighting prowess and potent magic to accomplish their goals. But they also use stealth – it is one of their most important weapons. Vendetta will not attack again tonight because we would be ready."

"Agreed," said Terion, holding out an arm to support Arianna. "Take us to Donaran. We must speak with him immediately."

They found him where Siranschae said he would be, and in about the same shape. He was propped into a corner of the room, snoring soundly, his fingers curled around an empty wine bottle that was cradled almost lovingly to his chest. He was a big man and, despite his apparent years with the bottle, was in remarkable shape. Armorless and wearing only a pair of leather leggings and battered boots, his powerfully-muscled chest rose and fell heavily as he slept. His hair was long and brown and wildly tangled, and he had about a week of beard growth on his face.

"I told you I couldn't vouch for his condition," Siranschae said apologetically as she walked across the room and unstrapped her weapon belt. She unsheathed her scimitar and threw the belt on the table, then took out a tattered cloth and quickly wiped the blade clean. "But after what just happened, perhaps you will have something that might shake him out of this funk."

"He's been like this for years?" Arianna asked quietly.

"Ever since the duels," Siranschae replied.

"Duels?" Terion put in quizzically. "I thought they only fought once?"

"Twice," she corrected solemnly. "The first time they battled several years ago, Donaran escaped before Draven could kill him. Fleeing was difficult for him to accept, so Donaran eventually challenged him last fall and they fought again."

"What happened?"

"Draven defeated him and then spared his life," she said, looking at the slumbering man with compassion. "I assure you it was not out of pity that Draven spared him – it was out of sheer spite. Draven wishes him to live with his failure, so would not allow him an honorable death."

"And so he drinks," reasoned Arianna.

Siranschae nodded, her face truly sad. "He seems to think he has little else."

Terion cleared his throat. "Well," he said, shaking away the despair that had crept into the room. "Let us see if we can find something more for him to live for."

Chapter 23

Terion stood facing the dark portal again, knowing that countless evil creatures stalked the deadly blackness beyond, waiting for the opportunity to slip through the gateway and into the land of the living where they might gorge themselves on the flesh and spirits of the unknowing and unprepared. And he was helpless to prevent it. He might destroy hundreds of the evil creatures, but in the end, he would fall and so would everyone else who dared to oppose the darkness.

"It is hopeless," came the soft female voice behind him and he turned quickly to face the speaker. The woman stood in the archway to the large chamber, her face still hidden within the deep shadows of her cowl, her slender hands clasped at her waist and barely visible in the folds of her black robes.

"It's only hopeless when everyone has given up," he answered firmly, again wondering just who this mysterious woman truly was and why he was so drawn to her.

The sorceress laughed lightly and Terion had a hard time believing that such a gentle sound could come from someone so evil. "Hope or no hope, you cannot stand against me."

"That remains to be seen," he answered defiantly.

She laughed again, amused at his boldness. "No, my dear Terion, that is where you are mistaken. What remains to be seen is whether you will stand with me in the end."

"I'll never join you," he snapped, almost too quickly—for there was that nagging doubt again. What if she was truly seeing something deep and dark within himself that he did not yet know existed? What if he was truly capable of turning his back on everything and everyone he believed in and embracing everything he abhorred?

"If you do not join me," she said simply, "then you will die."

"If I die, then so be it."

"You would perish foolishly and needlessly," she continued, raising a hand before her and causing him to take a quick step backward. "Fear not," she smiled at his agitation. "If I wished to kill you, there would be little you could do to stop me. You cannot know the power that I wield or the power that I will yet attain, Terion."

"Then what do you need me for?"

"I have already told you," she answered easily. "Join with me. It is the only way."

"It's the only way to damnation," he answered, his voice strong.

"It is the only way to survive," she corrected, raising her hands again. "Behold."

The air between the two of them shimmered into a thousand colors as she enacted her spell. Terion watched the rainbows of colors swirl and then begin to quickly coalesce into a more recognizable pattern. In a moment, he was staring down at a settlement overrun with Gol'Athi and U'Raati soldiers who were systematically plundering the town and chopping down the remaining inhabitants.

"Northern Outpost," she explained quietly, "fallen in the early spring." Her hands drew another design in the air. Quickly, the scene fell back into a chaotic swirl of color, before forming into another picture, this one of a much larger battlefield littered with hundreds of bodies of Doms and easily a thousand or more Rats, as a massive Gol army encircled the beleaguered city of Ithil Majeer. Two figures stood alone in the midst of the carnage and Terion watched as they engaged in battle, one falling quickly to the other in the warrior's challenge.

"The fall of Kelemaur," she continued and again shifted the scene, this time to show the once-great city of Ithil Majeer in ruins and wholly occupied by the forces of Draven. "Your allies are falling. They cannot stand against the might of my armies or the strength of my general."

"You show me nothing that I don't already know," he replied confidently. "I am well aware of Draven and of what he has done. But it doesn't change the fact that I, that we, will stand against you."

She laughed and once again turned the scene into the swirl of colors. "You will stand alone, Terion."

A low gasp of dismay escaped him as he stared at the scene, a tower chamber he had visited many times in the past. The lone occupant, though, was not found studying her tomes as she normally would be. No, this time she was lying on the floor, a thick line of red at her throat, her blood pooling beneath her body. "Keiran," he whispered. "So it was you that employed the assassin."

"Slain at my command," the woman said coldly, lowering her hands and allowing the scene to vanish. "As I said, you will stand alone."

He turned on her, his eyes narrowing angrily. "There will be other allies to stand against you," he growled.

"Then they will die, just as Keiran died," she answered plainly and pointed over his shoulder toward the gate. "Just as you will die."

He turned slowly and tensed as the reaver began to stalk toward him.

Terion sat up, instantly awake, the new dream still vivid in his mind. This one was different and he knew he was getting closer to the truth. But it was not the dream that had brought him awake – no, it was the intuition that something was suddenly very wrong in the real world.

The firelight was burning low, casting a dim glow and he took note of the forms of some of his companions, sleeping soundly on the floor around him. Notyet and Cavanah were in the adjoining room, but the youngsters were with him in Donaran's. Arianna was curled up asleep near Aylan, who sat propped against the wall nearby, his eyes closed in slumber and his spell book lying open across his lap. Donaran was snoring soundly now from his rumpled bed, his drunken stupor having passed and giving the indication that he might be able to converse with them when he awoke the next morning. Siranschae, however, was awake and alert, crouched near the door, her scimitar in her hand. She turned her head to regard him and Terion saw the fire in her eyes.

She comes again, the woman mouthed silently.

Vendetta was back.

Terion came to his feet, and swept up his blade. As he did, he noticed that beads of sweat were breaking out on his brow and he was suddenly aware of how hot it was getting in the room. He had only a moment to yell a warning before the wall directly behind him disappeared in a blaze of fire and smoke. And through the wall of flames came smoke-shrouded figures.

He immediately went on the defensive, picking off several sword swings as they came on. Two men quickly fell to his blade, but more came through the breach, rushing into the room in a wave. Terion recognized them as simple sailors and other ruffians, which should have bothered him, but he was too busy avoiding clumsy swings and thrusts to realize the significance of their overall lack of skill.

Siranschae held near the door only for a moment and then she was leaping toward him. She brought her scimitar around in front of a fighter, deflecting a sword thrust from one of the second wave of assailants. Spinning, she took the man across the throat with her blade and then moved to engage the next one.

Aylan had awakened at the first yell from Terion and had grabbed Arianna and thrown her to the middle of the room, even as his cloak burst into flames from the burning wall. A quickly muttered spell, though, left his clothing only smoking and he was otherwise unharmed. He kicked hard at the still snoring Donaran and then turned to lend his magic to the fray.

Behind them, the door to the room opened and a figure stepped in, all her enemies engaged with the ruse before her. Arianna was the only one to see her, the Tae girl climbing to her feet even as Vendetta entered the room.

The Vi'Raaji's whip snaked out immediately, encircling the young girl's throat and quickly cutting off any sound. Vendetta snapped the whip back, spinning the helpless girl to the floor. Even as Arianna hit the floor, Vendetta dropped her knee, crushing the young woman's throat closed. The light behind Arianna's eyes began to fade as Vendetta kept the pressure on the girl's windpipe.

It was Aylan that saved her through a stroke of sheer luck, having turned to avoid a desperate sword thrust. He quickly saw what was transpiring and gave a shout even as he began weaving a spell. Vendetta had no choice but to free the young Tae and roll to the side as several jagged shards of stone materialized in front of the young spell caster and flew through the air toward her. They crashed into the wall behind the assassin and splintered the wood, but she was already up and moving, her fine metal whip snapping out again. Aylan jerked his head to the side in pain, his cheek opened up from the whip crack and suddenly, the deadly woman was right beside him, her hand knifing for his throat.

The young mage would have died if not for the powerful hand of Donaran closing on the assassin's slender wrist and stopping the blow mid-strike. In a flash, she snapped her wrist down and twisted her body around, her other hand flashing forward. Donaran staggered backward, falling back across his bed, her dagger buried to the hilt just below his right collarbone. Vendetta spun again, catching Aylan's wrist and then twisting it down with a resounding crack of bone. The young mage's scream of pain was cut short as the heel of Vendetta's boot slammed into his ribs, snapping more than one and throwing him painfully into Donaran, who was struggling to get back to his feet.

When Terion turned, the woman stood before him, dark skin gleaming in the flickering flames, her pale crystal blue eyes locked with his. She immediately dropped him to his knees with a pair of sharp palm thrusts to his chest that drove the air completely from his lungs. In the next instant, she had circled an arm around his shoulder, her hand cupping his chin and pulling his head up. Her dagger magically appeared in her other hand and she placed it against his throat.

"Stand," she whispered harshly to him, even as Siranschae drove the last of the other attackers back through the smoke and dying flames of the breached wall.

When Siranschae turned around, she keenly felt the helplessness of the situation. Terion was still alive, though under the knife of the killer and gasping for breath.

"Hold," Vendetta challenged, pressing the dagger tighter against Terion's throat. "You would not wish to be the death of your friend now, would you?"

Siranschae stepped forward, her weapon before her, but stopped as Vendetta began to push the dagger home.

"I will kill him if I must," the assassin said calmly. "The bounty can still be claimed, even if I return only his body."

Siranschae lowered her scimitar and glared at the assassin. "I warn you. If you hurt him, I will see you torn to pieces."

"Threats do not become you," Vendetta replied coolly, moving backward toward the open door, the mage still under her knife. "Our business here is concluded. Tend to your companions and leave me to my prize." A moment later, she was gone through the door with Terion as her captive.

Siranschae stared at the darkened doorway, silently seething before Notyet stepped into the frame, dragging a bloodied sailor. The huge warrior angrily threw the wounded man on the floor before her as Cavanah crowded in behind him, looking every bit as angry as his friend.

"You said she would not attack again this night!" Cavanah growled.

"It would seem I have misjudged her," Siranschae replied quietly, before turning back to the others. "Come, we have wounded. When they have been tended to, I will go after her."

"And if she comes back again?" he challenged her.

"She won't, because she got what she came for. Now it's time to go take him back."

Vendetta seated herself easily on a rock some distance north of Haven, her hands resting lightly on one bare knee. She had been successful and taken her prisoner, but something about the female warrior bothered her. She respected the formidable woman, but there was something more to her, something intriguing, and the Vi'Raaji assassin did not yet know what it was.

"I wasn't aware that a Vi'Raaji witch had the magical strength to teleport two people, let alone yourself," Terion said curiously, looking up at her. He was sitting propped against another rock, his hands bound tightly behind his back with leather cords.

Vendetta smiled and slipped her hand into the low neck of her silken blouse, taking care that her prisoner's eyes followed her every move. She slowly withdrew the sparkling gemstone, holding it up for the man to see. "The Star Stone is quite a prize," she replied.

"I know who possessed that artifact before you," he said dangerously, his features darkening. "I will see her avenged."

"You are in no position to threaten me, Terion," the woman smiled, her features beautifully captivating and deadly at the same time. "But take some solace in the fact that Keiran did not suffer needlessly. I killed her quickly."

"I find that difficult to believe," he snapped.

"I had no quarrel with Keiran, so there was nothing to be gained by torture. I simply killed her because that was what was demanded of the contract."

"By whose orders?"

"You should already know that an assassin rarely knows the particulars," she answered, "All I can tell you is that the purse was rich and it was a challenge I chose not to reject."

"And the Star Stone?"

She smiled again, that entrancing look that had her prisoner silently doubting himself. "The gem was a bonus. Had I known she possessed such a grand item, I might have taken it from her a long time ago. Of course, right now its usefulness is rather limited, since I am burdened with you." Her statement was true enough. Free-range teleportation was one of the most difficult of magical spells and was accomplished only by master wizards, of which the Vi'Raaji were not. The same type of teleportation tied into a magical artifact was a feat nearly unheard of. The strongest of sorcerers could create magical gemstones that could teleport an individual from one place to a pre-determined location, but only once and then they were little more than burned-out chips of crystal. But only three artifacts were known that possessed the characteristic of free-range teleportation, allowing the user to transport themselves anywhere in the land they desired.

The Star Stone, the least of the three known teleportation gems, had only the power to transport a single person and could do so for great distances. More than one taxed the crystal immensely and Vendetta had only been able to get her prisoner and herself a few leagues outside the city. At the moment, the magical emerald's power had been thoroughly drained, but the assassin knew it would regenerate in time. She knelt down in front of the bound man, her face seductively close to his. "Tell me of your fighting friend," she purred, changing the subject.

"She is someone I have known for a long time," he said nonchalantly, staring back into the beautiful eyes of his captor and fighting to keep his gaze from straying elsewhere. He knew that Vi'Raaji witches were adept at using their charms, both physical and mental, to easily retrieve information and he did not want to divulge anything that she might not yet know .If Vendetta did not suspect the true nature of Siranschae, so much the better. With considerable effort, he pulled his eyes from her gaze and looked toward the glow in the night of what he was certain had to be Haven. "They will come looking for me," he said quietly, fighting to slow his pounding heart.

Vendetta leaned closer, her sensuous lips lightly brushing his ear and sending unwanted shockwaves through his body. "Then they will die," she whispered huskily, her breath soft on his neck. Finally, she stood and backed away, flashing him a sensuous smile. "Those who are still alive anyway," she finished with a wink and then turned away, positioning herself so that her prisoner would have difficulty not looking at her.

"I don't know who you're working for, but I have my guesses," Terion said, purposefully keeping his eyes on his feet. "And once I have dealt with them, you and I will have unfinished business to complete."

"You will know the identity soon enough," she said easily, kneeling down once more and this time, helping him to his feet. "Once I have delivered you, our business is complete. I doubt we will see each other again, as much as it pains me to admit that."

"Is it time to part ways already?" he asked, matching her sarcasm.

"Soon. We have but a short journey to get back to the docks. I do hope you don't get seasick, as the lake can be fairly rough."

"And if I resist?"

"I can just as easily deliver your head," she replied with a shrug, pulling her long knife from her blouse. Her blade went to his throat just as a loud roar split the night air. Vendetta spun instinctively, hooking her leg around the man's ankles and dropping him back to the ground. The movement brought her to a crouch, her leg pressed against the side of his head and her knife back at his throat. She had only a moment before her questions about Terion's female fighting companion were shockingly answered.

A huge bronze-colored dragon dropped onto a rocky outcropping only yards away, familiar eyes glittering fiercely at the assassin. The creature's head snapped forward, its powerful maw and dagger-like teeth snapping through the air where the woman had been kneeling only a moment before. However, Vendetta had spent a lifetime honing her ability to anticipate the movements of her enemies and she was already rolling aside, easily clear of the snapping jaws. She came up in a defensive crouch, one hand thrust forward and fingers splayed wide. Familiar missiles of green magic shot forward, strafing the head of the powerful creature, a beast the assassin knew she had no hope of defeating.

With a roar of anger and pain, the dragon's head shot forward again, this time stopping with its jaws wide open. Suddenly, the air was filled with a blizzard of stinging sand and small rocks, a debris-filled tornado that engulfed the assassin.

But again, Vendetta was prepared, enacting a spell of protection a moment before the dragon breathed. The deadly breath passed over and around her, the force of her magic deflecting most of its power. Had she not been protected, the dragon's blast would have shredded every last bit of flesh from her bones. In an instant, she was moving again, realizing that the huge creature was herding her away from her captive. A dive and a roll brought her behind a large stone as the remains of her protective spell fell away. Then she was standing, a throwing dagger in her hand. She flicked her arm forward, the blade flying straight and true toward the dragon's head.

Siranschae, though, was as good of a fighter in her natural dragon form as she was in her human guise and she quickly dipped her neck low, allowing the dagger to skip harmlessly off the iron-hard scales of her head.

"Now I know the truth about you," Vendetta said quietly to herself as she looked around for an escape. She saw it on a rocky bluff some distance away and cast her spell even as the dragon's tail came smashing into the stone she was hiding behind.

Siranschae lumbered forward, her head dipping low as she scanned the area where the now-shattered rock had been. A low angry growl escaped her throat as she realized the woman was nowhere to be seen. She allowed her vision to fall into heat-sensing mode, hoping to discern where the assassin might be hiding. But still she could see nothing and, finally satisfied that she had at least driven the woman away, she turned toward Terion. He was still lying in the ground, now half-covered by a small sand dune she had created during her attack on the Vi'Raaji assassin. But he was alive and looking at her with a grateful smile on his face.

"I trust that Donaran is not so badly hurt," he said shakily, knowing that if he had been, Siranschae would not have been nearly as effective in driving Vendetta away. The Arcai and their dragon companions were closely linked on what could only be described as a spiritual level and, if one was badly hurt or even killed, the other would be considerably weakened.

Siranschae brought her great head closer to her friend, baring her teeth in a dragon smile. "She stuck him with an Arcai blade and he is mad as a bound demon," she rumbled, her powerful voice similar to her human form, but rough and course. "But he will survive."

"And the others?" he asked hopefully.

"Some injuries, but alive. Had Vendetta not hired a bunch of novices to create the diversion, our casualties would be much worse."

"So that explains it," Terion said thoughtfully.

"Notyet captured one alive," she nodded. "Cavanah was interrogating him. From what I heard before I left, it almost seemed as if she wanted inexperienced fighters to come against us."

"Less chance of having her target killed, I suppose."

"Or she wanted to avoid killing anyone," the dragon countered. "Still, we are in no condition to defend ourselves if she comes against us again."

Terion nodded, pulling himself to his knees as best he could with his hands bound behind him. "For her to attack us twice in one night, someone is paying her an awful lot."

"Or the need is desperate," Siranschae added and then stiffened abruptly, her head darting about. Her dragon vision shifted through various modes of sight and she inhaled deeply, trying to catch the scent of the new presence she suddenly felt.

"What is it?" Terion asked quickly, seeing her agitation. "Is she back already?"

For a long moment, the dragon did not answer and Terion feared it was true. But a moment later, the dragon's head swung back to face him. "No. But I sense something else."

"What?"

After another pause, Siranschae simply shook her great head and did not answer his question. "We must be away," she replied and turned him around with one great clawed hand. A moment later, his bindings fell to the ground, neatly sliced by the dragon's razor-sharp talons.

"I trust your judgment," he answered, rubbing his sore wrists. "But it will take us some time to reach Taer Blys, longer depending on how badly hurt the others are."

"She is after you, Terion, not the others. I suggest splitting up."

"Are you saying you will fly me to Taer Blys?"

"Dragons are not prone to becoming carriages," she said, scowling at him. "However, circumstances being what they are, I will accommodate you if Donaran agrees. The others will have to catch up as quickly as they can."

"Fair enough," he nodded.

"Come, let's get back to the others. You and I should be gone at first light."

With that, the two set off back toward Haven at a jog, talking quietly to each other.

Some distance away, the Vi'Raaji assassin lay at the top of the rock face, feeling dirt and grit creep into her clothes and scratch her smooth skin, but caring nothing for it. Her sharp eyes were trained on the dragon and her former captive, some distance below. She had barely escaped, creating an extra-dimensional doorway that she had stepped through. It had nearly not been enough, though. Her back was still stinging from several shards of stone that had followed her through the portal and torn into her flesh.

Of more concern to her was the appearance of Siranschae. Vendetta realized the significance of the creature's arrival and now knew that Terion had taken up with the Arcai, Donaran. Truthfully, she could void her contract with her employer in Nykiva because of this new development, but the challenge of snatching him out from under the nose of an Arcai and his dragon was rather appealing. Of course, she would have to renegotiate the price, but that was secondary to the possibility of completing the task.

She watched Siranschae assume her human form again and her two enemies begin their trek back toward Haven. If it was even possible, it would take careful planning and great patience. "In time," she said softly as she watched them go. "In time."

Those words echoed clearly in the ears of the great black dragon that was watching her from a distance. Kraegor had already entertained and dismissed the thought of taking the woman right there where no one could bear witness. Having heard the entire conversation between his dragon sister and the swordsman, he knew who the assassin was and he was familiar with her history. He would certainly be justified turning her into a plaything before he devoured her. But he was also intrigued by her and her strange appearance in the currently unfolding saga.

He knew of Shayene's bid to capture Terion and have him join her in her quest to bring the lands under her sway, but her reasons were personal and she had not yet shared them with him. But he also knew she would never directly employ a Vi'Raaji assassin to accomplish his capture. Yet, here Vendetta was, indicating that she had been contracted to capture the man and the question on who might have orchestrated it intrigued him. It would make for some fine entertainment for him and he savored the chaos and subterfuge of having plots within plots. And while Shayene might not appreciate it once she found out, he certainly did. He was, after all, a dragon.

As far as Siranschae was concerned, he had no quarrel with her. By nature, dragons were not overly fond of each other, but they were also loath to engage in battle with each other. Their Arcai companions could fight among themselves as much as they wanted, for all he cared. But he would avoid engaging his own brothers or sisters, more out of pragmatism and sibling respect than fear.

So, he was content to watch Vendetta from a distance and more than once, he considered the fun he might have in his human form with a witch of such renown and beauty. "In time," he repeated the woman's own phrase in his mind. "In time."

Convergence

Part 4

When Worlds Collide

The bronze dragon, Siranschae, easily winged her way high in the dark sky, her incredible eyesight seeing everything in the pitch black of night. She was conducting another patrol of the surrounding lands around Taer Blys, as she had done every night for the past three weeks. Draven and his army were getting ever closer, along with the inevitable battle they could not hope to win.

Siranschae knew that they had at least a week, two at best, before Draven and his companion brought death to the people of Taer Blys. However, of even more concern to her was the presence that she continued to feel, shadowing her movements but always far enough away to avoid detection. It was a presence she had first sensed when she had rescued Terion from the witch, and it had come back many times since—there, but always invisible to her.

For a while, she had thought it be Draven's companion, Zarandrae, perhaps the most dangerous of their kind. However, when she flew over the encamped army of Draven three days before, she distinctly felt the greater presence of her stronger sister, intermingled with the faint and mysterious presence of the one that had been shadowing her. That meant only one thing – another dragon was somehow involved. And that disturbed her more than anything.

Tonight, she would share her concerns with Donaran and Terion.

Siranschae circled lower and then glided in for a landing, some distance south of Taer Blys. She landed in a clearing and seamlessly shifted back to her human form as she approached the small campfire crackling in the night.

"How went tonight's hunting?" Terion asked, looking up from a branch he had been distractedly shaving down with his dagger.

"Draven's advance scouts are not far from here," she replied, taking a seat next to the fire. "He is driving his army hard, so I believe they will reach Taer Blys in a week."

"Perhaps we should strike at them now," Donaran said quietly, eyes lost in the flames of the fire.

Terion looked up, somewhat surprised to hear the Arcai speaking. The half-god had said little in the three weeks they had been together. Siranschae had done most of the speaking for him, the moody warrior remaining mostly withdrawn. After the attack in Haven by Vendetta, Terion had told him the whole story of why they had sought him out. The Arcai had agreed to help them as the chance of facing his nemesis one last time and putting his personal demons to rest was too great an opportunity for him to pass up. But after that initial conversation, he had grown quiet and distant, preparing himself for the inevitable.

"We will gain nothing by it," Terion disagreed with a shake of us head. "Killing a few scouts will not slow Draven's advance on Taer Blys. Worse, it might reveal to Draven that the playing field has been somewhat leveled."

"That remains to be seen," Donaran snorted, rubbing his now smooth chin. The immortal had cleaned up quickly when they had recruited him and now his handsome face was bare and his hair pulled neatly back into a traditional warrior's braid. He was still armorless, wearing only his leather leggings and his worn boots. But he now wore upon each wrist, a glittering bracer crafted of a strange black metal alloy and inlaid with intricate silver runes. In addition, his huge curved sword, Whistler, was strapped to his back.

"Do you think Draven knows you are here?"

"He would only know if Zarandrae told him," Siranschae answered. "I don't believe she is aware of me, so Draven likely does not know yet, either."

"What will you do when you finally face him again?" Terion asked carefully. He knew the Arcai considered himself immensely dishonored because of his inability to defeat Draven not once, but twice. However, he probably felt more keenly the embarrassment Draven had heaped upon him by sparing his life the second time. There was also the matter of Zarandrae. While Terion knew little of the great blue's abilities while in human form, he knew with certainty of Zarandrae's nearly unmatchable power when in dragon form. There were sixteen original Arcai, each with a dragon companion, and of the sixteen, Zarandrae was the biggest and easily the deadliest. Were Zarandrae and Siranschae to meet in battle while in dragon form, he held little doubt which would emerge victorious.

"I will do what I need to do," Donaran answered. "I must face him one last time."

"Even at the cost of your life?" Terion asked pointedly.

"I will either kill him or be killed by him," the Arcai replied flatly. "This time, there will be no other outcome."

"And either way, your honor will be restored," Terion reasoned, nodding in agreement. "I suppose I cannot argue with that."

The Arcai managed a sad smile, the first Terion had seen on him. "Fate is strange, is it not?" Donaran said at length. "We are gods among men, but are not permitted to meddle in the affairs of mortals. Yet here Draven has betrayed that trust and gone to war with your people. And now I am aiding his enemies, again breaching the trust levied upon us by our godly parents."

"You are leveling the scales of justice, nothing more," Terion corrected him.

"It's possible. But it's more likely that I am betraying my oath just as badly as he is."

"You have not declared war on mortal man."

"No, but I am still involving myself in your affairs." The Arcai looked skyward for a moment, scanning the stars. "It's a paradox, a trap from which there is no escape."

"Perhaps for both of you," Terion agreed, his voice quiet.

Siranschae settled back on her elbows near the fire with a weary sigh. "The fates will play themselves out within a week. Regardless of the outcome of Donaran's fight with Draven, there is still the matter of Taer Blys."

"Cavanah has been shaping the fields beyond the city for a couple of weeks now," Terion answered. "We are as ready as we could possibly be, given the little time we have had to prepare defenses."

"If intelligence is to play any part in the defense of the city, you will pack your things and run to Nykiva as fast as you can go with anyone who will go with you," Donaran put in grimly. "Even if you could convince the Taes to defend themselves, they are too few and too unskilled to face thirty thousand Gol soldiers led by an Arcai warrior."

"You'll get no disagreement from me," Terion replied. "As many as we can convince to flee, we will guide to Nykiva. In the meantime, we have what soldiers have come to our call. It will have to be enough."

Donaran let his eyes drift back to the sky, but he said nothing for a long time.

"Do you sense it, too?" Siranschae asked after several minutes, breaking the silence as she continued to gaze into the night sky as well, hoping to catch a glimpse of their hidden shadow. He was there. She could feel him.

The Arcai nodded his head.

"Sense what?" Terion asked, following their gaze skyward.

"There is a presence," Donaran answered quietly.

"A presence?"

"There is another dragon nearby."

"That's not so far-fetched," Terion said with a nod. "Zarandrae is likely scouting."

"No," Siranschae corrected him. "I am certain it is not her. There is another."

Terion narrowed his eyes. "How can that be? There is only you and Zarandrae."

The woman chuckled softly. "There are sixteen of us, my friend."

"You know what I mean," he said, giving her a withering glance. "You and Zarandrae, Draven and Donaran, are the only immortal players in this game."

"Are you certain of that?" Donaran asked, his voice even.

The sudden indication that there may be more Arcai involved shocked the man into silence. But he could not bring himself to believe that yet another immortal had broken his or her covenant and was now involved in the downfall of humankind. "Could it be that this is coincidence – that there is simply another of your kind in the area?" he asked finally.

Siranschae shook her head. "No. Whoever it is, he has been with us since Haven."

"He?"

"Dragons know," she shrugged.

"And you are only now telling me this?"

Siranschae smiled again, ignoring the man's ire. "What would you have done, Terion? He is only watching – had he intended more, you would likely already be dead."

"I am more worried about what it means to have another

dragon in the mix," Terion lamented. "That would mean there is another Arcai involved, too."

"It may be nothing," she answered. "As with our companions, we try not to meddle in the affairs of man, but that does not mean we are uninterested in your race. Many times, I have watched your people just to watch and this may be just such a case, nothing more."

Terion shook his head. "These are not normal times, though."

"Your point is well taken," Donaran said, finally taking his eyes off the night sky. "But at the moment, we can do nothing about it. If our mysterious dragon decides to reveal himself, we will deal with it at that time, but we will certainly not seek him out. So for now, we proceed as intended."

"Agreed," Terion sighed, knowing the Arcai was right. If the mysterious dragon knew they were aware of it, it might decide to act differently and he could not think of any good outcome if that happened.

A number of leagues to the south, Zarandrae, in human form, sat quietly in her tent, her eyes closed as she focused on the two familiar presences she distinctly felt nearby. As the largest of her kind, her senses were the most fine-tuned of any of them, and Zarandrae could discern specifically which of her kin was nearby. She knew Kraegor's essence well. But it was not him that concerned her. It was the other one that she was unsure about. For many minutes, she concentrated, her spirit seeking out the other of her kindred. Then suddenly, her eyes snapped open, a smile coming to her face.

"Siranschae," she finally whispered in recognition.

Chapter 25

Cavanah adjusted himself in the crook of the ancient oak tree, fingering his crossbow as he stared across the large open meadow to the distant tree line. The main road cut a straight line across the field of high grasses and summer wildflowers, before disappearing into the trees of the southernmost edge of the Spider Forest. Taer Blys was nestled against the lower eastern edge of the forest near the start of the great river. The main road from the Tae city ran parallel to the river, leading from Taer Blys all the way to Kaylon Bay, passing through the major cities of Ithil Majeer and Toldon on its way, as well as dozens of smaller towns and settlements. It was the main road that the war machine of Draven was following, and the big tracker knew the point soldiers of the deadly army were not far beyond the line of trees at the other end of the field.

Since their arrival last month, Cavanah and his men had been preparing a bitter welcoming for Draven and his minions. Now, the field before him was filled with traps and pitfalls, and many defensive positions had been dug into the land all along the edge of the forest. Cavanah had nearly four hundred men stationed along the line they would hold, prepared to spring those traps when the time came.

While his preparation of a single area, instead of completely ringing the city with traps and defenses, suggested two-dimensional thinking on his part, it was the road before him and the surrounding fields where he was certain they had the greatest chance of hurting Draven's soldiers. He did not believe Draven would spend a week or more marching his forces through the heavy forest around to any other side of the peaceful city, when he could march the massive army right up to the front gate and through the city with little, if any, resistance.

The defenders of Taer Blys had not been lax and had prepared well in what little time they had been afforded. Oh, there was no hope of defeating the invading army and every last one of them knew it. But they could hopefully deliver enough damage that the invaders would have to delay their march on Nykiva, perhaps even until the following spring.

The first sounds of battle reached Cavanah's ears. That meant his advance scouts, about fifty strong, had encountered the first of Draven's Rats and the battle had begun beyond the trees .Cavanah pulled his dagger from his belt and reached over to a nearby limb where three ropes were tied off, each one running down the tree and through loops along the ground, out into the fringes of grass in the field. The big man sliced the dagger through the nearest rope and it immediately snapped downward and through the grass as a tall sapling, stripped of branches, sprang back up and out of the long grass. At the top of the sapling, a large red pennant flapped in the breeze.

Cavanah knew that nearly four hundred archers standing safely behind the deeply-dug trenches along the tree line were nocking arrows, having been given the first signal. Now they would all wait. There was no telling how long the initial fighting would remain beyond the trees, but he didn't think it would last long. His fifty soldiers would only be fighting a running battle, hoping to draw the enemy on and tripping the defensive traps as they retreated. It would be a brutally dangerous run.

It was less than fifteen minutes later when the first of them broke from the trees, running a carefully planned zigzag pattern along the road and through the grassy field, heading for the relative safety of the hidden archer line. Cavanah frowned as he counted less than twenty of his men returning. With more than thirty dead already, he found himself wondering if they had badly miscalculated.

The first of the attackers appeared from the trees. They were painted U'Raati savages, screaming and brandishing their weapons. Dozens began pouring from the trees, then hundreds. Cavanah placed his dagger against the second rope and waited until the field and road filled with Rats.

With a quick flick of his wrist, he cut the second rope and a second sapling sprang up near the first. This one was flying a green flag and the moment the pennant flew, the first volley of arrows flashed from the tree line. Many missed their targets; many more brought down a fair number of the savages. The pursuers paused at the unexpected attack and, in that brief halt, another major arrow volley felled many more. Then, in an almost unified scream of rage and battle lust, the savages came on again.

Cavanah placed the dagger against the last remaining rope and watched. Hundreds of Rats were now flying across the field and the distance suddenly seemed woefully small. In many areas, the attackers went down, the victims of arrows or deadly pit or spike traps that had been scattered throughout the field. Many more came on recklessly, heedless of their dead and dying companions. His mouth set tightly, he cut the final rope. A third sapling sprang up, this one flying a black flag. And with that, the big tracker quickly descended his perch.

At the appearance of the third pennant, half of Cavanah's archers grabbed nearby torches and flung them as far as they could into the grassy field, while the other half picked up arrows coated with pitch and set them alight. In moments, those flaming arrows were soaring over the heads of the enemy and landing behind the main body of the attackers. For nearly two days, Cavanah and his men had soaked the field in oil in preparation and now roaring flames were exploding both in front and behind the attackers. The Rats halted their charge and began trying to move back toward the road where there was less grass to catch fire. It was at this point that the wizards opened up. Fireballs, some large and some small depending upon the casting strength of the wizard, streaked out of the trees, slamming into groups of Rat soldiers or impacting with the oil-soaked ground. Huge patches of flames roared up, immolating dozens, and the U'Raati contingent completely broke apart. Hundreds of Rats went shrieking back toward the far trees, some trying to dodge the flames while others simply ran right through in a blind stampede to escape the inferno. A shout of victory rose up from Cavanah's men as they continued to rain arrows after the fleeing Rats, killing many more.

Cavanah stood on the road, grimly peering through the heat and smoke at the carnage. The route had been quick and complete and he believed it could not have gone any better. As far as he knew, he had only lost those few brave souls that had first engaged the Rats in hopes of drawing them into the field trap. Once caught in the trap, the Rats never even got close to the trees where he and his men were.

On the other hand, hundreds and hundreds of U'Raati savages lie dead or dying. It would bring a touch of hope to the defenders of the city proper.

Zarandrae changed all that in a moment.

The enormous blue dragon came over the treetops through the clouds of smoke, her massive form casting an immense shadow over the flames in the field. She opened her mouth with a roar and devastating lightning blasted forth from her deadly jaws. She strafed the tree-line as she came, her lightning blasting through trees, destroying anything and anyone in its path.

Cavanah could only watch in numb horror, unable to move until her lightning blasted into the ground in front of him, hurling him into the trees. And then she was gone, winging over the treetops as she sped toward the unsuspecting city. Cavanah was lucky. The blast had thrown him back, but he had landed in a thick patch of brush. He was quick to extricate himself, his body tingling with electricity and his hair standing on end.

He could not have known it yet, but the dragon's attack had killed fully half his men and it had lasted only a few seconds. Now he could only look across the field in despair as groups of black-robed figures stepped out of the trees on the far side of the burning fields. They began casting spells of their own. Swirling clouds of ice and snow appeared before the Gol war wizards and swept out across the fields, snuffing the flames as they passed.

Across the field, the tracker watched as Rat savages began slinking out of the trees again, this time following the wizards who were quickly clearing a path through the flames. And then he was running along the tree-line, yelling at those who survived to flee toward the city.

Terion gained the top of the wall along with Donaran and they could only watch as the huge blue dragon disappeared southward. Behind them and below, frantic orders were being shouted amid the screams of the dying. In that single assault, the dragon had obliterated half of the city's southern defensive wall.

"Perhaps it is time to meet my sister," came a female voice as Siranschae climbed up to stand beside them, her dark face grim.

"No," he said quietly. "She will not return, at least not in her true form. It would be too risky. The few ballistae are now manned and wizards are taking their places on the walls where they can. She attacked because she knew she could surprise us. She also knows that the surprise is lost now."

"Not that it makes any difference," the woman countered, looking around. "The wall is breached. She did a fine job destroying any hope we might have had."

"There never really was any hope," Terion said truthfully. "We could never have held Taer Blys in the end. Our only chance was to harass them a bit and perhaps force Draven to spend more time here preparing for his march on Nykiva."

"That's going to prove problematic now," she countered.

"You should flee," Donaran broke his silence as he fingered the hilt of his huge curved sword. "All of you. With the outer wall breached, we cannot mount any type of resistance, nor can we hold the escape tunnels for very long," he finished, referring to the network of deep underground passages and caves that led from the city and emerged a number of leagues safely to the northeast. Their plans had been simple enough – engage and hold Draven and his minions in Taer Blys for as long as possible and then escape underground, minimizing the risk of them being pursued and attacked in the open.

"He's right," Siranschae agreed, looking at Terion. "Begin the exodus, but keep to the trees and beware the sky when you emerge from the tunnels. Zarandrae's attack has proven to us that Draven has no qualms about turning her loose against mortals in her true form."

"But you will not leave with us," Terion challenged, looking at Donaran.

The Arcai shook his head. "My place is here."

"Even if you defeat Draven in the challenge, what will that gain us? The city is lost."

"I will not run from Draven," the Arcai answered flatly. "If I am successful, you will have the time you need to evacuate your soldiers and the rest of the Taes that will go with you."

"He will not honor the challenge, regardless of the outcome," Terion argued.

"If he cares for anything, Draven cares for his honor,"

Donaran continued. "If I defeat him, his army will hold for the required time."

"Is this the same honor that allows him to murder thousands of innocent mortals—the same mortals he has sworn to protect and guide as an Arcai?"

Donaran's face darkened, but he was silent.

"And if you fall to him?" Terion continued. "What then?"

The Arcai allowed himself to smile sadly at this. "Do not concern yourself with me. I am at peace with myself and my possible fate. But you do not have to die at Draven's hand and you can save many if you do not tarry."

Terion stood silently for a few moments, then nodded bitterly and turned away. In truth, he hated that they had to run before mounting any kind of solid defense. But the Arcai was right. They had no choice. They would have to move quickly once the battle began.

"Soldiers on the southern field!" a yell came from a warrior standing upon one of the few unbroken sections of the wall nearby.

Terion turned back and looked out across the field where they could see a handful of men coming toward them, seeking the safety of what remained of the city walls. Some were running; others were limping or helping wounded comrades along. There were a few dozen at most.

"Cavanah's men," Donaran said, his voice still quiet.

They watched as the first wave of Rat savages streamed out of the forest and toward the doomed city, shouting as they came on.

"Are all retreat plans in readiness?" Terion asked as a runner dashed up to him, ready for orders.

"Yes mi' lord," the young soldier answered breathlessly. "Those that have not already left are prepared."

"Send word to all leaders to begin evacuating immediately if they plan to leave," he said.

"Yes, mi'lord," the runner said again and then hurried off.

A shout from below caught his attention and he looked down to see a battered Cavanah looking up at them. "If you think I'm going to climb up there after runnin' my arse off, you're crazy," he called up loudly, breathing heavily.

Terion managed a grim smile and quickly descended, where he clasped hands with his old friend. "I'm glad to see you alive," he said warmly.

"It almost didn't happen," the big tracker replied angrily.

"Zarandrae?"

"The field trap worked flawlessly," Cavanah explained. "We inflicted heavy casualties on the Rats, but then that blasted dragon showed up. She killed hundreds of my men, Terion. It only took a few seconds."

"She did the same to the walls of Taer Blys, as you can see," he added sadly. "It seems we badly underestimated Draven and what tactics he would employ."

At that moment, the Gol'Athi war drums began to beat in the distance, signaling their coming and that of their general.

"Where are the little ones?" Cavanah asked.

"Aylan is on the wall," Terion replied with a sigh. "He will not be left out of the fight."

"As long as he knows when to run," Cavanah said gruffly. "What about the girl?"

"Arianna should be in the tunnels already," Terion replied, placing a hand on his friend's shoulder. "You should join her. You've done all that you can do at the moment."

"Bah," Cavanah snorted. "I've no intention of leaving just when things are about to get good. I'll find Aylan and make sure he's got someone watchin' his backside while he plays with fire."

"Why does that not surprise me?" Terion said with a smile. "Fight where you fight best, my friend. I'll see you in the tunnels later."

With a grunt, Cavanah hurried off and Terion rejoined Donaran. Below them, the Rat warriors were grouping themselves just out of bowshot, preparing for their first charge. Even as they did, the first lines of the Gol army appeared on the road behind them, marching forward to the beat of a thousand war drums, their armor and weapons gleaming in the sunlight. Thousands and thousands strong, they began to spread out off the main road and into the fields, separating into ordered columns and battalions behind the milling Rat line.

"It is time," Donaran said quietly as he turned to descend from the battlement.

Terion followed, leaving Siranschae alone on the wall. She knew her part in the battle and it was one that Terion knew she could not win. As he took the field, he silently prayed for her safety.

Nearly an hour later, as Gols were still moving into position and the Rats were working themselves into a killing frenzy, the drums suddenly stopped. Immediately, the air was split by a terrifying roar and, amid the cracking of tree trunks, the great blue dragon Zarandrae lumbered out of the forest, pushing trees aside as if they were matchsticks. She was far enough away that she was safe from ballistae and wizard spells, but she was no less imposing to the defenders of Taer Blys. Zarandrae roared again, stretching her great head forward, her jaws arcing wide, her huge teeth bared for all to see.

This time, there was an answering roar and the massive blue's sister, Siranschae, rose to hover over the gates of Taer Blys. Both dragons locked eyes, but maintained their distance. This battle, after all, was not about them.

At least not yet.

As the two dragons stared at each other, Draven finally emerged from the shadows of the distant trees. The Gol'Athi war drummers took up a furious cadence as the half-god walked toward the southern gates of Taer Blys, while the Rats chanted his name.

Draven walked slowly and confidently, the savages parting like water to allow him through. Daring to stride within bowshot of what remained of the city walls, he came to a spot between his still assembling army and the beleaguered defenders. Raising his massive sword in the air, he prepared to speak, but was suddenly interrupted by another roar from Siranschae.

The furious dragon landed her large bulk before the city gates, glaring at the Arcai with eyes that burned with hatred. "You risk much in waging open warfare on the race of man, Draven," the bronze dragon hissed, drawing her head back as if to strike at him.

"And you risk much more in siding with them," the Arcai scoffed, not concerned with facing down a dragon, as he knew the bronze would not attack him. "Now, where is your master, Siranschae? Has he run off and deserted you?"

Siranschae roared again in fury, but the deep voice of Donaran boomed out. "Draven!" Donaran shouted as he walked out from the gates of the city. He was dressed in plain leather leggings and high-topped leather boots along with his magical bracers, but his powerfully muscled chest was bare and he wore no helm. His huge, gleaming curved scimitar was held easily in his right hand and in his left, he held a long, slender dagger. "Your battle is with me!"

"My battle is with man! You are but a minor pawn in a bigger game, Donaran, and at the moment, you are in my way."

"I stand for Taer Blys," Donaran said evenly.

"You stand as their champion?" Draven asked smugly.

"I do."

Draven threw back his head and laughed before fastening a cold gaze upon his immortal brother. "Then consider yourself challenged, Donaran. Prepare for death."

"What will be, will be," Donaran answered calmly. "Twice you have beaten me in battle and my honor has been marked. But today, my brother, I shall regain that which I have lost."

"There is no greater honor than dying in battle," Draven answered with a sneer, bringing Dread around into a ready position.

"Whatever my fate," Donaran answered, swinging Whistler easily in his hand, "I am at peace at last."

With simultaneous shouts, both warriors charged forward, their swords crashing together in a shower of sparks. At the same time, Zarandrae leapt into the air with a roar of her own. Siranschae answered, meeting her dragon sister high above the battlefield. Teeth, claws, and swords rang against each other.

Two battles to the death had begun.

Chapter 26

Donaran backpedaled frantically from Draven's furious onslaught, parrying and dodging blows from the huge warrior's great sword. But a downward parry and a quick thrust of his scimitar suddenly had the bigger Arcai back on his heels, giving Donaran a small opening to immediately launch his own offensive.

Draven stepped to the side, allowing Donaran's deadly sword to thrust past him. His own blade was out of position, though, so Draven did the next best thing. He lashed out with his fist, catching Donaran in the side of the head and driving him sideways.

Bright flashes of light exploded behind Donaran's eyes, but he allowed his momentum to carry him away from Draven. Silently cursing his foolishness for falling into a two-dimensional fight, he brought his sword back into the ready position. With another shower of sparks, Draven's sword crashed into it, sending a ringing jolt down Donaran's arm. But the smaller Arcai shoved the attack to the side and spun low, slashing with his dagger. Draven skittered backwards, only just escaping from having his thigh opened to the bone.

Above them, the two great dragons circled and clashed, tearing with teeth and claws and clubbing with wings and tails. If the fight below was fast-paced, the battle above was truly dizzying. While neither dragon had the opportunity to use their terrible breath weapons, few things could penetrate a dragon's hide except for the teeth and claws of another dragon and both had opened up wounds on the other. Zarandrae, much bigger and stronger than her smaller bronze sister, was trying to work into a position to use her powerful tail to maximum effect. But the smaller and more agile Siranschae worked herself in closer to the great blue, accepting the teeth and claws instead, where she could return similar damage. Siranschae knew she could not defeat

Zarandrae. She had only joined in the battle to keep the bigger blue busy, praying that her companion would emerge victorious on the field below. If Donaran could land the killing blow, she would suddenly have the advantage and might be able to defeat Zarandrae when the weakness claimed her. If Donaran lost, however, it would not matter.

Back on the ground, Donaran turned inside of a particularly vicious thrust and swung Whistler around in a tight arc. Draven brought his bracer-protected forearm down to block, but Donaran shifted his body at the last moment, the blade slashing higher and catching Draven across his unprotected bicep. It was only a minor cut, but it drew first blood and a rousing shout from the city defenders, as both men once more moved back into their ready stances.

"Well played, my brother," Draven said with a smile as he brought Dread back around, tapping the hilt to his forehead in a quick salute to his opponent. "But you'll have to do better than that to defeat me," he said even as he launched another furious attack.

Donaran backed up, allowing the deadly sword to whistle past him, then darted in for a sure strike as Draven over-extended on the blow. He realized too late that he had taken the bait, for Draven continued on, allowing his momentum to bring him full circle, adding even more velocity behind the follow-up strike. Too late to back out, Donaran threw himself forward on the ground as Draven's sword sliced through the air above him, missing him by mere inches. But Donaran was on the ground and now at a serious disadvantage. He rolled over, bringing his sword up, only to have it swatted aside by Dread. Another desperate roll barely took him out of the way as the great sword plunged into the ground near his head. As Draven brought his weapon crashing down a second time, Donaran drove his dagger deeply into Draven's heavily muscled thigh. The blow was enough to throw the sword strike off by a bit, but not quite enough. The big blade tore deeply into Donaran's shoulder, even as Draven staggered backwards, the dagger protruding from his leg.

Donaran quickly rolled to his feet and immediately switched his sword to his other hand. The wound to his shoulder was serious, blood already running down his arm and back. He knew he was in trouble and the grin on Draven's face confirmed it.

"You cannot defeat me, Donaran," the huge Arcai said easily, reaching down and slowly pulling the long dagger from his wounded leg. With a smirk, he tossed the bloody blade to the ground before him.

Again Donaran drove in, fueled by the knowledge that his only way of defeating Draven was to take him by surprise. Draven turned sideways, accepting a minor nick across his midsection in return for being able to shove Donaran away, knocking him off balance again. He dropped his sword and pressed in, appearing to go after Donaran's legs and in doing so, presenting an irresistible opening at his head. In a panic, Donaran took it, swinging high and hard.

But Draven dropped easily to a crouch, then leapt towards Donaran, bringing his sword up hard. Donaran's eyes went wide as the deadly blade sheared through leather, flesh, and bone, opening him up from groin to throat. The Arcai knew he was dead, but for a single brief moment, he wondered why he did not feel anything. Then he sank to his knees and the light disappeared from his eyes. A moment later, his body slumped forward. Donaran was dead.

Draven stood for a moment, staring down at the body of his Arcai brother. Then he smiled and looked skyward even as Siranschae let out a terrible roar of distress.

The death of an Arcai had serious physical repercussions on his or her dragon companion, and at the point of the death of her companion, Siranschae knew she was finished. Immediately weakened by the loss of her bond with Donaran, the bronze dragon began to fall from the sky, her wings unable to keep her airborne. Zarandrae launched her final attack, slamming her tail into Siranschae's chest with the sound of thunder and shattering bones. The force of the blow sent the bronze dragon spinning through the air where she crashed into the town hall of Taer Blys, bringing the large stone and wood structure down on top of her in a roaring cloud of debris and dust. As the building collapsed around her, the last thing she saw was Zarandrae let loose with her devastating lightning breath.

Then she knew no more.

On the field, Draven watched the end of Siranschae in satisfaction and then raised his bloody sword high in the air. Immediately, the U'Raati warriors broke into a primal war cry even as the drums of the Gol'Athi split the air once again. "Slay them all!" the victorious Arcai screamed above the sudden roar of his army.

They needed no urging.

Terion looked at the terrible devastation where Siranschae had met her end. He could see no sign of her in the rubble. Fighting back the tears, he turned back to the battlefield. The Rats were already swarming toward the city's defensive positions and the Gols were marching forward. Shouts and screams went up from the field as the first combat was joined and bows began to hum from what remained of the city walls. He watched with growing rage as a number of the Rats hurried past Draven and tore apart the remains of Donaran and plundered what was left of his armor and weapons.

No, he thought. He would not allow it to be so easy. Donaran was dead and Siranschae had fallen, but he would ensure that the victory for Draven would be a bitter one indeed. Harnessing his mounting anger, he stalked out onto the battlefield.

Rats came at him from both sides and Terion was almost a blur as he parried and countered, dropping half a dozen savages. As he fought, he realized that Notyet was beside him, his huge sword sending Rats fleeing in terror; those that were not killed outright anyway.

The two warriors fought side by side, inflicting numerous casualties on the enemy, but there were too many and both men soon began to fall back, allowing the Rats to press forward. Behind the savages came Draven, stalking toward them and killing anyone who got in his way. Everywhere he looked, Terion could also see the Gol warriors massing for their charge and he knew they could not stand against them any longer on the open field. He turned and shouted the retreat. "Back to the gates!"

Nearby, Notyet heard his friend's shouted command and worked his way back toward the gate, keeping his enemies at bay with great sweeping arcs of his sword. As the savages pulled back, they began moving aside, opening a path between them. That's when he saw the reason why.

Draven strode toward him, his own huge blade covered in crimson, his cold eyes boring into him, daring the warrior to stand his ground. Notyet accepted the silent challenge and planted his feet firmly.

"You dare stand against me?" Draven growled as he closed the distance, bringing his sword into the ready position. The mute warrior would have surely died, but a flash of light and a small explosion filled the area between the two fighters with a thick, acrid smoke. Instantly, Terion was beside his friend, grabbing him urgently by the arm.

"Now is not the time, my friend," he said quickly. "We must protect those fleeing for the tunnels."

Notyet's eyes blazed angrily but he quickly realized it would be foolish to face the Arcai surrounded by enemy warriors. So he turned with Terion and the two began running back toward the gate with the rest of the survivors.

Behind them, Draven stalked through the blinding smoke as Rat warriors closed back in around him. Robbed of his fight with the big warrior, the Arcai began angrily putting his sword to work again on the few surviving defenders that still remained in his area, too wounded to flee.

From his perch atop part of the city wall, Aylan again surveyed the battlefield. While the ballistae and the more powerful remaining wizards kept the great blue dragon away, he concentrated his magic on the field below. He was drained both physically and mentally, but he stretched forth his hand again and launched another deadly lightning bolt at a group of Rat warriors. The bolt struck the lead Rat, fairly blowing the savage apart before the electrical current jumped and struck down several others. The rest scattered in a panic, trying desperately to get out of the young mage's range.

A few moments later, he heard the gates of the city slam shut as the last of the defenders made their way inside. Not that it would do much good, since Zarandrae had breached the wall in numerous places earlier, but at least it would force the enemy to crawl over broken wood and stone to get behind the walls.

Looking out over the battlefield, he shook his head sadly at the carnage. Hundreds of combatants lay dead and dying. The majority of them were U'Raati warriors, but there were a fair number of city defenders among them. The remaining Rats began swarming over the bloody field, stripping the dead and mutilating the dying. He had never felt so drained and without hope. His spirit had been trampled. His magic was nearly spent; his last spell had nearly caused him to pass out.

He leaned over, placing his hands on his knees.

"You okay, boy?" Cavanah asked gruffly from his perch several feet down the wall. He had a bow in his hand and a nearly empty quiver of arrows leaning against the battlement.

"I'll be...fine," Aylan replied between deep breaths, his eyes on the field. He was watching the Gol army far to the rear of the battlefield. But rather than charging the walls, they were beginning to pitch camp. "What are they doing? They have to know we cannot stand against a full attack."

"I don't know," Cavanah answered grimly, nocking an arrow and sighting down another Rat that was too close to the wall. "They have us at a huge disadvantage and Draven knows that," he finished, shooting the enemy soldier dead.

"Yet he does not press the attack," another voice said quietly, causing both to turn and watch as Terion climbed up to stand beside the young mage. He was disheveled and spattered with blood, but little of it was his own and he was mostly unhurt.

"Perhaps we stung him more than he had anticipated," Aylan mused.

"Or perhaps he plans something else."

"I don't suppose we'll have long to wait," Cavanah grumbled. "What about the evacuation?"

"It's underway," Terion replied tiredly. "Our friends are with them. Arianna should be in the tunnels already. Notyet is just plain angry."

"He wants to face Draven, doesn't he?"

"Aye," answered Terion bleakly. "You saw?"

"I did," the big scout replied. "You did right in stopping him. Draven would have cut him to pieces."

"Try telling him that," sighed Terion.

"If I get the chance, I'll gladly tell him what an idiot he is," Cavanah answered. "Then I'll have Aylan put a fireball up his arse."

Terion couldn't help but smile, but it was short-lived as a shout from below got his attention. "General Terion!"

"General?" Cavanah shot him a withering glance.

"Not my doing," Terion sighed and then looked down at a young man dressed in the white robes of a healer. "What is it?"

"Come quickly! It's the dragon," the young man exclaimed.

"Siranschae?" he asked, hope sparking.

"Aye! She's alive!"

Several minutes later, Terion was kneeling beside a makeshift cot in an infirmary, laying his hand gently on the damp forehead of Siranschae. Somehow, she had reverted to her human form. She had staggered out of the wreckage and right into the arms of one of the Tae healers, gravely wounded. Now she lay alert, but broken and dying.

"I'm sorry for your loss," Terion spoke softly to her, wishing there was more that he could do. Elated at the fact that she still lived, he also knew, though, that she would not likely survive the night. Her wounds were internal, ribs crushed from the force of Zarandrae's terrible blows. Blood flecked her lips and her breathing was very shallow. But her eyes were clear and she fought past the pain.

"He died...with honor," she gasped, every word a struggle. Tears welled up in her eyes and she was forced to finally close them. "He is...at peace."

"Can you do anything for her?" Terion asked, gazing up at one of the Taes, an older man in the white robes of a healer.

The old healer shook his wrinkled head. "I'm sorry, Master Terion. Her physical wounds are deep. It would take an empathic healer of great power to heal her now. And there is no one left in Taer Blys that can do that."

"Then make her last moments as comfortable as you can," he replied, climbing to his feet. Turning to Cavanah, he went on. "It is time to leave Taer Blys."

"And the walls?"

"They will be quickly lost," he answered grimly. "Pass the word. Pull them all."

"I'll get the boy," Cavanah said and then turn and left.

Terion paused once more to gaze at the tortured face of Siranschae and then quietly turned and left, the aged healer padding silently behind him.

They had only just gone when a small figure slipped into the darkness of the room and knelt down beside the dying woman. She placed one hand on the woman's forehead and another on her chest. There was a sharp intake of breath and a gasp of pain from the figure as the sheer gravity of the woman's wounds were made known to her. Then, closing her eyes, she settled in and began to work. She had no doubt that it would be a long and desperate struggle.

Chapter 27

"Shayene will not be pleased at the delay," Zarandrae—back in her human form—said quietly as the Gol generals took their leave of the impromptu war meeting in Draven's tent. The Arcai had pulled his generals together to discuss the cataclysmic ending of the dragon fight and its serious repercussions on their plans for a quick end to Taer Blys. Like Ithil Majeer, after the initial onslaught, the battle would have shifted behind the city walls as Shayene opened up a similar portal to allow her growing horde of undead to come through and destroy the inhabitants. Unfortunately, the death of Siranschae had changed all that and Zarandrae had been the cause of it.

"Such are the misfortunes of war, my dear," Draven answered, almost amused at what had transpired.

"She cannot open a gate into another part of the city?"

"She cannot reseed another gate without being here to do it," he answered with a smile. "This gate would have opened in the cellars of the town hall, the very building you sent Siranschae crashing into. It would be rather difficult to do that now that the building no longer exists, my dear."

Zarandrae straightened, her eyebrows furrowed in defiance. "I did not know. And even if I did, it was pure luck that sent her to her death through the walls of that particular building."

"Unluck," corrected Draven. He was obviously enjoying the whole scenario, despite his companion's discomfort.

"I do not understand why you find this amusing. Without the undead attacking from within, it will be a much more difficult battle. Even with the many breaches in the wall, we will incur more losses than we had anticipated."

"We have plenty of Rats to spare," replied the Arcai, placing a reassuring hand on her shoulder. "We will wait until nightfall and unleash them completely. The battle will still be won."

"Attacking at night is reckless, regardless of the outcome, Draven," Zarandrae said, a touch of uncertainty in her voice. "I do not believe Shayene will agree with this."

Draven only chuckled. "Shayene is not here. Besides, we are tasked to take Taer Blys as quickly as possible. A battlefield is ever changing, so a general must be able to adapt quickly and still conquer. Sending the Rats at night will be unexpected. It won't be the undead we had hoped to send against them, but it will be effective enough."

"Until the defenders have cut them all down," Zarandrae countered.

"I have little care what happens to the Rats in any event, my dear," Draven said with a smile. "They will be enough to overrun the city walls and open the way for the Gols to finish our enemies. If they all die in the attempt, so much the better. Regardless, the Taes and their allies will be routed and fleeing before the next dawn."

"And myself?"

"I would rather you stay in human form and safely away from any wizard or weapon that might take you out of the sky with a lucky shot," he said warmly. "Once they are on the run, I will give you leave to hunt them at your leisure. It's a long journey to Nykiva. I doubt many of them will survive with you dogging them the entire way."

"As you wish, my lord," she said with a slight bow of her head.

"Have no fear, Zarandrae. We will be on Nykiva's doorstep by fall. There, we will crush the Doms completely and finish this before the snows come."

"And the other races?"

"They will capitulate," Draven replied evenly. "Or they will die."

On the walls near the main gain, Aylan ignored his nearly overwhelming fatigue and stared down at the campfires of the enemy, thousands of orange flares in the darkening night. He was still only a young mage, but his former master had instructed him deeply regarding the ways of war—what was to be expected and what wasn't. Draven was doing what any competent general would be doing by marshalling his forces and settling them in for the night well away from the city walls. In doing so, they would be fresh in the morning and ready for a full day of fighting, while the beleaguered defenders of the doomed city would have waited out an entire night with no sleep or hope, making them ripe for the picking the following day. Surely, there was nothing odd about what was happening. Why then, were his instincts telling him that something was dreadfully wrong?

"You seem troubled, boy," Cavanah broke the silence as he climbed up broken stone to stand near the young mage and stare out across the battlefield from the wall.

"I certainly have no reason not to be," Aylan replied sourly. "And must you always call me 'boy'?"

The big tracker looked down at the young man and smiled warmly, before patting him on the shoulder. "You keep up with this battle mage shtick and I might have to start calling you something else."

Aylan smiled, but didn't reply. In the years he had known him, Cavanah always gave him a hard time, but Aylan knew that Cavanah's words were spoken out of genuine affection for both him and Arianna. In truth, the big man was fiercely protective of the two "young ones", as he referred to them.

"I reckon you're thinking about what happened in Ithil

Majeer," the big man went on, looking across the field, watching their enemies as they busied themselves with their camp.

"Maybe that's what's bothering me," Aylan agreed. "I heard the stories. I heard about the undead attacking from within the city itself."

"Aye, and Terion has all the soldiers he can spare covering the streets of Taer Blys."

"Do you think it will happen here?"

"Who's to say," Cavanah shrugged. "Right now, I'm more worried about what's going on out there."

"So you sense it, too?"

"Aye."

"Do you think Draven will attack at night?" Aylan asked skeptically. "It would be suicide, if he did."

"Or a calculated risk," Cavanah replied. "I'm certain that Draven doesn't want a prolonged siege of Taer Blys. It's in his best interest to take us down fast and get on his way to Nykiva. If he doesn't hit the capital before winter, he could very easily lose his war."

"Can Nykiva hold out for a winter under siege?"

"Probably easier than an army of Gols that are thousands of miles from their homes. If Nykiva forces a siege, they'll be better for it come spring."

"What about the Rats?"

"Well," Cavanah said with a yawn as he held his own weariness in check. "Ithil Majeer was taken from within by undead coming through a gate linked to the Wraithlands. It's long past dusk and that same help here doesn't appear to be forthcoming. The Rats would make a suitable replacement."

"So they're coming, aren't they."

At that moment, the drums of the Gols began in earnest and the air was cut once more by the primal war screams of Rat savages as they began their charge across the bloody field.

"I guess that answers the question," the young mage sighed, watching them come on.

"Time to go, boy," Cavanah said quietly, herding the young mage off the wall.

A moment later, they disappeared into the darkened streets.

Mindful of the fact that the walls of Taer Blys would be overrun in minutes, Terion took the infirmary steps two at a time. Most of the defenders—his soldiers, comrades, and friends—were already running toward the escape tunnels that would take them deep into the forest where they could regroup and flee toward Nykiva. Sadly, few of the remaining Taes would join them. They would wait for their conquerors. Thousands of them, pledged to ideals that mattered nothing to their killers, would be slaughtered. As badly as Terion wished otherwise, it was beyond him now. He had to concentrate on helping evacuate those that were willing to leave and the wounded that were unable.

That is what brought him up the steps and into the darkened room, where Siranschae lay dying. He doubted if she was even still alive, her wounds being so grave. So he was absolutely stunned to see her propped up on her elbows, looking around in bewilderment. Lying on the floor next to her was the very pale and unmoving body of a young Tae woman.

"Arianna!" he exclaimed in sudden shock, dropping to his knees beside her and gently turning the young girl over. Blood flecked her lips and a thin rivulet of crimson had run out of her mouth. His fingers quickly found her throat and he had to strain to feel the life beating ever so faintly within her. "What happened?" he asked, looking at Siranschae in amazement and confusion. "When I left you here, you were practically dead."

"I... I'm not sure," Siranschae said quietly, wincing in pain. "I was certain I was dying," She paused and looked at the young Tae. Realization flooded her mind. "It was her," she gasped. "She...healed me."

"Healed you? How?" questioned Terion, but the truth suddenly dawned on him and his mouth gaped open in astonishment. Everything about the young girl, her flight from home and her sometimes fierce reluctance to ever return, was finally made clear. "By the gods," he whispered in awe. "She's an empath."

The warrior quickly slipped his arms under the unconscious Tae and then stood up, cradling the young woman close. "Come. We must leave quickly. Are you able to walk?"

Siranschae nodded and climbed to her feet, grimacing as she did so. Because of Arianna, she was alive and standing, but her battered body still had a lot of work to do on its own.

"I'm not surprised that you still hurt," Terion went on, positioning himself so the human-form dragon could use his elbow for support. "Empathic healers are extremely rare and heal by drawing wounds into them and giving the injured a better chance of survival. But it's not instantaneous."

"I am well aware of how an empath heals," Siranschae replied with a painful whisper, tightly closing her eyes as she stood. "However, I did not know that any still lived."

"Few do," he agreed, "and none with great skills in the art. Certainly no one who could have managed this."

"Then it would seem that your wayward girl has kept her talents hidden," Siranschae added through clenched teeth. "An empath such as her would be treasured. Had the elders known of her power, she would have never been allowed to leave the city in the first place."

"So it would seem," Terion agreed, helping the woman take the stairs slowly down to the main level.

"Will she live?"

"I don't know," he answered softly, leading Siranschae carefully out into the streets. "Only time will tell."

Cavanah moved silently between the buildings, keeping to the shadows. All around him, he heard the invading savages hurrying up and down the blood-soaked streets, looking for stragglers and making sure houses and buildings were empty. In those that were not, the Rats were dragging out the survivors and brutally butchering them in the middle of the street. Men, women, and children were perishing under the weapons of the Rats and the streets were red with the blood of innocents.

"I feel so helpless," came a soft and sad whisper off to his right.

"I know how you feel, boy," Cavanah whispered back to the young wizard who was currently cloaked in an invisibility spell and closely following him. "But there's nothing we can do for them. They chose their fate. If we don't want to join them, we need to get to the escape tunnels."

"I know," came Aylan's disembodied whisper as a sudden nearby clash of steel had them pressing against the wall of a house until the skirmish moved away from them. "I just wish we could do something."

"Even if you do all you can, you'll never be able to save everybody that deserves to be saved," Cavanah said as he moved silently into the darkness between two large buildings. "Remember that."

He had taken only a couple steps before he stopped, his gaze hardening as he drew his sword and faced a shadow that had materialized in front of them.

The woman who was suddenly standing before him smiled, her white teeth glinting in the darkness. She stood in a sliver of light that revealed only muted outlines of her features, but what was visible was unmistakable. A metal whip was coiled at her waist and a long bladed dagger was in her hand.

"Well, well, well," Cavanah said guardedly, hoping that the young mage would remain hidden behind him. "Couldn't leave well enough alone, could ya?"

"I don't believe we have been formally introduced yet," she said, her voice low and husky.

"Doesn't matter," Cavanah replied, "because I know who you are. Pity I didn't get a shot at you back in Haven when you attacked my friends."

"I had no quarrel with you there anymore than I do here," she replied. "Providence spared you then. Do not tempt it this time, for I doubt it will be so kind."

"Spare me your threats, witch. What do you want?"

"I wish to speak with your friend," Vendetta answered easily, looking past him and turning the dagger over in her hand. "How we go about accomplishing that will be entirely up to you."

"I don't know what you're talking about," he answered, his own voice low and stern. "Now, unless you have a contract out on me, let me pass."

"And what makes you think I do not?"

"If you do, then make good on it," he snarled, leaping forward and thrusting with his sword. "If you can!"

As Cavanah rushed in, Vendetta skittered quickly backward, her free hand taking her whip from her belt. In a blur of motion, she looped the end around the big man's weapon wrist. Cavanah quickly planted his feet before clamping his fingers around the whip and pulling hard to counter her attack.

Not caught unaware, the assassin immediately released her hold, darting forward as she flung her dagger from her hand. Cavanah turned sideways to avoid it, but the throw was off to the right and would not have hit him anyway. Too late, he realized that he was not her intended target and the startled gasp of pain behind him confirmed his fears. Aylan began to materialize as he slumped against the wall, his invisibility spell failing, her dagger protruding from his shoulder.

In the next moment, the woman was on Cavanah, hands striking him like snakes. Her first shot caught him on the inside of his wrist, driving his sword arm to the side, while her second blow scored a solid punch to his chest. Cavanah staggered backward, the wind driven partially from his lungs. He began to bring his weapon back around, but again she was there, her booted heel connecting with his stomach. He struggled to retain his balance, but she came forward, hands and feet striking him at will.

Blow after blow caught him in the face and head and he found himself slipping to his knees in a hazy fog. He was vaguely aware of his sword being taken from his hand and hardly even felt the blade slide into his chest, piercing his heart. His last thoughts were of the agonizing sensation of her turning the blade inside him.

Aylan saw the woman withdraw the bloody sword from his friend's chest and toss it to the ground, before stepping forward to kneel down before his own helpless form. His magic was drained, his ability to defend himself gone. Grief overwhelmed him and tears ran down his face as he watched as Cavanah slumped to the ground and breathed his last, his blood staining the street.

"Are you well?" Vendetta asked, wrapping deceptively delicate fingers around the hilt of the dagger in his shoulder. Aylan stiffened as he felt as if his very life was being sucked away by the weapon. Then with a smile, she ripped the blade from his body. The light went out from behind his eyes as the woman's hand closed over the green gem she kept hidden inside her blouse. Putting an arm around the young man, she activated the item's powerful magic. In a moment, both were gone.

Chapter 28

Terion knew they were doomed the moment he felt the approach of the great dragon, Zarandrae, as she bore down on the far end of the Tae city. As she flew overhead, he could feel the power emanating from her, and he had to fight to stay on his feet and not succumb to the fear and hopelessness that washed over him. But she quickly passed beyond them and he realized she intended to destroy the entrance to the long tunnels that led deep into the forests, trapping the rest of the survivors in the city. As if to punctuate that thought, he heard her roar in the distance and in that roar, there was no mistaking the sound of her devastating lightning. The number of people that likely perished in that sudden attack caused him to cringe and he wondered desperately about his friends.

"She destroyed the tunnels," Siranschae said softly, leaning heavily on his shoulder.

Terion nodded, shifting the unconscious Arianna in his arms. Without the tunnels, the chances of him getting his injured friends out of the city were nearly non-existent.

"With the tunnel destroyed, Draven will find it difficult to follow the survivors without going well out of his way to cross the river," he stated, trying to sound positive. "That, at least, we can be grateful for."

"Why do it?"

"Draven's goal was to control Taer Blys and he now does," Terion replied. "His war machine would not be able to use the tunnels anyway, so destroying them causes him no issues, since his armies will have to cross the river far to the north. However, Zarandrae will have no such problem."

"She will pursue them."

"Most likely," he said somberly. "Without help, she can destroy everyone before they even get halfway to Nykiva."

A movement in the darkness brought Terion to a halt and he positioned himself in front of Siranschae, holding Arianna close. A moment later, the huge form of Notyet stepped out of the gloom. The man's blood-streaked features were grim as he walked slowly forward. In his arms, he bore the body of an old friend.

"How?" Terion whispered, his eyes brimming with tears. He couldn't believe it.

Notyet slowly lowered Cavanah to the ground. His face was hard and Terion had never seen his friend so angry. *It was the witch*, he signed rapidly. *I arrived too late to help.*

"And Aylan?" Terion asked, expecting the worst. He knew Cavanah had gone to fetch the youngster from the wall.

Taken, Notyet shook his head. *I don't know where.*

"Better her than taken by the savages," Siranschae offered. "Aylan is not dead."

"How do you know?"

"It is not in her nature. She took him for a reason."

"To do what?"

"To get to you," she answered, gripping his arm. "At the moment, though, there is nothing we can do for him. We must get out of the city while we still can."

Terion looked from her to the big warrior, knowing she was right. "We'll have to move quickly," he said softly, nodding his head toward Cavanah's body. "We will not be able to take his body with us."

I will not leave him in the street.

"No, we won't," Terion agreed. "The house across the street is open. Take him in and lay him on one of the beds. But be quick. We're not safe here."

With a scowl, Notyet effortlessly scooped Cavanah's body into his massive arms and hurried across the street. He was gone for several long minutes before finally emerging. He walked back across the street to Terion. *It is as he would want it to be*, he signed.

"We will avenge him, my friend," Terion said. "But for now, let's find a way to escape the city."

Nodding, Notyet pulled out his great sword and took the lead. Ducking in and out of alleys and buildings, they began their slow trek through the fallen city.

The Rats found them an hour later.

Notyet shouldered his way through the wooden door and into the warehouse, his bloody blade held out before him. Terion slipped in behind him with Arianna and quickly laid her down on the floor inside. Siranschae slumped down beside her. Terion peered back out into the darkened street as Notyet quietly closed the door to a crack.

They had fought a running battle with the Rats for the past fifteen minutes, with Notyet doing the fighting and Terion desperately trying to keep the injured women safely away from the savages. Moments ago, they had encountered two more Rats in the street. Notyet had quickly cut them both down, but not before one of them had called out to others nearby. That none of their enemies had seen them duck into the warehouse was a miracle.

"We can't stay here," Terion hissed in the darkness. "We are on the eastern edge of the city. If we can get over the wall, we can take shelter in the forest."

Notyet motioned to the door. Terion peeked through the crack and watched as several Rats appeared at the far end of the street. They were talking amongst themselves as they searched, but at the moment, they were too far away to hear. Their direction was unmistakable, though. They were coming directly toward the warehouse and as they approached, a larger group rounded the corner and joined them.

Terion grabbed his friend's arm and then pointed deeper into the warehouse. Without a word, the two warriors gathered up their wounded friends and began moving into the darkness. A few minutes later, the sound of the door being kicked open shattered the quiet stillness. Rat voices—a lot of them—could be heard from the front of the building.

"We're trapped," Terion whispered with a sigh, giving his friend a resolute smile. "It's here that we will have to make our stand."

And what of them? Notyet signed, barely seen in the dim moonlight filtering in through dirty windows high above.

Terion looked at Siranschae who was leaning against a crate, her eyes closed and her breathing ragged. Arianna was lying motionless next to her. Neither could defend themselves and he and Notyet would eventually fall to the superior numbers of their enemies. That would leave the two women helpless in the hands of the brutal savages. Terion had never felt more helpless. He knew what would happen to the women when he and Notyet fell. It was not something he was going to let happen.

As the dark thoughts swam in his head, there was a hiss in the darkness above them and then a whispered voice. "There's too many. You gotta run."

Terion and Notyet both looked up in surprise, but all they saw were shadows. "We can't," Terion whispered back. "Our friends are hurt."

More whispering sounded above them and this time it was several voices, small and high-pitched.

"We're not your enemies," Terion ventured quickly, hearing the

Rats drawing closer. They would find them in a matter of minutes. "Can you help us?"

"That depends," the first voice answered immediately in a barely heard whisper.

"On what?"

"On whether we can trust you."

Terion held his hands out. "We have nothing to hide. We fought to defend the city and we lost. Now we are simply trying to save our friends."

There were several uncomfortably long moments of silence before there was finally a rustle of movement overheard. A second later, a worn rope ladder fell to the ground. "Be quick," the voice said again, some urgency in it now. "They're coming."

Notyet grabbed Siranschae and hoisted her over his shoulders while Terion did the same with Arianna. It was a short, but precarious climb but after several tense moments, they slipped into an opening where they dropped to the floor behind another wall. Behind them in the shadows, several small shapes quickly pushed two wooden panels in place, covering the opening.

Their rescuers hurried past them in the gloom with a whispered "follow me." They were led down several darkened hallways and then down a short flight of rickety wooden stairs that opened up into a large room stacked high with old broken furniture and empty battered chests and crates. Their haven might have once been a warehouse, but had been converted over to housing by its current occupants: a small group of children that now stared at the newcomers with eyes that were almost feral.

"How many of you are here?" Terion asked quietly as he gently laid Arianna down on a tattered blanket, generously provided by one of the children. Nearby was a candle, one of several that were flickering in the darkness, and he moved it closer to the young Tae's face. Satisfied that she was still breathing, he finally looked at the boy who had rescued them—a child of perhaps ten years of age.

Above the waist, the boy appeared healthy, even strong—albeit dirty and grimy from a life on the streets. But where his upper body was strong and defined, his legs were withered and useless, crossed in front of him and tied together with filthy pieces of rope and tattered strips of cloth. He supported himself on his strong hands and arms and he moved quickly as he placed himself next to the injured girl.

"It varies," the boy answered with confidence beyond his young age. "Right now there's about a dozen of us."

Terion shook his head and looked around. He saw children tucked into chests and between broken furnishings, looking out at him with a mixture of fear and curiosity. They had each fashioned a living space of anything they could scrounge. "Where do you all come from?" he asked.

"Where do any street rats come from? Parents sometimes don't care. Other parents, like mine, sometimes wind up dead," he went on and, before the obvious question could be asked, he explained. "I was born this way."

Terion nodded with a small smile, but allowed the boy to continue.

"I was an only child and my mother took good care of me after my father passed on. But a couple years ago, my mother took ill and none of the healers could help," he sighed wistfully and looked away, as if seeing into his past. "Imagine living in a city full of healers and none had the skills to save her. So she died and before I knew it, I was on the street."

"You've done well to survive as you have," Terion said softly. He was well aware of the plight of lost and forgotten children in cities all over the land, even in one as peaceful as Taer Blys. "What's your name?"

"My given name is Anthony", the boy said, sticking out a strong and calloused hand, which Terion clasped firmly. "Everyone just calls me Toad."

"Toad?" Terion asked, managing to grin despite their predicament. "What kind of name is that?"

"I got it from my parents when I was very young, probably because I hop around on my hands to get where I'm going." As if to demonstrate, he took off across the floor, hopping along at an impressive pace. A moment later, he had swung himself up on top of the battered cabinet that Terion was leaning against. "I do alright," he finished with a grin.

"Well, Master Toad, we are deeply indebted to you," he said with a smile. "My name is Terion and our injured friends are Arianna and Siranschae. My large friend here is called Notyet."

"Why do they call him Notyet?"

"Notyet doesn't have a name, at least the way he tells it," Terion explained, throwing a wink at his friend who was clearly not amused. "Before he was born, his father kept asking his mother if she had picked out a name for him – or her, depending on what the gods blessed them with. His mother kept telling him 'not yet.' When he was finally born, his father asked again and his mother, having endured a particularly tiresome and painful delivery, shouted 'Not yet!' And that's what he's been called ever since."

"Really?" Anthony asked doubtfully.

"Really."

Notyet quickly flashed his fingers, calling Terion a particularly nasty name, before turning away to check on the wounded.

"Story aside," Terion said, his smile disappearing. "you have our thanks. Without your help, we would have been killed."

"The night's still young," another child spoke up, a bigger boy of about twelve. He stepped into the light of the candle and looked at Terion with distrust. "How grateful are you?" he asked suspiciously, an odd gleam in his eye. He appeared to be the oldest street orphan in the group and was certainly bigger and stronger than the rest of them, even if Anthony seemed to be their leader.

"What do you mean?" Terion asked.

"I reckon you've got some coins on you, right?" the boy continued, edging closer, his gaze darting back and forth between the companions.

"What we have amounts to very little," Terion admitted calmly.

The boy crossed his arms and puffed out his chest in an effort to look impressive. "Then maybe we should throw you back out on the street!"

"That's enough, Rubara," Anthony snapped angrily. "I know they're bigs, but I let them in because they were in trouble; same reason I let you in last month."

That seemed to deflate the boy and he crawled back into a huge broken chest, where he curled up on a pile of dirty blankets and tattered clothes and silently glared at the newcomers.

"Don't pay him any mind," Anthony said almost sadly. "We don't have a lot of contact with anyone other than other children and bigs aren't really that well-liked anyway. Ru hates bigs the most."

"Why?" Terion asked.

"I don't know for sure," Anthony answered thoughtfully. "Ru doesn't say much about his past or why he's on the street. But if you ask me, I think it's more because he's soon going to be a big himself and he knows he'll have to leave."

"Will you force him to leave?"

"No. He'll leave because he'll decide to. Bigs don't need other children."

Terion knelt down and looked at the bigger boy. "Look, Ru," he said gently. "We're not here to hurt you and we really are grateful for your help. But the city has fallen and enemy soldiers are in the streets looking for survivors."

"We'll get away," Ru snapped back.

"Not from these people," Terion shook his head. "They will find you." He stood up and looked around at the children. There were twelve that he could see, some as young as four or five, but none older than Rubara. He fought the desperation that again tried to seize him, thinking what would happen to them when the Rats discovered them. "They will find all of you."

"But what can we do?" Anthony asked. "This is our home. We have nowhere else to go."

"You will have to leave the city."

"All of us?"

Terion nodded, looking at Notyet, who's face remained grim as he knelt over Siranschae. "All of us."

The big warrior looked up and his fingers flashed. *We have two injured friends, Terion. Adding a bunch of defenseless children is going to make it impossible.*

And yet, we cannot leave them, Terion signed back.

No, we cannot.

"What are you doing?" Anthony asked, having watched the exchange closely.

"Talking," Terion answered. "Notyet doesn't speak with his voice. He speaks with his hands."

"And you can understand him?" Anthony asked, truly spellbound.

"I can," he nodded.

"Will you teach me?"

Terion smiled and tousled the youngster's hair. "Let's get out of Taer Blys first and then we can talk about teaching you how to sign."

"Fair enough," Anthony bubbled. "When should we leave?"

"As soon as we figure out the best way to get everyone out of here without being seen."

"Oh, that's easy," the boy replied. "We'll go out through the tunnels."

"The tunnels have been destroyed," Terion said grimly.

"Not ours."

"Yours?"

"We use the sewers to get around," the boy explained. "Easier to get away if we have to steal food."

"The sewers?" Terion asked, starting to smile. "What a brilliant idea, my little friend."

"There's a cistern in the next room," Anthony continued happily. "It's a bit of a drop, but we can take it out past the walls."

"Excellent," Terion smiled. "We should leave immediately, while it's still dark. Round up your friends, Anthony. Everyone must go with us."

The young lad scampered off to join the other children, talking quietly and excitedly about the grand adventure they were all going to depart on.

This will still be dangerous, Notyet signed.

"Immensely," Terion answered with voice. "That's why we need to leave immediately. If we wait and let Draven fully occupy the city, we'll have less of a chance to flee. There is also Arianna and Siranschae to consider. They need healers and the only ones left are with the refugees."

Less than ten minutes later, the two warriors had constructed a litter to carry Arianna once they had broken clear of the city. Siranschae was exhausted, but refused to be carried. With the little group of refugees ready to leave—only Rubara had needed to be convinced—Anthony led them through another long hall that opened up into a small stone-walled room. There was a hole in the center of the floor and they could hear the trickle of water echoing up through the darkness. A worn rope was tied off to one of four iron stanchions imbedded into the wall and it dropped into the blackness of the hole.

Anthony hopped over to the edge and peered in, then turned his head away as he wrinkled his nose in disgust. "It's not too far down but it's not the nicest smelling place in the city."

"Sewers never are," Terion said as he took hold of the rope and pulled hard to test that it was securely tied. "How long will it take to reach the outskirts?" he asked, swinging himself out over the hole and quickly beginning to descend.

"Maybe an hour or so; more if we take a wrong turn," the young boy answered.

Terion reached the bottom and peered up. "I cannot see anything."

"Look to your left and you'll see a small break in the wall," Anthony answered. "Inside, there should be a couple of pitch-covered torches and a flint."

Terion ducked away and a moment later, they heard him call out, "Found them." There was the sound of flint on steel and a torch flared to life. "You've been on more than a few underground adventures, haven't you?"

"Not much else to do," Anthony replied as he grabbed the rope and prepared to descend. "But it's hard for me to hold the torch, so I usually just travel in the dark."

"You use no light?" Siranschae asked weakly.

"Not unless I'm with someone else."

"How do you find your way, then?"

"I just do," he shrugged and quickly slipped into the hole.

One by one, they climbed down into the sewer, with Notyet helping the youngest and the wounded. After they were all beneath the city, they moved as one into the tunnels, following the young boy as he led them unerringly to safety.

An hour later, as they rested in a thick stand of trees a few hundred feet away from the sewer entrance, Terion stood apart on a small rise, sorting through the emotions he had held in check during their desperate escape. They had escaped, yes, but at what cost? Cavanah was dead and Aylan was a missing, likely a prisoner. How many more would they lose?

Notyet laid a huge hand on Terion's shoulder, knowing what the man was going through. "I have lost friends before," Terion replied quietly to the unspoken question. "But it does not make this any easier."

Notyet tapped him on the shoulder and then signed. *Cavanah died in battle. That is the best that any of us can hope for.*

Terion nodded. "Perhaps. But I wonder if he would have rather died in front of a roaring hearth with a plate full of roast mutton and a tankard of mead."

He would have preferred that, signed Notyet. *But he died defending a friend. There is no greater honor.*

"And his death will not go unpunished," Terion said, his voice suddenly hardening.

Are you going after the witch?

"I see no need to chase her. She will certainly come after me again and this time, she will have a bargaining chip."

She will use Aylan?

"Without a doubt."

What if you find her first?

"We have a duty to get these children to safety," he said, shaking his head. "Besides, I have a feeling she will find us long before we have the chance to seek her out ourselves."

Then we should get back on the road.

"Agreed."

Now comes the hard part.

"Aye," Terion said softly, looking to the east and toward Nykiva. Behind him, Taer Blys burned.

They would catch up to the rest of the refuges three days later.

Chapter 29

As morning dawned the next day, Aylan crawled slowly along the sandy floor of the cave, almost out of his mind with pain and despair, his body battered and his wounds exploited to new and previously unforeseen levels of agony. Predictably, the assassin's whip cracked again, opening up another gash on his already-savaged back and he rolled over, moaning in anguish. Forcing open his one good eye – his other having quickly swollen shut after a vicious snap of the assassin's whip across his cheekbone – he fixed the Vi'Raaji woman with a pitiable stare.

"Please," he moaned. "No more! I will tell you what you wish to know!"

Vendetta slowly coiled the fine chain links of the whip and hung it on the silvery belt that encircled her slim waist. "I never doubted that you would," she purred, kneeling down before him and placing a hand on the side of his battered face and brushing away some of the bloody sand that was sticking to it. She was actually rather surprised. She had been torturing the young mage for several hours and he had held out for quite some time before breaking. "If it is any consolation, stronger men than you have succumbed much quicker. You do yourself proud."

"Just promise to kill me quickly," Aylan croaked, coughing up blood as he spoke.

"And why should I kill you?" she teased, slipping her fingers into the top of her boot and withdrawing a small flask of liquid. She had taken him to the precipice. It was time to bring him back. "If I had a reason to do so, I would have killed you quite some time ago." She unstoppered the flask and held it up to his lips. "Drink this. It will help with the pain and begin healing your wounds. But I caution you. Cross me once and I will deliver thrice that which you have already suffered."

"I give you...my word," he gasped.

Finally, the beautiful witch poured a swallow of the liquid into his parched mouth.

The effect was immediate. Aylan sat up straight, his eyes wide and watering as the fiery brew went down his throat. He started coughing and sputtering and would have screamed if he had the air.

Vendetta sat back on her heels and watched with a smile. "Few people can take a shot of that and keep a straight face. Give it a few minutes and you will begin to feel better. Then we will talk."

The young man did indeed feel better as the power of the strange drink coursed through him. "What was that stuff?" he asked breathlessly.

"Velauri," she replied. "It's a healing draught that works on all but the deadliest of wounds."

"Why did you give it to me?" he asked, eyeing her suspiciously. As he did, he realized that his injured eye was beginning to open up as the swelling was absorbed by the healing properties of the potion.

The beautiful assassin hopped up on a stony outcropping of the cave wall and reclined into a comfortable position. Her black silken skirt slid off her leg, revealing itself to the young man. Whether by accident or design, Aylan could not tell, but it had the effect of raising some uncomfortable feelings deep within him.

"I have no intention of killing you, providing you cooperate with me. I do not intend any ill will toward your friend, either, short of capturing him and turning him over to my employer. What happens after that is not my concern."

"Who is your employer?" Aylan dared to ask, trying hard to keep his eyes locked on her face.

"Who I accept contracts from is my own business," she

answered, "and you would be wise to understand that I will ask the questions here."

Aylan nodded his head quickly. "I understand, but may I ask you one more?"

"Besides that one?" she replied sarcastically and then smiled. "Ask your question and I will answer if I feel like it."

"If you don't intend to kill me, what are you planning on doing with me? You did kill Cavanah," he pointed out bitterly, fighting back the sudden pang of grief.

"Your friend died because he saw fit to challenge me," she said indifferently, as if making a comment about the weather. "Had he stood aside as I asked, I would have spared him, for there was nothing to gain by killing him. As for you, as long as you cooperate and answer my questions truthfully, I will let you live and just use you as an asset to complete my contract. Once that contract is fulfilled, you will go free."

"You wish to use me in hopes of trapping Terion," Aylan said coldly.

"I do indeed," she answered. "However, I can just as easily accomplish the same thing with you dead. And I can also promise you that death would be a long time coming for you."

"Very well," he said quietly after a few moments. "What are your questions?"

"Simple ones, really. I desire to know what Terion knows."

"Hard to say. I've only been with him a bit more than a year and there's much that I am not privy to."

"Yes, but what does he know about what's happening around us today?" she pressed calmly. "More importantly, who exactly is seeking his capture? One would be a fool not to believe they were intertwined."

"You do not know?" the young man asked, one eyebrow rising

in surprise. The question shocked him and he realized that she was quite likely just as much a pawn in this game as Terion was. He wondered if he would be able to use that to his advantage.

"I would not ask the question if I knew," she answered slyly. "Or perhaps I do know and am merely gauging the truthfulness of your answers."

"I honestly don't know who is after him," Aylan answered.
"Why is it that you do not know?"

"I work through channels," she replied evenly with a shrug of her shoulders. "There are many layers to operations as delicate as this one. Killing him would be one thing, accomplished simply enough, but capturing a fighter as skilled as Terion is not something that is done easily. Or cheaply, I might add."

"Why do you think that I know who is pursuing him?"

"Because your little companionship sought out an Arcai, an Arcai who is now dead on the fields before Taer Blys. I wish to know the connection between this and Draven, particularly since Draven is behind the current war. Draven wouldn't busy himself with a mortal that posed no threat to his plans."

"Maybe it has something to do with Terion's dreams?"

"And what dreams are those?" she asked, truly intrigued. Dreams held a special meaning in her life, too, and she wondered if Terion's were as dark as hers.

Understanding that even if he said too much, there was no going back now, Aylan told her everything that he knew of Terion's dreams and how they were driving him. He spoke at length of how the dreams always ended with the mysterious sorceress urging him to join her and Terion's thoughts that they were somehow related to what was happening with Draven.

After he had completed his tale, Vendetta leaned back against the wall and was silent for some time as she considered what the young mage had shared. Aylan had to consciously keep his gaze focused on the far wall of the cave in order to ignore the alluring profile she cut. Whether it was a result of the potion she had given him, he could not be certain, but he found his gaze being drawn to her and it was enough to unnerve him.

"So, does Terion know who this sorceress in his dreams is?" Vendetta finally asked, wondering if he knew what she was beginning to suspect.

"I don't know," Aylan replied. "If he does, he has not openly shared it."

"What about you? Do you believe in the providence of dreams?"

"I suppose so," he replied. "I understand that in some cases, they can actually be prophetic."

"Is this the case with Terion?"

"I have no reason not to believe him, if that's what you are asking me."

"Perhaps this war is not about Draven," Vendetta stated. "Perhaps there is more to this war than what anyone believes."

"I don't understand," Aylan said, shaking his head in confusion.

"What do you know about the Arcai?" she asked, changing direction.

"What most people know, I guess," he answered, trying to keep up. "An immortal brother and sister for each of the eight gods, sworn to an oath of non-interference."

"A brother and a sister…"

Aylan's eyes immediately grew wide and he stared at the witch in complete fascination as her meaning became clear to him.

"It makes sense, does it not?" she smiled.

"The sorceress in Terion's dreams," he breathed. "It's Draven's sister, Shayene!"

"It would seem to be," she went on. "But even if that's the case, another Arcai involved in the affairs of man is rather difficult to believe, don't you think? What would even a single Arcai hope to benefit from waging this war, let alone two of them?

"Perhaps the Arcai seek to supplant the gods themselves," the assassin continued, talking more to herself now. "Conquering mankind would give them no end of followers and as they are already demigods, they would be uniquely positioned for just such a coupe."

Aylan stared at her in open amazement and she did not miss the meaning behind his startled surprise.

"I trust that is not something anyone has yet considered."

Aylan shook his head slowly.

"Consider what you know of the Arcai," she said. "An Arcai is but an infant god with the potential to become as powerful as his or her godly parent. Perhaps Draven and Shayene have discovered how to ascend to the heavens and replace the current pantheon."

Aylan nodded his head in amazement. He wondered if Vendetta would now abandon her contract, if only to better portray herself as neutral if a potential godly coup d'état was indeed underway.

"It also explains quite nicely how someone can afford to contract out for such a prize as Terion," she went on. "To an Arcai – particularly an Arcai that intends to become a god – gold would be no object. The question that remains, though, is what Shayene wants with a mere mortal like Terion." She slipped off the rock and knelt down in front of the mage. "Are you well enough to travel?"

Aylan nodded, puzzled. This was not exactly going as he thought it would. "I believe so."

She helped him to his feet with surprising gentleness. "Very well," she said, slipping her hand into her blouse and taking hold of the magical gemstone. "Let us go see if we can find your friend."

"Wait!" he blurted out before she could activate the magic. The woman paused for a moment, her pale blue eyes locking with his. "If you are correct, why go forward with capturing him? Why turn him over to Shayene?"

"Why not?"

"Surely aiding an Arcai who is attempting to overthrow the gods would bring about your annihilation if the Arcai are unsuccessful."

"Would my utter destruction be any less assured if it was brought about by an Arcai that was successful? An Arcai that I had betrayed?"

"I guess I hadn't considered it that way," he agreed.

"If the Arcai are indeed rebelling against their godly parents, we are all of us caught up in a conflict that we cannot escape."

Aylan had no reply to that, finding her words extremely unsettling.

"For now, I will continue on my path," she said softly, her thoughts casting back to a time when a dream-reading vampire had predicted her dire end as well as that of the world. There could be no doubt now. All of this, everything that was happening, was part of it. War was coming and it was not a war of men, but a war of gods. She would have to consider long and hard what side she would end up on.

Tightening her resolve, she willed the magical powers of the Star Stone to life. A moment later, they vanished in a flare of green light.

Chapter 30

The refugees were a week into their desperate journey to Nykiva and many were beginning to feel that they may have escaped pursuit when everything changed in an instant.

It happened as darkness descended and it manifested itself initially as a thunderous lightning bolt blasting down from the clear night sky, slamming into the rear guard of the fleeing survivors. Screams from the terrified and the dying erupted in the night and Terion knew immediately what was happening.

"Send word down the path to take cover in the forest," he snapped quickly to a pair of soldiers that were with him. "It's the dragon. She can see us in the dark but will have greater difficulty if we are hidden by the trees. Move!"

As the soldiers hurried off, he moved toward the wounded, not bothering to draw his sword. It would not matter if he did; he was not facing Rats this time. He had nothing with which to fight the dragon with and he knew it. For a brief moment, he wondered if they would ever catch a break, but he pushed the thought far back in his mind. He had a job to do and people were counting on him.

He had taken command of the rear guard after leading his friends and the small group of abandoned children safely out of Taer Blys, with Anthony's help, of course. They caught up with the surviving refugees a day later and made it their duty to see that as many people made it to Nykiva as possible. So he had organized the precious few soldiers still capable of wielding a weapon, and put them in charge of protecting the rear of the line.

Can we ground her? Notyet signed quickly, matching his strides as he thrust one hand out in order for Terion to see it.

Terion shook his head."I doubt it. We have few wizards

remaining and Aylan..." he swallowed the sudden lump in his throat, unable to finish the thought. "Let's just deal with her," he said and quickly began moving down the line of panicked refugees, urging them to hide while he fought back his apprehension for his friend.

The huge blue dragon banked wide after her initial strafing run and quickly determined the scope of the escaping survivors. Predictably, many of the remaining soldiers had been grouped to protect the last of the refugees, giving her an easy and irresistible target. So, she had struck with the full force of her breath weapon and then continued on in a wide, lazy circle, before preparing to strike again to finish off what little remained of the soldiers.

As she swung back toward her intended victims, she noted that many of the surviving soldiers were still grouped in the area, most of them aiding those that had already fallen. She steepened her dive, opening her mouth wide as she prepared to attack again.

Terion tensed, feeling the huge dragon's presence looming closer. Many of his men were still in the open, wounded and dazed from her attack, even as refugees were dashing into the safety of the trees. As Zarandrae approached, he realized that it didn't matter what he did now. He couldn't leave the injured any more than he could fight off a dragon. There was nowhere to run; no time to escape. With a deep breath, he closed his eyes, ready to accept the end.

Suddenly, behind him, the night was shattered by another terrifying roar and he felt himself thrown to the ground. Zarandrae pulled up sharply, jaws split wide, as another dragon, nearly the same size as her, faced her in the air. Terion looked up in astonishment. The dragon was huge, shining pearl white in the night sky, and astride his back was the figure of a richly robed woman, a staff held high in the air, a blinding light blazing from it. Her voice boomed across the heavens so that all could hear her. "Be gone, Zarandrae!" she ordered in a voice that sounded both soft and powerful." You have no business here!"

The huge blue dragon swung her head back and forth, as if contemplating her next action. One-on-one against the white, she would likely have decided to fight. But with the rider on his back, she would be at an extreme disadvantage. So with her own roar of defiance, she swung away and began winging her way back toward the fallen city, knowing the duo would not pursue her. Not yet, anyway. More importantly, Draven would want to know immediately of this newest entry into the war.

A few minutes later, the white dragon was circling riderless high above the earth keeping watch, while the woman who had been astride his back was now talking earnestly with Terion. She was beautiful beyond humankind and clad in robes of white, ornately marked with runes and symbols trimmed in gold and silver. Her features were flawless, with a thin circlet of silver around her head, keeping her flowing mane of raven hair out of her kindly face. In her left hand was her staff, a gleaming length of polished oak topped with the golden figure of a dragon with wings spread. The figure pulsed with a magical light, seemingly almost alive.

"Events are in motion," she was speaking sorrowfully to his question of why she had intervened, "that will ultimately draw all of us into the fray, whether we wish to be involved or not. Times have changed, Terion. For you and for us." Her eyes were sad, yet determined. An Arcai priestess, the woman was a close friend of Donaran and she had been aware of his death the moment Draven had slain him. It was his death that had thrust her into the conflict.

Terion bowed his head low in the presence of the powerful demigod. "You have our gratitude, Jayadra," he said somberly. "We owe you our lives. We could not have beaten the dragon back ourselves without the aid of Siranschae, and she is still too wounded to fight. Had you not arrived, it would have been a slaughter."

"I sensed Siranschae's presence earlier," the Arcai said hopefully, brightening for a moment. "How did she survive, when Donaran was killed?"

Terion allowed himself to smile briefly, glad to deliver a bit of good news for once. "She fought Zarandrae one-on-one and was gravely wounded when Donaran died. She was found by several healers. But she was in bad shape and we thought we were going to lose her."

"What happened?"

"She was healed by the hand of a truly brave girl who found a way," he answered plainly.

"But how is that possible? Humans have no power to heal dragons."

"This one does. She has capabilities beyond even the greatest of Tae healers, it would seem."

"She is a true empath then?" the woman guessed quickly, her eyes widening in surprise.

"Yes. But her unselfishness in healing Siranschae may have cost her dearly. I'm not sure if she'll survive."

"She was unable to overcome the wounds she took on?" Jayadra asked.

"Actually, she seems to have healed nicely over the past week.

She shows little in the way of outward injuries. But I'm afraid it may have been too much for her mind to overcome."

"Take me to her," Jayadra commanded quickly, "while there is still time."

Terion turned and hurried down the path, the others close behind. Five minutes later, Jayadra knelt down beside the comatose young Tae. The Arcai laid a hand on the girl's forehead and closed her eyes in deep concentration, reaching out to her mind with her own. After a long while, she reopened her eyes and looked up at Terion.

"She's alive," Jayadra said gravely. "But barely. Her body grows stronger, but her spirit is terribly wounded."

"Can she communicate?"

Jayadra shook her head. "Only general feelings. She's in agony and wishes release, but her empathic nature will not allow her to let go as long as her body strengthens."

"Is there any hope?"

Jayadra gazed thoughtfully at the stars far above. Then she brought her gaze back down and locked her eyes on Terion. "There might be a way, but it's an extreme measure and not my place to make such a decision. It's a healing draught of sorts."

"We have some of the most experienced Tae healers in our midst and we've already tried their most powerful potions and salves," he replied sadly. "Nothing has brought her back."

"This is not a medicine that you can make, and even the Tae healers have not the skill to brew it. Only I can. It is powerful beyond anything mortals can create. But because of that, it is also not *for* mortals. I cannot know what effects it will have on her."

"What is it?"

"It is made from dragon's blood," she answered softly. "I am certain my companion, Volsaun, would help, but I must still ask him to willingly aid the girl. If he agrees, I can brew it this very night."

"You mentioned that it's not for mortals," Terion repeated her warning.

"None have ever partaken of it. It is for Arcai only. It's power is beyond the normal frailties of the human body."

"But can it cure her?"

"It should," she answered. "But it is possible that its properties could overpower and kill her. As I said, it is not my place to make such a decision. You, as a mortal and as her friend, must decide if she should partake of it."

Terion ran a hand through his hair as he looked down at the tortured girl. "She willingly offered her life to save another," he finally said quietly. "If there is even the slightest chance you can save her, do it. And if it should ultimately bring about her death, that would still be a far better fate than suffering as she does now."

"As you wish," Jayadra nodded solemnly. "It will take me some time to prepare it. In the meantime, keep your people moving. Draven will not march any time soon and Volsaun will remain overhead to protect against Zarandrae. We will see you safely to Nykiva at the very least, before we decide our next course of action. I will return at dusk tomorrow."

"Once more, I give you our thanks," Terion bowed again. "For everything."

"We all do what we must," she answered softly. "Draven and Zarandrae have declared war not just on man, but on the rest of the Arcai as well. The boundaries are breached and there is no turning back. Before this is done, we will see a new age break on this world."

"Assuming we all survive the transition," Terion remarked darkly, once again thinking back to his dreams and the possible impending convergence.

True to her word, Jayadra returned at dusk the following evening, holding a small crystalline vial of a deep red liquid, the color and consistency of blood. Together with Terion, Notyet, and Siranschae limping along in her human form, the small group of friends bore Arianna high up into the hills, the Arcai feeling it would be better for all to administer the drought far away from the eyes of others.

Once they were secure within the shadows of a tight group of birch trees, they gently laid Arianna down upon the soft earth. Jayadra called forth a soft light that hovered magically overhead and then placed a hand beneath the unconscious girl's neck. Lifting her forward, she opened Arianna's mouth. With a final look at the others, she poured the contents of the small vial into the girl's mouth.

Instantly, Arianna's eyes flew open and she began to scream.

Chapter 31

Deep shadows cloaked the chamber, striving to blot out the pale flickering light emitting from candles scattered throughout the hall. On a dais near the back wall sat a grotesque throne, a macabre creation of magically-bonded skulls and bones of the dead. Reclining upon the ghoulish seat, Shayene stared hard at her brother.

"They were Taes," she snapped angrily after hearing his report of the battle of Taer Blys. "The cost was too high for taking a defenseless city!"

Draven bristled at his sister's rebuke. "They were well-prepared for us, as we knew they would be. Yet the battle was still won."

"At what cost?"

"At whatever cost was needed," the huge warrior answered. "War is forever fluid, my dear sister. We adapted and overcame, even with your pet's involvement."

"Terion is a formidable foe, more so than even he realizes," she said dangerously. "Do not underestimate him, Draven. He may not be a threat to you personally, but he can cause serious problems for us if he is not contained."

"I did not underestimate him," he growled in response. "I simply changed the strategy to deal with him and what happened. Taer Blys is won and my armies are preparing to march toward Nykiva. All is in readiness, as planned."

"Yet many of your soldiers were killed and he still escaped," she snapped.

"I was not under the impression that it was my job to capture him. He was driven away with the rest of the rabble when we took the city and our dead will be replaced with reinforcements from your gateway."

"The First Born are poor soldiers, Draven, and follow no orders. They are savage butchers that you cannot control and are used to break the spirit of our enemies, nothing more."

"I have plenty of my own soldiers to finish the campaign in Nykiva," he bristled.

"You have few Rats remaining and the Gols have taken heavier losses than you can afford. Do not forget that even with supply lines, you army is far from home."

"I have forgotten nothing."

"I would hope not. But as to the matter of Taer Blys, had you not destroyed the town hall, the First Born could have attacked from within as intended and far fewer of your soldiers would have been lost," Shayene continued to argue.

"That was an unfortunate accident. Zarandrae could not have known that you had seeded the portal in the cellar of that building. Even I did not know where the gateway was placed."

"Your companion is overzealous, is she not?"

"My companion is a great warrior," he snapped, leaning closer to his sister. "She fought Siranschae and defeated her while I killed Donaran."

"You seem pleased at your victory," the woman went on smugly.

Draven straightened. "Donaran involved himself in this conflict and I saw fit to eliminate him."

"As you should have," she replied, her voice finally losing its edge. "While I doubt the fool had any aspirations that would have threatened our long-term goals, killing him removes the possibility."

"Then you approve?"

Shayene stood up, her black silk robes whispering. "I do not approve of many things that have transpired. However, war being what it is, the objective was accomplished. We will simply re-evaluate the groundwork for taking Nykiva."

"We have ample time to do so," the huge Arcai agreed.

"When will you march?"

"One month's time," he replied. "There are two battalions of Gol reinforcements on the way and our supply lines are stabilizing. We can reach Nykiva before the snows come. Our enemies will not stop us."

"Then perhaps you should re-examine what your rather determined enemies are doing," a smooth voice interrupted and both Arcai turned as Kraegor the Black, in his black-robed human form, strode into the audience chamber. "There is a good deal of intrigue in this game that you both play and you are foolish to think that your enemies are incapable of disrupting your plans. Taer Blys should have taught you that."

"You have been away for quite some time, my friend. What news do you bring?" Shayene asked, ignoring his pointed comment.

"News of the most interesting kind, my dear," he replied.

Draven bristled inwardly at the reference the dragon bestowed on his sister. He did not trust Kraegor and had little love for any other dragon, save his own companion. But he remained silent.

"Speak then," Shayene said to Kraegor, seating herself back on her throne and focusing her gaze on him. "I am eager to hear your news."

"Very well," Kraegor began, smiling knowingly and anticipating the effect that he knew it would have on both Arcai. He cared nothing for Draven, believing the demigod to be bull-headed and stupid. And yet while he favored his companion fondly, sharing in everything with her, including the bed chambers, he took additional pleasure in knowing that she was not completely infallible. Should she succeed in her grand scheme, that would change, but right now it was a measure of comfort to know that he could still provide her information and guidance. "It seems that Terion has attracted the attention of another," he stated almost nonchalantly.

"Such as?" Shayene quickly pressed, knowing her partner's penchant for drawing discussions out long past the tolerance level of most people.

"A Vi'Raaji witch of some renown," Kraegor answered.

"Who?" demanded Draven.

"I'm certain you know of her," Kraegor chuckled. "Years ago, it was she who prompted you to embark on your ridiculous mission to eradicate your brothers and sisters."

"Vendetta," the huge Arcai seethed, clenching his fist in rage. It was no secret that he hated the Vi'Raaji assassin with every fiber of his being for what he perceived to be an affront to his own fame and warrior skills. She was after all, merely a mortal, but she had been the first to slay an Arcai. To him, it was a personal insult that he had no intention of ever forgiving until the day he slaughtered her on the battlefield. He suddenly felt that day might be drawing close. "How is the witch involved?" he demanded.

"Remarkable creature, that one," the dragon said almost lewdly. "She actually captured Terion in Haven when the man enlisted the aid of Donaran. But Siranschae was able to save him and Vendetta only just escaped."

"Does she still hunt him?" Shayene asked.

"She has yet to fulfill the contract," Kraegor answered. "As you were storming the walls of Taer Blys, she killed one of Terion's companions in the city and took one of his friends hostage. Even now, she plots to use the young mage in an attempt to capture Terion."

"How do you know of this and we do not?" Draven asked

suspiciously, folding his huge arms across his chest.

"Because I have been watching her," Kraegor answered with a wicked grin, his demeanor once again implying that he had a baser objective concerning the witch. "At least I was watching her."

"So, you lost her?" the Arcai warrior asked depreciatively.

"She possesses a great magical item that enables her to teleport without the powers of a wizard. But although she has escaped me for the moment, it is not difficult to imagine that she is preparing to trap Terion in Haven again."

"You said she tried and failed there once already," Draven said. "Why would she use the same tactic?"

"Because Haven is deserted now and most of refugees have already passed through."

"And Terion?"

"He tarries behind with what soldiers he has left, likely to ensure your soldiers don't catch them unaware. He would not expect her to strike again in Haven after having failed there once before."

"Her methods are not my concern," said Shayene with a dismissive wave of her hand. "However, who holds this contract is. By whose order does she hunt him?"

"I must admit that I originally wondered if it might be you that employed her," Kraegor stated plainly. "It would seem I was mistaken in that belief."

"Vendetta is not under my command and I do not wish Terion slain, if it can be helped," she warned. "I trust you will do what you can to ensure that he does not meet death before he has come to me?"

"Had the Vi'Raaji witch wanted him dead, she would have killed him in Haven the first time," Kraegor replied. "No, my dear, she wishes to capture him alive."

"Then find out who holds the contract," Shayene demanded.

"I have an idea who that might be," the dragon said.

"Who?"

"Balgar Mud."

"The leader of the Dom council?" Shayene spat. "You must be joking."

"Hardly, my lady," Kraegor replied. "Balgar leads the council because Keiran was murdered. It would take a supremely skilled assassin to accomplish that."

"And you think Balgar orchestrated it?"

"It's possible," Kraegor shrugged. "At the very least, I'm certain he knows something about it. He was, after all, the one who banished Terion from Nykiva."

"Terion is important to me, to be sure, but alive or dead matters nothing to what we are doing. Still, there is more in the balance here than you can imagine."

Kraegor inclined his head in a slight nod of agreement. "I understand his importance to you on a personal level. However, my counsel would be to simply allow things to progress. If Vendetta is successful in taking him, she will lead us right to whoever holds the contract. We can then act at the appropriate time and as needed, whether it is Balgar or not."

"So be it," Shayene nodded, somewhat mollified for the moment. "I will trust your judgment in this matter. Will there be anything else?"

"Indeed, there is one more thing," Kraegor answered slyly, casting a sideways glance at Draven. "There is another dragon involved in this conflict that may prove bothersome when the time comes to attack Nykiva."

"We are well aware of Jayadra and Volsaun," Draven cut in arrogantly, unwilling to give the dragon any measure of satisfaction.

"Neither is of any consequence."

"You would do well not to underestimate those of your own kind," the black dragon replied with a sudden scowl. "Or our kind."

"What's your point, Kraegor?" Draven asked icily.

"Volsaun is very capable of meeting Zarandrae in battle," Kraegor said slowly as if he was speaking to a young child. "We may be long lived, but we are no more immortal than you are."

"I need no reminders of what constitutes a threat, Kraegor. But I am quite confident that Zarandrae can eliminate those threats," Draven countered.

"Perhaps," Kraegor replied cryptically. "Of course, had she proven herself in the past to be a true dragon-killer, it might be a bit easier for me to accept your claim. As it is, she has killed nothing more than a few pathetic humans in this conflict – hardly a feat deserving of accolades."

"What are you talking about?" Draven demanded. "Zarandrae killed Siranschae in a battle seen by thousands over Taer Blys!"

"Are you certain of that?"

"I watched her die," the big warrior replied angrily.

Kraegor laughed again. "Then you would be surprised to learn that Siranschae travels with Terion, as alive as you or I and growing stronger every day."

"That is not possible," Draven snorted derisively, but inwardly wondering at the dragon's bold claim. He had seen Zarandrae's killing blow on the bronze dragon, but they had not found any evidence of the dead dragon in the ruins of Taer Blys. Zarandrae had told him that it was likely because she had changed back into her human form as she died and her body pulled from the wreckage of the building to be buried elsewhere. But she was certain her sister dragon could not survive the damage done to her and besides, Zarandrae could no longer sense her presence.

"Ah, but it is indeed possible, my overconfident friend," Kraegor countered.

"Enough," Shayene interrupted, holding up a slender hand to quiet the bickering. "You know this to be a fact, Kraegor?" she asked, looking directly at her companion.

The human-form dragon nodded.

"You have seen her?"

"I have. Before Volsaun arrived, I sensed her faint presence so I investigated closer. She is undoubtedly wounded, but very much alive. I am certain her dragon senses are considerably muted, but in human form, she is very much a capable warrior as her strength returns."

"Then you must eliminate her," Draven demanded, angry now at himself for claiming the dragon to be dead and even more so at Kraegor for slighting him in front of his sister.

"And why would I do that?" Kraegor asked as if he had just been insulted. "I have no quarrel with my own kind and will certainly not stoop to being your errand boy."

"That is enough!" Shayene snapped again. "I grow weary of this squabbling. If Siranschae is indeed alive, she is only a threat as a human on the ground. With Donaran gone, her dragon abilities will be greatly reduced, so she will remain in her human form. As such, she can be neutralized if and when the time presents itself. Perhaps she will even offer herself as champion of Nykiva and you can then deal with her at that time, Draven," she finished, speaking directly to her brother. "I trust you could then ensure she does indeed die."

The big Arcai hesitated and then nodded his acceptance.

"I want you to go back to Nykiva, Kraegor," she went on, turning to her companion. "Ensure that our associate is still in line with our plans. Promise more power and treasure, if you must, but make certain that we will have no problems. Those who survive our attack on the city will need a leader to act in my stead and eventually turn their hearts to me. I would know her reaction to your appearance, as well," she finished thoughtfully.

"As you wish," he answered softly, casting a final look of disdain toward Draven, before turning and departing quickly from Shayene's audience chamber.

"Your companion plays a dangerous game with me," Draven finally said after Kraegor's footsteps had receded down the hall.

"Kraegor is as loyal to me as Zarandrae is to you, Draven," she answered pointedly, her eyes still on the doorway he had left through. "Do not question that."

Draven wanted to reply, but carefully held his tongue. Instead, he switched subjects. "What about Branson and his outworlders? Have you recalled him yet?"

At this, Shayene's features darkened. "He and his people have vanished. I have not yet been able to locate them."

"You? How is this possible?"

"If they are still in Nykiva, they are carefully hidden from me."

"What about those that are still here?" Draven asked. "Surely you will kill them, as you said you would."

"If Branson has indeed betrayed me, I will kill them one at a time while he watches, so that he may understand the consequences. Then I will kill him."

"Then why bring the outworlders in the first place? I have yet to understand your need for them."

"They have powerful weapons."

"But you have not used them, sister," Draven said doubtfully. "Right after you brought them here, you forced them to kill each other until only twenty-five remained. Then you sent half of them to Nykiva with no supervision, while the rest wander around the castle growing soft and their equipment sits unused."

"I never needed an army of them," she replied. "Bringing them through the gate had the effect of weakening the barrier between worlds, which was what I wished. Sending Branson and some of his men to Nykiva has also accomplished what I intended."

"But you don't know where they are."

"It's not that I don't know where they are," she countered. "The better question is, who is hiding them?"

"You suspect the traitor?"

"The thought has crossed my mind," Shayene replied. "Kraegor will discover the truth."

"Very well," Draven sighed, unwilling to push forward. He had grown weary of her evasiveness and was suddenly ready to return to his soldiers and a task he understood perfectly. "I will return to Taer Blys to oversee preparations to march. Do you have any additional orders before I depart?"

"No," she said, shaking her head. "The timetable is yours, Draven, but I want Nykiva rushed before the snows come. With Taer Blys, Ithil Majeer, and Nykiva all overrun and under our control, the Dom'Ithi people will be unable to mount any type of a serious defense or counter-attack in the spring. We can then hunt them down and destroy those that still resist at our leisure, thereby strengthening the fealty of the other races."

"When will you seed the gate in Nykiva?"

"I will see to it when you prepare to march," she answered. "By that time, Kraegor will have ensured the compliance of our contact. In addition, the shorter the time the gate is in place, the less chance there will be of something going wrong."

"Very well," he answered, turning to depart.

"Draven," she said softly, halting him for the moment.

"Yes?"

"Take care that you do not underestimate those who stand against us. The involvement of Jayadra should not be treated lightly."

"I have no intention of letting her upset our plans," he assured her. "I will deal with her and her companion accordingly."

"Jayadra is a priestess of considerable power," she went on. "If she has agreed to protect Nykiva, that could swing the tide of battle significantly. You must take Nykiva before winter sets in. We cannot afford a protracted siege."

Draven shook his head and started back toward the doorway. "If she involves herself, she will die," he said and then he was gone.

"I hope you're right, my dear brother," Shayene said quietly to herself. "For your sake, you had better be."

Chapter 32

With a tired sigh, Terion leaned back in his chair near the window, staring into the fire's dying embers in the stone fireplace. It had been a long night and dawn was still several hours away. He felt that he had not slept for weeks and the cozy little room in the abandoned inn offered him little comfort.

He, along with Notyet, Siranschae, and about two dozen sappers, as well as Anthony who refused to go on ahead with the rest of the refugees, were holed up in Haven. On the morrow, they would begin working on the abandoned town, getting it ready for Draven's soldiers who would eventually be marching through it. The plan was to booby trap the entire town in the hopes they could cause some damage to their enemy before they reached Nykiva. It was a long shot, but Terion felt it was worth the effort.

Haven was already empty, the inhabitants evacuating it when Jayadra and her dragon companion, Volsaun, had urged them to flee toward Nykiva. This was after the people had initially refused Terion's pleas. The appearance of an angry white dragon had changed their minds fairly quickly and they had left immediately, accompanied by the Arcai, while many of the sailors had opted to just set sail for safer harbors, watched over by Volsaun.

Terion looked over at his companions, Notyet seated by the door and Siranschae reclining by the fire, her eyes distant. Anthony was curled up on the bed, sleeping soundly and Terion couldn't help but smile at the young lad. The crippled boy had turned out to be their savior, helping them escape Taer Blys when he could have remained a shadow and stayed out of danger. He had barely left Terion's side since they fled and the warrior had grown fond of the boy.

Anthony shifted in his sleep and Terion turned his eyes back to

Siranschae. "You are thinking of Arianna?" he guessed, speaking softly so as not to awaken the boy.

Siranschae nodded, but said nothing. She had not needed to. Everyone understood her concern for the Tae girl, as it was Arianna who had saved her by using her empathic healing.

"Arianna is a tough one. She'll be fine," Terion offered, hoping it was true. Upon receiving the healing potion from Jayadra, the Tae empath had gone into screaming convulsions that had lasted long into the night. When they had finally dissipated, she had lapsed into a deep sleep and she had been that way ever since.

"Jayadra said she will survive," Siranschae said softly. "But there is no knowing what the ordeal will do to her in the end."

"And so you blame yourself."

"She should not have healed me."

"Try telling her that when she awakens," Terion said with a smile. "Arianna is not your typical Tae. She's not likely to listen to you."

"When we return to Nykiva and put this war behind us, I will take her into my care, regardless of her condition," Siranschae said. "It is the least I can do for her."

"Then she'll be in good hands," Terion said with an appreciative nod. "But what of yourself?"

"I will survive my wounds. But you know what a dragon's relationship is like with our companion. With Donaran gone, I am severely weakened. I will physically survive, but I will not regain my former strength until Donaran is reborn and I am reunited with him."

"Will it be long?"

"I've no idea," she shrugged sadly.

"Will you know when it happens?"

"I will," she nodded. "That, at least, I can take solace in. Until then, you will have my sword in battle and whatever aid I may offer."

"I suppose it depends on the enemy," Terion said thoughtfully. "With Draven, things are pretty clear. But back home, things are...different."

Siranschae looked up from the fire, her eyes searching Terion's face. "Are you speaking of Jayadra's recent visit to Nykiva?"

"Yes," Terion nodded, thinking what a disaster it had been. Two days prior, Volsaun had taken Jayadra to Nykiva to meet with the Dom Council and have them begin preparations to receive a large number of refugees. Balgar had steadfastly refused, claiming that taking in so many people on the eve of war would be too much for Nykiva to handle. To make matters worse, while some of the council members disagreed with Balgar, enough of the others were obviously already in the man's pockets and sided with him, even when confronted by an Arcai. Jayadra had suggested that it was time to seat a new council, but many of those council members wielded considerable political might and would be able to call in any number of favors to keep themselves in power. And, there was no doubt that Balgar would go to any length to keep his own position as council leader.

But all that aside, even in the unlikely event they could pull off a peaceful change in council leadership, it would certainly be a long drawn-out process and would never happen before Draven and his soldiers descended upon Nykiva. By then, it would be far too late for any of them, resident or refugee.

So Jayadra had been forced to accept Balgar's counter offer, allowing the survivors from Taer Blys to set up camp outside the city walls and in the surrounding unprotected fields of Nykiva's farming community. Many of the more seriously wounded would be brought behind the walls and receive whatever treatment the Tae healers could offer, providing they accept Balgar's decree that those healers would remain in Nykiva.

Balgar had also been unwavering in his support that Terion stay behind in Haven and do what he could to delay Draven's army. What went unsaid, but easily apparent to the Arcai, was Balgar's hope that the man he hated so much would meet an untimely death.

Still, she had not lost every political battle to Balgar and his cronies. When the council leader had demanded that all arriving able-bodied warriors and soldiers conscript themselves into Nykiva garrisons in defense of the city, Jayadra had steadfastly refused, arguing that they would keep as many soldiers as were able to protect the refugees and the farmers that sheltered them. Her decision had enraged Balgar, but she had not relented and eventually returned to them last night with at least that notion intact.

"We are beset on both sides," Terion said. "Sometimes I wonder who the more dangerous enemy is."

"That would be Balgar," Siranschae replied knowingly. "There is nothing unknown about Draven. You know what his intentions are. You know that his armies are coming. You get none of that with your council leader and that makes him infinitely more dangerous."

"Normally, I would find that hard to believe," he said and then trailed off.

"These are not normal times, my friend."

An ember in the fireplace sparked and popped, startling Terion and he looked up. Notyet was moving his fingers, signing to him in the gloom with one hand as he silently took up his sword in his other.

Ready yourself.

Instantly, Terion was alert and a quick glance at Siranschae told him she had also caught Notyet's message. He stood up and lazily stretched, then walked over to check on the sleeping Anthony. Leaning over him, he pretended to tuck the blankets in around the lad, but whispered quietly into his ear, waking him up. "Under the bed, quickly."

As Anthony rolled off the bed and slithered underneath, a flaming object came crashing through the window, sending shards of glass and pieces of burning pitch flying through the room. The room door burst inward at nearly the same time and a trio of crossbow bolts flew into the room, imbedding themselves into the far wall where the swordsman had been seated.

Notyet leaped to his feet, swinging his huge sword as the first of the attackers burst in, assailants they had already faced one. He quickly stabbed forward with his blade, catching the lead man beneath his rib cage and running him through. The attacker's dying scream filled the room as more killers came at them, both through the door and through the now-shattered window. Notyet engaged a pair of enemies in hand-to-hand, not even having time to pull his sword free from the first man he had killed.

"Fangs!" Terion shouted, immediately putting his blade to use as two of the hired assassins squared off against him. These were seasoned fighters and he found himself doing his best to rapidly parry their coordinated attacks, unable to put forth any offense of his own.

Several more killers came in, only to face Siranschae and her curved sword. For all her injuries, she moved like the wind and quickly had a trio of assassins backing hastily toward the door. She might have turned the battle then, had a small throwing hammer not flashed across the room and struck her in the back between her shoulder blades, driving her to the floor and leaving her dazed and gasping for breath.

Another assassin followed the hammer throw through the window, gaining the middle of the room with relative ease. The new attacker was dressed differently than the others, his black clothing streaked with dark green and his arms accented with a pair of metal bracers. His face was masked with a hood that gave one the impression they were looking into the face of a huge serpent, but it was the bracers that told who he really was. They were in the shape of coiled snakes, the tails upraised at his elbows, giving the assassin a pair of deadly elbow spikes that could be used in close quarters fighting, while the snake's heads rose up from the killer's wrists.

Smoke from the growing flames billowed up around him and he looked down at the stunned Siranschae. Quickly dropping to a knee beside his victim, he drove his fist downward to plunge the bracer's fangs into the woman's temple and kill her. But before the blow could land, a tiny form latched itself onto the man's leg, swinging his body around and throwing the assassin off balance, causing the metal fangs to plunge into the wooden floor instead.

Anthony quickly let go of the man's leg and dodged back through the fighting as the man turned his full attention to the youth. Terion, working feverishly against the two assailants, had seen what had happened and worked his way closer. At that moment, the body of another attacker was flung across the room into the group, having been propelled there by an enraged Notyet.

Terion dropped down, sweeping his leg out toward the assassin who had just tried to kill Siranschae. The man easily jumped the leg sweep, quickly turning his attention to him. Terion had no chance to press his attack, though, as the other two killers worked their weapons back toward him. The mysterious assassin stepped into the fray intending to kill the swordsman first before finishing off the others. His fist drove forward, the deadly fangs of the bracer aimed at his victim.

Before the blow could land, the fine leather and metal links of a familiar whip circled around the killer's wrist with a crack, snapping his arm to the side. The Vi'Raaji assassin, Vendetta, stepped in from the open window, the body of a Fang slumping to the floor before her, his throat neatly slit .Her eyes glittered coldly as she stared at the masked killer in obvious recognition.

At that moment, Terion spun down a savage thrust from one of his opponents, forcing the surprised man toward the deadly witch. Unaware that Vendetta had actually just saved him, he followed the off-balance killer's momentum, intending to kill the woman before she could react.

But the witch's mind worked as fast as her body. Holding fast to the handle of her whip and hoping at least to take down the man that would have killed her contract target, she leapt backwards out of the window, free falling from the second story room to the road below. She landed lightly on her feet, releasing the whip as she did and pulling out her long-bladed daggers.

The masked assassin, knowing that to resist her pull on him would put him at an extreme disadvantage in the small room, followed her out and leapt far from the window, his arm still entwined by her whip. He landed in the road and rolled, already in a martial stance, prepared to fight. A twist of his arm and the whip fell free, leaving him unimpeded.

Terion came last, following his own opponent down and using the man's body to cushion his own fall. The Fang he landed on let out a single rattling gasp and was still and Terion rolled to his feet, facing the two killers.

"I had not thought finding you again would prove so easy," Vendetta said softly as she began circling to her left, one dagger poised behind her head and the other flat against her forearm. Her gaze was not on Terion, but on the masked assassin.

Terion held his sword ready, his gaze flicking from Vendetta to the other assassin, who still had not moved or made a sound. "You knew we'd have to come back through Haven," he finally said angrily, stepping cautiously toward her, his sword before him.

"I was not addressing you, Terion," she snapped impatiently, her eyes never leaving the other killer. "I have no interest in you at the moment, other than killing you if you persist in getting in my way."

In answer, the swordsman came forward in a lunge, feinting with a stab. But Vendetta arched her body backward, keeping her feet, and Terion's blade cut the air in front of her, slicing through the fabric of her blouse just below her breasts.

She snapped back upright, driving a dagger forward before Terion could get his blade around to defend. But at the same moment, the other assassin leapt forward, both hands striking at the witch with blinding speed. Vendetta parried away several successive strikes, before throwing her entire body backward into a flip in order to put a safer distance between her and her opponents.

The masked assassin used his momentum to move him closer to Terion and his next several strikes were aimed at the swordsman. Terion twisted out of the way and the man continued to drive him backward as he followed each strike with another, keeping him off balance.

Terion, recognizing he was in trouble, spun his body and dropped to the ground in front of the killer, but at least out of the way of his deadly bracers. The killer leapt upwards in order to drive the bracer's snake fangs into his throat, but Terion kicked himself back to his feet and whipped his elbow around hard, connecting with the side of the man's head.

The force of the blow was strong enough to knock the masked killer down, but he let the energy of the strike flow into his body and send him into a diving roll. In a moment, he was back on his feet again.

At that moment, Vendetta struck, green bolts of energy flying from splayed fingers and catching the masked killer across the chest and shoulder. The force of the magic sent the man into another quick roll, but once more he came back to his feet, relatively unaffected.

"Clever boy," Vendetta purred as she followed her magical strike in with a dagger thrust. She pushed her advantage, keeping the man off balance until his foot suddenly rolled over the handle of her discarded whip and he began to stumble slightly. She brought her dagger up for a killing strike, but Terion's sword intercepted her blade, knocking the blow aside.

Taking advantage of Terion's interference, the assassin spun himself behind the witch and drove the fangs of his snake bracer into her lower back. Immediately, Vendetta's dark skin began to pale, her breath coming in short gasps. The assassin pulled the weapon from her body and prepared to deliver another strike, when Terion thrust his own sword at the woman. But before the killing blow could land, Vendetta turned sideways and Terion's sword buried itself into the masked assassin's chest instead. He stumbled backward and then, instead of collapsing to the ground, he simply dissolved before their eyes, fading away into a wisp of smoke.

Terion was shocked enough that it almost cost him his life, but at the last moment, he parried Vendetta's incoming dagger strike with the hilt of his sword and then skipped back several steps. "Why aren't you dead?" he gasped.

"Not all poisons work the same way on all people," she replied quietly, beginning to circle again, both blades at the ready. True, the poison wouldn't kill her, but she knew her body would have to battle to overcome its effects, which were already dulling her senses.

"Why did he try to kill you anyway?"the fighter continued angrily. "Partners fighting over the kill, maybe?"

"Do you honestly believe any Vi'Raaji would ally herself with a

Dom'Ithi assassin?"

"Perhaps you're the first," Terion replied, quickly moving forward to attack. He struck three times in quick succession, but she parried each one aside. His fourth strike came from overhead and she caught the blade by crossing her daggers and locking their hilts. She shoved his sword and arm out wide and before he knew it, the heel of her boot was connecting with his jaw. The blow sent an explosion of stars through his head and he staggered backward.

Instead of finishing him, Vendetta spun one of her daggers back into its boot sheath and scooped up her discarded whip. "Enough," she said, fighting a wave of poison-induced vertigo. "I did not come here to kill you."

Terion shook his head to clear the cobwebs, his weapon held out before him. Behind him, Notyet came bursting out of the front door of the abandoned inn, streaked in blood and bearing down on the Vi'Raaji. "Hold," Terion said loudly, his voice unsteady. Notyet brought himself up short, staring at his friend in shock. Ignoring him, Terion directed his next comment to the woman. "What do you want?"

Vendetta reached behind her back, feeling the puncture wounds left by the assassin's deadly bracers. They still leaked blood, but she was gratified that they were not deep enough to pierce any internal organs. "Let us deal with the Fangs, first, then we can speak," she replied.

"They are dead," Siranschae said as she stepped out of the inn behind Notyet. Anthony was with her, his arms wrapped around her neck, riding piggy-back. He had a bloody gash across his forehead, but his eyes were alert. "What of the leader?" the dragon asked, her eyes darting around, but her concentration still focused on the killer.

"The one I...er, we just killed?" Terion stammered, remembering he had been trying to kill the witch instead.

"He is known as the Serpent and the thugs he employs are called Fangs," Vendetta explained. "Little is known about him, for he is rarely seen, leaving most of his guild work to those in his employ."

"Well, he's dead now, so won't have much to say to his employees."

"He is not dead," she answered, her voice bitter.

"How do you know?"

"He is not killed so easily."

"Is he Vi'Raaji?" Terion questioned.

Vendetta shot him a dark look. "He is a male," she replied, leaving it at that. Vi'Raaji males were the servant class in their female-dominated society. They were used for menial labor and breeding stock and little more. "He is also a Dom; one of you," she went on. "My people detest him. There is even a bounty for anyone who can eliminate him."

"Well, if he's not dead after I ran a sword through his chest, then he seems to know what he's doing."

"He is an amateur," she spit.

"He nearly killed you," Terion pointed out.

Vendetta's jaw clenched as she considered Terion's words and she had to grudgingly agree with the man. Having witnessed the Serpent's fighting prowess first-hand, she now knew she would have to be careful when dealing with him in the future. But that was a consideration for another time. "Whatever the case, we can table the discussion for later," she said. "We still have his soldiers to deal with."

"I told you," Siranschae snapped. "They are dead."

"No, dragon, that was just the beginning," Vendetta said, pointing past her. "Look."

As one, they turned and watched as several Fangs materialized out of the gloom, followed by nearly a dozen more. Behind Vendetta, more were coming down the street, every one of them with their weapons out.

"Their leader has left," the Vi'Raaji said. "But these are the execution squad. They remain committed to their master and will not rest until you are dead."

"Or they are," Terion said grimly.

"There are more than thirty of them," the witch said, her fingers reaching for the star stone inside her blouse. "This is a losing battle." But something held her back from activating the magical artifact and instead of escaping and leaving them to their fate, she pulled her blades and took her stance beside her enemy. "Pray for a miracle, Terion," she said softly. "We're going to need it."

Chapter 33

The Fangs came forward in an organized formation. They made no sound, moving silently and with a precision that was almost inhuman. Individually, any of the four adults they were trying to kill, could have successfully ended a one-on-one fight. But the sheer number of killers would be too much for them and they knew it.

Suddenly, a bright pinpoint of light, accompanied by a low buzzing sound that grew in pitch, caused both sides to watch in wonder as the spot of light suddenly grew into a circular hole that seemed to be cut right into the air.

The first man to step through the gateway was unlike anyone Terion had ever seen. He was a good head taller than him and was dressed in the strangest of clothing, gray-green cloth mottled with unequal patterns of black and gray from head to toe. Scars marred his face and he carried a black metallic weapon that was a completely alien. The stranger came through the portal quickly and was followed by a similarly dressed, ebony-skinned man. Without a word, they moved to either side of the gateway as four more came through. After the sixth man arrived, the portal shimmered and then popped out of existence. It was at that moment that Terion was introduced to heavy weapons from a different world.

The soldiers opened up with their weapons, magically throwing fire and thunder at the Fangs on all fronts. Flowers of blood appeared, stitching themselves across torsos and throwing bodies backward. Most of the assassins were cut down immediately. Several turned to run, only to meet the same fate. The fight was over in a matter of seconds.

"What in the…," Terion began in complete shock, but he could not finish as the leader slung his weapon over his back and barked orders to his men.

"Swan, check the bodies, make sure we don't have anyone that's going to pop up and surprise us," he said.

"Roger that," the man replied and then moved forward.

"The rest of you, I want a house-to-house search," the leader continued. "Make sure this berg is clear."

"We have about twenty men…holed up all over town," Terion said, still stunned at the incredible turn of events.

"If they're alive, I've got work for them to do," the man replied gruffly and then turned to another of his men, this one with a large black backpack that was slung over one shoulder. "Paris, you've got the ordnance. As soon as you round up any survivors and get them clear, start rigging the buildings. We've got twenty-four hours and then we need to start hoofin' it back to Nykiva. We've still got a lot of work to do to get our people back."

"Nykiva?" Terion asked in amazement, finally finding some level mental ground.

The man finally turned his full attention toward the warrior and stuck out his hand, gripping Terion's hand in an iron vise. "You're Terion, right? Name's Rick Branson. Ranora sends her regards."

"Ranora?"

"Long story, brother," Branson said with a smile. "Give me a few minutes to get things locked down and I'll give you the Cliff's Notes version."

"Cliff's what?" Terion was utterly confused now.

"Never mind," Branson said with a smile. "For once, I'm actually going to be the one explaining something in this world."

"It is apparently not your time to die," Vendetta said quietly, leaning close to Terion. She had watched the whole thing with rapt fascination and much more understanding than he and his friends were exhibiting.

Terion turned and looked at the Vi'Raaji, carefully considering her role in everything. His enemy stood before him. She had killed Cavanah, kidnapped their young friend, and could have easily killed him in Haven…twice now. Yet here she was, standing with him and his companions and would have fought alongside them, too, had it come to that.

"I know what you are thinking," she continued. "Once your friends have a moment to think clearly, things will change quickly and not for the better."

"What do you want?"

"A trade, Terion, nothing more," she answered simply. "You for your young friend."

"Aylan?"

"He is alive and safe for the moment," she offered. "Whether he continues in that condition will largely be determined by what happens when you reach Nykiva."

"And what needs to happen?"

"When you reach Nykiva, I will find you," she answered. "You will be alone and will consent to give yourself over to me. When you do, I will release Aylan unharmed."

"I'm just supposed to accept your word?"

"You have little choice, if you wish to see Aylan again."

"What about me?"

She shrugged, but Terion did not miss the flash of uncertainty in her pale eyes. "I will turn you over to my employer and complete the contract. What happens after that is not my concern."

"And if I refuse?"

"I have Aylan," she said knowingly. "You will not refuse. Besides, there is more going on here than you are aware."

"I think I have a pretty good idea of what's going on," he

replied, a trace of anger still in his voice.

"Have you deciphered your dream yet?" she asked, her question taking him off guard.

"I...my what?"

"Your dream," she pressed. "The dark sorceress that tempts you?"

"How do you know about that?" he asked incredulously.

"As I told you, Aylan is alive and well. He and I have spoken at length about your dream and how it fits into what is happening in the world."

"How's that again?" he asked, truly perplexed. "What do my dreams have to do with us? With this?"

"You believe that Draven acts alone," she explained quickly. "Aylan and I believe that he acts in accordance with his sister."

"His sister?"

"Shayene."

Terion was stunned that he had not considered the possible connection and now that the assassin had brought it up, it made perfect sense.

"There is much more you should know," she said quietly. "But now is not the place for this discussion."

As if to accentuate that point, Notyet suddenly focused on the witch, his features darkening. While Terion was able to have a conversation with her, Notyet's face told a different story. He would kill her if he could.

Vendetta saw it, too, and still hampered by the poison in her body, knew she was in no position for another fight. Besides, things had changed greatly in the past few minutes and she wasn't prepared to do anything until she had a firmer grasp on what it all meant. Turning back to Terion, she locked her gaze on his eyes. "Nykiva," she whispered and a moment later, vanished in a flash of greenish light.

"You let her go?" Siranschae asked incredulously, the magic having caught her attention.

"It seems I have little choice. She has Aylan."

"How do you know she hasn't killed him?"

"She needs him."

"Why?"

"Because it's the only way I will consent to surrender to her," he replied helplessly. "If I do when we get back to Nykiva, she'll release him."

"And you believe her?"

"I have no reason not to at the moment," Terion stated. "But that is a consideration for later. For now, we have work to do. Come, let's see what we can do to help our visitors."

Several hours later, the natives of the world were seated around a table in an abandoned tavern along with Branson and the man he called Swan, while the other four strange soldiers worked side-by-side with Terion's sappers, rigging the town for Draven's arrival. Notyet had raided the bar and everyone had a large tankard of ale, with the exception of Anthony, who was quite content to sit spellbound and listen as Branson told his tale.

The stranger—he called himself and his soldiers American marines—left nothing out when he told them how and why they were suddenly stranded in a world that was not their own. He explained Kraegor's appearance in their world and lamented his "stupid" decision to follow the man back here. He told Terion and his friends about Shayene forcing them to fight until only twenty-five remained and then sent him and nine others to Nykiva while keeping the other fifteen as hostages in her castle back in the Wraithlands.

"The witch took me apart first," Branson explained quietly, tracing a finger along one of the scars on his cheek. "She tore me up to make the others fall in line. After they did, she sent the ten of us to Nykiva to stand out. She wanted us to attract attention and we certainly did that during the bar fight. Afterward, I didn't know what to think."

"Is that when Ranora saved you?" Siranschae asked, amazed at what she was hearing.

"I'd hardly call it saving us," the marine replied and Terion detected a trace of bitterness in his words. "For the longest time, she kept me prisoner, telling me my friends were either dead or missing. For two weeks she had me believing that Swan had been executed and for longer than that, I thought Boozer was dead and Tuner had disappeared."

"Who are they?"

"Friends of mine from my world," Branson explained. "Ranora told me later that she had to know who I really was before she fessed up and told me the truth."

"And did she?"

"I have no idea," he answered with a shrug. "But I'm a lot closer to believing her now than I was a couple months back."

"What made you change your mind?" Siranschae questioned.

"It was when she brought Swan in during one of our sessions and told me I had earned some truthfulness from her. Couple weeks later, it was Boozer, although she's still nicked up."

"Nicked up?"

"Wounded," Swan answered sadly, his voice deep and rich. "Took a shot in the spine and she can't walk. Paralyzed from the waist down."

At that, Anthony perked up, leaning forward. "Is she okay?"

"No more than anyone else that can't walk," Swan said with a sigh.

Anthony swung his body up onto the table, plopping his bound legs down on the wood in front of the man. "I can't walk, either," he said, smiling widely. "I'll bet I can teach her a few things."

"You know, I'm probably going to take you up on that offer," Branson said, reaching out and tousling the kid's unkempt hair. "Tough kid like you could rub off on her a little. Lord knows, she needs some cheering up. She's pretty down right now."

"What about the one you call Tuner?" Terion asked.

"That's where things get downright strange," Branson said. "His real name's Eric. We call him Tuner because back on our world, he was my radioman. But he also seems to understand things and read things just a little quicker than anyone else."

"Yeah, and we couldn't call him Radar, because that's already been done," Swan added with a wry smile.

"Radar?"

Branson laughed. "Sorry, man, it's a M*A*S*H reference. I guess you'd have to be from our world to know what that means. But it's not important. Ranora kept Eric from me the longest. Kept telling me they were still looking for him, when it turned out she had him all along."

"Why did she keep him from you?"

"Because there's something special about him," Branson said thoughtfully. "You know that hole we walked through a few hours ago to save your asses out in the street? That was Eric's doing."

"You mean the portal?" Siranschae asked in astonishment.

"Yep, the very one. Ranora has this big mirror that she's been using to watch you and when those jackwagons out there were going to kill you, she had Eric open the gate so we could come through. She said he's the key master or something."

"Gatekeeper," Swan corrected.

"Right. A gatekeeper. And he can apparently open these magical gateways," Branson said. "I guess that's what started the whole thing in the bar with us. The guy that put Boozer down, tried to kill Eric and he snapped and freaked out. Popped a gate open that killed the guy and saved us in the end."

Terion looked quickly at Notyet, recognition coming to him.

Convergence, Notyet only had to sign one word.

"So let me get this straight," Terion said, turning back to Branson. "You and your people are from a completely different world, one where magic does not exist."

"At least not like in this world," Branson agreed. "We do science back home, not this hocus pocus crap."

"Yet one of your soldiers is able to open these gateways?"

"Yep and don't ask me how, because I don't have the foggiest idea."

"Can he open another one, so we can get home?" Terion asked hopefully.

Branson shook his head. "Not any time soon. That's the problem. It takes a lot out of him and he can only keep them open for a short time. Takes him a while to recharge his batteries, too."

"So what's next? Do we stay here and wait then?"

"Nope, we're going back on foot," the marine answered.

"All of us?"

"That's right," Branson said. "We should be there in about two weeks and when we get back, we get down to the serious work."

"And that is?"

"You're going to get to see my world."

"Your world?"

"Yep," Branson replied. "Apparently, Shayene left something there; something we can use against her. And we're going to go back and get it."

"But how? You have to have a gatekeeper for that."

"They have Eric," Siranschae added knowingly. "Is he that powerful, that he can already bridge worlds?"

"Ranora seems to think so. She can already see into our world with her mirror, but it takes one of us to be there with her because something about our thoughts helps her connect to it," Branson explained. "She's pretty sure that with the mirror and Eric juiced up to full power, he can open the gate to our world and we can get what we need."

"How does Ranora know what the object is?" Siranschae questioned.

"Lady, I've had a lot of really long days with Ranora," Branson said confidently, "and I'll tell you two things I know for sure. Number one, she's whip-smart. Number two, she's royally pissed off about Shayene and really doesn't like her, which suits me just fine because I've got some serious payback ready for what that witch did to me and my soldiers."

"So what happens when we get this thing from your world?"

"Once we have it, we're all going to go up to her place and thoroughly kick her ass," Swan spoke up, but there was no mirth in his voice. He was deadly serious.

"We're going to go get our people back," Branson added, somewhat more reserved. "Then we're going home."

Chapter 34

It turned out that the group had to only travel for five days before another portal opened up one evening as they gathered together and pitched camp. Branson heard the telltale buzz first and had everyone grabbing up their gear as fast as they were able as the portal shimmered open. Knowing it would only be open for a short time, he left four of his soldiers behind to escort the sapper to Nykiva on foot, before jumping through with Swan at the last second to join Terion, Notyet, Siranschae, and Anthony.

"If that thing snaps shut on you before you're all the way through, it's a one way trip," he breathed heavily, looking behind him as the gate popped out of existence. A moment later, he was clapping a young similarly-dressed young soldier on the back. "Nicely done, Tuner. You saved us some serious hiking."

Eric "Tuner" Johansson nodded, his young face bright red with exertion and streaked with sweat. "Yes...sir. Thank you...sir," he huffed.

Terion looked around at their new surroundings. Despite some changes, he knew immediately where he was. It was Keiran's former study and he remembered it fondly as being more cheerful during her reign as official arch mage of the city. Now, with Ranora in the position of head mage, the young enchantress had transformed it into a true chamber of sorcery. The shelves of tomes and books, some of them quite ancient, still lined the walls. But where there had once been chairs and lounges to relax in, now there were several tables covered with arcane apparatus, open tomes, and various other mystical objects. Most of the chairs and couches had been pushed to the outer walls and the stairwell in the back of the room that wound upwards to her private residence was now guarded by a huge stone golem.

Because golems of any type could only be created by the most powerful of wizards and were utterly loyal to their creator, Terion was shocked to see one in the tower of a sorceress so young. The human-shaped creature stood motionless, standing more than ten feet tall, and it completely blocked the stairwell.

Ranora herself stood nearby, an open tome on a table before her, and he noted that she had cast off her heavy council robes in favor of a sleeveless gown of black silk. The magical glyphs and tattoos that signified the strength of her arcane power encircled her hands and arms, covering her skin and disappearing beneath the folds of her gown. They were intricate and he suddenly realized that he was no longer looking at an apprentice, but at a sorceress of impressive strength.

"Well met again, Terion," she said warmly, reaching out and clasping his hand. "I trust you are well?"

"Thanks to you and your friends here," he replied, nodding toward Branson and then at Eric.

"Alas I couldn't have brought you back sooner. Eric is just now finding his powers."

"So I've heard," Terion said, looking closer at the young soldiers hands. There were no magical sigils present. "How is this possible?"

"All in good time," Ranora replied. "I'm not yet completely certain of a lot of it myself."

"Then start from the beginning," Terion stated. "Have you quit the council? You know you have broken Balgar's decree by bringing me back here."

"We live in difficult times, Terion," Ranora replied. "We make decisions we feel are the right ones to make. Nykiva falls more and more under the sway of politicians. Words of warning fall on deaf ears and do little more than earn you the contempt of the council leader and most members of the council. You, of all people, should understand this."

"Sounds like government in our world," Branson mumbled from nearby.

"Earth is not so different, no matter which plane it rests on," Ranora agreed almost sadly.

"Unfortunately, there is little we can do to change that here," Terion said bitterly. "Balgar rules nearly unopposed, now that you have stepped down."

"On the contrary," the sorceress countered. "I have done no such thing. I still serve, but I do so with an eye to the greater good. Your Arcai friend, Jayadra, suggested a logical course of action when she visited us last week and I agree with her. But disbanding and reseating a new council takes time and careful planning. And to be honest, replacing the council is not nearly as important as what we are dealing with right now."

"We are dealing with it because the council has failed to act on several occasions already," Terion said plainly. "Now, Nykiva will not have the strength to stand against Draven."

"Draven is but a part of the whole," Ranora explained. "Unfortunately, he is a lesser threat than his sister."

"So, you know that Shayene is truly behind this?" he asked, feeling somewhat vindicated for the trust he showed in Vendetta back in Haven.

"She is, and her obscurity gives her a perfect opportunity to hide behind her brother and his armies as they sweep across the lands."

"But why?" Terion asked. "That's what we can't figure out."

"I admit I don't fully understand her reasons, either," she replied. "But I do know some things that you do not."

"Such as?"

"Such as how she has accomplished what she has done so far," she said. "Are you aware that she had use of a powerful gatekeeper to open the hole to the Nether?"

"We suspected as much, or at least Aylan did. He figured that she used a gatekeeper to open an earth gate to the Nether, with plans of unleashing an army of First Born on our world," he said, deciding at that moment to keep his dreams regarding that matter, to himself. "But even if this gatekeeper did open such a gate, the sheer power required to open one to hell itself would mean he could only maintain it for a few minutes, no matter how strong he was."

"Unless it was made permanent," Ranora pointed out. "And I believe she has done just that."

Terion shook his head. "The only way she could accomplish that would be to sacrifice the gatekeeper."

"Correct, and to be more specific, it would have to be done with a particular artifact; an item known as Varankyl," she finished, reaching down and turning the open book in front of her so that it was facing the warrior.

"What's that?"

"It is everything we know about Varankyl," she replied, tapping the open page and causing him to look down at the illustration of an exotic-looking crystalline mace. "Also known as the Mace of the Damned, it is a sentient artifact, perhaps one of the most powerful in existence."

"Sentient?" Branson put in, clearly intrigued by the story. "You mean it actually thinks?"

"Yes," she replied. "It is a powerful relic created thousands of years ago and had a single purpose. It is said that the weapon could be used to sacrifice a gatekeeper, which would infuse an opened gate with the essence of that gatekeeper and that of the person sacrificing him or her, making the gate permanent, at least for as long as that person lived."

"You can't be serious," Terion scoffed.

"I am afraid she is completely serious," Siranschae finally spoke up, her features creased with worry. She stepped out of the shadows to stand beside Terion and picked up the tome. "Varankyl is a dragon-forged artifact that was created that way to ensure that few people, if any, would attempt such a deed. Indeed, most would not be willing to allow their life to be tied to a portal that others would want to destroy."

"Why would something like that be created?"

"Creating a sentient artifact is beyond mortal understanding," she replied, looking knowingly at Ranora who was content to allow the dragon to explain. "Varankyl was forged to be used in the event someone created a permanent gateway to another world. It was created to be the destroyer of that gate. However, during its creation, it gained sentience earlier than expected and gained the very trait it was being created to combat."

"You mean it does both?"

"Yes," she nodded. "Varankyl can destroy a gateway, but can also create it, too."

"How do you know this?" Terion asked.

"Because Varankyl was forged by all the dragons at the behest of the gods themselves. I know, because I was there," she finished softly. "It was not only our powers that created it, but Varankyl possesses a shadow of our souls."

"You mean it's part of you? Part of all the dragons?"

"Yes," she said sadly.

"So this thing was created thousands of years ago and you were there?" Branson cut in. "How old are you?"

"A tale for another time," Siranschae waved him off, then turned back to Terion. "The point is, if she possesses a gate to the Nether, Varankyl is the only way she could have created it and is the only way to destroy it, as well."

"Where's it been all this time?"

"Varankyl passed out of recorded history millennia ago," Siranschae insisted, "likely at the behest of the gods due to its chaotic sentience and additional power."

"Until recently," Ranora put in quietly as she picked up a small cloth-wrapped object that had been sitting on the nearby table. She slowly unwound the dark fabric and then held the item up for the rest to see. It was an object crafted of black crystal, a grinning skull adorned with sharp spikes resembling a crown. The base of the skull appeared to be broken off from a larger object, but the break was even and smooth, resembling that of a key.

"This is the head of Varankyl," she said.

"Where did you get this?" Siranschae whispered in astonishment.

"I got it," Ranora answered slowly, "when I took over Keiran's tower."

"You what?" Terion pressed, suddenly defensive. "What are you insinuating?"

"I am insinuating nothing," Ranora replied, her face stricken. "I found it here after Keiran's murder. I try not to think of the reasons why it could or should have been here."

"You found it here?" the warrior asked incredulously.

"Right here on this very table."

"And you're certain this is the artifact?"

"This is but half of the whole," the sorceress replied. "I have studied it, cast numerous spells on it, and I have spoken to it. Varankyl, at least part of his essence, lies within the piece. You are welcome to do the same if you do not believe me."

"She speaks the truth," Siranschae said, her eyes locked on the piece. "I can feel its presence. It is muted and considerably weaker than if it was united with the other half, but it is still very powerful, very old, and very dangerous." Turning back to Ranora, she continued. "Where is the rest of it? Varankyl was constructed in a way that it could be broken into two pieces, with each half housing part of its intellect. Separately, a strong mind can manage the individual pieces. Together, it is a powerful intellect that few would have the ability to master and it has likely grown stronger over the centuries."

"For a time, it was hidden," answered the sorceress as she carefully rewound the cloth around the item. "We know that the only way to destroy the gate is to use the weapon. And because of Varankyl's requirements, doing so could very easily destroy Shayene as well. With the gate, Shayene controls much power, but she is also vulnerable because its existence is tied to her own life. So she hid it in a place her enemies would not look."

"And you know where it is," Terion reasoned.

"I do," Ranora answered and swept her hand toward a mirror that stood against the far wall. It was encased in an ornately carved oaken frame, with randomly placed jewels imbedded into the wood, becoming part of an intricate design of vines and flowers. "This is the Mirror of Ataracus."

"I've heard of this," Terion said in awe, stepping toward it and running his hand gently down the wooden case. "Keiran possessed many artifacts, but I was unaware she had claimed this."

"She did not," Ranora said with a hint of pride as she joined him before the mirror. "I, alone, discovered the location of it several years ago and had it recovered and brought here. Keiran claimed it was too powerful for an apprentice to use, so I never got the opportunity to work with it." She paused before going on. "Now that Keiran is gone and I am master of the tower..."

Terion glanced again at her magical body markings and nodded satisfactorily. "You appear to be quite capable of mastering it today."

Ranora passed a hand over the mirror without answering. The surface immediately became cloudy, as if a roiling thunderstorm was brewing within. "For those not familiar with the Mirror of Ataracus, a short history lesson is in order to explain why it is absolutely essential to our plan," she said quietly, glancing quickly at everyone. "It was created over a thousand years ago by a powerful wizard bearing the name of the mirror itself. Ataracus created it to help him locate his known enemies and those who might challenge his power. In doing so, he was able to eliminate them and he soon became one of the most powerful men in the land."

"What happened to him?" Terion asked, unfamiliar with the lore behind the artifact.

"History only makes brief mention of his fall," she replied. "Ataracus was making enemies as quickly as he was eliminating them and one day, his tower was attacked by a large enemy force. They seized him and dragged him out to the courtyard, where they crucified him and then razed his tower. Afterward, the mirror passed in and out of history for several hundred years, before vanishing altogether more than six hundred years ago. It remained hidden until I came across it during my studies several years ago."

"So how does it work?"

"The mirror works on the principle of relations," she explained. "It can be linked to your consciousness, allowing you to see places you have been or people that you have met. As such, I was able to use this piece of Varankyl to forge a mental link to the other half of its intellect."

"So she forced it to tell us where the rest of its brain is," Branson added, having been present when she had accomplished the first feat.

"In crude terms, yes," she replied with a small smile. "But this you must know about Varankyl. It is a chaotic sentient, stronger than any of its creators had ever intended. It exists to cause problems and this earth gate offers no end of trouble. Varankyl dislikes being separated from itself and desires to be put back together. But once that is accomplished, it will turn against us and fight against closing the gate."

"So where is the other half?" Terion asked.

Ranora placed a hand on the mirror. The gray clouds within the reflective surface took on various hues as everyone peered a little closer at it. Then, the smokiness cleared and the sharp outlines of trees took shape, illuminated under a full moon. The line of trees were a short ways off on the other side of a river, the moonlight glittering on the surface of the water. It could have been any summer night on the bank of any river, except for the metal structure rising up out of the water on the far side of the river. It was illuminated by lights and was alien to everyone in the room except for the outworlders.

"Home," Swan said longingly, looking closer.

"That's our world," Branson added. "Ranora has shown it to us already. What we're seeing is the last place we were before we came through the gateway."

"What's that small tower out there in the water?" Terion asked, studying the image in the mirror.

"It's part of a submarine," Branson said, before catching himself. "Sorry, I forget where I am sometimes. It's an underwater boat."

"And Varankyl is there?"

"It's the most logical guess," Ranora stated. "I have tried getting a more specific location, but this is the best I can do. We are looking at a world different from ours and I am forging the connection through what I can sense from Branson and his soldiers. None have been on the vessel we are looking at."

"So you think it's there?"

"First place I would look," Branson added. "Just because we haven't been on the sub, doesn't mean Shayene or her toady didn't go through and drop it there."

"So she really hid the piece on your world," Terion said disbelievingly.

"She did," Branson said, staring at the image in the mirror. "And we're going to go get it back."

"When?"

"As soon as Eric feels he has the power," Ranora answered, turning to the young soldier and letting the image in the mirror fade away. "Opening up a gate that bridges worlds will be harder than anything else he has done yet."

"Give me a good night's sleep and I think I can do it in the morning," Eric said somewhat shyly.

"How are you capable of doing this?" Siranschae asked doubtfully. "I don't understand how a non-magical mortal can do such a thing."

"I don't understand it either," Tuner replied. "I can just feel it inside me. The mirror helps me lock on to where I need to open the gate to, so that helps a lot. I can already feel the connection, so I'm pretty sure I can swing it after I've rested a bit."

"While time is not a luxury that we have, I'm certain we can wait until tomorrow," Ranora said, before addressing them all. "You have all had a very long journey and faced difficult circumstances. You may all take your rest here. We will make the attempt tomorrow if Eric feels he can complete his task."

"Sounds reasonable to me," Terion said and Notyet flashed a thumbs up in agreement, before the others agreed as well.

"Before we hit the rack, I have a question," Branson suddenly interrupted, his brow furrowed in concentration. "Shayene doesn't have any power to open these gates herself, right?"

"Correct," Ranora replied.

"And to make this gate to the Nether or hell or whatever you call it, permanent, she would have had to kill the gatekeeper who opened it with this magic thinking mace, right?"

Ranora nodded.

"So if she killed him with it and then broke it after, how'd she get a piece of it through the gate into my world?" At the looks of dawning comprehension that appeared on the faces of those around him, he smiled grimly. "She couldn't have done it first, right?"

"There's another gatekeeper," Terion reasoned.

"There would have to be," Ranora agreed with a nod.

"Well, this just keeps getting better and better," the soldier muttered.

"We should concentrate on what we know for now," Ranora said. "We know where the other piece is. We can retrieve it and destroy the gate and hopefully Shayene along with it. Everything else is secondary."

"Ranora is right," Branson added, thinking again of going home, even for a brief time. "The faster we get this done, the faster we're on the road to Shayene's place to deliver a major-league asskicking. I have some people I want to get back." He turned to face Terion. "And from what I've seen of you in Ranora's mirror, you and I are going to get along just fine."

"I appreciate your sentiment, but I won't be going with you back to your world," Terion replied. "For the moment, my path lies elsewhere."

"Elsewhere?" Ranora asked sharply.

"Look," he explained. "All of this is fascinating and I know absolutely essential to facing Shayene. But if you've been watching us in your mirror, you know we're missing someone."

"Aylan," the sorceress stated emotionlessly.

"Yes, Aylan. And I can't leave him to die."

"Do you even know where he is?"

"I do," Terion nodded. "He's right here in Nykiva, a prisoner of Vendetta."

"Even if he is here, is his life more important than what lies before you? Before us?"

"It is to me," he answered curtly. "I gave my word to her, Ranora. My life for his. I won't go back on it."

"You realize what you are risking?"

"Maybe nothing," he said thoughtfully. "There has been a change in Vendetta. I hope she'll not only free Aylan, but that she'll allow me to go free as well."

"And if she doesn't?"

"Then I'll improvise," he forced a grin.

"What if she kills you?"

"She won't."

"Would you bet your life on it?"

Terion almost answered, but instead fell silent. He had to believe that something had changed in the assassin, that she understood the implications of fighting against those who would stand against Shayene. But even if she hadn't, he couldn't leave Aylan to die.

"I don't know," he finally said. "But I have to go to her. I have to make certain Aylan is freed."

"I am against this decision," Ranora said, her voice tense. "It jeopardizes everything."

"No, it doesn't," he replied. "I'm not needed to retrieve the piece of Varankyl in the morning. With luck, I can find her quickly, free Aylan, and convince her to let me go free."

"You cannot turn your back on your friends, Terion."

"Aylan is my friend, too," he said softly.

"Terion is right," Siranschae spoke up, placing a hand on the shoulder of her friend. "Let him go save Aylan, while we retrieve the piece of Varankyl. If he is successful, having Aylan and his magic with us when we go after Shayene will be most beneficial."

Ranora looked at each of them in turn, her jaw clenched and her eyes burning fiercely. It was easy to see that she did not agree, but she bit back her reply. "Very well," she said, her tone clipped. "One of my servants will see you out, Terion. The rest of you, I will show to your quarters. Let us put this night behind us."

At that, she turned away and walked out of the room. The rest followed after some hesitation. When they were gone, a young girl in a plain white shift arrived and motioned Terion to follow her. A few minutes later, he was standing outside in the night air as the main door was shut behind him.

He was alone. It was now time to find his young friend. To do that, he would have to find Vendetta. Somehow, he didn't think that would be a problem.

Chapter 35

In another part of Nykiva, Balgar's eyes suddenly snapped open in his darkened bedroom. He knew immediately he was not alone. He listened intently, hardly daring to breath, and for the longest time, there was only silence. But the terror within him grew. Just when he thought he might yell out in fright, a quiet voice spoke from the darkness. "I have been watching you, Balgar."

It was not the voice of the Vi'Raaji witch who had been writhing seductively beneath him in his dream, and Balgar immediately rolled his immense frame out of bed, his eyes darting around the room in panic. "Who's there?" he asked in a trembling voice.

There was no answer and he edged toward the cold fireplace as a terrible dread settled over him. Reaching the hearth, he took hold of the iron poker leaning against the stone. Gripping it tightly in his hand, he again looked around fearfully. "Show yourself!"

Silence.

Terrified, Balgar moved toward the door, ready to flee, when the shape of a man rose up in front of him. With a startled scream, he swung the fireplace poker. But the shadow reached out and caught the strike effortlessly in its hand, stopping the blow. Before Balgar could scream again, the intruder's right hand closed about his throat, cutting off any sound.

"I am disappointed in your lack of hospitality," the shadow said, easily lifting the heavy man off his feet. Then, with barely a flick of an arm, Balgar was sent flying across the room, crashing through one of the heavy wooden posts of his canopy bed. Balgar's momentum carried him over the edge of the bed, where he slumped to the floor, moaning in agony and holding tightly to an obviously broken left arm.

The shadow waved a hand toward the fireplace and fire sprang up anew within, feeding on nothing more than cold ashes. The flickering flames illuminated the shadow, showing him for who he was. Tall and dressed in black robes with silver arcane runes, he stalked toward Balgar. A sadistic smile played at his lips and his black eyes glittered in the darkness as he reached for the terrified leader of the Dom council. Sharpened black nails drew blood as he grabbed Balgar by the throat and hauled him back to his feet. Another flick of his arm and Balgar was sent crashing into the wall across the room, where he again fell to the floor whimpering and wailing.

Several easy strides had the intruder again standing over the fallen council leader. Once more, he reached down and yanked the man to his feet by his throat. "I trust you will answer my questions, will you not?"

Balgar's eyes were practically bulging from his head as he tried to nod and the intruder answered by practically throwing the wounded man into the cushioned chair beside the bed. "Good," he said. "I'm glad we have reached an understanding."

"My arm," Balgar moaned, holding it tightly to his body. "You broke my arm."

"I can do far more than that if you see fit to defy me," the man replied dangerously. To drive home his point, he grabbed Balgar's fingers, squeezing them in his own powerful hand.

Several bones popped audibly and Balgar screamed again, shaking his head almost violently. "No more," he pleaded. "I will do whatever you wish. Just spare me, I beg you!"

"Good," the man said. "Tell me, do you know who I am?"

Balgar shook his head.

"I am Kraegor. I trust that name is familiar to you?"

Balgar's eyes grew wide. He did, indeed, know who Kraegor was and the fact that a dragon had come calling on him terrified him beyond anything he had ever felt.

"This worries you, no?" Kraegor asked, shadows from the flickering fire dancing across his face.

"What...what do you want?"

I have been watching you, Balgar," the dragon said. "I have watched you and your council. I have seen things that bring questions. I will have answers to these questions."

"Anything."

"Good. You may begin by telling me of Terion."

Of all the things the dragon could have asked him about, this was one that Balgar had not anticipated. "I...I don't know," he stammered.

"Come now, did you not banish him from the council? Did you not have him pursued by a Vi'Raaji witch and by Fangs?" The flicker of guilt crossed Balgar's face and Kraegor caught it before the man could hide his complicity. "Ah, so I am not far from the mark," the dragon said with a smile. "Do you do this of your own accord?"

"I...I don't," Balgar trailed off, squirming as he tried to decide how to answer. What did Kraegor know and how much did he suspect? Would he kill him if he admitted it was all his own doing or would revealing his employer to the dragon save him?

"I will not ask a second time," Kraegor said, his eyes narrowing in anger.

"No," Balgar shook his head. "Well, yes. I mean, I took out the contract with the Fangs to kill him."

"And the Vi'Raaji?"

"I did not order that contract," he moaned, holding his injured arm. "I'm only the go-between."

"A go-between?" Kraegor mocked. "As powerful as you pretend to be, you are little more than a courier here?"

"I am only facilitating the contract," Balgar whined.

"And who holds this contract?" Kraegor asked. Balgar hesitated, causing the dragon to fasten his hand upon the man's good arm in a vise-like grip. "Answer the question or I shall snap your other arm like a twig. Who is your master?"

"Ranora!" Balgar nearly shouted, spittle running down his chin. "I swear it! It's Ranora."

Kraegor released Balgar's arm and straightened in surprise. "Ranora? The sorceress? Why?"

"I don't know," Balgar sputtered. "She only said that Terion must be captured. It was she who set up the meeting with Vendetta, I swear."

"Then you know the parameters of the contract," Kraegor said, leaning closer. "Speak them to me."

"Only that she was to capture him," Balgar admitted.

"All while you were trying to have him killed?" the dragon baited him.

"I hated him," Balgar managed to sneer. "I wanted him dead more than I wanted to see Ranora capture him. I was willing to pay a lot to have it done."

"And yet he survived twice," Kraegor said, his voice dripping with condescension. "Obviously you backed the wrong assassins."

"How was I to know..."

"That Vendetta aided him in Haven?" the dragon finished Balgar's question. "She did, you know. I believe she was rather upset that Fangs were attempting to kill the mark she was trying to capture. Tell me, Balgar," he hissed, leaning closer "What will Vendetta do if she captures Terion?"

"He is to be brought to me. Then I will facilitate handing him over to Ranora."

"And after that?"

"I don't know," Balgar replied, trembling. "I swear, she only said that he would be used as a pawn in a much larger game, one that would change everything."

Kraegor stood motionless, contemplating what he had just heard. Most things, his companion shared with him. But Shayene's fascination with Terion had puzzled him from the beginning. He had not pushed the issue, either, but he now wondered if that had been wise, particularly since Ranora was the one working directly with Shayene to set Nykiva up to be easily taken by Draven. The sorceress had been the perfect mole and now to find out that Ranora had been seeking to capture Terion herself spoke to a level of understanding on Ranora's part that could be very dangerous to both of them.

"Are you certain you know nothing more?" Kraegor finally asked, reaching down and gripping the wounded man by the throat again. Pulling him up so that his face was only inches away, he finished. "I would hate to think you were withholding information from me."

Balgar's eyes rolled as he shook his head over and over. "No! I am telling you...the truth. I told you everything I know! Please," he sputtered. "You're...choking me."

"I'm afraid, Balgar," Kraegor said, his voice low and measured, "that I must know absolutely everything."

"I have...told you...everything."

"We shall soon see," Kraegor responded, releasing the man's throat, but immediately fastening his long fingers on either side of Balgar's head. "How unfortunate for you."

Balgar screamed as Kraegor squeezed, pushing his iron-hard fingernails through man's skull. Balgar's shriek turned to a gurgle as Kraegor magically drew in all of the man's thoughts, discovering all that he wished to know. Surprisingly, Balgar knew little more than what he had already told the dragon, but that didn't stop Kraegor from relishing the process.

Several minutes later, he flung the dead man's body to the floor and casually licked the gore from his fingers as he considered all that he had learned. The initial thought that a human like Ranora could overthrow Shayene, was preposterous. Shayene was the most powerful sorceress in all the land. But while his companion's strength was increased because of the creation of the gate, she was also vulnerable because of Varankyl. Ranora had half of Varankyl already, a token given to her by Shayene for her service in ensuring that Keiran was eliminated and that Balgar mired the council in enough political maneuvering that they would not adequately prepare for Draven's coming. She had indeed been a valuable ally, but Kraegor realized that Shayene could never have foreseen the depths of the sorceress's ambitions. He wondered what Shayene would think when he confirmed that Ranora was indeed the traitor she was concerned about.

He finally turned to leave and then froze as a new figure rose up in the shadows of the doorway to face him. The intruder was dressed in the black clothes of an assassin, shot through with streaks of green. A serpent's mask covered his face and magical metal bracers in the form of striking serpents adorned his arms.

"I had wondered if I would find you skulking around here, brother," Kraegor said haughtily, unafraid and unconcerned at the man's sudden appearance. "Your pets seem to have not had much luck with killing Terion. But at the very least, they have been most amusing to watch."

Ignoring the comments, the figure walked past Kraegor, stopping in front of Balgar's body. He toed what was left of the dead man's misshapen head and then turned and faced the black dragon.

"Yours?"

Kraegor shrugged.

"There is nothing quite like a rich and greedy politician to keep my treasury full," the Serpent said softly. His voice was a guttural hiss, sounding more like a snake than a man. "Unfortunately, thanks to you, it appears I will have to find another to bend to my will in this city."

"Are you admitting that Balgar contracted you to kill Terion?"

"Does it matter?"

"No longer, it would appear," Kraegor said with a shrug. "But I warn you, your love of gold will be your undoing."

"And your devotion to your companion will be yours," the master assassin hissed.

Kraegor looked hard at the figure. "The world is changing, my brother, and it will be shaped by Shayene. With your employer dead, your part in this act is over, but you should consider well what part you will play in the future."

"I play what parts I wish to play and when I want to play them," the assassin countered.

"Your masquerade grows wearisome, Corosival," he said, using the assassin's true name, something no mortal in the world knew.

"To you, perhaps," came the reply. "But not to me. As long as there is greed and corruption in the world and men and women are willing to kill their brothers and sisters for gain, I foresee a long and fulfilling existence."

"Your companion might think differently."

"My companion need not know what I do in my spare time."

"And your interest in the witch?" Kraegor asked.

"You have eyes everywhere, just as I do," the other laughed, low and wicked. "But I am intrigued by that one. Perhaps I will arrange to meet her one-on-one, without interference."

At that, the leader of the Fangs dissolved into a smoky mist, before fading away into the darkness of the room.

Kraegor stood silently, considering all that had transpired. He could not help but smile. The subterfuge and deception that was going on was staggering. Shayene would not be happy that Corosival, a dragon like himself who had long been impersonating a human assassin, had attempted to kill Terion on two occasions. But that paled in comparison to the deception that Ranora had perpetrated, working for Shayene to give Nykiva up even while she was plotting her own coup d'état. Plots within plots were something that Kraegor could appreciate and at the center of it all was the witch, Vendetta. That was something he appreciated most of all.

With a grin, he waved a hand toward the fireplace. The flames died, plunging the room into darkness. He knew, though, the night was far from over.

Chapter 36

A short distance away, Vendetta stepped out of the darkness and looked around, listening for anyone that might be nearby. But nothing moved as she looked toward the darkened manor house, her mind still in turmoil. She had been in Nykiva for a few days now, her thoughts on the turn of events in Haven and even further back with her capture of Aylan and what she had discovered during their conversations.

The young mage was currently confined to a locked room in a house she owned deep in Nykiva, as much on his own word as hers. They had struck an understanding and he had come to trust her, as much as that was possible. Aylan knew she intended to free him when she found Terion, but he also knew the assassin was not certain that she would turn Terion over to Balgar. For Aylan, that was enough to keep him in her good graces. For Vendetta, it was enough to trust him to stay put and not use his magic to free himself.

It had also given her time to consider everything that had transpired since the day she had first agreed to work for Balgar and whoever his puppet master was. But too much had changed and her thoughts kept straying to her own dreams and her fateful encounter with the dream walker a decade ago. The vampire had known. He had seen her fate, a fate she had come to believe she was destined for. The question was, could she change it?

Still not certain what her meeting with Balgar would entail, she slipped through the shadows to a door set in the side of the large home. She froze, noting that it had not been pulled tight.

Drawing her blade, she gently pushed open the door. She was immediately struck by the thick and coppery smell of blood. Pushing aside her growing uneasiness, she moved through the house quickly and silently, counting three bodies on the ground floor, all of them servants and all with savage wounds that looked to have been made by claws.

She continued her search of the house and several minutes later, she found herself in Balgar's cold bedroom, staring thoughtfully down at the council leader's dead body. The blood and gore was fresh. The murder was recent, likely within the past hour or two.

"I trust this was not your work?" a voice said quietly in the gloom, startling the assassin.

Vendetta watched the speaker step out of the shadows near the window. The woman was a sorceress, judging by her garb, and it took a moment for Vendetta to recognize her. "Hardly my work, Ranora," she said, a steely edge coming to her voice. That she had initially missed the presence of the sorceress in the room, told her how much she had been affected by the events that were happening.

"I thought not," the enchantress said, stepping forward and willing a small sphere of red light into existence, bathing the room in a crimson glow. She was clad in sleeveless black robes and Vendetta could see tiny tendrils of arcane power arcing between her fingertips, as if she was sensing a fight.

"What are you doing here?" the assassin asked.

"I could ask the same question of you. I had hoped you were bringing your prize here, but I see you are alone."

"So you're the one behind all of this."

"If you are referring to the contracts that Balgar has been feeding you, then yes. You can understand then, why I am perplexed that Terion has not been delivered."

"I don't have him," Vendetta said, her eyes narrowing suspiciously.

"He left my tower several hours ago," Ranora said, not missing her distrust. "He seemed to think that his word to you was more important than a task I gave him."

"He is concerned about his friend. I would expect nothing less from the man."

"His friend became a liability for you almost a week ago," Ranora said, ice in her voice. "I'm surprised that you have not killed him already. It causes me to question your effectiveness."

"I don't care what you question. I have my reasons..."

"Your reasons truly do not concern me," Ranora interrupted with a dismissive wave of her hand.

"So, do you intend to kill me?" Vendetta couldn't help but smile at that. The thought of deadly combat immediately settled her nerves. Judging by the magical glyphs that covered Ranora's hands and arms, she had no doubt the sorceress was extremely skilled.

"As long as confidentiality is maintained, I am not interested in killing you," Ranora said, surprising the Vi'Raaji. "I may have need of your services in the future, after all."

"Then what do you want?"

"I still want Terion," Ranora replied evenly. "He said he would give himself over to you. When he does, I would like him turned over to me."

"If you already had your hands on him tonight, why not take him then?"

"That would seriously hamper my efforts to get his companions to carry out my task," the sorceress smiled. "Find him and then bring him to me, as originally agreed upon."

"For what purpose?" Vendetta asked, suddenly annoyed.

"Don't pretend that you don't know what's happening, witch."

"I know you play a dangerous game if you are indeed treating with an Arcai who has broken her oath of non-interference," she guessed.

"I do what must be done and hardly for the benefit of the Arcai," Ranora said coldly. "In the end, the fools of this city and beyond need to decide if they would rather be ruled by an Arcai with delusions of godhood or by one of their own."

"I fail to see how there is any difference. A tyrant is a tyrant, no matter the intentions."

"The difference is that while I agree that we must stop the Arcai, I will not have the rule of the Dom'Ithi people given back to an archaic, bickering council where the people with the most gold get their agendas passed."

"And you consider yourself as a better alternative?"

"I will destroy Shayene and present myself in her stead as a benevolent and fair ruler. The Dom'Ithi people do not trust the council anymore and would be far better served having their needs seen to by one person. Can you honestly find fault in that?"

"Whether it is you or Shayene imposing your will on a free people, it is still a dictatorship," Vendetta argued. "Regardless, you cannot defeat Shayene. She is an Arcai. You are a mortal."

"She is more vulnerable than you know," Ranora said smugly. "And with Terion, I will be able to get close to her and end this before Draven and his armies arrive."

"And what about Balgar?" Vendetta said, motioning toward the body of the council leader. "Have you factored in who killed him?"

At that, Ranora's features darkened. "Bring Terion to me," she said quietly ignoring the question. You have forty-eight hours to find him and complete the contract or the next time we meet will not be as pleasant."

A moment later, she vanished in a flash of magical light. Vendetta looked around the darkened room, lit now only by moonlight. The revelation that a relatively young sorceress like Ranora was behind what was happening was secondary to the belief that the woman could possibly pull it off. Vendetta had killed an Arcai herself a decade ago. What assurances did she have that the sorceress couldn't have the same success?

Before she could consider it further, flames suddenly snapped into existence in the cold fireplace and a long, low laugh filled the room. "My, my," a cold voice chuckled softly. "I must say that this has been a most illuminating evening."

Vendetta spun, searching for the source of the voice, but seeing nothing. A chill ran down her spine and she immediately began considering escape routes. A figure slowly materialized between her and the doorway, leaving the window as her only escape. "Who are you?" she asked, her voice quiet and steely.

"You don't know?" the man asked, his voice silky smooth and his eyes glittering in the shadows. "Perhaps that is not surprising, given the circumstances of our meeting here. But I certainly know who you are, Vendetta."

"So Ranora does intend to eliminate me after all," the Vi'Raaji reasoned, shifting her body into a combat stance.

The stranger chuckled. "Ranora is a fool. She has absolutely no idea what she has brought upon herself."

Vendetta instantly made the connection and her blood ran cold. "It was you. You killed Balgar, didn't you."

"Balgar had outlived his usefulness, as has Ranora, who I will deal with shortly. You, on the other hand, still possess potential and will serve me quite nicely."

Vendetta drew her weapons quickly and smoothly. "I serve no one. What contracts I accept are of my own choosing."

"Who said anything about a contract?" he laughed and then

vanished, instantly reappearing behind her and striking her with a force that threw her across the room. Pain exploded in her hip as she struck one of the broken bed posts and she twisted quickly to her side in order to keep her feet under her. She brought her blades back around as she faced her attacker.

The man smiled cruelly as he advanced leisurely across the room. Vendetta thrust forward with her lead weapon, but suddenly her movements felt leaden, as if she was barely moving. Her attacker clamped his hand down on her weapon hand and roughly pulled her to him, slamming his forehead into her face.

Stars exploded behind the beautiful assassin's eyes and he slammed his head into her face a second time, driving all the strength from her limbs. She felt blood flowing from a cut over her eye and from her nose and lips as she sagged in his arms, her weapons dropping from her nerveless hands. A moment later, he had bent her backwards over the bed, one hand closing tightly about her throat as the long-nailed fingers of his other hand tore the clothing from her body. His voice sounded far away as he spoke.

"I have watched you for some time, witch," Kraegor the Black said huskily, pushing her down on the bed as he slowly strangled her. "The time has finally come to take what I have desired."

She tried to scream as he violated her, but her voice was choked off. He took his time, and blackness claimed her long before he was finished.

Chapter 37

The next morning found Siranschae and Notyet standing before the Mirror of Ataracus along with Branson, who would accompany them through the portal. Ranora was nearby, speaking softly to Eric, giving him final instructions. No one was certain of success and even Eric, who felt stronger, was considerably less optimistic than he had been the previous night.

The night before, the group had thoroughly discussed who would return to Branson's world. It had been decided that Branson himself would go, along with the two warriors to provide any proof to Branson's story, should they happen to find themselves in the presence of others. In addition, Siranschae was better suited than any of them to handle the artifact. So the three would go together.

Eric would, of course, have to remain behind to open the portal and the plan was for him to open it again twenty-four hours later in the exact same place. This would ensure they had plenty of time to obtain the artifact, as well as give Eric the time he would likely need to recover from the task of bridging the two worlds.

"Is everyone rested and ready?" Ranora finally asked, her voice somewhat clipped.

"As ready as we can be," Siranschae answered, eyeing the sorceress and wondering if she was still upset that Terion had left to find and rescue Aylan.

"The plan is simple enough," Ranora stated, ignoring the dragon's look, "and hopefully without problems. If something does go wrong, you will have to adapt as well as you can. But return to the portal location by this time tomorrow."

"Understood," Branson said. "But this is likely not going to be as simple as stepping in, grabbing the thing, and coming home."

"Thinking there's going to be trouble?" Swan spoke up from his place lounging in one of the old chairs. He was less than pleased he would not be going back, but understood that in the event of any problems that kept Branson from returning, it would be up to him to effect the rescue of their people from Shayene.

"I'm always thinking there's going to be trouble," Branson shrugged. "It's been a couple months now since we left and that sub is still there. Either something is really screwed up back home or…"

"I was wondering the same thing, boss," Swan said with a nod. "Something ain't right."

"Unfortunately, we do not have the time to continue waiting," Ranora interrupted. Turning to Eric, she asked, "Are you ready?"

The young soldier-turned-gatekeeper swallowed nervously and nodded. Ranora faced the mirror and again waved her hand over the surface, letting herself fall into her magic. Immediately, the familiar clouds began to roll violently before suddenly dissipating and showing them once again the forest river. As the picture took shape, all eyes turned to the young gatekeeper.

"Here goes nothing," Eric said with a deep breath. He closed his eyes and fell into himself, reaching downward and mentally taking hold of the strange power that now pulsed within him. When he had it harnessed within his mind, he looked into the mirror, taking note of where he would place the portal. He then let the magic surge from his outstretched hands. The power flowed seamlessly from him, manifesting itself in crackling ribbons of energy that quickly twisted into a large circle. The portal started small and then expanded, reaching a diameter of roughly six feet. Beyond it, they could see the forest, exactly how it looked in the mirror.

"Let's move," Branson said quietly and then stepped through the gate. Notyet and Siranschae followed and as soon as they stepped

Convergence

through, the gate popped out of existence behind them with an audible crack of energy.

In Ranora's tower, those in attendance would watch the next hours through the mirror in dismay, cursing their short-sightedness and wondering about the survival of their friends.

On Branson's world, it happened with lightning quickness. The moment the gate vanished, automatic gunfire opened up and Branson found himself spun around as a round took him in the shoulder. Another pinged off of Notyet's armor-plated forearm as he dove to the ground, leaving a deep crease in the steel. Had Siranschae possessed her former strength, she might have taken dragon form right there. As it was, she was forced to pull her blade, even as shouts of "cease fire!" rang out around them.

With a grunt of pain, Branson hauled himself to his knees, pressing a hand against the ragged wound in his shoulder. "What the f…" he began, but another voice shouted him down.

"Don't move!" a soldier barked, stepping out of the trees, his rifle trained on Branson. Behind him and around them, numerous other soldiers appeared as well.

"Hold fire," Branson snapped back, looking up at an American marine that he did not recognize. He was rewarded with a boot to his chest, pushing him back down to his knees.

"I said don't move!"

"Fine," Branson sighed, looking at his companions. "You heard the man. Weapons down. We aren't winning this round."

"And yet, we must," Siranschae began, but Branson waved her off.

"Not like this. Trust me, lady. This op has been on the boards

401

the moment we stepped through the gate to your world in the first place. They were waiting for us."

"Major Branson," another voice called out and they looked toward the river's edge as several other solders moved up the path toward them.

"Lieutenant Davis," Branson said with obvious relief. "Good to see you again."

"You know, the first time I saw that happen, I couldn't believe what I was seeing," Davis said as he moved forward, flanked by several more soldiers, all of them with weapons out. "So I wasn't too surprised to see it again." He stopped in front of Branson, who was still on his knees. "You've been gone for a long time, major."

"You knew we would be coming back."

"With all due respect, I'll be the judge of what I know and don't know," Davis interrupted, his face grim. "As of this moment, you are prisoners of war and I can promise you that if you attempt to escape, the consequences will be severe."

"What the devil is wrong with you, Davis?" Branson snapped, glaring at the marine.

Lieutenant Davis knelt down before his former commanding officer and looked him directly in the eyes. "A lot has changed, sir. We don't know where you were or how you got back, but I'm fairly certain you're here to get this." He held up an item for all to see. While he might not know what it was, Branson did. It was the spiked crystalline rod of Varankyl. Branson tensed slightly and it was enough to confirm the man's suspicions. Without another word, he turned to his men. "Zip ties," he commanded. "Take them to camp. And get a medic on standby to patch up the major."

"Yes, sir," one of the soldiers replied and immediately he and the others quickly bound their prisoners and led them down the path.

Once at the riverbank, they were turned left and marched along the strip of rock and sand past the sub. A short time later, the camp came into view, a group of large canvas tents and a pair of white prefab buildings. Branson understood the significance immediately. Set up on the far side of the river as it was, it would remain out of sight to anyone coming through the trees toward the sub. The second thing that stood out was the red, white, and blue flag flying on a pole near one of the prefabs. It wasn't American. It was the red, white, and blue of the Russian flag that fluttered in the breeze.

"What's going on here?" he dared to speak, looking toward Davis. But Davis ignored him, instead speaking into his shoulder mounted radio. "We're inbound," he said tonelessly. "The major is secure." Without waiting for an answer, he switched it off and glanced at Branson, looking as if he was going to speak. Instead, he turned away, remaining silent.

"Not quite the return you were expecting," Siranschae said softly, earning a prod in the back by one of the soldiers with the barrel of his rifle. She snapped a glare at the man that told him she was more dangerous than he could ever imagine. He backed off immediately, clearing his throat.

"No," Branson shook his head, puzzled. "Like I said, they knew we were coming."

"Who's they?"

"These guys are United States Marines, so they're the good guys...or they were. Davis is...was one of my men. The others, I don't know."

"Quiet," one of the escorting soldiers snapped.

It was Davis that answered. "Regardless of our orders, *sergeant*, you are still addressing *Major* Branson. I would suggest you keep that in mind."

"Yes, sir," the man snapped to attention, clearly accepting the rebuke.

A few minutes later, they walked into camp. Without a word, a group of heavily armed marines quickly surrounded and escorted Notyet and Siranschae toward a tent at the far end of the camp. Davis handed Branson off to another pair of soldiers. "Patch him up," he said. "I'll want him in thirty minutes to begin interrogation."

"Yes, sir," both soldiers replied, guiding the wounded marine toward one of the pre-fabs, one with a big red cross on the side. Branson was deep into planning their escape before his foot even hit the threshold.

Thirty minutes later, Davis entered the infirmary to claim his prisoner. Branson looked up at him, clearly impatient. He might be the one due for interrogation, but he was certainly going to get some answers himself. The medic that patched him up wasn't American like the others. He was a Russian civy that did his job in silence while the American soldiers stood at attention near the door. No one had uttered a single word in the half hour he was there.

"Ready?" Davis asked, his tone emotionless.

"Has to be better than this place," Branson replied, sliding off the exam table and cracking his neck. His shoulder was patched—the Russian did a good job—and his arm was in a sling, at his own request. He had told the doctor that moving his arm felt like it was pulling the stitches, so he wanted it immobilized. The man had silently agreed, helping him sling it up. What he missed was Branson sliding in an empty hypodermic he had palmed from the tray during a coughing spell. It wasn't much, but he would find a way for it to make do.

"I'll swing you by the latrine before we get started," Davis said, opening the door to allow Branson to exit.

"I think I can hold it."

"Yeah, that's what they all say. I'd rather you get it done now before the colonel starts working on you. I really don't want to see you pissing your pants, *major*."

For a moment, Branson considered putting the hypodermic into Davis' jugular, but he quickly shelved the thought. "You've turned into a real prick," he said instead, deciding it would be better to goad the man into a mistake.

Davis ignored him and walked him down the path toward the river's edge. Before the trees gave way to beach, he turned him onto a band of dirt between several trees. Along one side was a deeply dug ditch and Branson immediately smelled human waste. Davis pushed him to the edge of the trench and then sidled up on the other side, a comfortable distance from him. "I hope you don't think I'm going to help you, major," he said. "One hand or not, you're on your own."

With a shrug of his shoulders, Branson unzipped and began to take care of business, Davis doing the same.

"Listen close," Davis said under his breath, eyes off in the distance. "Eyes and ears everywhere. Long story. Can you bug out?"

"Twenty-four hours from insertion," Branson replied, immediately understanding. "Same location. Can you get us there?"

"Hard to say, but will do my best, sir."

"I'll be needing that rod, too."

"I'll see what I can do."

"America?" Branson asked, fearing that everything had fallen apart in his absence.

"Still there," Davis reassured him, "but Russia is calling the shots on this op."

"We caved."

"Affirmative," Davis said, zipping up. "But you can't do the same."

Branson looked up.

"Russian colonel is coming in at fourteen hundred," Davis finished. "He's brutal, so watch yourself."

"Nothing he can do to me that hasn't already been done," Branson replied gamely, holding up one of his scarred hands. "Let's get this done."

Davis hadn't been lying. The Russian colonel, a bald bear of a man, used the first hour of their time together in the other white prefab building, just chatting back and forth, soldier to soldier. Branson had found it less than informative as the Russian wasn't keen on giving up any intel himself. After about an hour and not getting any straight answers from the American, the talk had given way to physical activities. One armed, Branson was in no position to resist and his enemy took his time just taking the occasional body shot, hard punches to the stomach or the ribs delivered at just the right intervals. And through it all, the Russian kept asking questions, speaking to him as if they were old friends.

It was the conversational pauses that turned out to be the colonel's undoing. Confident in his authority and his mastery of his wounded prisoner, he thought nothing of turning his back to Branson, as much to demonstrate his disdain for the American as anything. It was during one of those turns that Branson slid the syringe out of his sling. When the Russian swung back around, Branson buried it in the man's eye socket, driving it deep into his brain. He used the momentary surprise to lock his good arm around the Russian's throat, pulling him down to the floor and locking his legs tightly around the man, immobilizing him as he began to shudder.

It took a bit of time, but the Russian's body finally went slack. Branson didn't care if the man was dead or not, although if he was alive, the damage was severe enough that he wasn't worried about pursuit. Only the plunger of the hypodermic was visible in his eye. Slowly, Branson relaxed his hold, tensing for any sudden movement from his enemy. When none came, he climbed to his feet. Looking at his bandaged shoulder, he could see the blood beginning to soak through the gauze. He had popped the stitches. However, it would have to wait.

Taking a moment to arm himself with the man's sidearm, Branson went to the door. There were no windows in the prefab, so he had no way of knowing who was on the other side. He was mulling his next move when the door swung open and Davis stepped into the room.

If Lieutenant Todd Davis was surprised when he saw the Russian commander dead, he did not show it. He was even less surprised when Branson placed the barrel of the colonel's Makarov PM against his temple. Branson held it there for a moment, before pulling it away.

"Good to know my timing is spot on," Davis said quietly, shutting the door behind him. "He dead?"

"Doesn't matter," Branson replied. "He's not getting up any time soon"

"That leaves us with a big problem. If you have a twenty-four hour window from your arrival to evac, you've got a lot of time to kill before that happens. There's no telling what's going to go down in the next few hours."

"You going to tell me what's going on here?" Branson asked. "What's up with the Russians, anyway?"

"Politics and kowtowing to the enemy," Davis replied, his voice tense. "After you guys disappeared, we were quarantined on site for almost a week before any additional orders came down. Washington was fighting with the French and visa versa and suddenly the Russians were involved."

"Their sub?"

"So they claim and now they're running the op because of it." Davis looked hard at Branson, before continuing. "And just so you know, that op has changed drastically since you left."

"Meaning what?"

"Meaning you're it now," the lieutenant replied. "Shortly after you left, some jackass in DC uploaded video of our encounter with the alien and the gate to YouTube and all hell broke loose. Everyone's trying to play it down and has been for the last couple months. In the meantime, they've got a hundred mile perimeter set up around this location, patrolled by more air and ground assets than we had in Iraq. We are completely locked down in here, or at least we were until a few hours ago."

"They've been waiting for me?"

"You or someone to come back through a portal. That rod I showed you showed up out of nowhere on the sub about a month ago, so we knew someone was coming back."

"Well, this can't get any worse," Branson grumbled. "What's with our troops here, if the Russians are running things?"

"Command transferred out the rest of our battalion and left me with mostly unknowns," Davis replied. "We're here providing the muscle while Russian and American scientists are working on the sub, supposedly in some great exercise of multi-national unity. That's what's being pitched to the public anyway, but that's a load of garbage."

"What about the French?"

"Oh, you know them. They're whining twenty-four seven, but no one's listening. Any of them left on your end?"

"One," Branson replied, suddenly thinking of the men back on the parallel world. "It's a helluva story and not a pretty one."

"I judged that by your scars," Davis said. "Anyone ever tell you that you look like Frankenstein?"

"Yeah, I've already heard it. I'll tell you about it later."

"Might not have a chance. I'll be honest, sir, I don't trust any of our guys over here. Washington has me in charge, but I'm just a piece on the chessboard. These guys aren't answering to me. They've got someone else pulling the strings."

"Which complicates things."

"Immensely," Davis agreed. "I can keep things calm for an hour, maybe two. No chance I can keep it on the down low until your evac."

"That might be all I need," Branson said thoughtfully. "We might be able to move up the time table. You have that rod on you?"

"It's in lockup."

"Can you get it?"

"Yeah."

"Do it," Branson said. "You up for coming back with us?"

"You mean through that gate?" Davis asked incredulously.

"It might be your only chance, if you're going to help us."

"Well, that depends on what else you need."

"I need my friends back at the rendezvous point along with that rod, nothing more. Anyone at all here that you can trust?"

"Maybe one or two, tops."

"That'll be enough," Branson said. "Get my two friends to the evac point, yourself included, with the rod, because I sure don't want to have to come back. Get someone to create a diversion on the other side of the camp to pull my guards and anyone else that will follow. I'll do the rest and meet you there."

"Not very foolproof, sir."

"It'll have to do. Just do what I ask and let me take care of the rest."

"I'll do my best," Davis said. "What's your timeframe?"

"With the colonel dead, there's no time better than the present. Now get going. Say what you have to say to the guards out front about the colonel beating my ass into the ground. Just make sure whatever you pull on the other side of camp is enough to get people running."

"What if they don't leave?"

"I've got the colonel's sidearm," Branson replied. "I'll improvise. But make sure you and my friends are at the evac point."

"Yes, sir," Davis nodded, snapping off a salute to his former commanding officer, before slamming the door shut behind him.

Listening at the door, Branson could only hear muffled voices as Davis said something to the guards, and then silence. Now he would have to wait.

It took about an hour and Branson was starting to worry, when the first explosion finally rattled the prefab. It was followed by two more. Branson pulled his arm out of the sling and grabbed the door handle. He counted to five and then swung the door open wide. As Davis had feared, both guards had remained at their post as others were running toward the smoke rising above the trees on the other end of camp. Branson improvised by shooting both of them.

Rushing out of the building, he tucked the Makarov into his pants and snatched up one of the Marine's M16's and began running the other way. Predictably, shouts followed him. He made the beach before the first shots rang out. Ducking into the trees, he moved as quickly as he could, trusting his instincts to find the exact spot that Eric would open the gate. That was the part of his plan he wasn't certain about and he had invested a considerable amount of faith that on the other side, Ranora and Eric had been watching what was happening. He had to believe they were preparing at that very moment to open the gateway.

Bullets flicked through the leaves of a tree off to his right and he crouched lower, moving quickly. He didn't want to return fire, at least unless he was forced to. Let them wonder for the moment.

It took him about five minutes to reach the designated spot and when he did, he was alone. Davis was nowhere to be seen, nor was Notyet and Siranschae. He knew the ramifications of that and while he would certainly mourn the loss of the two strangers, none of this would matter without Davis and the artifact.

Taking up a position behind a large oak, he peered around it and down toward the beach. He heard shouts and issued orders, but the gunfire had stopped. They were searching for him and he knew that it wouldn't take them long to find out where he was.

He was contemplating his strategy in the inevitable firefight when automatic weapon fire lit up the forest again. He heard a grunt and muffled curse—definitely American—before his companions burst through the brush several feet away. Notyet had been stripped of his armor and was wearing only a pair of marine trousers and boots. Siranschae still had her armor, but neither had their weapons. Between them, they were supporting Davis, who had a hand pressed hard against his gut, a stain of red growing on his uniform.

"Where's...the gate?" Davis wheezed, his eyes squinted tightly against the pain.

"Give it some time," Branson replied, sending several bursts of automatic weapon fire back toward the beach. He purposely aimed high, hoping only to buy time. He wasn't ready to gun down other marines. At least not yet.

Return fire had them all hunkering down behind trees, with Siranschae helping put pressure on Davis' wound. "Your friend will die if we don't get him help," she said.

"He's gut shot," Branson said tonelessly. "If we take him back, your world doesn't have the ability to heal him. He needs to stay here and hopefully the Russians will get him to a surgical hospital."

"Yeah…" Davis started to reply, before coughing cut him off. Blood dribbled down his chin. "That…ain't happenin'."

More gunfire erupted and Branson knew the soldiers were moving on their position now with the cover fire in place. It was now or never.

Fortunately, at that moment, the portal snapped open with a high pitched buzz right behind him.

"Go!" he shouted, spraying return fire in a wide swath back toward the beach. Then they were moving, with Notyet grabbing Davis and diving through the portal. Siranschae followed with Branson the last to jump through. As he did so, the portal popped out of existence. American marines converged on the clearing seconds later.

They had just escaped.

Chapter 38

Branson immediately dropped to his knees beside Davis, his hands going to the man's belly wound. Pressing hard, trying to stop the bleeding, he said quietly, "Well done, lieutenant. Now hang on, let's see about getting you patched up."

"How...did you...know?" Davis coughed weakly.

"I didn't," Branson answered. "It was a calculated risk."

"You have the artifact?" Ranora said urgently, kneeling beside them, her gaze on Branson.

"I'll worry about that when I get him stabilized," Branson snapped, glaring at the woman.

"Let me," a voice said softly, breaking the tension and causing them all to look up. There were others in the room that had not been there when the trio had departed. One of them, a young girl appearing pale and robed in white, stood with her fingers laced in front of her. "Let me," she said again.

The huge warrior, Notyet, placed his hands on her shoulder, his face both joyful and anxious. He didn't need to sign his question.

"I am alright, Notyet," Arianna said with a gentle smile, her first after weeks in a coma. "Now that I know, it's much easier. I can help him." She paused and looked at Siranschae. "Like I helped you."

Arianna knelt before the wounded marine. She took Branson's scarred hands in her own, lifting them gently from the wounded stomach of the other soldier. At her touch, Branson felt electricity shoot up his arms, coalescing into a burning feeling in his own wounded shoulder. A moment later, it passed as she released his hands and went to work on Davis. As she did, Branson realized the pain in his shoulder had diminished considerably.

On the floor, Davis was fluttering in and out of consciousness as the white robed angel pressed her delicate hands against his torn stomach. A groan escaped both of them simultaneously as the empathic healer realized the scope of his wound. He had lost a lot of blood, perhaps too much. For a moment, she faltered, wondering if she had the strength. But she quickly pushed those thoughts aside. She had shown her strength once and survived. Now, a new power flowed within her own blood and she felt it enhance her empathic abilities. Silently, she went to work, feeling the man's wounds with her hands, seeing them in her mind. Slowly, she began to heal him.

The others watched in rapt silence, Notyet with the concern of a father, Siranschae with what looked like a mother's love. Branson could only stare now, leaving his soldier in the hands of the young girl, not much more than a teenager. The rest looked on as well – Boozer seated in a chair with Anthony on her lap, Swan behind them alongside Eric, who looked like he was ready to collapse himself from exhaustion. Even Ranora marveled inwardly as she watched Arianna work, her fingers pressing against the wound and even dipping into his torn flesh. Where she touched, the blood lessoned and the flesh began to heal into shining scars.

It took some time and when it was over, Lieutenant Todd Davis was sleeping, his eyes closed in peaceful slumber. His belly was healed, a large somewhat star-shaped scar all that remained of the bullet wound. Arianna slumped to the floor, only to have Siranschae sweep her up in her arms.

"Her room?" the human-form dragon asked, turning to Ranora.

"Yes, of course," the sorceress said, breaking out of her own trance. She motioned toward the door where one of her servants had been standing. "Follow the girl. She will take you to a private room on the other side of the tower." She beckoned another servant forward.

"Prepare a room for the outworlder. He will likely sleep for some time."

"Yes, mi'lady," the young girl said and then hurried out of the room.

"It would seem you have been successful, Rick Branson," Ranora said, turning her full attention back to the soldier.

"You watched," he answered, suddenly feeling very tired.

"We did."

"I was gambling on that," he added. "If you hadn't been, that would have been the end." He turned away from her and went to Eric, clapping the young man on the soldier. "Well done, Tuner. I owe you. We all do."

"Thank you, sir," Eric said, blushing slightly.

"I assume you will want to be with your people," Ranora went on. "All of you have performed admirably and now should take your rest. I have work to do on my own." She held up the haft of the enchanted mace, gazing at it.

Branson looked at her, his eyes narrowing. How she had gotten her hands on the artifact, he didn't know. He was certain that Davis had it in his possession when they came through the gate. Now here she was, holding it aloft like she had procured it herself. It made him more than a little angry, but he stayed silent.

"Once I have completed the task of reforming Varankyl, it will be time to end this," Ranora said, returning Branson's hard stare. "Prepare your men and what others will agree to go with you. We will assault Shayene's stronghold in the Wraithlands in two day's time."

"You have an army to go with us?"

"Why would I need an army when I have you?" she smiled. "An army will attract attention. Our best chance of success lies in a small party that won't attract the attention of her own forces."

"Which are likely to be considerable."

"All the more reason to go with stealth," Ranora said, addressing them all. "Now go, I have much work to do."

With nods and words of acceptance, the various individuals departed, Ranora's servants leading them out of her study and to their rooms in the far wing of the tower complex.

Branson was the last, pausing at the doorway to turn and look at the enchantress. "I wonder, lady," he said quietly, "if you're telling us everything."

"And what would I gain by keeping anything from you?" she answered. "You have performed brilliantly, better than I could have hoped. Because of you and your friends, I have the artifact and can now reform it."

"To do what really?"

"To destroy the one that would destroy us," she replied coolly. "Isn't that what everyone wants?"

"I want to get my people back."

"The only way to do that will be to destroy Shayene and the only way to accomplish that, will be to destroy the gate, making her vulnerable. That is what Varankyl will do."

"And then?"

"You can kill her," Ranora shrugged. "If the destruction of the gate doesn't kill her outright, she should be robbed of all powers. What you do with her at that point, I care not."

"As long as my people are freed."

"If they are still alive, they will be," Ranora said. "I give you my word."

Branson stood for a few more seconds, searching her face. Finally satisfied, he left the room, letting the door shut behind him.

When he was gone, one of Ranora's servants appeared from

the shadows near the stairs where she had been watching the entire time. Like the others, it was a young girl, but instead of plain nondescript servant clothing, she was clad in unadorned robes of black silk. The markings of magical glyphs adorned her fingers, creeping onto her hands. She was young in the art and looked at Ranora expectantly.

"Prepare the lower chambers," Ranora said softly. "The time has come to reform Varankyl."

"What of Terion?" the young girl asked. "Do you intend to wait for the assassin to bring him to you?"

"If she does, so much the better," Ranora replied, looking at the piece of artifact she held in her hands. "It would make things much easier to have Shayene preoccupied with him while I destroy the gate."

"And if she doesn't?"

"No matter. I have plenty of others who will do my bidding."

"Very good, mistress," the young woman said with a smile, bowing low as she departed.

Ranora paid her no heed. The young apprentice would do as she was commanded. And once she completed the preparations, the girl would find herself one of those fools that Ranora intended to throw against Shayene. There were other potential apprentices, to be sure, including one nearby who didn't even know it yet. She would consider that more fully once Shayene was removed. For the moment, the youngster would have to wait.

Chapter 39

That evening, Terion found himself crouched in the shadowed gloom beneath an ancient oak tree, staring up at the outline of the manor house, considering his plan and wondering again if his concerns were correctly placed. He did not yet know the outcome of the task Ranora had sent his friends on, but that didn't stop him from wondering. He wished he could have accompanied them, but he owed a debt to the young mage who called him friend and followed him, no matter the danger.

Aylan was somewhere in the city, if he were to believe the assassin and he had no reason to doubt her after her actions in Haven. Except that she had not found him as she had told him she would. He had searched for her himself, making himself visible in taverns and inns, hoping she or one of her contacts might see him and bring him to her. But there had been nothing.

It was that which had brought him to Balgar's mansion. Balgar Mud was a slimy bureaucrat and quite possibly complicit in Keiran's murder. Terion had not been able to find Vendetta, but he was almost certain that Balgar might be able to change his fortune. His only concern was being able to do that without killing the man, particularly if he found him guilty of what Terion believed he had done.

Sequestered in the shadows, he wondered again at the darkened windows of the manor house. He had been hidden here now for more than an hour and in his time, he had seen no lights, nor any movement from the house. It had gradually escalated his concern until finally, he could wait no longer.

Loosening his weapons, he moved toward the house, keeping to the shadows and out of the moonlight. He reached the front of the house and quickly hurried around to the side, heading for the servant's entrance. There he found the door ajar, leading into darkness. Nothing moved inside.

Pulling a long-bladed dagger, the swordsman slipped into the house. It was silent as a tomb and Terion could smell death as he stepped across the threshold. He padded softly down the hall, looking in the first room he came to. It was the kitchen, but the fires were cold and no lamps were lit. By the light of the moon streaming through the window, he could see the body of what he presumed was the cook, lying stretched out on the preparation table, the man's throat torn open.

Not bothering to investigate, he quickly checked the rest of the ground floor, finding the bodies of two more of Balgar's servants, both of them brutally murdered, their blood drying and crusted. He quickly ascended to the second floor, cringing at the slight creak of wood. But nothing stormed out to meet him and he quickly made the landing and began moving down the hall, checking the rooms as he went. The first two appeared normal, nothing out of place. But when he opened the door at the end of the hall to what was Balgar's huge bedroom, he was stunned at what he found.

He could see Balgar's corpse tossed unceremoniously to one side of the room. Where the man's head should have been was only a misshapen mass of bone and flesh. But the real shock was the figure on the bed. She was bound hand and foot to each of the four corner posts of the bed and her black silk clothing had been shredded, leaving her mostly naked, her skin ashen where it wasn't bruised. It was obvious what had been done to her and Terion shook his head angrily, despite the troubling animosity he held toward the Vi'Raaji witch for the murder of his friends. No one should have to suffer the degradation she had suffered before death, and he found himself hoping that she had died quickly.

He stepped into the room and walked over to the bed. Looking briefly at the woman's bruised face, he used his dagger to sever the bonds that held her, intending to wrap her in a blanket and give her some dignity when her body was found by authorities.

That was when her hand weakly closed on his wrist and he nearly shouted with fright at the sudden realization that she was not dead. Instead, she was looking up at him through tear-filled eyes, utterly helpless and at his mercy. He thought back to their battle and her willingness to kill him, as well as the deaths of Cavanah and Keiran. He knew he should hate her; should avenge the deaths of his friends right now, but he also could not forget the change he had seen in her in Haven, her own confusion and her willingness to aid him. Conflicted as never before, he let his emotions take hold and bear witness to the truth. He was looking no at a deadly assassin, but at a woman who had been savagely assaulted.

He gently drew the edge of the bedclothes up, covering her nakedness. Her hand reached weakly for his throat and he caught her wrist, momentarily thinking she was trying to attack him. But she was whispering, her voice cracked and broken. "Boot," was all he could hear and he looked down at the floor. Her nearly knee high leather boots lay next to the bed. Just inside of one, he saw the top of a stoppered vial secured by a small band. He quickly withdrew it and put the vial to her lips, letting the liquid pour into her mouth.

The reaction was immediate. She sat bolt upright, her eyes going wide and her face reddening. Her long fingers gripped the bedclothes tightly as the powerful potion worked its way into her, beginning to heal her wounds, both outside and in. After a few minutes, normal color began to return to her skin. She finally turned her face toward Terion, her pale blue eyes shining in the gloom. "Thank you," she whispered, pulling the bedclothes tighter about her and drawing her legs underneath her, but making no other movement.

Terion nodded, still very much conflicted and at a loss on what to say. "Powerful brew," he finally stammered, looking away.

She slowly returned the nod, equally at a loss. Here was a man she had tried to kill and for the first time in her life, Vendetta did not know how to react. Part of her was screaming that she should put a dagger into his heart so that none would know what happened, while the other half was reminding her of the honor of her people, an honor which helped her aid the man and his friends in Haven. In the end, it was the latter half that won out.

"I am indebted to you, Terion," she finally said softly, her voice husky and raw as she turned away and looked out the window. "Honor demands…"

"What would you know of honor," he snapped, letting his anger take control for a moment. "You are an assassin. You killed Keiran, Cavanah…me, if you had been given the chance."

"I cannot change the past," she said simply, her eyes surprisingly sad. "I cannot change who I am."

"Did you kill Balgar, too?" he pressed.

"No." Her voice was quiet, leaving something unsaid.

"But you know who did," Terion said, his voice softening as he realized the tenuous situation they were in. "Was it the same person that did this to you?"

She whirled to face him, her own eyes suddenly blazing in anger. "It was," she snapped viciously, one hand unconsciously reaching for a weapon that was no longer there. "Does that please you, Terion? Do you consider your friends avenged now that I have been violated so? It would have been better if he had killed me."

Terion leaned forward, his hand closing on hers. "I did not mean to imply I was happy at what happened," he said gently. "You are an assassin, by trade. You have killed those that were close to me. Killing you in battle would be one thing, but this…," he trailed off, unable to finish.

"It is the way of my people, Terion," she said quietly, her voice distant.

"You chose to be an assassin," he reminded her.

"You know nothing of me," she responded bitterly. "I did not choose my path as a child, much like your people do. I was taken from my family at a very young age and trained in the arts. While Dom children were playing imaginary games, I was plying a trade that was forced upon me. I was one of the youngest to ever pass the final test of the Harrowing and I accepted the calling because it was required of me…because it is my heritage."

"And because you're good at it," he added.

She looked at him, a mixture of anger and helplessness. "I cannot change who I am," she repeated.

"You cannot change who you were. But one can always change who they will be." He picked up her discarded blade, then presented it handle-first to the startled Vi'Raaji.

Uncertainty clouded her face, but she slowly took the dragon-forged blade from him and held it before her.

"I am familiar with some Vi'Raaji customs," he went on, turning his back to her. "So, I offer you a choice. You can either kill me and depart with no one the wiser about what has happened to you or that I freed you."

"And the other option?" she asked guardedly after a long silence.

"You can tell me your birth name," he answered without pause, hoping against hope that he was making the smart decision.

Vendetta froze. "You have no idea what you are asking," she

whispered. "Or risking."

"I risk it because I'm certain I know how you will react," he said, purposefully keeping his back to her. Outwardly, he was quite calm, but inwardly, he was wrestling with his decision to test her like this. Indeed, Terion knew well that honored Vi'Raaji such as Vendetta held their real names secret to all but the closest family members. As they came of age, those that successfully navigated the Harrowing and progressed down their chosen path – or not chosen, according to her – were given a name by the mistress who gave them their final test and their given name was forgotten, stricken from the records of their people. Vendetta was no different and she would hold honor high among her priorities. Now, he was asking her for the equivalent of a life debt – a pledge that she would serve him. He held himself still, his eyes fixed on a point on the wall above the mantel, and waited. The seconds turned into minutes and still, the feeling of a dagger sliding into his heart never came. Finally, as he was about to face her, she spoke.

"Avenrael," she finally whispered.

Smiling to himself, he turned and looked at her. She had bowed her head and her dagger was laying on the bedclothes. He had been right.

"Avenrael," he repeated. "That's a beautiful name."

She looked up at him and there was a hard edge to her voice when she spoke. "I am trusting in your honor as I have never trusted another before. If you betray me, Terion, there will be no end to the pain I deliver to you and those close to you."

"I understand and I give you my word, Avenrael, that I will never betray your trust."

In a flash, she had retrieved the dagger from the bed and now held it against his throat. "You will also swear to me that you will never utter my given name again. It is enough that you know it. But you must never speak it again. Swear this."

Terion swallowed audibly, but managed to smile. "You have my word…Vendetta."

Her features softened and she laid the blade back on the bed. "So what happens next?" she asked quietly, still obviously uncomfortable.

Terion stood and walked toward the window. Peering into the night, he considered the task ahead. With or without Varankyl, they would have to find a way to confront Shayene. A sudden thought came to him and he turned quickly to look at the woman. "Why would Balgar contract with you for my capture? The man hated me as surely as anything."

"Balgar was only the go-between," she answered. "And he was dead when I arrived here."

"He was a traitor then?"

"I could not tell you where his loyalties were, but they were obviously not with you or the council. It was through Balgar that I took the life of Keiran. As a matter of fact, it was he who let me into her chambers and he was present when I completed the contract."

Terion reddened with anger as the woman went on.

"It was also Balgar who ensured the Keiran would not be able to work any magic when I confronted her. He gave her a Vi'Raaji potion that temporarily inhibits arcane abilities."

"And so you were able to kill her quickly then," Terion snapped, fighting to know where to direct his anger.

"She did not suffer, if that's what you mean," Vendetta answered softly. "The contract was only for her removal, nothing more."

"You said Balgar was the go-between. Who was his master?"

"I only found out recently," she answered. "It was the sorceress, Ranora."

"Ranora?" he asked in shock, his eyes wide. "The arch mage of Nykiva? You can't be serious!"

"She was here when I found Balgar," the woman continued. "She revealed herself as the one behind the contracts and demanded that I fulfill the remaining contract by returning you to her."

"Do you still intend to?"

"Don't insult my intelligence," she snapped.

"Sorry," he said quickly. "That was not my intention. What about Balgar?" he changed the subject. "Did she kill him?"

"No."

"Then who?"

Vendetta lowered her eyes, unconsciously pulling the blankets about her even tighter. Terion, understanding the words not spoken, placed a hand lightly on her bare shoulder. "I know what he did to you and for that I am truly sorry. I really am. But I need to know."

"It was Kraegor," she finally answered, her voice husky as tears welled in her eyes. "He told me who he was as he…as he…"

"Kraegor the Black?"

A silent nod.

"Kraegor is Shayene's companion," Terion said, as much to himself as to her. "So all along, it has been the Arcai that have been manipulating the strings of deception. Shayene and Draven, with Ranora acting in their stead right here within the city – it all makes sense now."

"It is not as simple as it seems," Vendetta countered. "Ranora is not allied with the Arcai."

"So she truly does intend to go against Shayene?"

"There are some things she saw no need to hide from me. She

believes she has the key to defeating Shayene."

"She may, at that," Terion mused, considering the story of Varankyl. "What about Kraegor? Did he say anything else?"

"He did," she replied after a deep breath, her voice low. "He was quite boastful during..." she trailed off again.

"I understand," he said gently. "I know how difficult this must be for you, but did he speak of the coming attack on Nykiva?"

She nodded. "I heard some of what he said, but not all. Draven marches on Nykiva with the full force of his army. In addition, you must know that Shayene has assembled an army of First Born in the Wraithlands. She intends to unleash them within the city when Draven attacks with his armies."

"It will be like Ithil Majeer," he replied, nodding his head in understanding. "She will have a portal somewhere within the city that she will send the undead through. The question is, where will it be?"

"Ranora's tower."

"Are you certain?" he asked, hoping beyond hope that she was correct.

"He mentioned that the height of Ranora's betrayal would be that her tower would serve as the focal point of Nykiva's destruction."

"But would Ranora not destroy the gateway?"

"She would if she was alive at the time," Vendetta answered. "Kraegor will see to it that she's not."

Terion stood up quickly, everything settling into place. "So Kraegor will move on Ranora, if he has not already. I must get back to her tower."

Vendetta grasped his arm. "I have been here for the better part of a night and a day, before you rescued me, Terion. You may already be too late."

"I have friends there. I have to know what happened! And that gate has to be destroyed!"

"No," Vendetta countered.

Terion turned a hard look on her. "If we do not, Nykiva will be overrun by the First Born as soon as Draven attacks."

"Think about it a moment, Terion," she said quietly. "Destroying the gate will not eliminate the problem. It will only postpone the inevitable. Even without the undead attacking from within, Draven leads an army far vaster than what Nykiva can field. A protracted siege is well within his military capabilities and it is something that this city will not survive."

"So what do you suggest?"

"It seems clear to me that, to kill the snake, you must cut off its head. Regardless of what she plans in the aftermath, Ranora's intentions were correct. She intended to go directly to the Wraithlands and destroy Shayene."

"True," Terion answered, catching on.

"So why not locate the gateway and use it to our advantage?" Vendetta went on. "We can have the gate destroyed after we enter it, to prevent the First Born from coming through into Nykiva."

"That might work, but we would be trapped on the other side."

"If we are unsuccessful, it won't matter anyway," the woman replied. "But if we manage to defeat Shayene, we can return to Nykiva at our leisure. There are other paths out of the Wraithlands. They may be difficult, but they are accessible."

"That makes sense," he said after a few moments, looking into her eyes. "You act as if you intend on joining me."

"I said I will serve you, but you may find some difficulty in getting your friends to accept the current situation," she said quietly, reminding him that there would be repercussions from the sudden alliance.

"Perceptive," he answered truthfully, "but I will make sure they understand."

"We will see," Vendetta said, getting to her feet to face Terion, the blankets still wrapped tightly around her. "I wonder how you intend on telling them, though. Facing them and Ranora at the same time seems to be somewhat problematic to me."

"I will deal with Ranora first," he said. "I knew Keiran for a very long time. There are things about her tower that I doubt Ranora is even aware of."

"A back door perhaps?" she allowed herself a small smile.

"Or two," Terion replied. "There is a great cavern beneath her tower. It houses a small underground lake. Very few people know about it."

"You are one of those?"

"One of a select few," he agreed. "Ranora undoubtedly knows about it, too, but I would be willing to bet that if Shayene plans on unleashing her undead horde in Nykiva, the gate will be located there."

"And if it's not?"

"At least it will be better than knocking on the front door," he said lightly. "I'd prefer to have some advantage when I confront her."

"And what of your friends?"

"I'll figure that out when the time comes."

"Very well," the assassin said softly. "I will trust that you know what you are doing. But I must first retrieve some suitable clothing. Turn around."

Terion hesitated for a moment and then turned away from the woman.

Behind him, Vendetta let the blanket fall to the floor, leaving only the tattered remains of her clothing to cover herself with. "I will meet you at Ranora's tower in a short time." She walked over to the window and leapt up onto the sill, grateful for the shadows of the night. Normally, she would not concern herself with hungry eyes on her body and admittedly, had used her beauty to her advantage many times in the past. But after her ordeal with Kraegor, it would be some time before she would consider following that path again. "Terion?"

"Yes?" he answered, not daring to turn around.

"Aylan is alive and well and in the city. You will find him in a small house behind a tavern known as The Whistling Ghost. The door is unlocked."

"Why would you leave your prisoner free to leave?" he questioned.

"Aylan and I have reached an understanding," she said softly. "It is based on trust...much like the one we are forging."

A moment later, she disappeared into the night, leaving Terion alone with his thoughts and no short supply of confusion. It would take some time for him to figure everything out with regards to the assassin. But in the meantime, he had one friend to rescue, before finding out if his other friends remained safe.

Chapter 40

Ranora walked along the stone walkway that circled the enormous pit beneath her tower of sorcery. She was in the very lowest subterranean level of the tower, one known only to a privileged few, a cavernous pit that fell for hundreds of feet into a crystal clear lake of freezing water. A stone stairwell ran downward, cut into the rock and circling the cavern several times before reaching the bottom of the pit. The entire grotto was lit dimly by torches spaced evenly along the walls, flickering with a magical light.

During Keiran's reign as leader of the council, the woman had found solace on the edge of the silent lake, a perfect place to meditate. Now, with Keiran dead and Ranora in power, the unpolluted rock and water in the pit had become a source to increase the younger woman's magical strength. Standing along the walkway at various intervals were nine golems carved from the pristine stone below, created through the earthen magic that ran strong beneath the waters. They were motionless, but their eyes glowed with an inner fire, indicating that they were very much alive.

Ranora had mastered the art of their creation some time ago. However, as an apprentice, she had been refused by Keiran to dabble in the powerful magic used in building them. But unbeknownst to her former master, Ranora had not only mastered the creation of the mindless constructs, she had discovered the way to truly give them a life of their own, a process that would have horrified the arch mage.

Shortly after Keiran's murder, Ranora had requested ten of Nykiva's strongest soldiers to attend a feast on the pretense that she intended to form an elite garrison of soldiers for the defense of the city. After feeding them and giving them drugged wine, she had her servants bind them and bring them to the pit, where she performed a horrifying ritual of dark magic that had filled the cavernous room with screams of agonizing death. Removing the hearts and brains from the still-living soldiers, she married their flesh to her stone creations, creating golems of unmatched savagery and intelligence and malevolent intentions. There were nine present on the walkway, while the tenth stood guard over her private chambers. All ten would be a small part of the surprise she held for Draven's advancing army, for one was more than a match for tens of dozens of the most well-armed soldiers. But that would happen after she faced Shayene and she wondered again if Draven would even continue his campaign with his sister dead.

Confidence drove her as she took her place before the stone table on the edge of the pit. From there, she would be able to draw the elemental power from the lake, which she would use to fuel the shielding she would weave about herself before she attempted to unify Varankyl. She was well aware of the artifact's sentience and its ability to ensnare those that came in contact with it. Split as it was, she could handle the thing's intelligence and had indeed already earned some mastery over it. But combined once again, she knew she would have to be ready for the psychic onslaught it would unleash.

Lying on the table on opposite ends were the two halves of the artifact. Ranora ignored them as she began calling upon her power. It drew strength from the earthen magic that ran so richly through the rock and unpolluted water of the lake. Feeling the power build within her, she wove a psychic defense against the artifact. As it settled around her, she began to reach out with her mind, feeling the tendrils of power emanating from the two halves of Varankyl.

You perform a rich service in reforming me, Varankyl said in her mind, the voice seeming to echo into both ears.

"I am reforming you to serve me," she replied aloud, willing her own mind to overpower the growing strength of the artifact.

You will wield me.

"I will."

You will throw down the Arcai and take her place.

"I will."

You will find me a willing participant in your game, the artifact teased.

"And why would I believe that?" she asked, pulling the two halves of the weapon together until they were mere inches apart.

I will repay Shayene for splitting me in the first place, it said and Ranora sensed the bitterness within the sentient artifact. *Allow me to show you what I am capable of.*

Before the sorceress could react, the will of Varankyl rose to a crescendo in her mind and she felt herself nearly overwhelmed. Her psychic barrier began to unravel and she had but a moment to wonder at the artifact's sheer power. Then the mace snapped together, the two pieces coming together with a click, leaving the weapon whole on the table before her. Varankyl uttered a final thought, *I am yours*, and fell silent.

Ranora stumbled backward and sank to her knees, gulping in great breaths of air, trying to shake away the fog within her. The power of the artifact had nearly overwhelmed her. All her preparation and study had not prepared her for the truth of it. And yet, it now lay before her, quiet and willing. Pulling herself back to her feet, she stared at Varankyl for the longest time, studying the black crystalline lines and edges. It was a truly beautiful piece of workmanship and the power that lay within was startling. But it was hers. It had said as much. Slowly, she reached out, laying her hand on the pommel. It was cold; bitter cold and she felt the magic thrum within it. Strengthening her will, she hefted it in the air. It was surprisingly light for its size and density and even as she felt its power, she knew it had spoken truthfully. It was indeed, hers.

"If I hadn't seen it with my own eyes, I would have a hard time believing what I just witnessed," a low voice sounded from the shadows to her left.

Ranora turned slowly as a familiar swordsman stepped into the soft glow of the candles, his sword held out before him. If she was surprised to see Terion, she did not show it. "I see that Keiran must have shared some knowledge of the tower with you before her death."

"She was a dear friend," he said coldly, "and you killed her."

"It was the assassin that committed that deed," she replied.

"At your behest."

"Semantics," she shrugged, then made a show of looking around. "Since you are back, I am assuming you found your wayward charge?"

Aylan stepped out of the shadows behind him, his face set in stone, the white lines of new scars shining in the torchlight. His hands were raised and power flickered at his fingertips.

"You deem it wise to threaten me?" she laughed with a shake of her head. "You are but a boy."

"You're not much older than him," Terion reminded her, stepping closer.

"But immensely more powerful," she whispered, her own hands coming up. Immediately, a globe of energy materialized around Aylan, trapping the young mage in magical bands. Terion darted forward, but Ranora swung Varankyl up before her, feeling the magic hum through her body. "Don't," she warned.

"How could you have fallen so far?" Terion asked sadly, halting immediately. He recognized the power in her and realized just how much trouble they were truly in. "What turned you into such a monster?"

"Hardly a monster," she countered. "History will remember me

434

as a savior, Terion. I have done what needs to be done and regret nothing. Now that I have Varankyl, we can move against Shayene to deliver the final blow."

"We?"

"You and your friends will accompany me to the Wraithlands," she stated matter-of-factly.

"You presume much."

"I know much, where the will of Varankyl is involved," she corrected him, holding the mace before her.

"If you possess so much power now, why do you need us?"

"Because Shayene is seeking you. I will use you as the bargaining chip and your friends to prepare the way. That is why I had Balgar broker the deal with Vendetta to capture you." She looked around. "Where is the witch, anyway? I hope you didn't kill her."

"Her whereabouts are her own business. I'm more interested in how you intend to use me to get to Shayene."

"It will allow me to get close to her," Ranora replied. "For some reason, she covets you, Terion. I don't know why and I certainly don't care. I only care that you will give me the opportunity I need to finally confront her."

"And do what?"

"It should be obvious," the sorceress smiled. "It is time for the Arcai to die."

The sound of clapping hands behind her caused her to whirl around, her eyes going wide with surprise as Kraegor the Black stepped out of a darkened alcove and onto the circular walkway.

Terion's gasped in shock as he recognized the newcomer, but the dragon ignored him, his black eyes boring into the sorceress. "Well done, Ranora," Kraegor said, his voice dripping with sarcasm, his lips curled into a perfectly evil smile. "In one fell swoop, you have managed to eliminate the greatest threats to our success, you have taken possession of the one item that could undo us all, and you have even prepared Terion to be delivered alive back to Shayene. Truly, we could not have done this without your valuable assistance."

"What are you doing here?" Ranora snapped, clearly not afraid of the appearance of the human-form dragon. "We have no more business."

Kraegor held up his hands, his black robes revealing his bare arms and clawed hands that began to glow with arcane power. "On the contrary, I am here to reward you, my dear Ranora," he replied smoothly, smiling widely. "Shayene so values her loyal allies and would certainly not wish for me to pass up an opportunity to repay you generously for your actions."

He thrust his hands forward and bolts of green energy shot toward the sorceress. But Ranora was already moving, throwing her robes around her as a shield. The cloth had been heavily enchanted and absorbed the bolts as they hit. She continued her pirouette, coming back around to face the dragon, immediately thrusting her own hand forward. A powerful wave of force rolled into the man, slamming him backward toward the edge of the pit.

Kraegor quickly recovered, his eyes blazing with anger as the young sorceress dropped to her knee and placed a hand on the ground. She muttered a quick incantation and Kraegor felt his feet begin to sink, as the rock floor beneath him turned to mud. A moment later, she intoned a second spell, turning the mud back into stone and trapping the man up to his ankles.

"Foolish mortal," Kraegor hissed, dropping low and placing a hand on the ground in order to steady himself. "Do you really think you can defeat me?"

Ranora ignored his threat and waved a hand toward the nearest golem. "Kill him," she commanded. Immediately, the creature turned its ponderous bulk and, with deceptive speed, started toward the trapped dark wizard.

Kraegor watched the oncoming monster almost impassively. In his natural dragon-form, the golem would be little more than a pebble to his might. But in his human form, he was vulnerable. Acting quickly, he began the transformation into his true self even as the creature reached him. He felt his bones began to transform and lengthen and the stone entrapping his feet began to crack. But the crushing blow came far too quickly as the golem swung a huge arm and blasted him fully in the chest. Kraegor felt the cracking of bones for only a moment, before being launched over the edge of the pit, where he fell into the icy water far below.

Ranora heard Kraegor's dying shriek and then the splash, before silence descended across the cavern. Turning, she walked back toward Terion, smiling arrogantly. "That will make destroying Shayene that much easier."

Terion did not know what to say. This young sorceress, little more than an apprentice not that long ago, had succeeded in taking possession of the one item that could stop the demigod. She had destroyed one of the most powerful dragons in the world in mere seconds. It was almost too impossible to believe.

"Kraegor was a fool to underestimate me," she said, reading the look on his face. "Will you be as great a fool as he?"

The warrior began to say something, when his voice froze. Behind Ranora, the fully transformed Kraegor rose up out of the pit on massive wings, green eyes glittering with fury, his huge maw split wide, baring dagger-like teeth. The dragon's head shot forward as he twisted his neck, his massive jaws snapping shut on the young woman's body. Ranora only had a moment to register her surprise, before her severed head fell to the floor, along with what remained of her legs and arms.

Freed from her magic, Aylan stumbled to his knees and Varankyl rolled under the stone alter as Kraegor straightened his huge bulk and raised his head, gulping down the woman's torso.

Terion stared at the dragon in fearful fascination as it regarded him, eyes gleaming. "Fear not, mortal," Kraegor growled, reading the man's fear. "For you, there is a higher purpose. In a moment, you shall find out what that is."

The dragon twisted in the air, its great tail slamming into the stone golem with the force of a thunderclap. Stone constructs like the ones that Ranora had created were built for their durability and near imperviousness to physical damage. But the strike of a dragon's tail could bring down mountains, and the golem was reduced to rubble in a moment. The dragon, in his rage, turned on the other ones and delivered the rest of Ranora's creations to a similar fate.

Several minutes later, Kraegor was back in his human form, standing on the stone landing. Stepping over the grisly remains of Ranora, he stood before Terion. "Such will be the fate of all who oppose Shayene."

"So what happens now?" Terion said, fighting hard to keep his teeth from chattering in the presence of the dragon.

"Your presence is required in the Wraithlands," Kraegor answered.

"I won't join her," Terion said quietly, recalling the dreams that seemed to have heralded all of this.

"That is not for me to comment on," Kraegor shrugged, reaching into his robes and pulling out the green emerald known as the Star Stone.

Startled, Terion looked at the gem and then at Kraegor's face. "I've seen that before."

"I'm certain you have. But the witch will no longer require it."
He took hold of Terion's arm in a grip like iron. "The stone is powerful
enough to get us clear of the city. From there, we will return to the
Wraithlands by wing. That will give you time to rethink your position."

"I will not join her," Terion repeated. "There is nothing that
will sway me."

"We shall soon see," Kraegor said. "We shall see."

A moment later, they were gone.

Chapter 41

Aylan climbed to his feet, the shock of what had just happened still heavy upon him. Ignoring what was left of the traitorous sorceress, he walked toward the edge of the pit, still trying to comprehend it all. Terion was gone, taken by the dragon. But at least he was still alive. How they would go about rescuing him was another matter entirely. He just knew he wouldn't be alone when he went after him.

He reached the edge of the basin and then slowly descended the stairs toward the lake, his eyes never leaving the figure that stood silently next to the water. She was staring at something; something he could not quite see. The young mage felt a pang of sadness as he reached the stone platform and the assassin still did not move.

He paused, his mind still not completely made up about her. Vendetta had killed his friend, Cavanah. She had taken him prisoner and savagely tortured him for information before ultimately together, they began figuring out what was really happening with Shayene. Then suddenly, Terion showed up and freed him from captivity, apparently with her blessing.

After Terion had found him, Vendetta had met them both back at the tower and showed them the secret way in, knowledge Ranora had provided her through Balgar, as the young sorceress plotted the murder of Keiran. Now, the Vi'Raaji witch stood on platform, staring into space.

Or was it space?

As Aylan stepped toward her, he finally noticed it—a tiny ripple in the air before her, no bigger than a fist. He looked from the fissure to her face and his confusion grew. It was a face stricken in a way that made his heart break and he wondered at the tears that coursed down her cheeks. It was a side of her he had not seen.

"The dragon has taken Terion to the Wraithlands," she said softly, her tone giving away nothing.

"It will be a long journey to retrieve him," he said, watching her closely. "And I will need allies."

"You have friends, Aylan, and there are other ways to travel," she said, pointing to the ripple, drawing his attention to it.

"What is that?"

"It's a portal," she replied, rubbing a hand across her cheek and wiping away the tear, hiding her emotions once more. "Look, but do not get too close."

Aylan did as she commanded, leaning forward and studying the apparition. It was indeed a portal, but it was barely the size of the diameter of his wrist. He peered into it, seeing foggy darkness beyond. He could see shapes moving about in the shadows and could hear an occasional moan or scream from things best left to the imagination. Straightening, he looked back at the assassin.

"It is a seeded gate to the Wraithlands," she explained. "With it in place, Shayene can expand it with little more than a thought, no matter where she is. This is how she intends to defeat Nykiva. By attacking from within."

"And it works both ways," Aylan reasoned, looking closer. As he did, he saw a tattered skeleton rise up before the hole and thrust out a bony hand. Aylan stepped back quickly as the skeletal arm flayed around, seeking to grab something living.

"Let it be," she breathed, her face suddenly close to his. "If aroused, it could bring others to the hole and that might alert Shayene."

Aylan took a moment to compose himself and cleared his throat. "So, is there any way to get through it from this end?"

"The gate can be forced open by someone with similar abilities – a powerful wizard or another Arcai."

"Of which, I am neither," Aylan lamented.

"There are others," she began, but was interrupted by the sound of a sword being drawn from it scabbard.

They both turned at the same time, as the huge warrior, Notyet stepped from the stairs and onto the stone walkway, his eyes fixed in a rage on the assassin who had killed his friend. Spaced well apart along the stairs were the others, their footsteps having been magically silenced as they positioned themselves. Now, weapons and spells were prepared and all were eyeing the Vi'Raaji.

"Wait!" Aylan shouted, his voice echoing through the caverns. Vendetta had not moved to draw her own weapons and he quickly stepped in front of her. "Hold your weapons. There is much you do not know."

Notyet scowled at him and the young mage was taken aback by the hatred in his mentor's eyes.

"You would be wise to speak quickly," the Arcai, Jayadra, said from her perch on the stairs, her normally calm demeanor stern and dangerous. The demigod had her own personal reasons to hate the assassin and far above her, the massive head of Volsaun, her fearsome white dragon companion, peered over the edge of the walkway, his own glittering eyes fastened on the god-killer.

"You must not harm her," Aylan said, mustering all the courage he could find. "We have a common goal."

"A common goal?" Siranschae questioned bitterly, her scimitar held ready as she stepped off the landing to stand beside Notyet. "Regardless of what happened in Haven, she's a killer, Aylan. By what witchcraft has she ensnared you?"

"I have not been ensnared," he said evenly and much to the amazement of the others, he drew his dagger and planted his feet in a battle-ready stance, willing his magic to life. "And I will defend that which I believe should be defended," he said as arcane energy began to bathe his hands in light.

"No," Vendetta broke the tense stand-off and laid a hand on Aylan's shoulder before stepping in front of him. "This must not happen." Turning to the young mage, she spoke so that all could hear. "I do not fault your friends for their hatred and distrust of me, nor should you. I have killed your companion; I took you prisoner. Their hatred of me has been well-earned and I cannot allow you to sacrifice their friendships for my sake."

"But Terion…" Aylan began.

Vendetta shook her head and then walked toward Notyet and Siranschae. "I will not fight you," she said simply, her voice strong as she drew her Arcai-forged blades. She tossed them on the ground in front of Notyet. "Kill me if you must," she offered, then fell to her knees in front of the huge warrior and dropped her head.

Notyet came within a hair's breadth of lopping her head off. But it was the pained, almost agonized, expression on Aylan's face that caused him to instead sheath his huge sword and take a step backward.

"Let them speak," Jayadra said quietly.

Vendetta climbed back to her feet almost wearily and Aylan stepped up beside her.

"It's a long story," the young man said finally, sheathing his dagger, "and much of it still unknown to me."

"And you expect your friends to trust you?" a strangely dressed man quipped, stepping off the ledge to stand beside Notyet. He was almost as tall as the huge warrior and Aylan shook his head. He had never seen the man before in his life.

"Apparently, I'm missing a lot more than I thought," Aylan said. "Who are you?"

"Branson," the man replied, "and that's another long story. But first, you. You best get to explainin' things, boy."

"Tell them," Vendetta spoke up softly. "Leave nothing out. They deserve to know why they are placing their trust in you." She paused before finishing. "And in me."

"Very well," he said and began to explain. He told them everything that had happened after he had been taken prisoner by the assassin, including what they began to figure out together. He told them how he had come to trust her, a trust that had born fruit when Terion showed up to release him. Terion hadn't told him much about Vendetta, but what he did say, Aylan related. He finished up with their confrontation of Ranora and her death. When he was done, silence reigned as each of the companions considered his words, weighing them against being able to trust a life-long killer.

Eventually, Arianna broke the silence. "I will trust her," the Tae empath said simply. "I have no reason to doubt Aylan, as he has been like a brother to me."

"Tell me, witch. What is your interest in Terion?" Siranschae asked the assassin, her voice still clipped and challenging. "Do you still seek to collect a bounty on him?"

"This is no longer about a contract," Vendetta answered softly, her eyes locked on those of the dragon. "I owe Terion a debt. It is a personal matter."

"A ruse?"

"A rape," the Vi'Raaji said bitterly, refusing to back down.

Silence again descended until Aylan quickly spoke up. "Look," he said somewhat impatiently, "Terion is in the Wraithlands. Shayene is, too. We are going to have to go there ourselves if we intend on getting him back and ending this thing with Shayene, if we even can." He paused and looked around, taking in everyone's eyes. "You know her history. I cannot think of anyone else I would rather have beside us if we are going to do this."

"Well spoken," Jayadra nodded after several moments of uncomfortable silence. "I am inclined to trust your judgment in this, young wizard. You are a testament to your master." Resting her eyes on the Vi'Raaji, she asked. "You will aid us, Vendetta?"

"I have pledged my loyalty to Terion," the Vi'Raaji answered softly. "In doing so, my loyalty is to his friends as well. I cannot change what has happened in the past," she went on, pausing to look at Notyet. "But I can determine what path I will follow. If I can help get him back, I will do so without hesitation."

"Again, well said," the Arcai said and then looked around. "Does anyone oppose this?" While there were still looks of concern and some outright distrust, no one spoke. "Then it is agreed. For better or worse, we are in this together now and we must move quickly. The bulk of Draven's army is but a day's march from the gates of Nykiva."

"Draven has moved faster than we anticipated," Siranschae added, more for Aylan than anyone else. "We are pressed and it is a long journey to the Wraithlands."

"Not if we use Shayene's portal," Aylan said, pointing to the small shimmering hole in the air behind him.

"A portal?"

"A seeded gate," Vendetta corrected. "I imagine Shayene created this one with the intention of opening it when Draven attacked with his army. It would allow her to send thousands of undead through in order to attack the city from within."

"That was how Ithil Majeer fell so quickly," Aylan added. "We just need to be able to open it from our end and walk through."

"I can open it," Jayadra said plainly. "But understand that I will have to destroy it immediately after you have gone through."

"You're not coming through with us?" Branson asked.

"It has to be destroyed," she answered, "and it can only be done on this end."

"That might make things a bit more difficult," the marine lamented. He had grown to like the Arcai priestess and her dragon. He knew how much her powers would aid them, because he also knew what Shayene was capable of. Facing her without some serious firepower was not a prospect he was excited about and he shivered in spite of himself.

"It cannot be helped," Jayadra replied. "If the portal remains open, creatures from the Wraithlands will begin coming through into Nykiva. It would be catastrophic to the city. Besides," she said, her voice lowering, "someone must be here to answer Draven's challenge."

"You?" Siranschae asked, looking up sharply. "With all due respect, my lady, you are a priestess. Your skills are no match for Draven's abilities with a weapon."

"A priestess, yes," Jayadra agreed. "But I am capable in battle." Above her, Volsaun growled his agreement. "Besides, there is no one else. It may buy us some time, but it will not matter if you are not successful. Draven is not the key. Shayene is. She must be stopped."

Turning to the others, she addressed them all. "Your journey will be extremely dangerous. I will ask for no one to go. If you wish to remain here, I will only ask that you do what you can to aid in the defense of the city."

"I will go," Aylan said immediately, stepping forward.

"I want to go, too," Anthony called out from his perch high on the stairs. When the boy wasn't spending time with Branson's injured friend, Boozer, he had been nearly inseparable from the rest of them and the thought of everyone leaving on a grand adventure without him, was rather disheartening.

Jayadra smiled and shook her head. "I absolutely forbid it. You will be needed here and Terion would never forgive me if I allowed you to go after him. If you wish to help, Anthony, conscript yourself into the service of the city healers. I fear they will need all the help they can get when Draven arrives."

"I will go," Arianna said, her voice strangely husky and Siranschae quickly indicated that she, too, would also go. Notyet also quickly signed his insistence on going, still eyeing the assassin carefully.

"Well, I'm definitely in," Branson added. "I've got people stuck in that witch's castle that I'm getting out." Turning to Jayadra, he went on. "Swan will stay here with Davis and the rest of our soldiers. We have only a couple weapons from my world, but that will give you some firepower, if you need it, when Draven gets here. They can take up sniper positions and put a dent in his flunkies."

Seated on the ledge above, his feet dangling over the edge, Swan snapped off a quick salute. "Good hunting, bro. Bring'em back home."

"All of us," Branson agreed, nodding to his friend. "We're all coming back."

"Then prepare yourselves," the Arcai said. "It is time to leave."

Chapter 42

Deep in the Wraithlands, Shayene was preparing herself for the final confrontation, as well, a battle that would have a very different outcome than the one sought by her enemies.

"Are you certain of your course?" Kraegor asked, watching her closely and searching for any sign that she might consider abandoning her plan. He was still hesitant about the danger involved in what she was getting ready to do, as concerned for himself and the loss of his power as he was for her well-being. He knew what would happen to him if she died and he wasn't at all happy about the chance she was taking.

"It is the only way," Shayene answered softly. "The convergence must occur if I am going to bring down my mother."

"What if they manage to kill you before you escape?" he asked. "They are going to be formidable, particularly if Jayadra is leading them."

"She won't be."

"How do you know?"

"Because she is the only one who can open the seeded gate," she answered. "Then her sense of honor and duty will force her to destroy it, so she can protect the city. No, my dear Kraegor, they will come through alone on their quest to stop me and rescue Terion. Jayadra and Volsaun will remain in Nykiva."

"You still seem resigned to this foolishness," he sighed, "so I will not question you further. I pray you have planned for every contingency."

"I have," she said. "What of Varankyl?"

"I left it, as you instructed. I imagine Siranschae will be strong enough to avoid being possessed."

"She will," Shayene reasoned. "She will be the one to destroy the portal, I'm certain. I don't care what happens to the others, but she must be allowed to complete the task."

"And who will be the one to destroy you, when your Arcai powers are stripped by its destruction?"

"It will not come to that," she smiled and then reached up to pat his cheek. "Have faith, Kraegor. All is proceeding according to plan."

"And Terion?" he grumbled.

"It's time I paid him a visit – a real visit this time. I trust he is unharmed?"

"He's fine," Kraegor shrugged. "I left him in the portal room, so he could watch our army come forth." He chuckled as her face darkened in anger. "Fear not. I placed him in a siphon sphere. The First Born cannot touch him."

"For now."

"Then perhaps you should go to him before his energy runs out."

Shayene shook her head and brushed past him. He watched her go, carefully considering his own part to play in what was to come.

Terion raised his head wearily and watched as several more rotting zombies emerged from the black portal to the Nether. They shambled over to him, mouths gaping hungrily. But when they could not reach him, they shuffled past his prison and disappeared down a long corridor, obeying the control that was exercised over them once they arrived through the gate. It was the same with the hundreds of other First Born that he had watched emerge from the gateway and with each one, his heart sank even more.

He looked around half-heartedly, but knew there was nothing he could do to free himself. The sphere that held him was a flawless globe of energy felt like glass to his touch. When Kraegor had first imprisoned him without taking any of his gear, he had tried hacking through the magical barrier with his sword. But he quickly realized that the sphere drew power from him, and his exertion only seemed to increase the rate it sapped his energy. So he halted his attempts, but it was soon obvious that the strange sphere was feeding off his life force anyway and he felt himself slowly weakening, both in strength and human spirit.

That was when he finally saw her.

Shayene practically glided into the room, her cowl drawn over her head, hiding her features in shadow. She stopped in front of him and then slowly removed her hood, staring up at him with deep gray eyes. Her face was smooth an unmarked, her pale skin perfect, and her long dark hair fell well past her shoulders. Terion would have considered her beautiful, if he did not already know her heart.

"At long last," she said, smiling as she looked him up and down. "It has been quite some time since I last saw you, my dear Terion."

"You visit my dreams quite often," he said carefully, giving her a questioning look. "It hasn't been all that long since the last one."

Shayene laughed lightly and turned to regard a rather large scarecrow that was just emerging from the portal. "True," she said, before turning back to him. "But I am not referring to the prophetic dreams we have been having. I was actually referring to the last time we were together. Tell me, Terion. What do you remember of me?"

He didn't answer—couldn't answer. That she had referred to *his* dreams as *their* dreams, confirmed to him that she had actually visited those dreams somehow. But her inference that she knew him beyond the dream world had him frantically thinking back, trying to discover if there was more.

"What do you know of our past?" she pressed.

"Not much, really," he finally answered, deciding to play along and see where the conversation went. "I know about you because I dream about you. I know you are an Arcai that, up until now, honored the god's code of not interfering with mortal man."

"That is true," she affirmed. "But what about *our* past?"

"That's about all I know," he shrugged. "You're an Arcai, so we don't have a past. If not for my dreams, I would have never given any thought to you."

"Likely because it has been many years since you have seen me. The mind of a child is largely buried and forgotten in the mind of an adult."

"I don't know what you're talking about," he huffed. "I don't know you beyond my dreams and nightmares."

"No, you simply don't remember me, Terion," she said, her voice soft.

"And I suppose I should?"

"As I said, the mind of a child forgets many things," she shrugged. "But perhaps I can help you remember." She paused, taking a minute to walk around his globe, her head bowed. When she began to speak, her voice was soft and contemplative. "You said something about the Arcai honoring the god's code of non-interference. I once held those covenants dear, Terion. Did you know that?"

"What changed?"

"Nearly three hundred years ago, I would have never considered abandoning my covenants with the gods," she explained. "I was much like any mortal wizard or sorceress—reclusive, happy to be alone, desirous to learn all that I could about the art. I had built a tower of sorcery high in the mountains in the frozen lands far to the north. There, I was content to delve into my magic well away from humanity. I left mankind to their own devices. I was at peace."

Shayene crossed her arms and seemed to shiver, but continued, her voice far away. "There came a morning that dawned crystal clear one deep winter day. I remember it as if it was yesterday. I decided to free myself from the confines of my tower and take a walk about the pristine and untouched frozen land about my tower. I walked for nearly an hour, losing myself in the beauty of the mountains and I eventually found myself on the edge of a high precipice, overlooking the land for miles all about. It was truly an breathtaking sight and I was suddenly aware of what it took to create such scenic beauty. I felt as close to the gods as I ever could."

"Was that when you decided to become one of them?" he asked, unable to mask his angry sarcasm.

She shot him a truly venomous look as she answered. "Three centuries ago, subjugating mankind was the last thing I would have ever thought about."

"And now?"

She turned away. "As you know, Terion, Arcai are immortal in a sense that their spirit is undying and time does not affect us like it does you mortals. But even with our strengths and our near immortality, our bodies can be broken and we can die."

The realization of what she was talking about suddenly hit him. "That's what happened to you, didn't it. You died. How?"

She turned back to face him and he could see the pain in her face. "The cliff face gave way," she said bitterly. "The weather had been somewhat warm for that part of the world and it had weakened the ice. I fell over a thousand feet, where I would lay among the rocks and boulders for some time, my body shattered and broken. Kraegor found me several hours later, but there was nothing he could do to save me. I died in his arms, my spirit freed until the moment my mother would ensure that I was reborn."

"You died in an accident," Terion said. "Accidents are nothing more than acts of fate, whether you're a mortal or an Arcai."

"All true," she agreed, her features hardening again. "However, when mortals die, their spirits are free to return to the gods; to their creators, where they attain their reward of eternal life, for good or bad. But for an Arcai, the spirit is reborn soon after and we start over again on this earth. It is both a blessing and a terrible curse – a blessing because it is immortality of a sort and a chance to live among mortals forever, superior in every way. But it is a curse because we are never afforded the opportunity to return to the gods, as mortals are. We can never return to our makers as our final reward."

"But why bring war to man? It was not mortals who caused your death," he argued.

"I do not bring war to mankind *because* of mankind," she snapped angrily. "I bring war to mankind to subjugate you, to claim your worship. And I do this so that I may take the throne of my mother, Karasika."

"But why?"

"Because after my death, my spirit was left to roam for more than two centuries," she nearly spit in anger. "My mother did not see fit to attend to my rebirth and, for all those long years, I wandered alone, cut off from everybody and everything and unable to communicate, even with my companion. That is a very long time to fan the flames of hatred and plenty of time to realize the path to revenge."

"And now you intend to usurp your mother. Isn't that a little extreme?"

"I intend to usurp all the gods," she stated flatly, whirling around and pointing to the gate as more of the First Born emerged. "I will shatter the race of man, and those few who survive will have no choice but to worship me. The worship of mortal man gives the gods their power, Terion. You know this."

"And without it, they lose their power," he reasoned, beginning to truly understand.

"The Arcai are more a prisoner of our existence than anyone could ever hope to understand. So I intend to escape that existence, to never have to worry about being abandoned again."

"So it's all about revenge."

She twisted back around to face him, her face a mask of fury. "Not revenge, Terion. It's about two hundred and fifty years of nothingness."

Terion shook his head sadly. He could almost sympathize with her and likely would have, had she not set about on a quest to destroy mankind. "So what do you need me for? In my dreams, you're always asking me to join you. You know that's never going to happen, no matter your reasons."

"Your skill with the sword is well-known, Terion, and you have the mind of a general. It would be of great advantage to me to have you by my side. But there is another reason I have sought you out."

"And why is that?"

She turned away in silence and for some time did not speak. When she finally turned back to face him, her eyes were haunted. "You were little more than a baby when I last saw you."

"I'm not following you," he said carefully. "How could you have seen me when I was a baby?"

"After Karasika finally saw fit to rebirth me, I was given to my mortal father near the city of Nykiva. When I was about seven, my stepmother gave birth to a son. I left within a year to be taken in as an apprentice to a wizard living in the city."

Terion froze, unable to speak.

"That's right, "Shayene went on, seeing that he was beginning to understand. "When I left home, you were but a baby, so you probably do not even remember me."

"That's not...possible," he was finally able to whisper.

"Oh, but it is, my dear Terion. You are indeed my brother. We share the same father, you and I."

"No," he snapped. "That's not possible! My parents died before I was ten, but neither ever spoke of you. They never told me I had a sister."

"Nor would they. I am the daughter of a god, an Arcai borne of a union between Karasika and my mortal father; your mortal father. It is not something they would speak of, even to their only son."

"You lie," he snapped back, even as he began to realize the truth. The familiarity that he had felt every time he saw her in his dreams began to coalesce and suddenly he remembered her when she was a child, bending over his crib and speaking softly to him as she caressed his check. He saw her kneeling beside his mother, their hands working the earth of the flowerbeds that surrounded the little cottage they lived in. He saw her and their father examining the runic symbols and glyphs that had appeared on her small hands, placing her firmly on the path to the arcane. He saw it all. And he knew.

"Yes, my dear brother," she said softly, waving a hand in the air, causing his magical prison to disappear. She reached forward and touched his cheek, much as she had done when he was a baby. "We are reunited after so many years, Terion. Join me. I will make you a god and we can rule this world as brother and sister for all eternity."

Terion sank to his knees, despair and anguish washing over him, and did the only thing he could do. He wept.

Shayene watched him silently, then placed her hand gently on his head. She felt the old feelings of love and protection she had felt as his older sister grow stronger and she recoiled slightly. But then she quickly turned it into a resolve and a silent promise. She would prevail upon their bond as brother and sister and she would force him to her side. She would make him join her.

Or he would die.

Convergence

Rick Branson examined the mace in his hand one more time, taken by Jayadra from Ranora's private chambers only a few short minutes ago and given to him. He would have preferred going in with guns blazing, but he had to admit that Jayadra was right when she explained that his guns would have little effect on the undead. So, he had opted to lead with the mace and he gave it a few experimental swings, getting a feel for it. He felt confident it would do the job. Looking around, he saw that everyone else was prepared, weapons at the ready, with looks of concern or fear on the face of each of them.

Vendetta stood near him, her expression still guarded, her long bladed daggers in her hands, while Notyet flanked him on the other side, his huge sword resting point first on the floor as he made last minute adjustments to his chain armor. Behind them stood Aylan and Arianna. As neither were close quarters fighters, the group would move through the portal quickly in a diamond formation, with Branson in the lead, Vendetta and Notyet on the sides, and Siranschae bringing up the rear. That way, they could maintain a four-point offensive and keep the two young ones safely within their perimeter. From there, Aylan could use his magic as needed and Arianna could offer healing. More importantly, Siranschae carried Varankyl in a loop at her belt. She had found the artifact underneath the stone table Ranora had used to reassemble it, left there when Kraegor had returned to the Wraithlands with Terion. For the dragon, she found it curious that Varankyl seemed almost dormant, clearly unable or unwilling to fight a battle of wills with her. But there was something else about the artifact as well that she did not miss—the low buzz of power deep within. It appeared to be waiting.

"Ready?" Jayadra called out from her position on the stairs.

Volsaun remained at the top of the stairs, his huge reptilian head hanging over the edge, his glittering dragon eyes fastened on the tiny point of magic that would become a portal into the Wraithlands. In the event that the little group of companions were suddenly overwhelmed and the First Born came pouring into the chamber, he would fill the whole pit with his icy breath, destroying anyone or anything that happened to be in the area.

Branson knelt a safe distance away and peered through the tiny portal again, absently tapping the mace on the stone floor. He could see a pair of skeletons milling about near the portal. Beyond them, he could see various shapes moving within the foggy gloom, but there was no way to ascertain how many others were in the immediate vicinity. Standing up, he cast one more quick glance at his companions and then nodded toward Jayadra. "Open it," he said.

The Arcai priestess raised her arms and power began to form at her fingertips, arcing back and forth in blue and green flashes. A moment later, the tendrils of energy leapt from her fingers, connecting with the tiny portal with the sharp crack of lightning. The portal before the companions instantly grew in size until it measured some twelve feet in diameter, and Branson was moving even before it had completely opened. He led with his weapon, slashing across and crushing the skull of the first skeleton as Notyet barreled into the other one, driving the hilt of his huge sword into the creature's skull.

"Move!" Branson shouted as more shapes began to materialize out of the gloom. He rushed forward, bashing his mace into the bones of another pair of skeletons and then ducking to avoid the snapping jaws of a vicious scarecrow. He pivoted immediately, swinging his mace and crushing the monster. The marine continued working forward, his mace making grim work of the advancing monsters.

Beside him, Notyet was cleaving advancing zombies and

skeletons in two, dropping eight of them in less than a minute. Suddenly, another scarecrow darted in, claws finding a hold on the links of his chain mail. The strength of the First Born creature pulled him quickly forward. Notyet saw the huge fanged jaws open wide before the head of the creature vanished in the sizzle of thick green liquid. He flung the monster to the ground and whirled around to see Vendetta launch another stream of magical acid at another nearby scarecrow, burning the creature's leg off. With a grim smile and a blooming sense of trust in the witch, he launched himself into the fray again, his sword tearing into the swelling ranks of the undead.

With Notyet safely back in the fight, Vendetta whirled around and shattered the chest and ribs of an advancing skeleton with a well-placed kick. An expert martial fighter, trained to never waste any type of a movement in battle, she continued her spin, easily taking the head from the shoulders of a zombie with one of her razor-sharp blades. As the creature fell away, her hands shot forward, fingers splayed, and greenish lightning lanced out from her slender fingers. The arcane energy crackled through the air, the chain lightning dropping a dozen of the creatures.

Siranschae was faring just as well, feeling the thrill of the fight as her scimitar hummed through the air, slicing into the approaching monsters. Her dragon-heightened strength increased as the fight wore on, giving her hope that her powers were slowly returning.

From the center of the fighting, Aylan and Arianna stood back-to-back, turning as one to monitor the fighting. There was little they could do as the four warriors gradually widened the area around them, although Aylan would occasionally let loose with a bolt of lightning if a creature seemed to be getting too close.

Behind them, the gate to Ranora's tower winked out of existence and they were alone, fighting the growing horde. It was a fight that would eventually turn against them and they all knew it. But at least Nykiva was safe.

Having closed the portal and silently wished the companions luck, Jayadra joined her companion on the stone landing and waited while Volsaun transformed back into his human form. In his human body, he was a giant of a man — extremely muscled, and clothed in the skins and furs of the northern barbarians. His skin was dark brown, almost leathery, and his crystal blue eyes shone fiercely. A huge two-handed hammer was slung on his back and there was no mortal in the world who could heft its incredible weight.

"I still say you should permit me to face Draven," he said after his transformation.

"You would consign me to face Zarandrae then?" she gave him a half-smile as she answered. "This close to victory, you know she will be in the fight."

"I would see this war finished," Volsaun growled.

"If our friends do not succeed in the Wraithlands, it will matter little what the outcome of this battle is. It will be the end of the Dom people."

"Shayene will not find so easy of a campaign against the northern people," Volsaun said dangerously, the dragon having spent many of his centuries among the icelanders. "If the Doms do fall, the Gols will not be so willing to do battle with them."

"With some luck, it will never come to that," she replied quietly and then stopped, listening intently.

Volsaun had already heard it himself. "War horns," he said darkly. "Draven has arrived."

Chapter 44

As her magical hold on the Wraithlands picked up on the growing disturbance in her domain, Shayene glanced once more at Terion and then snapped his prison back into place with a mere thought. She then waved a hand before him, causing the air to shimmer, before solidifying into an image. Before them, they watched as Branson and his companions cut down the advancing First Born. She turned as Kraegor strode into the room. "They have arrived," she said as he paused to look at the vision in the air before them.

"The gate?"

"Destroyed after they come through."

"I counseled you against bringing Terion here and letting them find the portal," the human-form dragon said, casting a deadly look at the imprisoned warrior. "It seems that I was correct."

"This is not about me," Terion interrupted, feeling a slight surge of hope after the devastating truth about Shayene had been revealed to him. "They've come to stop you, but you can still end this. If you are truly my sister, you won't do this."

She turned to look at him, her countenance unreadable.

"What of the gate?" Kraegor interrupted impatiently. "You still have not explained to me how you intend to redirect the First Born without the portal in place. Without it, our attack plan is altered, perhaps irreparably."

"Only the attack on Nykiva is altered," she answered, still looking at Terion. "I trust that Draven will suitably compensate for the loss of the First Born."

"And if he cannot?"

"He will commit everything he has to the taking of Nykiva, with or without help. He will not fail. Once he is successful, his forces can occupy the city and spend the winter resupplying and reinforcing."

"The Gols will suffer great losses against Nykiva without the aid of the undead," Kraegor pointed out. "It will seriously hamper our plans to turn them westward in the spring."

"Once Draven takes Nykiva, there will be little need to field a massive army in the spring. Nykiva is the key today, Kraegor. Destroy that and the Doms will fall, with the rest of the races following. As Draven is so fond of saying, warfare is always fluid."

"And what of Terion's companions?"

"You know what is at stake here," she said knowingly. "They must be allowed to reach the chamber."

"You are certain this must happen?"

"Trust me, my dear Kraegor," she said, reaching out and affectionately patting his cheek. "Now go. It must not be too easy for them or they may suspect."

With a nod, Kraegor turned away and stalked out of the chamber.

Terion looked at Shayene, his eyes narrowing. "I...don't understand."

"You are about to learn that things are not always as they seem," she answered chillingly, pointing to the vision that still shimmered in the air. "Your friends have come because I wished it. They will certainly die in the end, but they have a task to perform first."

"You mean...this is all just a ruse?"

Shayene only smiled.

Having fought their way clear of the initial surge of undead, the companions hurried toward the fog-shrouded outline of the tower. The First Born were still all about them, but had grown wary and were keeping their distance now. The companions quickly reached a pathway that circled around into the rocks and led toward a wide gate at the top of the hill, its iron portcullis raised high.

"Looks like they're expecting us," Branson said sarcastically, pausing to look at the others.

"That is of great concern," Vendetta said softly, peering into the gloom. "The First Born appear to be moving off."

"Maybe they're scared," Branson retorted.

"They are killers," Vendetta said, shaking her head. "They exist to slay and feast on the living. They would not willingly avoid us."

"Unless they were being controlled," Siranschae said with a knowing nod.

"She knows we are here," Vendetta said after a moment, turning her gaze toward the open gate at the top of the hill. She caught the movement high above a split second before it disappeared behind the tower. The meaning was immediately clear. "Run!" she shouted.

Without hesitating, the group broke into a run, hurrying up the path. They were only halfway up when the huge black dragon soared into view, pulling up in a glide on huge wings. His fanged maw opened wide and a stream of poison spewed out of his mouth.

Vendetta threw up her hands, desperately calling forth a spell. A pulsating greenish disc shimmered into existence above them as the venom rained down. It hit the magical shield fully, splashing and sizzling as it flowed over the edges and onto the ground. Arianna screamed in pain as a large glob of the thick viscous fluid landed on her lower leg, dissolving skin and flesh.

"Run!" Vendetta shouted again as she shunted the magic to the side. "I don't have the power to create another one!"

But they would not make it. The dragon reached them well before they made the door. As the others ran toward the door, Aylan stopped and turned around. He knew he was going to die, and vowed he would do so honorably and perhaps save the lives of his friends. As the dragon soared in, he dropped to a crouch, one hand behind him and the other outstretched. He called forth the magic within him, feeling the runes and glyphs on his hands and wrists expand further down his arms as he cast the spell. Arcane energy formed in his trailing hand, before twisting around his body and blasting toward the dragon from his outstretched hand, forking into two powerful bolts .

Kraegor twisted his huge body in the air to avoid the magical lightning. He only avoided part of the spell. One of the bolts shot harmlessly past his head, but the other blasted through his leather-like wing, burning a hole in the membrane. The huge dragon pulled up, roaring in pain.

Aylan, for his part, was already running, elated but nearly exhausted from casting such a powerful spell. He stumbled near the entrance and would have fallen had Notyet not caught him. As the big warrior dragged him into the entrance, he turned to see the huge dragon once again bearing down on them, opening his mouth as he came.

"Here he comes!"Aylan yelled, diving into the darkened passage with Notyet right behind him.

The poison shot in, only to impact with another wall of magical green energy. But unlike the first shield the Vi'Raaji witch had created, this one immediately faded. The venom came through, splashing the ground and the walls. But the shield had been enough to allow the companions to get out of harm's way.

Vendetta staggered against the wall and started to fall, her strength gone. But Branson was there and slipped an arm around her waist, holding her steady until she got her feet back under her.

"Thanks," the marine said with a smile. "In my world, we'd call that 'saving our collective asses.' You okay?"

She returned a weak smile and struggled to shake off the lethargy. "Give me a moment to regain my strength, though it is doubtful I will have the ability to cast any more spells," she said quietly.

"We'll make do, but we'd better move fast," he added, pointing back down the passage to where they had just come from. Kraegor had landed on the ground outside and was already metamorphosing back into his human form. "I think we pissed him off."

Jayadra stood on the battlements atop the city gates and surveyed the land beyond. Gol forces were moving into positions, while a sizable contingent of Rat savages danced about singing songs of war and clashing their weapons together while their shamans worked them into a frenzy. Large Gol catapults and ballista were being wheeled into place near the rear of the enemy lines and ladder men and grapplers were grouping together for runs at the city walls.

"This dude has to know he's going to get a lot of his soldiers killed if he comes right at us," Swan said from his position near Jayadra's side. He was in full tactical gear now and had his weapon slung over his shoulder. Almost a dozen other marines were stationed all along the wall, waiting for his signal to open fire.

"I doubt Draven cares much what happens to his soldiers, now that he has reached the end of his campaign," the Arcai answered. "He intends to finish this as quickly as he can. With the gate destroyed, he may act desperately."

"What about the challenge?" a new voice asked.

Jayadra turned to face the speaker. Myngar, the council finance minister, had just assumed the temporary role of head of the council and also spoke for the people of Nykiva and his burdens of late had been great. The toll could be seen on his normally passive face as it was now lined with concern and his eyes were dark and sunken. To his credit, he had proven to be a wise leader, and had immediately ordered the Tae refugees brought behind the city walls as he ordered their own soldiers to prepare for battle.

"He will challenge," the priestess answered softly, "and we will answer."

"And if you fail?" Myngar countered almost feebly.

"We do not have that option," Volsaun answered instead, glaring at the man. "You would do well to retreat to the battle chambers and let us handle Draven. Your generals will need your leadership."

"I did not ask for this," Myngar answered sharply.

"But it has been given to you," the dragon replied evenly. "And you accepted it. See to the defenses of the city and we will see to our own tasks."

"Very well," Myngar nodded slowly. "Luck be with you." With another look at the vast army spreading out before them, he departed the battlement.

"Are your men prepared?" Jayadra asked Swan, her eyes scanning the enemy, looking for the man she would have to face in battle.

"Armed and waiting for my signal," the marine replied. "But there's only twelve of us, ma'am, and we have only a limited amount of ammo. I'd give a month's pay to have my hands on the weapons we left back in her castle. With what we have, we could kill a couple hundred. But you see what's out there. It's not going to make a difference in the end."

"Then we need to end it now," Volsaun growled.

At that moment, the war horns of the Gols sounded and a huge shape appeared over the trees, gliding in effortlessly to land on the ground, far out of bowshot. Draven made a show of dismounting from his huge blue dragon companion and shouts of praise erupted from the lines of his soldiers. He raised his huge sword high in the air, the morning light gleaming from the blade, prompting another roar of approval.

Looking toward the city gates, he strode forward as Zarandrae transformed into her imposing human form. A minute later, she joined him, gazing up at the two figures atop the battlements.

"Jayadra," Draven called out smugly. "I had expected as much."

"You lead an unjust war, Draven," the priestess countered, gazing down at the challenger. "You have forsaken your oath of non-interference and you use your god-given strength to subjugate those who cannot hope to stand against you. You cannot be allowed to continue."

"Donaran thought much the same as you," Draven smirked. "He now lies dead on the fields before Taer Blys, food for the carrion birds."

"He is Arcai," the woman replied, her voice like ice. "In time, he will return."

"Perhaps," Draven smirked. "But then again, we live in a time of great change."

"In that, we agree," Jayadra replied. "It is no secret that your actions have angered the gods. Perhaps the time has come for the end of the Arcai – the end for all of us."

"Or perhaps the time has come for the end of the gods," Draven replied, still smiling.

"You speak blasphemy now," Jayadra shot back angrily. "Make your challenge and be done with it, Draven."

Draven smiled again and raised his sword high. "Consider yourself challenged." With that, he brought his sword down and immediately the horns of the Gols began blowing wildly. Screams and shouts erupted from all along the battle lines and the huge force began moving toward the city walls as siege weapons of all types began their barrage from both sides of the wall.

The battle for Nykiva had begun.

Branson led them quickly through the passages, seeking always for stairs that would take them higher, pointing them in the direction he remembered her main chamber to be. Three levels up, they charged into a small group of zombies and quickly cut them to pieces.

"We're heading in the right direction at least," he said, stepping over the corpses of the undead. "I'm guessing we'll encounter more as we go, but we should have no problem with smaller groups of them."

"But they delay us," Vendetta cautioned, her voice uncertain. "Kraegor is coming and we are in no position to challenge him. We must find Shayene quickly."

They hurried on and after several minutes, they emerged into a large chamber.

They had arrived.

Terion stood across the room, encased in a glowing blue field of energy, gazing at them with a look of despair. A woman stood next to him, her face hidden by the shadows of her cowl. Her hands were tucked into the sleeves of her robes, but there was no mistaking who she was. Across from the chamber entryway was the black earth gate, the portal to the Nether. But most imposing of all was the creature that was standing before it. It was a First Born nearly twelve feet tall, a mass of rotting flesh and splintered bone. Its red-rimmed eyes burned with hatred and its face was split with a mouth full of jagged teeth. The reaver, a thing from the darkest of nightmares, stood staring balefully at the companions.

"It is so good of you to grace me with your presence again, Rick Branson," the woman said softly, reaching up with delicate hands and removing her cowl. Her gray eyes sparkled and she flashed a radiant smile, but her appearance did little to mask the malevolence that emanated from her. "I give you high marks for making your way back to my chambers."

"You had to know I was coming back," he snapped, fighting the urge to rush forward and smash her down. Instead, he let his companions move out around him, taking up positions and preparing to fight. If they were going to defeat her, they would have to do it together. "I'm not about to leave my men behind."

"It would have been better for you if you had," she replied. "After I deal with you and your friends, I will happily keep you alive so that you can watch me turn your soldiers into something that will better suit my own needs."

"You're deluded if you think we're just going to roll over and die for you."

Shayene laughed. "Do you really think you can stop me?" she asked, making a point to look back at Terion's prison and then at the reaver that stood silently before the portal. "I control power far greater than anything you can imagine and will soon claim the power of the gods themselves."

"I don't give a damn about your gods, lady," he snarled. "I just want my people back."

"You underestimate those who stand against you, Shayene," Siranschae added from her position at the chamber entry.

"No, it is you that underestimate us," a dark voice said as

Kraegor materialized directly behind Siranschae and grasped her wrist even as he spoke. Power flared down his hand, blasting the woman backward against the wall, her weapon clattering away from her and Varankyl sliding free across the floor.

"Kill them all," Shayene said, her smile vanishing as she raised her hands, summoning her own power.

The reaver moved forward, even as additional shapes materialized out of the blackness of the portal.

Jayadra picked herself up and grabbed the mace from her belt. Volsaun was already standing, his huge hammer in his hands, looking up at the shattered battlement where they had just stood. A well-aimed catapult shot had taken it out and very nearly them with it. Swan was picking himself out of the rubble nearby, swearing angrily and ordering his men to open fire. His soldiers wasted no time, firing down on the enemy, picking their shots carefully to conserve their limited ammunition.

"Perhaps we were wrong about him making the challenge," the Arcai said, brushing shards of stone and dust from her robes.

"He has betrayed the honor of the challenge," Volsaun growled.

"Then let us make certain his betrayal does not go unanswered," she answered, turning to face the gates. Behind her, three hundred of Nykiva's mounted cavalry were ready, warhorses stamping impatiently. "Open the gates!" she commanded and immediately the enormous wooden gates began rolling backward, pulled open by a dozen men each. On the field beyond, charging Rat warriors screamed in glee and surged toward the opening gates, but with a roaring battle shout, the heavily armed cavalry charged forward, splitting into two columns as they thundered past Jayadra and Volsaun and onto the battlefield.

The cavalry charge was devastating as the Dom horsemen impaled Rat warriors on spears, hacked them down with swords, and trampled them beneath the hooves of warhorses. Above them on the battlements, Swan's men provided devastating cover fire as Jayadra and Volsaun walked purposefully forward, weapons at the ready.

Draven and Zarandrae stood waiting for them.

With shouts of challenge, the four combatants threw themselves into the fight. Draven leapt forward, bringing his sword in a powerful overhand slash, but the priestess brought her mace up, deflecting the blow. She reversed the direction of her smaller, lighter weapon, swinging for Draven's unprotected ribs, but the huge Arcai spun to the side, causing the weapon to simply whistle through the air. He brought Dread around in a deadly slash toward the woman's head, but she was already moving out of range.

Volsaun and Zarandrae clashed together in a fury born of a long-time hatred for each other. Their momentum carried them into each other and each caught the weapon wrist of the other, halting the blow. As dragons, they were a near match in size and strength, with Zarandrae being only slightly larger. But in their human form, Volsaun stood nearly a foot taller than the seven-foot Zarandrae and he used his size and strength advantage to throw the woman violently to the ground. But where he was bigger and stronger, Zarandrae was much more agile and experienced in her human form and she rolled through the throw, coming to her feet even as the huge barbarian slammed his war hammer into the ground where she had been only a moment before.

Draven drove forward, his huge blade cutting through the air, causing Jayadra to retreat. She ducked two slashes and parried away a third with her mace, before dropping to a knee and digging her fingers into the ground as she intoned a spell. Immediately, thorny vines sprang up around the feet and ankles of the huge Arcai, wrapping themselves quickly around his feet and twisting about his legs. But it did little more than slow him down as he growled and ripped his legs free.

For the priestess, however, the reprieve was what she was hoping for and she dropped low, swinging her mace under the blade of the big warrior. It cracked solidly against his hip and drove him backward a step, but Draven shrugged off the blow with a growl of anger and came on.

Nearby, Volsaun was pressing his attack on Zarandrae. He, too, had struck his opponent a glancing blow with his huge hammer, but Zarandrae had rolled with the impact and was now working her sword easily against his heavier blows, parrying them away. It was on one such parry that she quickly reversed her movement and drove the point of her blade forward. She would have taken Volsaun in the heart, but a quick shift of the barbarian's body caused the weapon to slice into the heavy muscle of his shoulder instead. Volsaun threw himself backward, turning his hammer inside to deflect her follow-up thrust. But now he was on the defensive, parrying and dodging strikes that were coming quicker and quicker.

The two pairs of combatants fought on, while all around them, the battle continued to rage and soldiers on both sides continued to die.

Chaos reigned within the chamber in Shayene's keep as the combatants engaged one another. With Siranschae out of the fray, Kraegor got off another blast of lightning, catching Aylan squarely in the chest and blasting him backward. But the young mage pulled himself to his knees, energy crackling across his body as his own magical wardings shorted out. He countered with his own spell of lightning, causing the human-form dragon to stagger back and seek shelter behind a stone pillar.

Notyet had quickly intercepted the reaver as it entered the fray, but a spell from Shayene caught him in the shoulder and he let out a silent scream as the flesh began to wither along his arm, turning putrid green as festering sores erupted in his flesh. The monster would have had him, had Branson not shouldered him aside and crunched his mace into the creature's leg. But the creature was unaffected and a moment later, the marine felt himself flying through the air after having been clubbed heavily across the chest by one of the reaver's huge arms.

Vendetta darted to the side on the pretense of engaging the scarecrows that had suddenly come through the gate, but she only offered a token slash across the eyes of the nearest one as she pulled out a small glass globe. Turning to duck the deadly claws of a another scarecrow, she threw it with perfect accuracy at Terion's prison. The globe impacted with the confines of the wizard's magical prison, exploding into a cloud of glittering dust. The blue energy of the field sputtered several times and then disappeared altogether as the dust absorbed the power of the imprisoning spell.

Terion was moving almost before his prison had disappeared, grabbing Shayene's wrist and disrupting her next spell. She screamed at him in anger and the newly freed swordsman responded by punching her in the jaw.

As the fighting continued, Siranschae slowly regained her feet, one arm hanging limply, broken from the force of Kraegor's initial spell. After picking up her sword with her good hand, she stepped in front of Kraegor. "You have disgraced our kind," she said, her sword held out before her.

"Not true, my dear sister," he replied with a wicked smile. "I intend to raise our kind to a new station. You, unfortunately, shall not accompany me."

His hand lashed forward, razor-sharp nails tearing deep gouges in Siranschae's cheek. But she was moving, too, her blade coming up in an attempt to disembowel the man. Kraegor, however, simply vanished and the blade passed harmlessly through the air. A moment later, he reappeared at the side of the woman, his hand clamping down on her wounded arm.

Siranschae bit back the pain and she lashed out with the hilt of her sword. It caught Kraegor directly in the face, but he only smiled and wrenched violently on the woman's broken arm. Pain washed over her and she sank to her knees, only to have Kraegor fasten his other hand about her throat and lift her high in the air.

"Pathetic," he hissed, squeezing tighter and taking no small amount of pleasure in seeing her eyes bulge. "I would have allowed you to live, had you not thrown yourself in with this lot."

"You...cannot..." Siranschae began, but Kraegor tightened his grip even more, strangling her.

"I can do whatever I wish," he snapped and then threw her body across the room where she slammed into the wall with a sickening crack.

As Siranschae slid to the floor, bloodied and unconscious, Aylan hit the dragon with another powerful lightning bolt, blasting him to his knees. The young apprentice advanced, bringing his hands together as he followed up with another spell. A thunderclap of sound exploded through the chamber and Kraegor was thrown backwards, pinned against the wall by the young mage's spell. But the dragon suddenly vanished once again. Aylan had no chance to react as the dragon reappeared behind him and clubbed him to the floor with a fist to the back of the neck.

Branson had recovered quickly from the blow the reaver had given him and was on the offensive, slashing at the huge creature as he moved. But he pressed his advantage one too many times and ended up too close to one of the scarecrows. The vicious creature lunged forward, its fanged jaws ripping into shoulder. He yelled in pain as he turned to fend off the attack, but in doing so, left himself helpless to the reaver's next attack. Its huge hand closed about his chest, crushing him as it lifted him up.

Notyet, still reeling from the death magic that continued to consume him, lunged forward, half blinded with pain. His sword drove deeply into the creature's bowels, but it did nothing but get the monster's attention. With a roar, it lashed forward with its other hand, claws tearing out the big warrior's throat. Blackness took him as he fell, his life pouring from his ruined throat.

In that moment, Arianna was there, a strange guttural roar issuing from her throat as she faced the monstrous reaver.

On the fields outside of Nykiva, the advancing Gols had hemmed in more than a hundred of the Nykiva riders, while the larger force was thundering back towards the gates of the city. Soldiers manning the battlements were loosing a rain of arrows and automatic weapon fire on the enemy, covering the retreat, but there was little they could do to save those riders who had been trapped. Slowly, the Gols began decimating the trapped cavalry, cutting down horse and man alike.

As the retreating riders galloped back through the gates, the deadly battle between Arcai and dragon continued. Jayadra was bleeding from several slashes on her body and Draven was spitting blood from internal bleeding caused by a particularly nasty hit to his ribs from Jayadra's mace. Nearby, Volsaun and Zarandrae were equally wounded in their titanic struggle against each other.

Seeing Jayadra stumble slightly in their fight, Draven feinted with a thrust to draw her mace up and then went into a full spin, bringing his weapon across the woman's chest. Jayadra just managed to deflect the blow, but the force of the slash jarred the weapon from her hand. Dazed, she stumbled to her knees. Sensing victory, Draven laughed and wrapped his free hand in the woman's long hair. Then, he drove his knee hard into her face, snapping her head back. As her eyes glazed over, he struck her again several more times before finally letting her sink to the ground.

Blood flowed freely from Jayadra's battered face as she lay at Draven's feet. Her nose was broken and one eye was swollen shut, the orbital bones shattered, but still she clung to consciousness. Her world was spinning and she could barely make out the form of Draven standing above her, raising his sword high to finish her.

Nearby, Volsaun saw his beloved companion fall and turned to help. But Zarandrae, sensing his distraction, suddenly pressed her attack, driving forward with three quick thrusts of her sword. The first two came up short, but the third one found its mark, driving deeply into the barbarian's chest. Volsaun lunged forward with his free arm, his own hand clamping down on Zarandrae's sword hand, pinning it to the pommel. He felt his lungs begin to fill with blood and knew the battle was over. Zarandrae stared at him with cold hatred and then ever so slowly, as his strength slipped away, she began to turn her blade.

In Shayene's tower, all eyes went to the young Tae empath as she roared again in fury. But instead of a young woman, the Arianna that was facing the huge monster was now a monster herself. Her smooth skin had been replaced with glittering white scales and her fingers had lengthened considerably, ending in wickedly sharp light-blue talons. Her face was the most remarkable change, however, seemingly caught somewhere between human and reptile, as human eyes stared out above a mouth filled with tearing teeth.

The reaver released its hold on Branson and lashed forward, but Arianna was already moving, almost a blur as she struck with terrifying ferocity. She caught the monster's arm and shoved it aside as if it were nothing. She roared again, but this time, a stinging storm of ice and frost issued from her oversized mouth, blasting directly into the monster's face. Tissue blackened and fell away even as Arianna leapt on the creature, claws from both hands and feet tearing into the reaver. Her head snapped forward and a moment later, she tore away the monster's ice-blackened face.

With ponderous slowness, the reaver fell backward. Arianna held on, continuing to tear at the monster as it collapsed to the floor. A moment later, she leapt away, leaving the thing dead in the middle of the chamber. But as she landed, she stumbled and crashed into the wall, her strength suddenly leaving her. Slumping to the floor, her reptilian features began to fade, being replaced again by the soft skin and beauty of the young Tae woman. As her features returned to her human form, she crawled forward, finally collapsing on top of the body of Notyet.

The whole thing had lasted only seconds and left everyone in shock, but with the monster destroyed, it was Branson who recognized the opportunity. Struggling to breathe through cracked ribs, he stumbled forward, sweeping Varankyl up in his hand. He knew immediately that he had miscalculated as the sentient artifact suddenly awakened and launched its own mental assault on him. He felt numbing coldness worm its way up his arm and into his chest as the will of Varankyl smashed through his mind. His strength leaving him, he stumbled sideways and fell to his knees, feeling his chest tighten.

Seeing what was about to happen, Shayene screamed in rage and flung Terion to the floor. On the other side of the room, Kraegor made a wild leap toward the marine who had taken up the artifact. But Vendetta was there, suddenly rising up behind the dragon and driving her blade deep into his back. With a roar of rage and pain, Kraegor spun around to face the woman, only to find her other blade suddenly buried to the hilt in his chest. He felt the pull of the blades – weapons he himself had forged a decade ago – as they fed on his life force.

Vendetta stared into the face of the man who had violated her so savagely and felt no compassion; no remorse; no rage. She felt only a peaceful calm as she wrapped her arms tightly around him and pulled him close, ignoring the feeling of his hot breath in her face and the hard strength of his dragon-enhanced body once more against her own. Closing her eyes in acceptance, she used all of her strength to fall backward, pulling Kraegor with her. As Kraegor let out a single echoing scream of "NO!", the thick blackness of the earth gate swallowed them up.

And with the last of his failing strength, Rick Branson threw Varankyl.

Jayadra stared up, seeing the sword of Draven raised high, ready to be plunged down through her body. She saw the wicked gleam in his eyes and suddenly, the implication of what would happen if Draven was successful, rang loud in her mind and her thoughts and vision suddenly cleared.

Her hand darted out even as she called forth the spell. As her fingers closed about the man's muscled calf, the powerful life-stealing magic went off instantly, drawing off some of the huge Arcai's life force and instantly healing some of her own wounds.

His strength suddenly drained, Draven gasped in horror and stumbled backward, trying to keep his huge sword raised above him. Her strength returning, the priestess climbed to her feet and swept up her fallen mace. Draven tried to thrust his sword forward, but his movements were sluggish and she easily swatted his lunge aside, then spun full circle, her mace smashing into his chest. Bones shattered and internal organs were ruptured as he dropped to his knees in shock, blood running from his mouth. His strength gone, his sword dropped from suddenly lifeless hands. He looked up one more time as Jayadra brought her mace high above her head.

"For all of us," the priestess said softly before the mace fell. A moment later, Draven was dead.

Zarandrae saw the death of her companion a moment before the weakness took her and she fell to the ground, leaving her sword imbedded in her opponent's chest. Her eyes locked on Draven and she could not help but stare at his ruined body, all thoughts of combat and victory driven far from her mind. She was unaware of Jayadra standing nearby, pulling the sword from Volsaun's chest and placing a healing hand on the wound. She was oblivious as together, the two then lifted her up and bound her hands tightly behind her. And she cared nothing for the ringing sound of war horns, signaling the arrival of a new army.

Branson's strength deserted him as he threw Varankyl toward the earth gate. It fell short, hitting the floor and skidding the last few feet toward the portal before disappearing into the blackness.

The effect was instantaneous. The room filled with the wailing screams of the First Born reverberating from the gate as it began to shimmer violently within the stone framing of the wall. The blackness swirled faster and faster, growing smaller as it picked up speed. The shrieks and moans turned to little more than echoes and, a moment later, the earth gate was gone.

Shayene stood motionless, feeling her powers drain swiftly away with the loss of the gate. She was calm, though, knowing that it would be a temporary weakness and that this was what had to happen. Although she lamented the loss of her companion, this was what everything was all about. The creation of the gate and its subsequent destruction by the very item that created it would bring about the convergence in short order. And the convergence was the key. When that happened, when the barrier between worlds was no more, she would move to claim victory over the gods themselves, not only in this world, but in the other as well.

But first, she had to survive. She had to escape. That thought sent her running out of the chamber. She was acutely aware of footsteps pounding behind her, gaining as stronger legs drove them harder than she was able. But it would not matter. Her salvation was close enough and she turned the corner and ran into the designated room. Her power fading quickly, she whirled around, bringing her arms up before her for one last spell. Arcane power flickered and nearly died at her fingertips, before flaring one more time as the spell completely drained her. But it had been enough as thick strands of viscous webbing stretched themselves across the doorway, blocking entry into the room.

Close behind her, Terion skidded to a stop before he ran into the magical webbing. He was familiar with the spell and knew that to touch it would stick him fast. Likewise, weapons were useless on it, so he could go no further. On the other side, Shayene summoned enough strength to look up and smile. Her visage was pale and drawn, her skin wrinkled and lined with years upon years of age that had suddenly manifested themselves upon her as her magic failed.

"It ends here, Shayene," Terion said gravely, staring at her between the strands of magic. "It's over."

Shayene only cackled and pointed a bony finger at him. "You have won the day, Terion, as was intended. But the war is far from over and that is something you cannot win."

"It's over," he repeated. "You've lost. We have beaten you."

"You seem to think you understand what's happening, Terion," she countered. "I assure you that you have no idea what is coming."

She turned and it was at that time that Terion noticed the room itself. Against the far wall, a huge tapestry depicting a woodland forest hung, concealing most of the wall. Before it was an altar of stone and upon that alter lay the body of a young girl, not more than ten or twelve, her corpse draped with a silk sheet. Much to his sudden horror, however, he realized the girl was not dead, her eyes staring wide-eyes in terror as Shayene, now an old hag, loomed over her. Terion could not know it, but the child was the youngest daughter of the old gatekeeper, kept alive and bound by Shayene for the darkest of purposes. And now that purpose suddenly grew clear.

"No!" Terion yelled, realizing what the fallen Arcai intended to do. "Don't do this!"

Shayene ignored the warrior, purposefully moving around to the far side of the altar, giving Terion a clear view of what was about to happen.

"Don't," Terion warned again. "I beg of you. She's only a child."

"It is far too late for that," Shayene replied, looking straight at him as she placed a hand on the young girl's forehead. She smiled, showing yellowed and aged teeth, now elongated into fangs. "Her blood is on your hands, Terion. You have brought this fate upon her." With that, she leaned forward and plunged her fangs deep into the girl's throat.

The scream that followed would haunt Terion for the rest of his days and the vision of the young girl shriveling and dying as Shayene feasted upon her blood would terrorize his dreams until he died. Mercifully, it was over quickly for the young girl, the Arcai needing every precious drop of blood as she greedily fed on her victim. A minute later, Shayene straightened above the withered corpse, her features once again young and radiant. Blood dripped from ruby-red lips and when she smiled, yellowed teeth were now white beneath a coating of blood, her canines long and sharp.

"You would forsake mortality for this?" Terion asked quietly, shaking his head in grief.

Shayene threw back her head and laughed, her voice once again musical but dark all the same. "I was never mortal, brother," she said, walking back to the tapestry and taking hold of its fringed edge. "Such is the curse of an Arcai, as you well know. But do you honestly think I would wait hundreds of years again for my mother to decide to rebirth me in the event of another accident?" She laughed bitterly. "I chose this path not long after I left our home, Terion. It is a different existence, to be certain, but one that lends me great power and strength."

"You are an abomination, Shayene," Terion said, tears appearing at his eyes. "You were my sister. You could have been so much more. Now, you are nothing but a monster. You have lost everything!"

"On the contrary, I have been thwarted here only for the

moment and again by design, my dear brother," she replied, ripping down the cloth with a flourish. "But I am far from defeated and what I intend to be when this is all over is like nothing that you can even comprehend."

Terion gasped at what he saw, for behind the woman, the wall was not a wall, but another gateway. It was a much smaller earth gate than the first, but easily large enough for a person to cross. However, instead of the inky blackness of the Nether, he saw the shadowed outlines of trees and plants, and in the distance, the shoreline of a river.

Standing within the gateway on the other side where three figures. Two of them wore the uniforms of United States Marines, something he had recently become familiar with. The third was clad in tattered gray robes, his skin sallow and his eyes downcast. His hands were manacled together in front of him with strange bands of metal.

"While there are precious few ways to destroy someone like me," Shayene said, looking back at him as she stood on the edge of the portal, "one must first know where to look."

With that, she stepped backward through the gate and into the forest. For a moment, she locked eyes with Terion one final time and the man thought he detected a glimmer of remorse. But it was replaced with a cold evil as she waved a hand before her as if to say good-bye.

A moment later, the earth gate winked out of existence.

If Shayene's defeat in her tower of sorcery was complete, it was made even more decisive on the fields before Nykiva as the large host of Vi'Raaji witches descended upon the flanks of the Gol army with a vengeance. Thousands strong, magic and weapons alike tore into the rear of the invading army. Many Vi'Raaji fell. But for each one that was slain, many more Gols fell dead and in time, the battle became a route.

From the ruined gates and walls of the city, the beleaguered soldiers of Nykiva rallied at the sudden turn of events, charging forward on horseback and on foot. With Draven slain and the surprising appearance of the Vi'Raaji, the Gol army was caught.

Still, Gol'Athi warriors were among the fiercest of fighters and the battle raged throughout the rest of the day and deep into the night. Finally, as morning began to dawn and the true scope of the death and destruction became apparent, the Gol generals finally signaled their surrender.

The aftermath of the battle was dreadful and the fields about Nykiva were soaked with blood. Thousands upon thousands lay dead, more Gol'Athi than others. Of the U'Raati, not a single savage remained. The Vi'Raaji losses were not nearly as steep, but more than a thousand witches had been slaughtered on the battlefield, though still far fewer than Nykiva soldiers.

As the morning sun dawned overhead, Myngar, flanked by Jayadra and Volsaun, accepted the sword of the Gol'Athi general Tanth in surrender. The surviving Gols, as part of the terms of surrender, immediately begin the long and arduous work of burying the dead. For three weeks they would labor, creating massive burial mounds on the fringes of the forest, before being freed to return to their own lands, their weapons and armor left behind as penance for their deeds.

But the wounds left on the land would remain for years, at least until the day the Cataclysm would arrive and change everything.

Chapter 45

Deep in the Wraithlands, Terion stumbled back into the main chamber of Shayene's keep, still shocked at what had transpired. As an Arcai, Shayene's powers were nearly unmatched. As a vampire, he could not even begin to imagine what his half-sister was still capable of, even with the loss of her companion. And now she was free and he had no way to go after her.

However, for the moment, the threat was eliminated and his friends needed him. He paused to gaze around the chamber, eyes wet with tears of sadness, for even though they had stopped Shayene, much had been sacrificed in attaining it.

Branson would survive. He was conscious, muttering curses from his own world, and shivering with a cold that he could not seem to shake. But he lived and his actions concerning the destruction of the earth gate would make him a hero in this world, once the historians and lore masters got a hold of him.

Vendetta was gone and Terion could not help but feel a pang of sadness at her death. She had offered the ultimate sacrifice and, in doing so, had likely saved them all from Kraegor. As far as he was concerned, she had righted her past wrongs with her actions in the chamber and he would hand down no condemnation against her.

Siranschae was seated with her back to the wall, tears in her eyes as she stroked Arianna's hair, who lay dead in her lap. Oblivious to Terion or the others, she sang softly in a voice barely above a whisper and in a language known only to dragons.

Terion watched her for a moment, but his gaze was suddenly drawn to the face of Notyet, who lay nearby. The huge warrior's eyes snapped open and his hand immediately went to his torn throat. To his surprise, his fingers pressed against scarred, but healed skin and he sat bolt upright in surprise.

"By the gods," he exclaimed in a voice raspy and new. "I'm not dead."

"Notyet?" Terion questioned incredulously, his own eyes widening in surprise.

"By the gods," Notyet repeated, holding his throat gingerly as he looked at Terion with wonder-filled eyes. "I can talk."

Terion rushed forward and knelt beside his friend, grabbing the huge man in a hug. "I thought you were dead!" He shouted, not bothering to hide his tears.

"I was," the warrior replied, his new voice rich and deep, and then turned and looked at the fallen Arianna. Siranschae still stroked the dead girl's hair and forehead, oblivious to them. "It was the young one. She saved me."

Terion nodded sadly. "It was the empath in her. She gave her life to save you. And in doing so, it appears that she restored your voice."

Terion gingerly helped his friend to his feet and then walked over to where Aylan was laying on the floor. He was relieved to see that the young mage had survived the battle, though he was somewhat singed for his efforts, his robes still smoking. As Terion helped the still groggy young man to a sitting position, he inadvertently pushed one of the sleeves up the young man's arm. Startled at what he saw, he pushed it up further, noting that the magical runes and glyphs that signified a wizard's power had grown, moving up his arms from his wrists and well past his elbows, the mark where all wizards moved beyond their apprenticeship.

"Well, look at you," Terion managed a smile, looking Aylan in the eyes. "All grown up and ready to take on the world."

"I feel like I already have." Aylan winced, looking at his newly marked arms. "I wonder what my master would say."

"Loken can no longer be counted as your master," Terion replied, tapping the glyphs on his arm. "It's time for you to forge your own destiny. If you wish to remain with us, I would be honored to have you."

"We should consider going home," Notyet interrupted, still marveling at his newfound voice. "We're not safe yet and it's a long way back to Nykiva. There will be a lot of First Born to fight through and they'll likely be around for a long time to come."

"We'll need to rest first," Terion countered. "We should be safe enough if we set up camp in a side room of the castle somewhere. We're in no condition to fight right now."

"We can camp back in the cells," Branson said through chattering teeth. "Shayene said it's warded from her creatures. Besides, I need to get to my people."

"Fair enough," Terion replied and together, they began to move deeper into the castle.

A short time later, they had found the cells and joined the rest of Branson's soldiers, eleven of them in all. When Branson asked about the other four, they only knew that Shayene would occasionally summon one and they would not be seen again. Terion, alone, understood what that meant.

After the reunion was over and explanations given, they settled in for some much needed rest, intending to begin their journey back to Nykiva on the following day. It was only when they were finally relaxing that Terion realized they were missing someone.

"She's gone," Notyet said quietly as he walked over and took a seat next to his friend, confirming his thoughts.

"Siranschae."

"Aye."

"When did she leave?"

The big warrior shook his head. "I don't know, but she took Arianna with her."

"She's a dragon," Terion said thoughtfully. "And there's more mystery about them than is known. Our quest is finished and she knows that we're safe. She had charged herself to be Arianna's guardian and will continue to honor that."

"I'm going to miss the young one," Notyet said softly. "I owe her my life."

"We all do," Terion agreed, thinking back to how the young Tae had taken on the huge undead monster and killed it. He shivered to think what might have happened to them had she not done so. How she had done it, though, was nothing short of amazing to him and in time, he would share that tale with Notyet. He was pretty confident that the story of Arianna, the half-dragon, was nowhere near finished.

Almost twenty-four uneventful hours later, the survivors, bolstered now by eleven freed and heavily armed soldiers, passed out of the gates of Shayene's keep and picked their way carefully down the path into the fog-shrouded gloom of the Wraithlands. They traveled carefully, always alert and prepared, but although they sensed movement and heard noises within the darkness, the First Born and whatever else prowled the shadows left them alone.

Half a day later, they were met by Jayadra and Volsaun, as well as Eric, who opened a gateway and before the sun set, they had all returned safely to Nykiva.

As evening fell the next day, Terion stood alone on a broken parapet, staring sadly out over the battlefield as Gol prisoners labored under armed Nykiva guards, burying the dead. Behind him, the various celebrations within the city were in full swing, but he could not share in the joy. His own thoughts were still in turmoil and he would be a long time accepting that a half-sister he had never known, had been responsible for so much death and misery. There was no logical reason for him to take on such a mantle of guilt and he knew it. But that didn't help him.

Much of those last few moments before Shayene escaped troubled him deeply and a dreadful unease had been growing within him ever since he saw her for what she truly was. Because of it, he had decided to tell no one until he could relate the tale to Jayadra, the one person who would understand the possible implications of what had happened.

But that would have to wait. While thousands had died, thousands more had been wounded and the Arcai priestess had been hard at work with the Tae healers.

Still, there was much to celebrate with the defeat of Draven and the Gol'Athi surrender. It was a significant occurrence, too, for the Gols would take decades to regain their strength and the Doms knew that meant years of peace. Gol messengers, under Dom guards, had already been sent west and south under Nykiva escort, signifying the surrender and ordering the end to the occupation of Dom and Tae cities and villages.

Additionally, the Gol generals were busy signing the formal documents of concession within the Dom council chambers as Myngar spelled out the terms of their surrender. And knowing the wily finance minister, Terion had no doubt that the man would likely extract heavy reparations from them before the dialogue was completed.

"The celebration continues and still you persist in staying in the shadows," a voice said quietly as footsteps padded up the cracked stone steps to the battlement.

Terion turned and smiled tiredly as Aylan joined him. "We paid dearly for it, my young friend," he said. "The gods know, we earned it. What about you? Why are you up here with me when you could be back with those who are celebrating?"

"I've been thinking about what you told me back in Shayene's tower," the young mage answered. "About joining you."

"The offer stands."

"I appreciate that more than I can ever convey, Terion. The time I have travelled with you and Notyet has been some of the best days of my life."

"But you're staying here," Terion guessed.

"Myngar has asked me if I would take Ranora's place," Aylan nodded.

"So, you get all powerful on us and jump at the first open wizard tower that presents itself, is that right?"

"I will stay with you if that is what you wish."

"No," Terion smiled, patting the young man on the shoulder. "It's time for you to make your own path. You've earned this, and Myngar's trust in you is well-placed."

"Do you think I'm ready?"

"Are any of us ever truly ready for what we face?" Terion answered truthfully. "Still, if you believe you're ready, you'll do well."

Aylan was silent, staring out at the moving torches of those working on the battlefield as he considered his future and what had transpired. He had been called in front of the council earlier in the day and had been shocked when the council formally requested that he take up residence in the city's tower of sorcery as Nykiva's chief wizard. He had argued that only an arch mage given that title by the Consortium could claim a tower of sorcery, but those concerns were quickly dismissed. Myngar assured him that the Consortium would have to grant Aylan the title of arch mage and back his appointment. So he had accepted, though he had done so with more than a little apprehension.

Terion, seeing the young wizard wrestling with the responsibility that had been placed before him, continued. "Despite your misgivings, Myngar thinks you're ready for this or he would not have made the request. Your time has come, Aylan, and you deserve the honor placed before you. I only ask one thing of you as you take your new position."

"Anything," Aylan said, suddenly feeling much better about things.

"Take care of Anthony. We owe that kid everything for getting us out of Taer Blys. I don't want to see him wind up on the streets. I only ask that you give him a place of honor."

"He is a remarkable child," Aylan grinned.

"Careful now," Terion chuckled. "You're not much older than him."

"You have my word, Terion. I will have him moved into his new quarters by sundown. But only if you agree to one thing."

"And what's that?"

"You have to join the celebration," Aylan replied matter-of-factly. "At the very least, you must listen to Notyet."

Terion groaned good-naturedly. "Has he even shut up yet? He's been at it non-stop since the Wraithlands. If Eric hadn't shown up and opened the gate, I might have had to leave him."

"Have you heard his singing?"

"Oh no."

"Oh, yes," Aylan replied with a smile. "He is fairly set on singing every ballad that has ever been written and he's doing so quite badly, I might add."

The following afternoon, Terion found himself in the Dom council chambers, speaking quietly with Myngar. Jayadra had been kept busy throughout the previous evening, so he had sought out the leader of the council first thing. He had arrived as Myngar was greeting a middle-aged, but beautiful and regally dressed woman, and the eight well-armed young women warriors who accompanied her.

Upon his unexpected arrival, the queen of the Vi'Raaji bade him sit and the three entered into discussions that lasted well into the afternoon. Terion learned much that morning as they spoke of the arrival of the Vi'Raaji army and their role in defeating the Gols. He was not surprised to hear that it was the late sorceress Ranora who had been responsible for their inclusion in the battle, her own answer to Draven's march. The woman had been ambitious to a fault and he was impressed that she had seen fit to seek the aid of the Vi'Raaji. It was, after all, a perfect match. While the Vi'Raaji were hungry for power, ruthless, and even occasionally cruel, they were not inherently evil and would stand to gain much with the defeat of Draven and the Gols. Knowing what he did of the dead sorceress, Terion had little doubt that Ranora was able to appeal to everything the Vi'Raaji were.

But as he feared, when the discussions finally came to the terms originally set forth by Ranora for the Vi'Raaji aid, they came as a complete surprise to Myngar. But the council leader, ever the gracious diplomat, gingerly worked around the potentially dangerous differences, heaping praise on the Vi'Raaji fighters and formally pronouncing Vendetta a heroine to the people of Nykiva for her actions in helping to defeat Shayene and Kraegor the Black.

In the end, the queen left with her entourage, with an acceptable draft of Myngar's revised terms and with a promise that the Dom leader would visit Ravenspire in two months' time to ratify the terms and a treaty between their two people.

As servants escorted the nine women out of the council chamber, Myngar finally leaned back in his chair, threw back his head, and exhaled an exhausted sigh. "By the gods, I am not cut out for this," he breathed deeply, staring at the ceiling.

"You sound like Aylan," Terion replied with a smile. "He's fairly uncertain about his appointment, too."

The man waved a hand in the air. "He is a fine wizard and I have little reason to be concerned."

"He will serve Nykiva well," Terion agreed, "much the same as you are a fine diplomat and a capable leader and will serve our people well."

Myngar sighed again. "I suppose that is debatable, but there is little I can do about it anyway. While I did not seek the position I have, I will uphold the duties and serve to the best of my abilities."

"You'll be fine, Myngar. However, even with the victory over the Gols, the times are likely not to get much easier for a while. Few would be capable of accepting the reigns as you have and we are honored as a people to have you as our leader."

Myngar laughed, but it was a warm sound. "Save your praise, Terion. Half the job of a diplomat is to avoid trouble and I have been lucky so far."

"You did well enough with the Vi'Raaji queen and that was no easy task," Terion stated. "With several thousand well-armed Vi'Raaji soldiers camped in the woods all about Nykiva, a single misstep on your part could have plunged us once more into a terrible battle, one that would have cost many, many more lives."

Myngar smiled. "Well, if that had happened, we could have rearmed the Gols and had them fight for us."

"Interesting observation," Terion laughed softly.

Myngar cleared his throat and then sat up straighter as a pair of servants entered the room, bearing a tray of fruits and cheeses, along with a flagon of wine. Without a word, they set the food and settings down and departed quickly.

"So, what will you do next?" Myngar asked, taking a bite from a shiny red apple. "Will you remain here in Nykiva?"

Terion shook his head, having already decided on his next course of action. "I am going to head south. I intend to seek out DesertSpeake."

"Loken's tower? Whatever for?"

"For two reasons," Terion answered. "I need to tell him the news of his apprentice. I think…I hope he will be pleased to hear about Aylan's new task."

"And the other?"

"I'm going to take Eric with me," Terion explained. "I've already spoken to Branson about it and he agrees. Because of Eric's powers, he could be in grave danger if we're not careful. Loken is one of the most powerful mages in the land. Eric will be safe there and Loken will know what to do with him."

"Won't Branson and his people be returning to his world?"

"Most of them will, but several of them have decided to stay here, including Branson and Eric."

"Whatever for?"

"Branson seems to think his world is in worse shape than this one," Terion shrugged.

"How is the outworlder doing anyway?"

"There is little change in his condition. Varankyl damaged him in some way that he cannot seem to warm himself even by a fire. Perhaps that will change in time, but for the moment, he said if he went back to his own world like that, the doctors there would have him locked up running tests on him for the rest of his life."

"I can't begin to imagine what that means," Myngar sighed.

"There's a lot of things I don't understand, either," Terion said thoughtfully. "A lot of things."

That evening, Terion sat in quiet contemplation with the Arcai priestess, Jayadra. Up until now, he had said nothing to anyone else of Shayene's escape and what he witnessed. Even his companions only knew that she had escaped through a gateway. He had just finished relating the full tale to the Arcai and he was not at all encouraged by her reaction.

"This is most distressing news," she said softly, her gaze locked on the fire that crackled in the fireplace.

"There was little I could do," Terion admitted. "My sister is defeated, but she planned well for the possibility. It's almost as if she knew what was going to happen."

"Perhaps she did."

"She *was* already a vampire," he agreed. "But even if that was part of her plan, that's not something that someone can just decide to do. It takes another vampire to make one and, quite frankly, I can't see there being one that would be a match for an Arcai."

"That is not entirely true," Jayadra replied. "Vampires are extremely rare, because it takes one to create one. But there is a way for an arch mage of great power to transcend mortality and become the worst of the undead. It is a difficult transcendence and requires the greatest of power and the ultimate sacrifice. Few in all the land could even attempt it, and survival is doubtful at best."

"Like a lich," the swordsman said.

"This is far worse than a lich, Terion," she replied. "A wizard who quests for continuing power and knowledge can traverse the path you speak of, becoming an undead lich of great power. But it does not have to be a wizard devoted to the black arts of death to follow that path. Whoever it may be, though, as a lich they are to be greatly feared and sometimes their quest for power causes them to seek the subjugation of others."

"Is that not what Shayene has done?"

"Shayene does not thirst for the same power that draws a lich," Jayadra answered. "She wishes instead to supplant the gods themselves."

"But that's what I don't understand," Terion replied in exasperation.

"She is an Arcai and that presents opportunities that mortals do not have," the priestess explained. "Simply stated, because of our immortal parentage, the Arcai become the logical successors to the gods, should the gods ever lose their power."

"You mean to tell me that she is capable of that?" Terion asked sharply. "She can actually become a god?"

Jayadra nodded. "When the gods gave us life, they did so knowing that we could attain the power to be as they are and given the right circumstances, one of us could attain even greater power than they have."

"One god to rule all?"

"There is only one true God," the priestess answered quietly and solemnly. "But as you know, there are numerous gods for our world, just as there are numerous gods for other worlds. And like the Arcai of our world, there will be Arcai of other worlds, too. Shayene hopes to evolve from her current station as an Arcai and become a god of this world, perhaps even the only god of this world. That is why her departure into another world is so distressing. There is no telling what kind of effect that might have on their world." She paused before finishing. "Or ours, for that matter."

"Why do the gods not act, then?" he snapped. "Are they so uncaring about what happens on this world that they would ignore something that threatens even their own existence?"

"They are very much aware of Shayene and her ambitions. But the gods believe in fate as much as mortal man and will not interfere, even if it means their own demise. Before time itself came into being, the One passed a decree among the gods of each world that their power would grow and wane with the belief or unbelief of those who worshipped them. But with that decree, they were commanded to never directly interfere with humanity on the penalty of banishment, forced mortality, and eventually death."

"But I still question how Shayene can become one," he pressed.

"The Arcai are not constrained by mortality. It has always been within our power as children of the gods to draw mortal man to us as worshippers. Until now, none would have ever dared to attempt such a thing."

"Why not?"

"Because to fail would mean our ultimate end," she answered. "The gods still maintain a measure of control over us in that we are dependent on them to be birthed and rebirthed, should we somehow perish. That is what Shayene experienced long ago and why today she seeks to become a god. She also knows that, should she perish now, Karasika would never consider allowing her to be rebirthed again."

"So she decided to become a vampire instead, ensuring her own immortality in a sense," Terion reasoned, "providing no one hunts her down and kills her."

"True, but it is more than that," Jayadra explained. "If she has truly followed this path, she possesses powers far beyond that of a normal vampire or that of an Arcai, for that matter. As an Arcai, she can command mankind. A mortal man will find that he must either bow down and worship her or she will simply consume his blood and soul and then control him as she controls the First Born. Either way, she grows in strength from those who will follow her."

"So it's not over, is it?"

"Not at all, Terion," Jayadra said softly. "It is only just beginning."

Epilogue

Many miles from Nykiva and deep within the Spider Forest, a woman sat on the pebbly beach of a small lake hidden away under a thick canopy of trees, absently trailing the slender fingers of one dark-skinned hand in the cool water. She had been here for several weeks, a place she had come to many times as a Vi'Raaji child. It was her safe haven and, ultimately, it had been her key to freedom.

She was lithe and finely muscled, a beautiful face framed by long, light-colored hair that had been pulled back in a ponytail. Crystalline blue eyes looked down thoughtfully at the object in her other hand and she turned the brilliant emerald Star Stone between her fingers as her mind continued to relive the recent past.

She knew that the horrors and terrors of the Nether would haunt her for the rest of her days. But she was safe now, far away from that living nightmare and from the thing that had brutalized her, safe because fate had smiled upon her and delivered that which had saved her.

Gazing once more at the powerful artifact, she finally stood up and slipped the magical gemstone into a hidden pouch within her black silk blouse. Barefoot, having no need of weapons or armor where she was, she walked slowly along the beach. She felt stronger than she had the past few weeks, the temporary sickness having passed only a couple of days ago. But her mind was still in turmoil.

As she walked, she put her hand to her belly again. Her stomach was still flat and toned, with no hint of the life beginning to grow within her, but that was not surprising. She knew it would change soon.

And she knew whose child she carried.

It was something that Vendetta…that Avenrael…had not yet

come to terms with.

***

He lay stretched out along the rocky plateau high up the mountainside, shrouded in darkness and surrounded by the unearthly screams and wails of the First Born. He rumbled painfully, deep within his throat again, as the changes continued to course through his body, slowly transforming him into the creature he would become.

He had thought himself dead when he had been dragged into the darkness during his struggle with the Vi'Raaji witch. But he had quickly remembered the artifact he had previously taken from her and had taken it in his hand as the hordes of undead closed in around them. But the woman was quicker, driving her blade deeper into his chest, a weapon he himself had forged a decade ago specifically for her. She had used it to kill the Arcai, Jayra, an event set into motion by Shayene herself. Now she was using it to kill him. As the magic siphoned his life away, the Star Stone dropped from his weakened fingers. Then, he could only watch as she snatched the glowing emerald and spun away from him. A moment later, she vanished, the defiant glare of her pale blue eyes the last thing he saw.

And then they were there. Creatures and monsters of unspeakable horror fell upon him, crushing him to the stony ground as they tore away his flesh and feasted on his blood. He could only scream helplessly as the undead ate him alive. But it was as the cold hands of death were beginning to close tightly about him that he found the strength to fight back.

The transformation lent power to his limbs and he began to tear at his attackers, the sharp bones of his hands, then talons, tearing dead flesh and shattering brittle bones. He fought his way clear, gaining the base of the mountain he now lay upon. It was then that his defense became his offense. He lashed forward, rotted dragon teeth tearing the head from a nearby ghoul, before he fell upon and devoured the creature's body. The putrid taste of rotting flesh and diseased blood did nothing to stop him and in a rage, he began to consume others.

For weeks, he rampaged among the hosts of the First Born until, finally sated, he crawled to the plateau and collapsed. And there he lay, feeling the unholy strength continue to flow within him. His powers had been changed, both in body and in the arcane, having been heightened to a fearful level, even to him. His flesh was mostly gone and he still marveled at how his bones held together with only bits and pieces of rotted flesh and dangling sinews. But hold together they did and as he stretched one great wing, he felt strength surge from within.

He rumbled again, this time in a deep, unholy laugh that rolled down the mountain as thunder, and he drew himself up to his full and awesome height. In this world, nothing could oppose him. In the world of the living, his brothers and sisters would be mere toys to him, and even the Arcai would now bow to his greatness. But he would have to be patient. The earth gate was gone. However, time meant nothing to him now, as immortality had taken on a whole new meaning. In time, he would find his way back. All he had to do was find Varankyl. He knew the artifact was here somewhere within the Nether. He just had to find it.

With that, Kraegor the Blacks stretched his wings and leapt into the air with a roar, beginning his search once more.

Coming Soon!

Mirror, the Earth War Saga, Book 2

The epic tale continues with the shocking birth of *Avenrael's* twins, *Fyre* and *Rayne*. The bittersweet event tears open the weakening barriers between worlds, freeing *Kraegor* from Hell and casting *Avenrael* and *Fyre* into a strange world where they have no hope of escape.

While *Terion* and *Rick Branson* set forth on a quest to rescue *Fyre* and her mother, *Notyet* journeys with a surprising ally to rescue *Rayne*. Meanwhile, *Shayene* continues her quest to usurp the gods, while *Kraegor* begins training the living weapon he will use to bring down the barriers between all worlds, leaving only Hell remaining, and he, its only ruler.

Antivirus

Homeland Security Agent Rick Alders lives a relatively peaceful life in his home town of Helena, Montana. His idyllic existence is shattered when a top-secret government black ops project known only as The Horde, is activated during the presentation of a breakthrough technology that would bridge the gap between our reality and the unknown of cyberspace. As Agent Alders plunges deeper into a nightmare he never could have imagined, he finds himself pitted against a malevolent intelligence with a single purpose — the annihilation of the human race.

www.ingramcontent.com/pod-product-compliance
Lightning Source LLC
Chambersburg PA
CBHW020823030726
47496CB00001B/65